THE NORTHERN LIGHTS SERIES

THE CAPTAIN'S *Bride*

A NOVEL

LISA TAWN BERGREN

WATERBROOK
PRESS

THE CAPTAIN'S BRIDE
PUBLISHED BY WATERBROOK PRESS
12265 Oracle Boulevard, Suite 200
Colorado Springs, Colorado 80921

The characters and events in this book are fictional, and any resemblance to actual persons or events is coincidental.

Scripture quotations are from the King James Version.

ISBN 978-0-307-45806-3

Published in the United States by WaterBrook Multnomah, an imprint of the Crown Publishing Group, a division of Random House Inc., New York.

WATERBROOK and its deer colophon are registered trademarks of Random House Inc.

146484122

For Dan, Cara, and Madison Grace Berggren,
With love

Acknowledgments

My appreciation goes out to the people who graciously read this manuscript as a first draft and gave me their input: Lois Stephens, Joy Tracshel, Jana Swenson, Leslie Kilgo, Rebecca Womack, Ginia Hairston, Mona Daly, Cara Denney, Liz Curtis Higgs, Francine Rivers, Rebecca Price, Dan Rich, Jeane Burgess, Diane Noble, and my husband, Tim. In addition, Paul Daniels of the Evangelical Lutheran Church of America archives in Saint Paul assisted me in finding authentic wedding vows and burial services for the time period. And I cannot forget Judy Markham, editor *extraordinaire*. She, and the editors who have preceded her—Shari MacDonald and Anne Buchanan—helped mold me into a better writer. You *all* helped make this book a better one. Thanks.

n e w   h o r i z o n s

June–September 1880

o n e

Elsa Anders knew she would remember everything of this moment, even as an old and bent woman. The scent of sea and wild clover, the vision of seven peaks about her, the feel of the cold North Sea's stiff wind that would leave her cheeks chapped and rosy come morning. This high up, it was cold enough to make her nose run. She reached for her handkerchief, but as usual, her father was already ahead of her, offering his instead. She took it gratefully, feeling the impact of the realization that he might never hand her anything again. For she was going. Far away and forever, it seemed.

Papa himself was uncommonly quiet tonight, Elsa mused, undoubtedly dreading what she herself dreaded: parting. In two days, she was to wed her beloved Peder. Her heart skipped at the thought of it, and her breath became even more labored. *Peder, oh Peder.* Her darling, who had finally come home to claim her as his own! Her heart swelled with pride at the thought of him. He had stood so proudly at the helm of the *Herald* as it entered port last week! Such a vision he was: all manly man, standing several inches taller than her own impressive height. His long brown hair had a slight rakish wave to it, and on top, the sun-bleached highlights common to sailors. In the year since she had last seen him, his face had matured. Lines at his eyes had deepened, and his skin was tanned to a golden bronze. How could such joy walk hand in hand with such sorrow? How could she walk by his side while leaving her entire family and the only home she had known for her twenty years of life?

Elsa looked west and then east, crying out silently to God. *Please, Father, tell me this is right, tell me this is good.*

There was no moon, but Elsa needed no illumination. She knew the landscape by heart. A million stars glittered high above the mountains that towered over Bergen and the darker, winding coastline of the Byfjorden. Turning a corner around an outcropping of rock, she could see below her the ancient city of Bergen, its warm lights twinkling softly. The town had once been the biggest trade port in Norway, surpassing even Copenhagen in the Middle Ages. In recent years, the pace had slowed, shipping traffic had moved on, and Bergen was left to find its own way in a new age.

Silently, she and her father reached their destination and sat on a large, flat stone and looked to the heavens. The two of them had come to this spot countless times, this place that Elsa, as a child, had named Our Rock. Her father, a slight man with a bone structure that Elsa had inherited, took her smooth hand in his withered, arthritic-bent one. Elsa thought that if she could travel back forty years, their fingers would be nearly identical: long and thin, yet strong. Perfect for a career as a shipwright, which was what her father had worked at for decades, forming, modeling, building ships. The longing to draw her own plans—or anything else for that matter—gripped her as she stared at the stars. But her destiny lay elsewhere. She was to be Mrs. Peder Ramstad, and she would find her fulfillment in that. Yet the ships in port called to her. Many were majestic vessels, and Elsa could see them in her imagination, crashing through a cyclone's worst wave, brave and formidable. . . .

Her father cleared his throat as if to speak, and her attention immediately focused back on home and the present. How could she leave her dear old father? The agony of it threatened to break her heart. Oh, why could her parents not come with them to America? Why did she have to leave her loved ones to have another?

Elsa could hear him take in a breath, and then, after a moment, sigh heavily. An old ship designer who married his beloved Gratia years behind most couples, Amund Anders had started his family late in life. Somehow, Elsa intuitively knew that this made it harder for him to let any of his brood go. And she was going. Her heart beat triple fast again at the thought of it. In two days' time she would wed. The day after, she and Peder would sail for America.

Her father tried again. "Elsa, my sweet, many dangers are ahead of you. Are you certain of this path?"

"As certain as I can be, Papa. I know that I love Peder with all my heart."

Amund harrumphed, then remained quiet for a moment. Then, "Love is a good thing for a young heart. But it is not always the best compass in trying to find one's way. This immigration"—he cast about for the right word—"*fever* is like the smallpox. It threatens Bergen like the angry blisters the pox leaves on one's skin."

"Or perhaps it is like scarlet fever," she answered carefully, "leaving one with a new appreciation for life."

Her father nodded, relishing her banter. Elsa knew how he would miss their intellectual sparring. Her older sister, Carina, seemed to have not a thought in her head, while her younger sister, Tora, was too busy to stop and indulge in the pleasure of conversation and discussion.

"Papa," she began, looking toward the skies again, "I must know. Do you disapprove of Peder?"

"Do I disapprove?" he scoffed. "I disapprove of the fact that he is taking my darling daughter away from me. I disapprove of the fact that you will not be here to comfort me in my old age. But of the boy himself? I cannot disapprove. The boy . . . the *man* is like a son to me." Amund turned to Elsa and cradled her cheek in his hand. "I am so happy for you, Elsa. I am happy that you've found your own beloved as I found my own in your mother. But permit me to grieve. I promise. On your wedding day, I will celebrate your union and not grieve any longer. But tonight, please allow an old man a bit of sadness."

A huge lump grew in Elsa's throat, and tears welled in her eyes. How did she know that this was right? Did she truly know Peder anymore? They had been inseparable as children, but he had been off to sea for the last ten years. Oh, but when he had come home, all the old feelings were there, along with something new. There was a maturity and solidity about their love now, built upon a lifetime of friendship and, over the last three years, a courtship of letters. Yes, Peder was the man for her, her beloved.

"You haven't thought more about going with us," she said carefully.

"No. You know my feelings, daughter. Bergen is where I was born. Bergen is where I will die. Your mother and sisters and I are where we are to be. You, my sweet, have been called to a different path."

Elsa knew her father's answer by heart. He had proclaimed it three years ago when their pastor, Konur Lien, had first raised his proposal of going as a large group to the new Promised Land, as he had called it. Together they would be stronger, more successful. Together, they would flourish. He had waved a letter from Peder, promising to take them to America. Their departure date was set for June 1880 and had set the town abuzz not only because of the excitement but also because of the sheer bravado of such a letter sent from a second mate who planned to be a captain.

"The pompous boy who would be captain," people had called Peder Ramstad. Elsa had defended him, sticking her nose in the air as if to say they knew not of whom they spoke, but privately fretted that they were right. Who had Peder become? And were his tender words, written in his strong, manly script, a passing fancy or the seedlings of love? Gradually, Elsa found strength in her trust of the man who found a way home to visit at least once a year. Still, for years she had wondered and waited, looking to sea, hoping against hope that each day would bring Peder home to her for good or that he would take her with him the next time he departed.

"What are your hopes for the future, child?" her father asked, interrupting her daydreaming.

"My future?" She paused to think before speaking. "A good marriage to Peder, lots of children, a good home." And maybe a career as a shipwright or an artist, she mused silently, yet unable to voice it. A woman's career was never a point of discussion in the Anders household. She sighed. Perhaps it would not be welcomed in Peder's home either.

"They are good aspirations," he said in approval. "You will make your mama and me proud."

His uncommon words of praise again brought Elsa near tears. She looked at him, squinting, trying to see what he must be feeling by his expression, but the light was too dim. Suddenly, a green light shimmered on the horizon, lighting up the entire mountain range. "Papa, look!" The lights grew, sending streaks southward toward them and then filling the streaks in with horizontal waves of red and purple, reminding Elsa of the inner iridescence of a seashell. The movement was like a tiny wave upon the sand, uneven in its climb, ebbing and flowing.

"Ah, yes!" her father cried, leaping to his feet and dancing a little jig. "It is appropriate for such a night as this. Do you remember what I told you as a child?"

Elsa stood beside him and hooked her arm around his thick waist. "I do. You said the lights were symbolic of God whispering to me."

"Yes," he nodded in approval. "They are a hint of heaven's

splendor." He was more visible now in the soft light from the north. Twin streaks of glistening tears ran down his weathered cheeks, and at the sight of them, a lump rose in Elsa's throat.

They stood there silently for a moment, looking toward the fjord that reflected the aurora borealis in unearthly hues. "I will always cherish these memories, daughter. Thank you for making an old man's life so full of joy."

"Oh, Papa . . ."

"Remember your old father when you see the lights, will you, Elsa?"

"If you will remember me."

He turned toward her. "You, Elsa, will never be out of my thoughts for more than a day. I will pray for you and yours every day, as will your mama."

"And I for you."

Father and daughter embraced while the northern lights continued to dance high, high above them.

Kaatje Janssen smiled, thinking of her dear friends marrying on the morrow, the beautiful northern lights she had witnessed with her husband last night as they lay together under the spring night sky, and Pastor Lien's sermon to come this morning. It would be his last in Bergen. As she finished her chores in the kitchen and began to prepare for church services, she caressed the slight bulge beneath her apron. Her belly was hardening and her hips widening by the day. Last night she was sure that her amorous husband's warm hands would at last discover the treasured secret her womb held.

Oh, how she had prayed to the heavenly Father that Soren would be pleased! Perhaps this was just what they needed to solidify their marriage and stay his wandering eyes. She finished the breakfast dishes and wiped her hands on her apron, smiling again as her fingers brushed her stomach. Today would be a good day to tell him. If she waited until they boarded the ship, he might be angry.

As she dumped the wooden pail of dishwater outside their tiny cottage, Kaatje glanced toward the barn, situated just beyond the house. She would miss this cozy home and their small farm, but what she and Soren needed now was a new start, for themselves and their baby. A girl? That would be nice. But a boy would be so helpful to Soren as he plowed the new soil that was said to be as fertile as Eden. At least a boy would be of some help in five or six years. But she was getting ahead of herself. Where was that man, anyway?

With a smile, she wound her creamy blond hair up into a knot and set out toward the barn to get Soren. He only had a few minutes to wash up and change for church. Humming, she walked across the spring grass in their yard, feeling cool, damp strands against her skin where they cleared her slippers. Low voices inside the barn brought her to an abrupt halt. She swallowed hard.

A low moan, a soft giggle. Soren's husky voice, the way he used it when he wanted Kaatje. *No. Please, God. Please, Father in heaven. Not again.*

Steeling herself, she took hold of the barn door and pulled it open. The creaking and groaning silenced the couple's noise and movement as Kaatje's eyes scanned the dark interior, fighting to adjust to the poor light. What they found confirmed her worst fears. In a stall, her handsome Soren, the man no woman could seem to refuse, stood very near Laila, who looked at Kaatje with a horrified expression. Laila's milking apron straps were off her shoulders, her dark hair pulled from its knot, and it took Kaatje only half a second to understand what had transpired.

"Elskling!" Soren began, his face a mask of consternation. "My love, this isn't what it looks like." In three powerful strides, he covered the distance between them while Kaatje fought for the energy to move. She felt numb, like a bird frozen in the snow. His hands were on her shoulders, moving down to cover her arms, as if he intended to hold her there until she understood. But she understood. She understood only too well.

"Oh, Soren," she breathed. Kaatje glanced up to meet his fiery blue eyes, normally so bright and gay, but already steeled for the argument they were sure to have. A sudden bolt of fury broke Kaatje from her dreamlike reverie.

"You told me it was over! That there would be no others ever again!" She wanted to spit in his face and struggled to escape his giant hands. "Let me go! Your hands are defiled! You do not deserve to touch me!"

Her words seemed to pierce his defensive armor, and the blush of excitement on his cheeks faded to pale gray. He ducked his head and looked down at her like an errant schoolboy confessing to a schoolmarm. He knew that look always melted her heart. Quick tears laced his lashes. "You are right, *min kære*," he said humbly.

Behind him, Laila edged out of the door and fairly ran for home. She was little more than sixteen years of age, compared to their own twenty, but age did not seem to matter where Soren was involved. He had the powers of the wind, seeming to gust in and capture any female heart he could, surrounding, pulling, easing them away from their moorings. And he seemed to have a distinct preference for brunettes.

"No," Kaatje said, brushing wisps of hair from her face. "No more, Soren. I will not forgive this." She shook her head as if deriding herself. "When you wanted to hire a milkmaid, I fought off my feelings of fear and suspicion. But I was wrong! It was not fear . . . it was God! The Lord was trying to warn me that there cannot be a woman within sight for you! The only way you could stay true to me is if we were alone for a hundred—no, a *thousand*—square miles!"

She whirled and stomped away from him, tears blinding her path. *Not again, God! Oh, I can't bear it!*

"Kaatje!" Soren cried, his voice cracking like a scared child's. In moments he had her in his arms again. He spoke in broken English as she struggled to get away. "I am sorry. I am so sorry! I don't know what is wrong with me! It is like an illness! I am sick. You must help me to get better!"

He knelt before her, crying, his blond curls pressed against her abdomen. Kaatje, still shaking with anger, fought off the urge to place her hand on his head. Soren lapsed into Norwegian as he begged her forgiveness. "Please, Kaatje. Please forgive me. It will be better in America. I promise. Please, please." His sobs and their native tongue—largely unspoken in their house since they had committed to go to America and had taken up English lessons—tore at her heart in a new way. She had never seen him so completely broken. Everything in her pulled Kaatje toward comforting him. But he was the one who had wronged her! Was this simply a new tactic? Just then, she glimpsed the figure of Laila in the distance as the girl ran over a hill and out of sight. Kaatje pulled at Soren's hands, wanting only to be away from him.

But she was too late. His eyes lit up through his tears and he glanced at Kaatje in wonder. She made another half-attempt to wrench free, but her strength seemed to be gone. She had waited so long for the joy of this moment! His large hands wandered over her stomach, searching, clarifying, frantic in their questioning. One more glance into her eyes and all his questions were answered.

Soren jumped up with a tremendous shout, then reached down to lift her in the air, spinning her around until she felt dizzy. His exuberance melted the edge off her anger. Crazily, a smile edged her lips.

"Soren, let me down," she said wearily.

"Oh, yes, yes," he said contritely, immediately doing as she bid. "I must be careful with you. With both of you."

She glanced away—embarrassed that she was forgiving him yet again—and moved toward the house, but Soren gathered her up into his arms again. Kaatje gave in to the embrace, sorrowfully longing to be reassured, longing for her husband. With her head resting against his chest, the tears flowed while Soren once again promised undying faithfulness.

"Father, you must let me go," Tora Anders railed, pacing as her father sat at the breakfast table, serenely drinking his coffee.

Elsa closed the door of their modest home behind her and remained quiet, listening to her sister and her father rehash an argument that had grown old. It was no use trying to sneak down the hall without disturbing them. From the kitchen, the front entry was visible, and both her father and Tora had glanced over at Elsa.

"No, Tora. You are sixteen and will do as I bid until you marry and have a good man to look after you. I will not be sending you off alone without proper supervision."

"Proper supervision? What is Elsa?" Tora cried, gesturing toward the door and her older sister. "I do not know of anyone more proper than she." *Ah,* Elsa thought, hiding a small smile. *She has changed tactics.* Earlier Tora had tried to get the whole family to go, then to convince their father that she was old enough to handle herself. Now she had given in to the last ploy—that he would entrust her to Elsa's care, a thought that had previously made her younger sister shudder.

Quietly, Elsa observed father and daughter. Tora had inherited Papa's olive skin—and the dark, chestnut hair he once had—as well as large, expressive eyes that often spoke more loudly than words. In her father's Elsa saw a menacing storm cloud that could always make her turn away. But not Tora.

"We will not talk of this again, Tora. I have decided."

"Decided?" Tora said, her voice high and tight. She stood, placing her hands on her hips. Her skin blanched and her hair, in contrast, seemed to darken to the color of night. She and Elsa shared only one physical characteristic: startlingly blue eyes, inherited from their mother. Now, in anger, they looked like the color of a turbulent sea in winter. "How can you decide? Perhaps I will go anyway, in spite of your decision. What would you think of that?" she challenged, tossing her head.

Her father stood quickly, bumping his chair over in the process. Even after years of stooping over his drawings, he was a tall man. Yet Tora stood her ground, staring up at him in open defiance. It was at that moment that their mother chose to enter the kitchen and gently edge between the two.

"Tora, sweetheart," reasoned Gratia, "I know this is difficult for you. But Elsa is going on to a new life. She must have some time alone with Peder for a bit before she takes on any family responsibility." Her face took on a merry look. "Besides, she might soon have a baby. She cannot look after you too."

"Oh!" Tora said in frustration, her hands balled into white-knuckled fists. "You all treat me as such a child! I will go to America. You will see. One way or the other, I will get there!"

With that, she edged past her sister and slammed the door behind her.

Elsa's mother sighed as her father sat down heavily. "She's a wonder, that one," Gratia said, as if commenting on the impish tactics of elves instead of their daughter.

"Perhaps I should allow her to go and sleep easier at night." Amund glowered. "Is it my judgment that I should raise three daughters?" he asked, gesticulating toward the ceiling.

His wife ignored him. "Come," she said to both him and Elsa, "We must go if we are to make it to church on time. Now where is Carina?"

"May I drive, Father?" Peder Ramstad asked, gently touching Leif Ramstad's shoulder.

Leif turned to regard his son, studying him eye to eye, and then nodded once. He immediately climbed into the elaborate surrey's second long seat, ducking to avoid the fringed roof, joining his wife,

Helga, and their daughter, Burgitte. All were impeccably dressed, as suited a wealthy family in Bergen on a Sunday morning. Peder's older brother, Garth, heir to the Ramstad shipping fortune, took the front seat beside Peder. "Your last day at home, eh, little brother?" He clapped him on the back as Peder shook the reins, sending the matched span of geldings into a quick trot toward church.

Behind them was the large family home that bordered the shipyard and faced the North Sea. Peder glanced back at the house, which had been built in the Italianate style after his father had returned from an inspirational trip to Europe. Peder had to laugh when he considered that at home he longed for the sea, and while crossing the Pacific, the Atlantic, the Indian Ocean, or elsewhere, his thoughts often pulled him home. At sea, he could mentally trace the low roof and overhanging eaves with decorative brackets, the entrance tower, the round-headed windows with hood moldings, the arcaded porch, and his bedroom on the second floor.

It was from that bedroom, as a young lad, that he had watched ship after great ship, built and launched from Ramstad Yard, and longed to go on each one. Over the past decade, he had done just that. Now, at twenty-four, he had accomplished his second goal at an uncommonly young age: captaining his own ship. And he had done so by stubbornly refusing a position on any Ramstad ship; never did he want anyone to attribute his success to anything other than hard work and well-deserved rewards. The *Herald*, a bark-rigged clipper, sat proudly at Bergen's docks, awaiting those immigrants who would accompany them in two days' time to America. But the most important passenger would be his wife.

He smiled as the sweet, warm coastline air filled his nostrils and the surrey glided over the macadam road toward town. She had never left his thoughts, it seemed. Like his childhood home, he was irresistibly drawn to Elsa Anders. In all his years away from Bergen, she had filled his nights with elaborate, fanciful dreams. At sea, facing the doldrums, Peder had filled his days with decisive plans for the future.

On the still waters, safely past the Roaring Forties, Peder would stare out to sea and imagine his beloved as a mermaid, her corn-silk hair floating in exotic waves about her sculpted face, her blue eyes matching the water around her, beckoning him to join her. Long ago he had decided he would return to Bergen and claim Elsa as his own. But not until he reached a position of influence. Not until he was captain and could build her a decent home. How he had prayed that her heart would not, in the meantime, favor another!

Peder had returned as often as he could, signing on for ships with routes that ported at Bergen. And each time he had found Elsa more beautiful, inside and out, than he had remembered her. He had last left her a year prior, promising to return for her as captain of his own ship. Others had laughed, but not his beloved Elsa. She had nodded once and said, "I will see you then, my future husband." The secret had remained theirs until a fortnight past. Then, all of Bergen learned that the captain had returned for his bride.

Leif's gruff voice shook Peder from his daydreaming. "You should not be going again, son. You have had your journeys and adventure. Garth could use your experience at sea to our advantage at Ramstad Yard. Together, as brothers, you could build our company to new heights."

Peder glanced at Garth, who met his look. He spoke to his father over his shoulder as he drove. "Garth knows quite enough about running the family business. And as much as I want to run a yard of my own, I believe I must be in America. Father, you should see it—"

"Pshaw," his father exclaimed. "What could America have on our Bergen? Here, we have a port over four hundred years old. There, the entire country is barely a hundred. Who can find confidence in a government so young?"

"Governments come and go, as we have seen here," Peder said. "But I tell you, I love the democratic constitution of the United States, and I would die to keep her free." He swallowed hard. Then, lowering his voice, he said, "I want something of my own, Father. I

13

always have. First it was captaining my own ship. Now I will build another Ramstad Yard. In America. I will make you proud, Father, as Garth will continue to make you proud here."

Garth clapped Peder on the shoulder with an understanding smile. "I envy you, little brother. Such freedom."

Leif groaned from the backseat. "You young men don't know what you have. When Amund and Gustav and I were at sea, we had to entertain thoughts of how to begin our own yard when we had nothing. You, at least, come from a position of power and money. It is an edge that I envy. Not the freedom."

"Yet you are an old man who has had his share of freedom," piped up Peder's mother, Helga. She was a strong, stalwart woman who had had much to do with the success of Ramstad Yard. She leaned forward between her boys, a hand on each. "He talks like a big man, but once he had dreams that were as frivolous as a child's."

Leif let out a sound of muted outrage as the rest of the family laughed. At heart, the big man with the tough exterior was as soft as a loving old hen.

"At least you men have the choice of whether or not to go," Burgitte joined in. "I think it is most unfair that I must wait for a man to take me away."

"Knowing you, Burgitte," Peder said, smiling, "you will find just the right man to take you exactly where you want to go."

"Yes," Garth said, turning around. "You, baby sister, are as weak and mindless as our dear mother."

Returning his smile, Burgitte batted away his hand, which threatened her with a pinch. "So I know my own mind. Is that a sin?"

"Oh no," Peder said, catching sight of his bride-to-be in the church courtyard. "On the contrary. It is an attribute."

❧

Karl Martensen took the bentwood butter box from his father's hands and spread the white, creamy mixture over his mother's fresh-baked rolls. Sonje Martensen finished placing food on the table and passed wise eyes over her son.

"What is bothering you, child?"

"Mother, I am not a child. I am a man of twenty-four."

His mother continued to study him, and he looked away, knowing that she was memorizing his features as if she would never see him again. All three of the Martensens had ash blond hair and large bones, but it was his father, Gustav, that Karl most resembled. Karl glanced at his father, who was leaning over his plate, silently shoving food into his mouth. It was as if he was looking into the mirror and could see his own reflection thirty years hence. Hopefully his hair would not recede as his father's had. Gustav's nose drooped a bit at the end, and his cheeks sagged as if weighted. In contrast, Karl's mother, who sported her own lines of aging, had pink, rounded cheeks and gentle smile lines at her eyes and mouth. Karl glanced from one to the other. He hoped he would inherit his mother's lines more than his father's. *I must smile more,* he silently reproved himself.

As if signing on for the effort, he smiled purposefully and said, "Will you always think of me as a boy?"

"Yes, my son," Sonje said, leaning over to hold his arm softly. "You age, but so do I. So I will always feel old and you will always feel young." Her look sobered. "So tell me what is bothering you."

A quick image of Elsa Anders burst through his mind. She had stood on the hill of the peninsula as Peder and he had brought the *Herald* to port. Even at a distance, Karl had recognized her proud stature and golden flying hair, a dark blue cape at her shoulders to guard against the early summer's evening breeze off the water. *Away,* he willed the image. *Away.* Instead he focused on today. "It is . . . it's just that . . ." he cast about for the right words and then urged confidence into his tone. "You see, I have become a Christian."

Gustav Martensen looked up at his son for the first time and quit chewing. He dropped his knife noisily on his plate as if in disgust. "No son of mine will be a lousy, two-faced, hypocritical Christian."

Karl lifted his chin and did not blink. He stared back at his father, refusing to look away as Gustav had routinely made him do as a child. "I am sorry, Father. I'm afraid I'm a grown man and can do what I wish. And I am sorry the Christian faith fills you with such memories of anger. It is not all about that. It is not all about grandfather and the way he was. You should know that from knowing your Christian friends like Amund and Leif."

Gustav stood, trembling with anger. He shook his finger at his son. "You will not disrespect your elders in my home!"

"I mean no disrespect," Karl said, wiping his mouth with the rough, cloth napkin and methodically laying it beside his plate. "Thank you for breakfast, Mother. Would you care to join me for church? We're late, but we can still make it."

He glanced at her, but she was seemingly struck mute. He softened his gaze and his tone. "I am sorry, Mother, I should have told you days ago. But it never seemed right. Today is Sunday. The Lord's day. I should worship."

His father glared at him as if he wanted to spit in his face. His features contorted as he struggled to find the right words. "I always lamented having but one son. Now I know why. I risked not having *any* when my boy defied me." With that, he walked out, slamming the cottage door behind him.

Karl closed his eyes. *Father, let me understand and love him anyway,* he prayed. *Reach out to him. Pull at his heart, as you did mine.*

When he opened his eyes again, he met his mother's soft gaze.

"I was a Christian once," she began.

t w o

*E*lsa watched out of the corner of her eye as the Ramstads arrived in their fancy surrey, noting the luxurious morocco leather and rich satin. Peder's father, Leif, after years of struggling financially, was given to frequent splurges in style, witnessed by their home and carriage. In comparison, the Anders family had always lived frugally, stepping up to a nicer home as the girls got older, but never living outside of their means. Not that they had the means of the Ramstads—Elsa's father had always been a partner at Ramstad Yard, but owned no more than 10 percent. What would it be like, as Peder's wife, to be a part of the Ramstads' fortune?

She fingered her long hair nervously, which she had done up on top but left flowing free in back. Seeing Peder, Elsa felt her heart catch and a small shiver run down her back. Tomorrow that handsome, grinning man would be her husband!

Kaatje Janssen walked up beside her and gave Elsa's hand a squeeze. Elsa glanced down at her friend and then back to Peder. "Oh, Kaatje, how could I be so blessed?"

"He is a wonderful man. I am so happy for you, my friend."

Something in Kaatje's voice caught Elsa's attention. What was it? Sorrow? No, Kaatje wore a small smile, as if she harbored a secret. "What is it, Kaatje?"

"I have news," she said, breaking out into a full-fledged grin. "I am expecting."

Elsa squealed and pulled her much smaller friend into an embrace. "That is wonderful news! A new life for a new country! Oh, Kaatje, can life get much better? Where is that husband of yours? I must congratulate him!" She glanced around and found Soren, talking animatedly with her sister Tora. Her eyes narrowed, and she glanced guiltily toward Kaatje.

Kaatje sighed as her smile faded. "There is one other hope I have for America," she said so softly that Elsa had to bend forward to hear. "It is that my husband will cease to have eyes for anyone but his wife."

Elsa felt her intense sorrow and agonized for her. She took Kaatje's hand. "Perhaps this child is just what he needs. Being a father will make a man out of your husband," she said. "And maybe a better husband out of the man."

Their conversation was cut short by Peder and Garth's arrival. "There is my sister-in-law to be!" boomed Garth. He nodded to Kaatje in friendly greeting and then took Elsa's hand in both of his, cocking an eyebrow at his younger brother. "I never thought you would marry first. Nor find favor with a woman I always had an eye on."

Elsa felt the slow burn of a flush climb her neck. "Oh, Garth, stop it. You know you never gave me the time of day. You have always thought Carina was the sun and the moon."

Garth let her hand go as he searched the churchyard for her older sister. "I do care for her," he said. "She is simple. Uncomplicated." He found Carina and his eyes softened.

Would Carina ever see him? Elsa wondered. Her older sister was always hard to pin down on any subject, let alone love. Perhaps she would grow old as a spinster, living with their parents until they passed on.

"I believe it is the sense of peace I get around her," Garth added. "I can see coming home to her at the end of a busy day at the yard and finding a sense of . . . *stillness.*"

Peder clapped his brother on the shoulder. "Keep up this reverie and we will consider including you two in a double wedding tomorrow."

"Ah no," Garth said with a laugh. "Just a young man's dream. Maybe someday. But I'm afraid you'll be the only Ramstad to marry for a while." Garth turned his attention back to Elsa. "Carina is peaceful. But life with *this* Anders girl will be an adventure."

Elsa smiled, feeling her blush climb again.

Peder placed a warm hand at the small of her back, and she glanced up at him, a bit shocked at his forwardness in public. "That is my hope," he said. "To adventure forward with my wife beside me."

"And I with you," she said, relishing Peder's words. After a quick glance around the yard, she stood on tiptoe to give him a surreptitious kiss.

Pastor Konur Lien and his wife, Amalia, greeted Kaatje, Soren, and each parishioner as they entered the spare sanctuary that doubled as a schoolhouse. They would return for the wedding tomorrow. Kaatje smiled, thinking of Elsa and Peder. They were a good match and would no doubt find much happiness in marriage.

Then her smile faded as she thought about her own marital life. Would she and Soren ever find their footing again? As they sat down on the wooden pews, Kaatje contemplated their own beginning. Two years ago, Soren had been her world and she seemed to be his. Out of all the young women who populated the cottages that surrounded Bergen on acres of rolling farmland, Soren had chosen her to be his wife. He had always been popular with the girls, and Kaatje's heart had thrilled when she learned that he wanted to court her. In her naiveté, she never dreamed that she would not be the last.

Kaatje unconsciously placed her hand on her stomach and rubbed it in a small circle. She hated to leave the only home she had ever known, but farming here was an endless chore, with no hope of getting ahead. Most of the farmers she knew worked until they could do so no more, only to hand off most of their income to wealthy landowners who lived in the heart of the city, never appreciating the beauty of the land about them.

In America . . . in America, one could *have* a hundred and sixty acres as his own. Imagine that! They were giving it away and only expected the new Americans to do what she and Soren had always wanted to do: work their own soil. Kaatje sighed, finding hope again in their future. A hundred and sixty acres was bound to be a long way from any other women. Better yet, perhaps the other settlers would be male, going ahead of their wives and families to make a home out of a homestead.

The church service began with a hymn of hope and praise, led by Amalia Lien's clear, sweet soprano and the pastor's off-key, booming bass. Pastor Lien was in rare form today, clearly excited about their upcoming trip. Peder Ramstad had wisely sold Konur on the idea of immigration first, and Konur, in turn, had helped sell the idea to many of his congregation. Although they intended to split up into two groups, one heading to a place called Maine to work on a new shipyard, and the other to a place called North Dakota to work the land, they were leaving together in spirit. And that was bound to make them stronger.

"I know that my Redeemer lives . . . He lives to wipe away my tears; He lives to calm my troubled heart; He lives all blessings to impart." Kaatje found strength in the words of the hymn as they sang two verses in Norwegian and two in English. She would focus on the hope of the future, the promise of her Redeemer. For in both, she would find her true happiness. Kaatje wiped away her tears as the congregation finished the hymn and sank once more to the hard benches.

"This morning, I want to introduce the new pastor to the congregation that will remain here. I am honored to present Pastor Maakestad, just arrived from Christiania." The people applauded and wove their heads back and forth, trying to get a good look at the youthful man. He seemed terribly young in comparison to Konur's fifty years, probably just out of seminary, Kaatje mused. She found comfort in the fact that the pastor who had baptized her as an infant would be going with them on their new venture. They would still be able to worship together in North Dakota!

As the new pastor spoke, Kaatje sensed the sorrow within the group. For half of them would be departing shortly, and the other half would remain. It was sad, but part of life, she supposed. Once again she wished her parents had lived to immigrate with her. It would not be nearly as hard. A pang of sorrow crossed her heart. Who would care for their graves? Who would go and talk to them? She sighed at her own foolish thoughts. She could still talk to them. They were as bound to hear her in America as they were in Bergen. And what did they care of their graves? They had gone on to paradise! Which was what North Dakota sounded like to her—nearly heaven.

She thought back on the American railroad pamphlets that Soren had brought home to study. According to the promises made within, one only had to set a seed down and it became a garden! How could they fail on land so fertile? Why, it sounded almost easy to grow an entire crop there!

Pastor Lien read from the Bible and then launched into his sermon on new beginnings. A new start, Kaatje thought. It *would* be like springtime—for both of them. She glanced up at Soren with a smile and saw his eyelids begin to droop as they customarily did in church. Setting her lips in a grim line, she gave him a swift jab in the ribs. That will do, she thought with satisfaction as he gave a soft "oof." Yes, it would be a new start for them.

Tora was so relieved when church was over that she nearly ran down the aisle. She needed to get out in the fresh air, to think clearly, to lay her plans. She was almost at the door when she heard her friend Laila call her name. "Tora!"

She turned and searched the sanctuary for her school friend. The two looked very similar with their dark hair and sculpted faces. Many times people had mistaken them for sisters. A brief feeling of sorrow passed through Tora's heart. She would miss Laila. But she dismissed the feeling right away. Laila was a poor milkmaid. She, Tora Anders, would be a great lady someday.

Laila reached her, her cheeks flushed a ruddy hue. "I have something to tell you!" she said excitedly, taking Tora's hand.

Tora's heart skipped a beat. She loved secrets, and judging from Laila's face, there was much to tell. "Come on," Tora said, pulling her around the group at the door and out, without greeting Pastor Lien and the new minister. "I have something to tell you too!"

They ran down the steps, as giddy as twelve-year-olds, and settled under a huge pine that bordered the yard. There, Laila turned toward her with big eyes. "I've been kissed!" she said.

Tora smiled, feeling wise and maternal. "Well, it's high time, I'd say. Who was it?"

Laila's face fell. "That's the horrible part."

Tora felt a shiver up her arm and grew more interested. "Who? Who is it?"

Laila's eyes searched the courtyard and settled on Soren Janssen, talking with some other farmers. "Isn't he . . . beautiful? I love his curly hair and those broad shoulders, and you should see the way he looks at me with those deep blue eyes!"

Tora watched the man along with Laila. Within seconds, he scanned the group congregating outside of church. When his gaze reached the two girls, his secret smile was meant for Laila. But Tora felt his eyes studying her too. Another shiver ran down her back, and she tossed her head as if even the idea of flirting with him was repugnant.

"He is leaving, Laila," she said. "Besides, he's married."

"Yes, but I don't think he loves Kaatje." Her voice held such hope.

Tora scoffed at her naiveté. "Laila, he does love her. He just has a taste for more than one woman."

The girl turned shocked eyes on her. "More than one? Is that possible? I thought he loved me!"

"No, dear," she said, feeling all the condescension she heard in her own voice. "You were convenient, available. But he's leaving in two days—with Kaatje."

Laila's face grew red as she held in the tears that pooled in her eyes. "But he said I was beautiful! Like a ripe peach!"

"Oh, you are beautiful, Laila," Tora said, surprised by a sudden rush of empathy for her friend. "Someone else will discover you soon. You'll see."

Laila turned away as the tears cascaded down her cheeks. She wiped them away with the back of her hand and nodded quickly. "And what is your news?" she asked after a moment.

"I'm leaving on the *Herald* too," Tora said softly. This time she boldly met Soren's roving glance.

A church picnic followed services that day, honoring the immigrants and celebrating their last meal together as a congregation. Peder ate his meal as a guest of the Anders family and could not stop smiling at Elsa. "Mrs. Anders, that was a wonderful meal," he said, settling back, full and satisfied. "I can only hope that my bride will be as good a cook as her mother."

"Ah, pshaw." Gratia Anders waved his praise away. "There is no cooking when it comes to this picnic. I think that even Tora could fix this sort of meal."

The family laughed, and Tora, for once, simply smiled along. She was acting very amiable today, Peder thought, and was relieved. Elsa had told him the stir her younger sister was making about going with them, and he was worried. He didn't want her on his hands. She was trouble from head to toe, that one. Not like his Elsa. His eyes were drawn to his beloved once again. What would it be like to hold her in his arms at last as a husband held his wife? Moreover, what would life be like with her day to day?

He popped another piece of flatbread in his mouth and stood. The other men were heading back into the building for their final meeting. In two days' time, all these people would be aboard the *Herald.* As the captain, he would lead today's meeting.

Before he joined them, Peder knelt and took Elsa's hand, bringing it to his lips. "Tomorrow, my bride?"

She smiled and looked down prettily, and Peder's heart swelled with pride. "Tomorrow, my groom," she said, bravely meeting his gaze again. He stared into her eyes for a moment, hoping she could read his mind and be reassured by his thoughts. Like a flower, she was just beginning to bloom. What would she be like as a married woman and a mother? He hoped their children would inherit her intense blue eyes rather than his own muddy green.

Peder stood then and nodded to the other Anders women, then held out his hand to Amund. "Sir. Thank you for welcoming me into your family."

"Glad to have you, my son. My daughter has chosen well." Amund gripped his hand firmly for a moment longer than necessary and stared intently into his eyes. Peder had no problem reading his mind. *Treat her well. I am entrusting her life to you.*

Peder returned his future father-in-law's gaze until the older man released his grip and looked away. One thing Leif Ramstad had always taught his sons: A man never looked away from a challenge. And Peder wanted Amund Anders to have faith in the man he had become. Peder knew that Elsa was Amund's favorite daughter, although the man would never admit it. And he wanted both Amund and Gratia to have confidence that she would be safe and happy when they waved good-bye to her.

With one more tender smile toward Elsa, he turned on his heel and climbed the church steps. Inside, he walked the wood floor to the front, taking stock as the others moved to their seats. Of the people that would help build the American Ramstad Yard, there was Bjorn Erikson, Kristoffer Swenson, and Mikkel Thompson, all of whom had families. Of those who would make their way west to North Dakota, there was Soren Janssen—a man who troubled Peder—and Birger Nelson, a shepherd who would leave his sheep behind, but not his wife, Eira, a natural healer. Einar Gustavson was also a good, strong farmer. Nels and Mathias were young, single men who intended to make their way on the prairies of North Dakota, as did Nora Paulson, the teacher who had taught all the immigrants English. Together with the Liens, the children, and Karl Martensen, their group numbered twenty-one. Searching the crowd for Karl, he decided his friend must not be coming and began the meeting.

～≈◯≈～

Sonje poured another cup of strong coffee for her son and herself as she gazed out the window. With Gustav still absent, she dared to speak openly.

"Your father," she said, cocking her head toward the door as if visualizing him leaving again, "is afraid. He is afraid that he made the wrong decision in dishonoring God so long ago, but is too proud to admit it."

"And you, Mother?" Karl asked quietly. "How could you turn your back on Christ?"

"I am a married woman, and I had to abide by your father's decision."

A rush of anger flowed through Karl. "How? I admire your respect for my father, but how? If you've seen the face of God, how can you turn your back?"

With wise eyes, Sonje studied her only child. "Like anything, it becomes easier with time. When I was a young woman . . ." her voice trailed away as she looked out the window. "It was harder. Gustav and I attended church each week. But then your father's father came to live with us."

"I remember him. A little."

"Yes, you were quite young. I am surprised you remember him at all. In public, he said all the right things, but in private, he was a mean man who used the faith in evil ways. Even as an old man, he seemed bent on belittling your father, much as he had your grandmother. Poor dear. She was a wonderful woman. He destroyed her."

"How?"

Sonje shook her head. "It is not my place to tell you specifics. But I will tell you that she had planted a seed of faith in Gustav that was just beginning to sprout in those early years with me. Away from his father, he could tend the garden—and I could see it." Her eyes were cloudy with tears, as if she were witnessing a scene from their life twenty years past. "I could see that he was going to become a man with an impressive faith. It brought us ever closer." A single tear dripped down her cheek and glistened in the window's light. "And then your grandfather tore it all down. I've been trying to pick up the pieces ever since then—to hold us together as a family."

Karl reached across the table and held her wrinkled hands in his own. "But Mother, you know it is not enough, do you not? I appreciate all you have done for me. But Christ calls constantly. Do you not hear him? Regardless of Father's decision, you need to stand up for your faith. I don't know much, but I do know that."

His mother nodded, two trails of tears glistening now. "I know, Karl." She removed her hands from his and padded to the window. Outside, Karl glimpsed his father, coming in for his noontime meal. "I've heard God calling me for some time now," she said. "I guess I just needed time to gain strength for the fight." She turned back to him. "For now, I will find solace in the fact that you have found God. Someday you must tell me how."

"I will."

"Was it Peder?" she dared ask, just as Gustav opened the door.

"In some ways," Karl said, turning to face his glowering father.

"Are you still here?" Gustav thundered. "Out! At once! You are no longer welcome in my home."

three

✦

"It is stunning," Elsa said in gratitude, standing back from the altar and hooking an arm around each of her sisters.

Indeed, the church looked like a reflection of the hills that surrounded it, artfully decorated with wildflowers. There were the rosy red of heather, the purple of lupine, the gold of buttercups, and the white of daisies and caraway. Carina, dear Carina, had walked high into the hills to gather Elsa's favorite, pink and purple fireweed. On either side of the altar was a small tree, mounted in a pail of sand, decorated with *prestekrage*, the white flowers that looked like Pastor Lien's clerical collar. In each of the six windows stood a fat candle that Gratia Anders had hand dipped, with flowers all about them. Although it would be a morning wedding, as was traditional, Elsa had wanted candlelight.

"It is beautiful!" Carina exclaimed, clasping her hands.

Tora moved away, suddenly conscious that she was being friendly with a sister who had refused to help her. Elsa ignored her withdrawal, not wanting anything to shade the light of this day. The morning had begun with a traditional wedding breakfast, a hearty

27

stew served to both the Anders and the Ramstads at the bride's home. They had kept Peder blindfolded throughout, determined to keep him from seeing his bride until the wedding. He had laughed along with the rest, accepting help from his mother in feeding himself, yet had borne it all with a quiet dignity. Watching him had made Elsa's stomach tighten and her hands shake, thinking of how beautiful her husband-to-be was, inside and out. Had she ever been as sure of anything as she was of him? Elsa thought not.

"Come," Carina said gently, pulling at her younger sister's hand. "We must get you home and dressed. The processional will begin very soon."

Elsa nodded and walked out behind her sisters, then turned back once more to look at the sanctuary. She would leave now as an Anders. The next time, it would be as a Ramstad. "Thank you, God, for this happiness!" she whispered, elated. Nothing compared to the joy of this day.

At home, Carina and Tora hustled her into her bedroom and into the clothes that their mother had so lovingly laid out for her. Along with the rest of the wedding party and congregation, Elsa would wear her *bunad,* the traditional costume of Bergen. But as befit a grown woman, she would wear her hair in a graceful chignon instead of a long braid, along with her great-grandmother's wedding cap—worn by her grandmother and mother before her—and the wedding brooches passed down through her family.

She giggled as Carina pinned yet another *sølje* to her vest, making six in all. "It's a bit gaudy, don't you think?"

"Nonsense," Carina said gently. "It befits a bride to wear all the special jewelry she can get her hands on." Elsa shifted in her chair, and the tiny gold and silver streamers from each pin jingled softly against the pewter buttons of her vest.

"There, you see?" Carina said. "It sounds like bells from heaven, far, far away."

Tora snorted from her perch on the bed. "You mind your manners,

Tora Anders," Gratia said, shaking a brush at her youngest. "This is Elsa's day, and I do not want you to put a damper on it."

"I would never think of such a thing," said Tora, putting on a hurt expression.

"Do not let her fool you, Mama," Elsa said. "She helped decorate the sanctuary, and it is lovely."

"She even went up into the hills to get the fireweed you love," Carina added.

"Tora did that?" Elsa asked in surprise. "I was sure it was you, Carina. Thank you, Tora. See, Mama? She is not as disinterested as she pretends."

Gratia hid her smile from Tora and finished her work on Elsa's hair. Then she gently placed the cap on her daughter's head, tears of joy and sadness intermingling as she did so.

"Oh, Mama," was all that Elsa could say, feeling herself choke up too.

Gratia wiped away her tears and smiled at her daughter in the mirror before them. "There you are, more beautiful than ever."

"They have arrived!" Carina said, turning excitedly from the window. "They're all here! Are you ready, Elsa?"

Butterflies flitted about in her stomach. "As ready as I ever will be," she said, swallowing hard. Taking her mother's hand, she stood and looked once more in the mirror. Her long skirt was a thick black wool with fine embroidered work at the bottom. The traditional white blouse hugged her arms and breasts, and over it was a matching vest to the skirt. White stockings and black slippers completed the ensemble. But she had to admit, the jewelry and wedding cap made her feel like Norway's queen.

And it was a good thing. For when her father opened the door to her groom and shook his hand, she felt as if he were a king. Peder too wore the Bergen costume, but he loomed larger in the doorway than she remembered, and his outfit was new, since the one from his adolescence would have been much too small. His image echoed the rest of the men, but Elsa thought she had never seen a finer form. Broad shoulders filled his white shirt that billowed at the arms and came down to a fine, fitted cuff. He wore a black vest with gold buttons, and the matching knickers and white hose hugged his thickly muscled legs above big, black shoes. His wide belt was an ornate masterpiece with dangling metalwork.

Amund Anders turned from Peder, kissed his daughter, reached for her hand, and placed it in Peder's. They grinned at one another for a long time, relishing the moment, and then Gratia pushed them out the door. They led the processional of people walking two by two and talking among themselves. All were in a festive mood, and Elsa felt very loved. How could she do without these people? Only the promise of Peder's love kept her feet moving to the church, where Pastor Lien met them.

"O God, we commit these children to thy tender care," he prayed after the opening hymn. "Walk between them, O Lord, for all their days and nights together. Hold them fast in the love that only thy Son Jesus could represent, and give them long life and a fruitful union. These things we pray in thy name, Father."

"Amen," said the people.

Pastor Lien leaned forward and smiled at the young couple before him. "I ask thee, therefore, Peder Leif Ramstad, in the presence of God and this Christian assembly: Wilt thou have Elsa Anna Anders, here present, to be thy wedded wife?"

"I will," Peder said, staring into Elsa's eyes.

"Wilt thou live with her according to God's holy word, love and honor her, and alike in good and evil days keep thee only unto her, so long as ye both shall live?"

"I will," he repeated, his eyes never wavering.

Pastor Lien turned to Elsa. "In like manner I ask thee, Elsa Anna Anders: Wilt thou have Peder Leif Ramstad, here present, to be thy wedded husband?"

"I will," she said, her voice surprisingly strong and sure. She wanted Peder to feel all the assurance she had in her heart that this was right, that she wanted nothing else.

"Wilt thou live with him according to God's holy word, love and honor him, and alike in good and evil days keep thee only unto him, so long as ye both shall live?"

"I will," she stated, hoping her eyes conveyed to Peder all the love she felt.

"Forasmuch as you have consented together in holy wedlock, and have now witnessed the same before God and this Christian assembly, and have joined your right hands in token thereof, I pronounce you man and wife. In the name of the Father, and of the Son, and of the Holy Ghost. Amen. What God hath joined together, let no man put asunder."

The pastor turned to Peder. "The rings?" he whispered. Peder fished for them in his pocket, then pulled out the two simple bands.

"Repeat after me," he directed Peder, handing him Elsa's ring. "Receive this ring . . ."

"Receive this ring," Peder said, his eyes glistening with joy as he stared down at her.

"As a pledge and a token of my love and faithfulness."

"As a pledge," he said slowly, as if thinking over each word, "and a token of my love and faithfulness."

As if in a dream, Elsa, as Peder had before her, repeated Pastor Lien's words and slipped the ring on his hand. They then remained side by side, kneeling before their pastor, as he went on to preach about Adam and Eve, Paul's letter to the Ephesians, and loving as Christ had loved. Elsa only heard snippets of his homily, thinking more on her elation at being Peder's bride, having his hand in hers, and their future in America. Pastor Lien's hand on her head brought her back to the present.

"Let us pray," he said. "Lord God, heavenly Father, thou who didst create man and woman and didst join them together in marriage, thereby signifying the mystery of the union between thy dear

Son Jesus Christ and his bride the Church: We beseech thee in thine infinite mercy, let not this thy blessed work and ordinance be brought to naught among us, but graciously protect it. Through Jesus Christ, thy beloved Son, our Lord. Amen."

"Amen!" Peder repeated with gusto, making Elsa want to giggle.

"Peace be with you," Pastor Lien said, smiling at both of them.

"And with you," Peder said with a nod.

"The Lord be with you!" the pastor said to his congregation.

"And with thy Spirit!" they said as one.

"The Lord bless thee, and keep thee. The Lord make his face to shine upon thee, and be gracious unto thee. The Lord lift up his countenance upon thee, and give thee peace. Amen."

Pastor Lien gestured to Peder to help Elsa rise, then placed a hand on each of their shoulders as they turned to the congregation. Spontaneously, the people began to applaud and cheer.

"I would like to introduce Mr. and Mrs. Peder Ramstad!" Pastor Lien shouted happily over the mayhem.

The traditional wedding luncheon was another picnic, held on the hillside near the rock where Elsa and her father had enjoyed so many times together, watching the great aurora borealis. High above the city, the group reveled in the perfect summer weather, under clear blue skies that met purple granite mountains, and surrounded by the full bloom of wildflowers. Far below them, ships entered and exited the port on gray-blue waters, and yet none of the sounds of commerce could reach them today.

"It is like being in heaven!" Elsa said, taking her younger sister's hand.

Tora shook her off, feeling half-bad about it, but not in any mood to be gay. She wanted to give in, to celebrate with her sister, but could not get past the wall of resentment inside. She could feel it—choking, heavy—and blamed Elsa for its presence. *They* could all be happy. Why not? They were leaving on the morrow with family blessings, while she had been reduced to sneaking aboard the ship like a common criminal! Had Elsa stood up for her, Mama and Papa would have given in. But she had not.

Elsa gave her a hurt look and turned away, obviously trying not to let Tora affect her mood. Tora did have to admit that her sister looked fetching. The red and the black of her *bunad* brought out her blue eyes and the ruddiness of her cheeks. She looked like the quintessential bride, with tendrils of white-blond hair escaping her knot beneath her bridal cap and dancing in the breeze about her face. The traditional costume was tight and accentuated her enviable figure. Fortunately for Tora, she did not have to physically compete with Elsa. She was reasonably sure of her own attractive image. It was Elsa's newfound status as Peder Ramstad's wife that Tora envied.

Tora's mother had found a central location and spread out her part of the wedding feast. There was fish of all sorts—cod, capelin, herring, mackerel, salmon, and trout—cooked in a variety of ways and chilled for the luncheon. In addition, there were whipped cream cakes, tortes, smørbrød, thick cream to pour over fresh strawberries . . . the delicious dishes went on and on as others spread out their own blankets and added their offerings to the fare. Finally, the medley of dishes stretched for twenty feet, for a crowd of perhaps fifty. There would be plenty to eat. Tora turned away as the group sang the doxology as grace. The thought of food, or any more prayer, disgusted her. There were plans to be made.

She eyed the crowd, searching for that one young man she had spotted earlier, a sailor on the *Herald*. There he was, she noted as the crowd sang "Amen." Tall, gawky, and struggling with the last vestiges of acne, the boy blushed clear up to his hairline when he met Tora's mastered gaze—forward, yet coquettish. Oh, this will be simple, she thought. This will be much too simple!

Peder nearly choked on his salmon when Garth came to the punch line of his bawdy joke and slapped him on the back. Burgitte handed

Peder another glass of lingonberry juice and smiled benignly at both her brothers. The Ramstads were sitting with the Anderses, and the two families melded comfortably, as they had for years. Only Tora was missing; Peder had seen her disappear over the hill some time ago with one of his sailors. The conversation was lively. Amund espoused that, as old friends, this seemed like a logical end, that their children should marry. *It sure feels right to me,* Peder thought.

He gazed at Elsa with such happiness in his heart that he feared tears would come to his eyes. She was elegant and beautiful. And she was his. He glanced around for their old friend Karl. He should be there with them, Peder thought. After all, they had played together as children, and through ten years of sailing on the same ships, Karl had become as close to him as his brother, Garth. Peder's eyes found the Martensens, higher up on the hill. As usual, Gustav looked grumpy, even in the midst of the festivities, and Sonje bravely put up a false front of joy. Catching Peder's eye, she raised a glass in greeting. He mouthed "Where's Karl?" and Sonje pointed down the hill.

There by an old pine was Karl, talking with several of the men who would sail with them—Bjorn, Kristoffer, and Mikkel. *Making plans, as usual,* Peder thought with a smile. It wouldn't be long until Karl captained his own ship. He was certainly as capable as Peder. Despite Peder's best efforts to make his own way, the Ramstad name had afforded him a slight edge. Still, it wouldn't be long before Karl had his own place of authority. He was bright and ambitious. But ambitions should be set aside today. All were to drink and be merry—not work!

Peder was rising to go rout out his friend when his mother called to him. "Peder, wait a moment. Your father and I would like to share something with you and Elsa."

The seriousness in her tone stilled Peder. "Yes, Mother?"

Helga looked to his father, and on cue, Leif Ramstad spoke. "At long last, your mother has convinced me that you deserve the same as your elder brother has received. Although Garth comes into a ready-made business, we are prepared to help finance your American enterprise. It is our wedding gift to you."

Peder heard Elsa's quick intake of breath but did not turn from his father. "I . . . I do not know what to say, Father, Mother. Other than thank you." He shook his head. "You are most generous. But I must talk it over with Karl. All along, the two of us have planned this venture as a sixty-forty split. Your gift would change things drastically."

Leif nodded sagely and patted his son's knee. "You are wise to think it over. But I would not think it wise to turn down the opportunity our gift affords you. It is a leg up on a business in which it is increasingly difficult to turn a profit. Find a way to break the news to Karl, son." Leif smiled and pointed at Elsa. "You have a wife to care for now. Perhaps children soon. You need to think ahead."

Peder swallowed his irritation. Did his father think of him as a boy? Peder did not like the thought of his father controlling him through his financial gift, but he was right. It was tough to make a go of a shipping business these days, especially in sail. A man needed any edge he could find. But Karl would not like it. He would not like it at all.

When he rose, he gave Elsa a reassuring smile and tenderly tucked a golden tendril of hair behind her ear. "I won't be long. I just need to talk to him."

"I understand," she said, smiling into his eyes.

Peder turned and walked down the grassy slope toward the pine grove where Karl and the men still spoke animatedly. On the way, friend after friend stopped to greet and congratulate Peder on his good fortune or offer up a bawdy joke on marital activities. After years of life with sailors, the humor did not offend him, but he rarely joined in. The closer he got to Karl, the more clearly he saw what might transpire if his friend knew the truth. He might leave and start his own company. After all, Karl's heart was in steam, not sail, and the only reason he stayed with Peder and his vision was friendship and lack of funds. And Peder needed him. No, perhaps now was not the right time. Once aboard ship, then he could break the news.

Peder plastered on a smile as he joined the men. They greeted him loudly, and for the first time, Peder realized that they had been dipping into the homemade reserves. After a moment, Tomas, the town doctor, joined the group and Peder turned away from the men with relief.

"Now, doctor, it is imperative that every man, woman, and child be thoroughly examined tomorrow morning," Peder said, hearing the commanding tone that had made him a good captain enter his voice. "Watch specifically for signs of cholera and consumption. I've seen corpses swell so big, no coffin could hold them. I want none of that on my ship. These people will get to America before they face new miasmas," he told the doctor, referring to the bad air that carried disease, "not die aboard the *Herald.*"

"Aye, aye, Captain," Tomas said with a friendly smile. He leaned toward Peder with a look of semiserious conspiracy, then glanced at the loud group of men ten paces away. "But I honestly think that the only illness you'll see could be politely attributed to seasickness."

Karl took another swig from Bjorn's jug and watched with watering eyes as Peder took his wife in his arms. *Dear Father in heaven, how am I to stand this?* Contrary to what Karl had hoped, the drinking had not made things better; it had simply made things more *present.* Instead of putting distance between him and Elsa, it seemed to call him closer to her, increased his longing to take her into his own arms. How was he supposed to work with Peder? To have Elsa in such close proximity? And what kind of friend fell in love with his best friend's woman? Perhaps it was hearing about her for years from Peder on dull, quiet seas. Hearing her attributes bragged about, hearing her letters read aloud. Somehow along the way, Karl had imagined that Elsa would be his. How could he have let it happen?

As the sun grew low in the sky and people gathered in close for a few last celebratory dances, Karl swallowed hard. The sad fact was that Elsa had never given him a second glance. Peder was always the captain of her ship, and Karl nothing more than the first mate. It was as it should be: She was married to the man she had always loved. After all, she barely knew Karl the man. They had been friends as children, but it was Peder who had courted her for the last three years via letter and the occasional visit. Karl only knew Elsa the woman because Peder was so open in sharing his love for her, and through that sharing, Karl had fallen for her too. It was not fair, but it was fact. Yet that knowledge didn't make it easier for Karl.

She was a wonder to watch as Peder swung her around in the traditional wedding dance of Bergen. Later, amidst the warm, glowing light that each person contributed in the candlelight dance, her eyes sparkled as she looked up into Peder's eyes. It was too much for Karl. He could not watch any longer. His only hope was to focus on Christ and pray—pray with all he had in him—that his Savior would cast away these feelings that threatened to undo him. He turned and walked away, and was surprised to find his father walking in silence beside him.

"I thought you had disowned me," Karl said, no malice in his voice.

"I have. Yet I still need to keep you accountable," said Gustav.

Karl pulled up short in a clearing not far from the candlelight dance. He peered through the deep shadows, trying to discern his father's look. "What do you mean?"

"I mean that it does not honor your *faith* to covet another man's wife."

Was it so obvious? Karl quickly looked away, embarrassed to be read by his father. "I know. It is something I will conquer. I never intend to get between them, only serve them as a friend. Peder needs me. We are building a business together."

Gustav took a step closer to his son. "You are the hypocrite my father was. Claiming to want to serve your friends by staying near them when the best way you could do so is to go away." He paused and his tone softened. "Run, son. Run far away. The love of a woman is a powerful thing. Time and miles will heal you."

Karl looked up at him, wondering at the care in his voice. Was this the same man who had thrown him out yesterday? What kind of witness to Christ was it to remain in a position that might ultimately endanger his dearest friend's marriage? But he was so close to fulfilling his dream! Peder and he would build a business that would make him a successful man. As a full-fledged partner. Not dependent on a Ramstad as his father had always been and always resented. Karl had worked long years to come to this place. Where else would he have the opportunity?

"You are wrong, Father. I have the power of Christ within me. He defied Satan; so will I defy these feelings and prove to you that a Christian man can be pure and honest, not two-faced."

Gustav Martensen laughed in derision. "If I live to see it proven true, we will talk again. But mark my words, Karl. You are on a dangerous path. Come back to Bergen in the years to come and show me you took the high road, and I will allow you in my home. Unless you prove that to me, you are not ever welcome here again."

f o u r

*E*lsa looked over at her friend and gave her a quick squeeze. Kaatje looked as frightened as Elsa felt as she stared at the *Herald,* a medium-sized, bark-rigged clipper. The ship, of which Peder was so proud, was majestic.

Kristoffer Swenson, the second mate, stopped beside them and looked up at the ship. "She'll boast twenty-one sails once we're on the open sea," he said briefly. Kristoffer was not given to long speeches, but a kinder man would be hard to find. And his obvious love for the ship, reflected in both his words and his lean face, made Elsa and Kaatje smile.

As the passengers from Bergen continued boarding the ship, Astrid Swenson, Kristoffer's very pregnant wife, stopped beside Kaatje. "You are not nervous, are you?"

"Ah, no," Kaatje said. "Terrified."

"Pshaw," said Kristoffer. He pointed up at the port side of the *Herald.* "She's the best down-easter Maine has to offer. Her steel hull can tolerate any transatlantic wind. Don't you ladies worry," he said, placing a lean arm around Astrid. "I would not be taking my wife and sons along if I weren't confident they would arrive in Boston."

Kaatje looked down, a bit embarrassed that Kristoffer was referring not only to his son Knut, but Astrid's unborn child as well. But he was so exuberant, so sure, that the women all took confidence as they looked up to the ship again.

Soren joined their little group and was almost knocked over by three-year-old Knut, who was running around and around his parents, begging to go aboard. Soren laughed his great belly laugh that always beckoned everyone else to join in and echoed Knut's request. Together the adults glanced back at Bergen and then climbed the gangway with Kristoffer leading the way—all except Elsa.

She turned and clung to her mother, reluctant to part, wanting to memorize the feel of being in her arms. It would be a very long time, if ever, before they saw each other again. Her mother obviously felt the same, for she embraced Elsa with a ferocity that threatened to crush the air out of her. But she welcomed it. Despite the agonizing departures occurring in every family's circle, the air about them was bright and sparked with excitement. Elsa battled the feeling that they were all just going away on holiday, not wanting to forget any important face, not wanting to forget any important words.

"*Adjo,* daughter, *adjo,*" Her mother said over and over again. Her repeated good-byes tore at Elsa's heart. Sobbing, Gratia wrenched away and into Carina's arms as Elsa went on to her father. The old man wiped his watering eyes with an almost angry hand and then pulled Elsa into his strong arms as fiercely as had her mother. She closed her eyes and tried to memorize his smell—a curious but perpetual mix of wood, soap, and ink. It was difficult to differentiate it from the briny, fishy odor that permeated the docks, and that pained her somehow. She pulled away but held on to her father's hands, feeling the ache in her throat beginning to build, and not wanting to give in to the sobs that would beg her heart to stay in Bergen forever.

Elsa looked down at those wizened hands, virile despite the age spots that covered them, afraid to look into her father's eyes. Over the years, his fingertips had grown permanently black, stained by the ink of his trade as a shipwright. Oh, how she would miss those hands! His reassuring pats, the way he used them to gesture his feelings and emotions.

"Elsa," he said softly, pulling away one hand to raise her chin.

Reluctantly, she raised her eyes to meet his. Tears flowed freely down his face now, and that was the end of Elsa's reserves. She tried to smile through her own tears. "Good-bye, Papa," she managed, feeling like she was strangling.

"*Adjo*, sweet one. Go with God, and he will see you through. Remember the lights, eh?"

She nodded, swallowing hard. She knew she had to tear herself away. It was her duty to be on board and greet the passengers while Peder saw to other things—an initial act of partnership. Thankfully, at that moment he appeared, and simply having him near seemed to shore up her crumbling walls. She raised her chin, gave her mother another quick hug then said brief good-byes to her sisters as Peder said farewell to her parents. Then, resolving not to look back, she walked in front of her husband and up the gangway to the ship that would take her to her new life.

Karl was at the top and stretched out his hand to help her over the side and down the three small stairs. Peder told Elsa that he needed to speak with Kristoffer and check on the crew's progress in stowing the last of the luggage. She nodded and turned to greet those who were boarding. All she wanted now was to be off. The wait for their departure, with her family and beloved homeland still beckoning on shore, would seem interminable.

"You will be back," Karl said quietly, his voice as always reminding her of cello tones.

She glanced up at him in surprise. "Whatever do you mean?"

"I mean that captains often bring their wives along on voyages. We will not be gone from Bergen forever. And as the yard grows and more ships are deemed seaworthy, will not the chances of that simply grow too?" His smile was gentle and reassuring.

"Oh, Karl," she exclaimed, giving his big, rough hand a quick squeeze. "You cannot fathom what that does for my heart! Do you think Peder would really allow me to go along? And that you will return to Bergen? He has told me that trade in this port has been steadily dying. Everyone goes to Copenhagen these days, he says."

A shadow crossed Karl's face before he responded. Then, as if forcing a smile, he said, "I am confident that, given time, you can convince your new husband of most anything. It will be difficult for you to be away, Elsa. But think of it as an adventure. A journey of such wonder that each moment is something to treasure as a gift from God. Even when things are difficult, it helps me to remember that."

His look was distant as he gazed out over Bergen, and Elsa wondered about this old childhood friend who had become a man in his years at sea, right alongside her own husband. She studied him for a moment, noting the boyish look he still held through the eyes and nose, even though his jaw had grown strong with manhood. He had grown muttonchop side-whiskers that he was somehow able to carry off, and he had the body stature befitting a first mate—no, a sea captain. Peder was right. Karl had the countenance to command his own ship. It was good that Ramstad Yard would soon build him one.

Elsa's attention was diverted by the pilgrims who were entering the ship one by one, carrying the trunks to which they would need access during the voyage. The rest of their luggage had been stowed the day before. As the captain's bride, Elsa was already beginning to feel responsibility for her townspeople.

"I am so happy that so many will come with us," she said to Karl after greeting Kaatje and Soren with mock-formal handshakes and laughter. Departing was difficult, but the thrill of going was undeniable.

"It is good in many ways," he said. "You all will find support in one another. And you'll be glad for that. Peder and I have seen many immigrants return home, despairing from being so cut off from all they knew. It can be overwhelming."

"But their English lessons," interrupted Nora Paulson saucily, their stout teacher of three years, "will be their mainstay." She cocked her head and, with a grin, hopped down the stairs and onto the ship. "I wanted my first steps to America to be without trepidation!"

Karl laughed, and Elsa joined in. Behind Nora was her giant of a beau, Einar Gustavson, who lugged an enormous trunk on his back. Einar shook his head at Nora's antics. "For years now," he said haggardly, yet with a twinkle in his eye, "she bothers me to go to America, go to America. Now I go along and what does she say? She wants me to build her a schoolhouse so she can teach. She tells me it will be alongside *our* beautiful farm in this place they call Eden. The woman does not even bother to wait until I ask her to marry!"

Nora smiled benignly as she stood with hands on hips. "If I wait for that moment, Einar, I will be old and gray. If you will not make plans, then I must."

Einar raised his eyebrows and cocked his head toward her while still looking at Karl and Elsa. They laughed again. "You had better get to that proposal, Einar," Karl said. "Or Nora is bound to ask you."

Nora snorted at that, as Einar set down the trunk with a loud *clunk.* "That will certainly be the day," she retorted. "No, no, this stubborn farmer is free to do as he wishes. If he does not move soon enough, I will simply find another farmer in North Dakota who would be proud," she paused to give Einar's brawny shoulder a slap, "to find a teacher as his wife."

"You see what I have to put up with?" Einar asked woefully. "How is a man to ask this woman to marry him when she never gives him a chance? For years now, it has plagued me."

Elsa laughed again at his antics, appreciating the release of tension. Feeling the headiness of the moment, she blurted out, "Well, for heaven's sakes, Einar. There is obviously going to be no perfect moment. Ask her now."

Nora looked up at Einar with a cocky smile, seemingly daring him to do it. Behind them, other townspeople gathered, chuckling at the scene.

Einar looked around, blushing a purplish-red at the neckline that made Elsa immediately sorry for her forwardness. But to her surprise, the big man knelt right there and took Nora's hand. "Nora. We go to a new land. A new place. Will you be my new wife?"

Nora laughed nervously, obviously as surprised as Elsa that he had taken the bait, then offered them her own surprise. "*We're going* to a new land," she corrected in a softer voice than most had ever heard from her. "And I would love to be your wife."

The group erupted into a cheer and quickly spread the news down the gangplank. On the dock, their nearest and dearest echoed their approval.

Elsa smiled. It was a good beginning to their new venture. Surely God was smiling down upon them.

Kaatje's stomach had lurched with excitement as the tug hauled them out of the port and then released them. Karl yelled, "Unfurl the sails!" and within minutes, it seemed, the crew had the square-sailed ship clipping along out of Byfjorden. At first, the salt-laced air, the brisk breeze whipping off the water and ruffling the sails until they billowed like enormous feather pillows, invigorated Kaatje. But as the *Herald* left the sheltered fjords and encountered the first of the sea's endless waves, her stomach turned turtle. It was with some embarrassment that she vomited all over the ship's wooden deck, and the only consolation she could find was that she was only one of many.

Now she moaned as bile rose again in her throat. She concentrated on the glass prism in the ceiling above her, the only source of daylight for belowdecks passengers, and prayed that God would settle her stomach. Karl, God bless him, had loaned her his tiny cabin so that she could at least find privacy in her misery. She was just wondering if Norway was still in sight and lamenting that she was not

above deck to say one last good-bye, when Kristoffer arrived with
Astrid in tow. One look at the woman's face, and Kaatje wordlessly
got out of bed and offered her friend the lower bunk.

Gratefully, Astrid sank onto the bed, too exhausted to protest
Kaatje's kindness. Feeling sick again from being vertical, Kaatje gave
her a quick half-smile and climbed the hand-hewn mahogany steps
to the top bunk. Just lying prone with her eyes closed seemed to help
her stomach, and surprisingly, moving closer to the ceiling seemed to
de-emphasize the *Herald*'s rocking. She listened to Kristoffer speak
reassuring words to his wife. Then he rose and stood beside the
bunks, his head at about Kaatje's level.

"I am sorry, Kaatje," he said, keeping his eyes lowered in defer-
ence to her modesty. "Karl mentioned you were here. The hold is full
of passengers who are faring about as well as you two. I thought it
would be better for Astrid—in her condition—not to be with so
many other sick people."

"No, no," Kaatje managed, waving off his apology. "Astrid has as
much right to this cabin as I do. We'll get along. I can imagine you're
needed above deck."

"Well, yes," he said, fidgeting, obviously feeling torn as Astrid
threw up in the tin bucket Karl had left beside the bunk. "I need to
go rescue Elsa from our little Knut, and Karl is bound to be looking
for me."

"Go, my love," Astrid said, leaning back against her pillow. "We
will be fine. Two pregnant women know how to deal with upset
stomachs."

"Aye," Kristoffer said softly. "I will send someone with clean
buckets and cool cloths shortly."

Kaatje closed her eyes, feeling a bit pained as she heard him give
Astrid a quiet kiss. Soren had yet to check on her.

Her mind raced as she thought about Elsa and Peder's wedding,
and her own nuptials two years past. She smiled as she mentally
traced Soren's image: his new sideburns, like Karl's, which he assumed

was American fashion, his wild, unruly hair parted on one side. Kaatje thought his new look far too sophisticated for a man who wanted to farm, but anything new was welcome. It just added to the celebration of rebirth—new look, new choices, new land, new life.

Their own wedding had been nowhere near as elaborate as the Ramstads', but the day had resurrected a hundred memories. Had Soren once looked at her the way Peder drank in Elsa's image? Yes. Did she once look up at Soren with all the trust and admiration that one could see in Elsa's eyes? Indeed. Could their love be rekindled after such a thorough dousing, after such betrayal? Yes, they were going to a land of new beginnings. Anything was possible. Still, would it be enough? Kaatje decided she had no choice but to trust in the Lord and her husband. With that thought in her head, she escaped into blissful sleep.

Having heard nothing for hours, Tora decided it was safe to move about. She smiled to herself, utterly exultant that her plan had worked. How surprised her parents and her sister would be when they returned to their home and found her gone! And how simple it had been! On the day of the wedding, Tora had coerced Vidar, a silly sailor boy whom she had wound around her little finger, to help her forge a plan. He had known the inner workings of the ship and the best way to sneak her aboard. It had only taken one kiss to convince him.

They had added an old trunk to Elsa's belongings, placing it close enough to be construed as one of hers, yet far enough away that Elsa would not notice it. Vidar had taken part in the loading of the passengers' luggage, so he made certain that the trunk holding Tora was loaded on top of the others. "Careful," she had heard his muffled voice say. "I think that one's full of cut crystal."

In her opinion, the sailors who carried her trunk did so with all the care of those carrying straw bales, but she had ended up in a perfect position. As soon as she felt the rolling of the open sea, she had escaped her cramped quarters and felt around in the darkness to get a sense of her surroundings. Finally, sure that she was the only living thing in the cargo hold besides the squawking chickens, grunting swine, lowing cows, and a few rats, she pulled a candle from her pocket and lit it.

In the soft, flickering light, she stifled a small "oh." The ship seemed enormous down here, and not the least bit comforting. The huge cargo hold rose up through a portion of all three decks and was filled with crates and barrels and trunks of various sizes. She was at the bottom, with the stairs rising not far from her perch. The wide-stepped staircase led up to the huge cargo hold doors that allowed sailors to load and unload the *Herald*. The candle shed little light, and a shiver ran down her back as she squinted, trying to peer into the farthest reaches of darkness to reassure herself.

How she longed to climb the stairs, bang on the doors, and surprise them all with her presence! But no, she told herself, she must stay put until she could hold out no longer. By then, it would be impossible for Peder to turn the ship around.

She shivered again and raised her candle in search of the other trunk of clothes Vidar had smuggled aboard with her. Tora discovered it two chests over and immediately rummaged through it for her cloak and some of the food she had hidden there. The night watch, which she assumed she would hear, had not begun clanging their bells, her only way to ascertain the time. She assumed it was about noon and time for lunch. She would call it that, anyway, until she knew better.

Nothing in her life had tasted better than the remains of Elsa's wedding feast, which Tora had smuggled away with other precious stores. Yesterday it had tasted dry and flat; today it was like manna from heaven, as Mama would say. The thought of her mother brought Tora up short. She was sorry to cause her pain. But Papa was getting his just desserts. The old man had forced her to this. Yes, today, her first day of freedom and new life, all food tasted like manna.

After supper on the second day of their voyage, Peder pushed away his inexpensive porcelain plate and Cook, a man whom Peder liked to joke had come as cheap as the dinnerware, immediately cleared it away. Peder watched the old Chinaman move, his feet shuffling along, as Karl and Kristoffer debated the profit potential of different cargoes and Stefan—Peder's steward—looked on. Although his cooking skills left something to be desired, Cook was indispensable. In all the ten years Peder had traveled with the man, earlier as second mate, then as first mate, and now as captain, he had never known him to show up late from port or shirk his duties in any way. One thing he would grant, Chinamen knew how to pull their weight.

Peder glanced down the elegant mahogany table to his wife, who watched Karl and then Kristoffer speak, seemingly delighted by their banter. She was a quick study, and he could almost see her mind working as she considered first one man's comments and then the other's. When either man glanced at her, Elsa nodded politely, obviously listening, but not intruding.

He watched as Karl glanced at Elsa and saw his first mate do a double take. Peder smiled. He knew that Elsa's unfaltering blue-eyed gaze was enough to make any man take a step back. Her eyes begged one to stare back into them, as if one could ascertain his future simply by staring into their blue depths. "Gypsy eyes," Peder had whispered to her during their first night together. She had demurred, calling Tora the gypsy. But underneath the blond halo that glistened in her hair from the cabin's candlelight chandelier, she was a gypsy. And Elsa's eyes were only the beginning of her siren's call for him.

As Elsa dropped her gaze in embarrassment when Karl did not look away, Peder cleared his throat. For an instant, he thought he saw a guilty look cross Karl's face as he glanced up at him, but immediately dismissed the idea. He knew Karl had always had a mild crush on Elsa. What man in Bergen who knew her had not? But Karl was Peder's best friend. He knew his bounds.

"We need to review our supplies," Peder said to Karl and Kristoffer, returning to the conversation at hand. "I want to know before we near Scotland if there has been any oversight in planning."

"Why not review them right now?" Kristoffer asked.

"It could take us hours," Karl said.

"Let's go and get it done," Peder said with authority. "Kristoffer, I want you to take the helm and see out the port watch. We're near the shoals that we've been studying."

"Aye, aye, Cap'n," Kristoffer said with a curt nod, then turned to Elsa. "If you wouldn't mind . . . if it wouldn't be too much trouble," he said with a hesitant smile, "could you look in on Astrid tonight? I think she and Kaatje would welcome a woman's touch."

"Certainly, Kristoffer. I meant to get there all afternoon, but your boy kept me busy."

"I appreciate you looking after Knut," Kristoffer said, clearly unsettled at having to rely on others. "I know he is not the easiest child."

"Not at all. I love being around little *gutts*. They're not much different from you big boys, you know."

The three men laughed, and Karl and Kristoffer said good night to her as they left the cabin. Peder stayed back to give her a quick kiss.

"I will not be long," he whispered.

"Hurry back," she responded, giving him a meaningful glance.

He raised one eyebrow at her and followed his men out the door.

Out on deck, Karl took a deep breath, appreciating the fresh breeze on his face. These dinners in the captain's quarters with Elsa were bound to get more and more difficult. Perhaps he would suggest to Peder that the captain should entertain other passengers on a rotating schedule, making them all feel welcome. He sighed in relief. Yes, that would certainly be an idea that Peder would find appealing and would rescue Karl from such close proximity to Elsa.

It was a beautiful summer night on the sea, and several of the passengers were strolling around the deck, studiously keeping away from the rigging as instructed. There was nothing more irritating to sailors than landlubbers underfoot.

Karl nodded to two sailors, and the men immediately hurried over to join him. Without a word, just a look that would soon earn Karl his own captain's position, they unhooked the cargo hold doors and, with a *heave-ho!* pulled open first one mammoth door and then the other. Another sailor hurried over with a kerosene lamp, and Peder and Karl carefully stepped down the stairs. They had just reached the hull floor when Karl was sure he heard a muffled sneeze.

"Did you hear—" he began.

Peder held up his hand to still Karl's voice, obviously listening with a straining ear. But with the noise of the waves against the hull, the animal sounds below, and the wind in the sails above deck, it was difficult to hear anything else. After a moment, Peder shrugged, and they moved to the port side to review foodstuff supply inventories. In the dark, even with the help of four lanterns, it was a difficult, tedious process.

"Perhaps we should have waited until the morning," Peder finally said with a sigh. Karl could almost see that he was thinking about Elsa waiting for him in the captain's cabin.

"Perhaps," Karl said noncommittally.

It was then that they heard another muffled sneeze, and Peder whipped around to look at his first mate. Karl nodded.

"That is it, then," Peder said, a little louder than was necessary. "Let's give it up until we have some natural light to aid the process."

"Aye, aye," Karl said. They clambered up the steps, stomping loudly so that the stowaway would hear them. But just before they reached the top, Karl suddenly sat down with darkened lamp and flint in hand, and understanding immediately, Peder said, "Come,

Karl, join me in my quarters. I believe something interesting has transpired, and I wish to fill you in."

Obeying Karl's silent gesture, the confused sailors on deck closed the heavy hatch doors above their first mate. As they were securing the bulky iron fasteners, Karl stealthily crept down to the bottom deck. He sat there for an hour in the darkness before he heard any more stirring. It was larger than a rat, to be sure, and too far from the stalls to be an animal. The *Herald* definitely had a stowaway. Who? He was wary, to be sure, and Karl wondered if the stowaway had a light source. If not, his night might be spent observing an eye-draining dance of shadows.

He heard movement again, and his scalp tingled in anticipation. The stowaway was making his way somewhere when he ran into something heavy. At the sound of the soft cry and mumbled swear words, Karl's eyes widened in surprise. It was a woman! Sure enough, she lit a candle and bent to take off her slipper and examine her wounded toes. With her back to him in the dim light, it was difficult to see who it was. But she was small and shapely, and Karl was mesmerized by the whole scene playing out before him.

Peder would have her hide. Two days out, and with no time to lose, they could not return her to Bergen. She slipped on her shoe and turned toward him. His breath caught. Tora! Make that two people who would have her hide, he mused.

Casually, he flicked the flint and spark met wick. As the flame caught and grew, so did the lamplight's reach. Below him, Tora froze. Karl raised one eyebrow. "I don't believe we have you on the manifest as part of our cargo, Miss Anders. Would you care to greet the captain and explain why you are down here among the chickens?" He rose and stepped down to her side.

Tora closed her mouth, lifted her chin, and stared into his eyes with a calm expression plastered on her face. Karl chuckled under his breath. She was a vixen, this one. She used her eyes with more power than any woman he had ever seen—and she was all of sixteen.

"I assume, since you have nothing better to do than sit there preying on innocent women, that I'd be better off with my brother-in-law?"

Her look was clear, and Karl found himself doing a double take. The shape and depth of her eyes so resembled Elsa's that for a moment he fancied himself looking at her sister. He gave her a laugh devoid of cheer. "It is you that the world has to watch out for, Miss Anders," he said, "for I'm afraid it is you who preys on the innocent."

She shook her head as if dealing with a fool, picked up her skirts, made her way to the stairs, and climbed them. "Summon your sailors, first mate. I have no more time for idle banter with you. We might as well get this over with . . . unless . . ." she turned to him, her look beguiling. But she was no more than a child learning to use a woman's body.

Disgusted, he stood, climbed the stairs past her, and banged on the doors above them. "You were brought up to be better than this," he said.

The doors opened, and Tora whisked upward, ignoring the dumbfounded sailors' gazes. She turned briefly to Karl as he took her arm and headed her toward Peder's cabin. "Do not presume to lecture me again, Mr. Martensen. Although you are right on one count: I was born for better. And I shall have it in America."

The few remaining passengers above deck stopped to gawk as Karl knocked loudly on Peder's door. "Captain, I found our visitor."

Peder opened the door with a grim expression on his face. Seeing Tora at Karl's side, his expression grew decidedly more angry. Karl felt Tora shrink at his side, leaning slightly into him as if her strength waned. He resisted the feeling of protection rising in his chest. Were all men such saps that young women could twist their hearts with a small movement?

"Come in," Peder ground out through clenched teeth.

They entered the cozy three-roomed cabin that was not as luxurious as the prosperous captain's quarters many ships boasted, but still attractive. The sitting room had paneled walls, gas lighting, book-shelves, two upholstered chairs, a love seat, and a potbellied stove. To the right was the attached dining room for six, and to the left, behind a closed door, the bedroom.

Karl pulled Tora into the sitting room and plopped her down on a chair as he would a child. Peder went into the bedroom and returned almost immediately with Elsa.

"Tora!" Elsa cried. Her hand flew to her mouth. "How could you? You impudent child!"

Tora lowered her face prettily and worried a lace handkerchief in her hands. "That is exactly why I *had* to leave, Elsa." She raised her head to look at her sister, and Karl had to admire the dramatic tears she had worked up. She was a piece of work, this one. "I thought that you, of all people, would understand. They think I'm a child!" She rose and paced before the stove. "But I am a grown woman, capable of making my own decisions!"

She hurried over the few paces to her sister and took her hands, trustingly looking up into her face. "Oh, please, don't send me home, Elsa. I promise I'll be nothing but a help to you and dear Peder."

Karl looked over at his glowering friend. While Elsa seemed in a quandary, as if moved by her sister's speech and a little pleased to have a family member with her, Peder was stoic.

"I assume that if you are a grown woman capable of making a grown woman's decisions then you have come with enough money to pay for your passage," Peder said in a low voice.

Tora's brow furrowed. "No. Is it not perfectly horrible? I begged Papa to send me. And he would not! I was reduced to this . . . this . . ."

"Stowing away," Peder said.

"Well, if we must call it that, yes. I brought my own food supplies."

"Enough for five weeks of travel?"

Tora faltered, then stubbornly lifted her chin. "I will manage."

Peder glanced at Karl, and Karl shook his head. He seriously doubted Tora carried enough food and water to make it across the Atlantic.

"We will manage," Elsa put in. "But hear this, dear sister: You will take an active role in making it work."

f i v e

s soon as Cook had cleared the dining table and departed with the lunch dishes, Nora Paulson sat down with Elsa and her English primer to work on her language study as they had done three times a week for the past three years. Once aboard the *Herald,* Peder had decreed that only English would be spoken. This would help train the immigrants in their new tongue so they would be prepared for their new world. With this mandate, Nora was a busy woman.

Elsa leaned over the book with Nora, familiar with the lesson, as she had worked it through many, many times. Many parts of the troublesome new language still gave her pause, but she was slowly learning the ropes, as the sailors said. She looked over at her sister, who sat pouting in the corner of the sitting room. She had been that way all morning. Tora was angry at Elsa for sending her to sleep in the hold. As the last "passenger" to board, she had been forced to sleep in a makeshift bunk closest to the crew quarters' wall, the noisiest.

"Tora, come in here. If you are to make your own way in America, you'll need to know the language."

"I know enough," the girl said in saucy tones, but perfect English nonetheless. "Elsa knows no more than me."

Elsa's mouth dropped in surprise. Up to then, she had only heard her sister speak in their native tongue. Then she began remembering how Tora always wanted to tag along to Nora's house when she had her lessons, and how she was always somewhere nearby when Nora came to the Anders' home. It had never made sense to her then; now it did.

"Elsa knows no more than *I*," Nora corrected her. "Come in here and join your sister. We'll review pronouns."

"I do not believe I want to do that," Tora said, her chin held high as she carefully selected her words. "But I do wish to understand some things. There are some funny rules to this language. For instance, take the different sounds O-U-G-H takes. 'A rough-coated, dough-faced ploughman strode through the streets of Scarborough, coughing and hiccoughing thoughtfully.' Does that make any sense whatsoever?" she asked, her countenance proud over her mastery of the language.

Tora had always been bright, Elsa mused, but this was amazing. Still, her uppity manner was irritating.

Elsa looked at Nora and then back to her sister. "Nora, would you excuse me? Perhaps another passenger would like to exchange their lesson time with mine so we could meet again later?"

"Certainly," Nora said. Clearly Tora agitated her as much as she did Elsa. If she weren't the captain's sister-in-law, Tora would certainly have received a solid dressing-down by the teacher.

As Nora left, Elsa rose, pausing to take a deep breath to try and still her anger. She reminded herself that she was a married lady and strove to picture herself as such, thus maintaining some hold on her fury. She walked into the sitting room and sat daintily on the richly upholstered rococo love seat. "You and I must speak, Tora."

"About what? Your husband said quite enough last night." She tossed her head, refusing to look at her elder sister.

"No. He did not. You have intruded upon us and our new marriage, assuming I would care for you. To compound the problem, you are penniless. Peder is trying to build a new business; he does not need another mouth to feed."

"I did not realize I would be such a burden," Tora spat out. "There you were, bemoaning the fact that you had to leave your whole family behind."

Elsa swallowed hard. "I did leave my whole family behind. You, dear sister, are a stowaway. That is a criminal offense on most ships. You're fortunate that Peder is not planning to enter a British port and dump you off."

"Do not do me any favors," Tora said, leveling her cool gaze at her sister.

Elsa snorted in disgust. "You are . . . I will tell you something. I *won't* do you any favors. You will eat from your food supplies until they are gone, and when they are, I will feed you because I have a charitable heart."

Tora said nothing.

"You are an impudent, willful child, Tora. But you have made an adult decision. I plan to hold you accountable for it."

"Fine."

"I hope you'll continue to think so. Peder and I will see you after dinner tonight. Until then, you may go back to your bunk or roam the decks. Just stay out of the way of the sailors. In fact, stay far away from the sailors, period. Which reminds me, Peder wishes to know the name of the sailor who helped you sneak aboard."

"I do not recall."

"He means to give him ten lashes and leave him ashore at the next port. You deserve lashes too. If you won't give him the name, perhaps such measures will be necessary."

"Do not threaten me," Tora said with indignation, standing up with fists clenched.

Elsa sighed. "Listen to me, Tora. A captain is lord of his domain. He can do as he wishes. And since the *Herald* is a rather small domain, it is imperative that he maintain control. Can you imagine what would happen if all sailors got it in their heads to sneak their girls aboard? Chaos. And it will not happen here, for Peder is too good a captain to allow it. Give me his name. I'll plead his case, asking Peder to simply put him ashore, not whip him. The boy must be simple—it is obvious you used him."

She saw a small smile of victory flicker across her sister's face. Despite everything, Tora was pleased with herself. It took every ounce of reserve in Elsa to keep from throttling her.

"He thinks he knows who it is anyway. He saw you disappear with him at the wedding. Papa would be livid if he knew! Give me his name, Tora."

Tora stood and flounced out her skirt, avoiding Elsa's gaze. "He means nothing to me. His name is Vidar."

"I suppose you take pride in using this young man?"

Tora simply stared back at her in silence.

"It is not something to be proud of, Tora. Someday your ways will catch up with you." Getting no response, Elsa sighed again and said, "You may leave."

As her sister left through the small cabin door, Elsa muttered to herself, "Your ways will catch up with you sooner than you think, dear sister."

Three days out and still my stomach soars with the ship, Kaatje mused. She supposed that if she weren't pregnant, her stomach would have adjusted to the movement of the ship on the sea, much as others' had. But she and Astrid were still battling to keep down the broth that various women brought them and, between naps, trying to entertain one another with stories. She had always liked Astrid but had not known her very well; now she felt they were close friends.

A quick knock at the door was followed by Soren entering in typical exuberance. "Good afternoon," he said, bowing gallantly at the hip. "Is there anything I can get for you ladies of leisure?" He came over to the bunk and gave Kaatje a brief kiss on the cheek.

"Oh, Soren," Kaatje said. "Tell us about what you can see from above deck. We're feeling a bit closed in."

"It's wonderful! It is so marvelous that I'm considering quitting the land and sailing with Peder and Karl and Kristoffer. What a life!"

Kaatje frowned. "What? Quit farming? But our land . . . our dreams . . ."

"Oh, Kaatje, I'm only joking," he said, smiling into her eyes. "But you should see it. We're nearing Scotland; you can see it in the distance. She rises up out of the gray, swirling seas like a great, green turtle."

Kaatje giggled at his wild gesticulations and imitation of a sea turtle.

"Last night, I coerced Karl into letting me climb to the crow's nest."

"I knew you would."

"You could see for miles!" he said. "On one side, there was a great school of fish swimming alongside the *Herald*. On the other, two dolphins! It's like we're a part of King Neptune's watery universe!"

Kaatje smiled at his picturesque enthusiasm. She should have known. Soren had fallen for the sea just like he did any new thing in his path.

"And your English lessons, Soren? Are you working with Nora and the others?"

"English! Just listen to my new words! When the *sperra,* or should I say 'spar,' becomes entangled with the rigging, they say it's 'running afoul.'" He paced, puffing out his chest, enjoying the captive audience. "When they say 'to be all at sea,' they mean confused. When things are slow, the sailors get together and 'spin a yarn,' meaning to tell stories. Oh, this is a grand place, America."

Kaatje giggled, feeling energized just having him near. "We are not in America yet."

"I feel like we are. As soon as we entered the *Herald,* we were in a different world."

"I feel it too," she said, looking at him with love in her heart. It was if he had been born anew, baptized into a new country. Oh maybe, just maybe, this would work!

"I better go and let you rest. I'll just take these," he said, bending to retrieve the tin pails.

Astrid made a weak protest.

"No, no," Soren said, grinning. "There's not room to swing a dead cat in here, and you need to get rid of this foul-smelling stuff. I will be right back."

As he closed the door behind him, Astrid's weak voice carried up to Kaatje. "He's like the wind, that one."

"Yes, he is."

"How do you keep up with him?"

"I don't, I fear. Sometimes I worry I'll lose him. That I can't keep up, and someday he'll just run off, like a kite that's lost its string. I've had dreams that I run and run to try and catch him, but he just keeps smiling that impish grin of his and disappearing again. It makes me feel nearly hysterical. I wake up covered with sweat."

Astrid was silent for a moment. "You cannot live in fear of losing him, Kaatje. I know. Watching Kristoffer go to sea all these years put the fear of God in me. The months apart, the concern that he'd never come home again, threatened to sicken me. Finally, Pastor Lien gave me a prayer that worked for me. Gave me some measure of peace. Maybe it would work for you."

"I would like to hear it." Kaatje stared up at the glass prism above her, which looked like a huge, faceted diamond. It had been placed upside down through the wooden deck above, leaving it flush with the flooring and pointing down toward the passengers below. Each facet of the six sides shed a shard of light, and in some ways, it re-minded Kaatje of Christ. It comforted her to think of it that way, at any rate.

"Pray with me, Kaatje," said Astrid then plunged into her prayer. "O God, we ask that thou wilt be with our husbands, whether we are near or far from them. Protect them, Father God, giving them an extra measure of wisdom before they act. Thou art the author of peace and lover of concord, in knowledge of whom standeth our eternal life, and in whose service is perfect freedom. Defend us, thy humble servants, against all assaults of our enemies, so that we, surely trusting in thy defense, may not fear the power of any adversaries; through the might of Jesus Christ, thy son, our Lord. Amen."

Kaatje swallowed hard. Never had she heard anyone pray with such sweet assurance that God was listening. It was as if Astrid believed God was her friend, not . . . *God.* Kaatje was just working up the courage to ask her about it when there was another knock, and Soren burst through the door again. He was opening his mouth to say something when he gave Kaatje an exaggerated "shh" with his finger and pointed down at her companion. Obviously, Astrid had drifted off to sleep as soon as she finished praying.

Soren set a pail down beside Astrid and another on a peg beside Kaatje's bed. A faint whiff of salt water wafted over her, and she gave him a grateful smile, her lids heavy.

"Maybe you need some rest too," he said.

Kaatje nodded sleepily. A nap sounded enticing. The conversation with Astrid had left her weary. In fact, it seemed difficult to remain awake anymore. Before Soren could kiss her again, she was asleep, dreaming of mighty angels around her husband, protecting him from something she could not quite see.

With the help of two sailors who looked at her alternately as both a tiresome child and a tempting mistress, Tora retrieved her meager stores of food. That evening she ate alone on deck. Sitting in the forecastle—or fo'c'sle, as the sailors called it—with her back to the foremast, Tora could ignore the problems at hand. From her vantage point, all that lay between her and her American dream was a steel bowsprit stretching out to the open sea, seemingly pointing the way home. The truth was that her food provisions would run out within days. She would be forced to go to Elsa and ask her for help. Tora cursed softly under her breath and leaned her head back against the mast. How Elsa would enjoy that moment. She thrived on feeling superior to Tora. Well, she would see who would end up on top. She might be the captain's bride now, but Tora had bigger goals in mind. Someday, Elsa would come to her.

For now, she choked down dry flatbread with water and forced herself to think of the future instead of her meager meal. Looking far out to sea, she observed the different patterns on the water, caused by either wind or current, she could not tell. Away from the ship, it was more difficult to discern the swells that plagued the *Herald.* If she kept feeling this nauseous, she wouldn't need any rations from her miserly sister. But she was happy for the wind. The wind that filled the topgallant, topsail, and forecourse sails above her, like clean sheets in a spring breeze, and meant that she was inching her way to America.

"Pardon me, miss," said a sailor at her elbow. She dragged her eyes away from the horizon to the pesky man.

"Yes?"

"Cap'n wants to see you. I have orders to escort you to his cabin immediately."

Tora looked him up and down, idly wondering if it was worth the effort to sweet-talk him into taking her for a walk instead of to the captain. But his face was resolute, and he studiously avoided her gaze. There was little doubt he knew she was the stowaway and the cause of Vidar's imminent departure.

"Very well," she said, rising to follow him.

He led her to the captain's quarters, where he left her in the sitting room and then departed immediately without a word. Tora, despite her resolve, felt her mouth water at the smells of roast beef, onions and vegetables, and fresh bread. It just made her angrier that her sister could deprive her so. She was family! She should be treated like the princess to her sister's queen!

Tora saw Elsa lean over to one end of the table, hidden behind the cabin wall, no doubt to tell Peder that his sister-in-law had arrived. Elsa wiped her mouth with a cloth napkin and then set it to one side. She rose and entered the sitting room, followed by Peder and their dinner guests, Einar and Nora, and Birger and Eira Nelson. After polite good-byes, the foursome departed quickly, as if wanting to get out of the way of the executioner's blade.

As the door closed, Peder spoke. "Vidar has been punished for his indiscretions."

"I know. I think it is a barbaric practice," Tora said huffily. She looked at Elsa with accusation in her eyes, blaming her for not intervening as promised.

"Not as barbaric as some captains," Peder said. "I have known a few who would have thrown him overboard, and you as well."

Her heart skipped. "You wouldn't dare."

"It is not a matter of daring, Tora; it is a matter of doing." He stared at her, and she noticed that the deep smile lines that were almost always present were conspicuously gone. His dark green-brown eyes stared at her dully. His mouth turned down at the corners. Obviously Peder Ramstad was a man one should not cross. Even her most potent little-girl glance, known to melt the toughest of men, failed to soften his gaze. She squirmed and looked to Elsa for relief.

She was little better. "I have found a decent answer to our dilemma," Elsa began, folding her hands in her lap.

Observing this composure, Tora had to admire her sister a little. Since her engagement, Elsa had gained an adult countenance that made her seem secure, peaceful, sure of herself.

"An answer? To what?" Tora inquired.

"To how you should pay for your passage, just as the other good people aboard ship have done."

"I will repay you, Elsa. I promise—"

"Kristoffer Swenson has stepped forward and offered to pay for your passage. In return you will care for young Knut for the duration of this trip and assist Astrid with Knut and their new child once in Maine. For six months."

Tora was dumbstruck. Her mind raced as she searched for a good argument. "That's nothing more than indentured servanthood!" she cried.

"You deserve much less generosity," Elsa calmly informed her. "Men who stow away and are not thrown overboard are often not only flogged, but sentenced to seven years of servitude aboard ship. By all rights, Peder could make you work for him until you turn twenty-three."

Tora stood, her fists clenched at her sides. "I would like to see you try and flog me," she said to Peder. "I know of at least four men aboard this ship who would stay your hand."

Peder's look turned from formidable to glowering. He too rose, towering above Tora's slender frame. "Do not make mutinous threats, Tora. A ship is a different world from Bergen. There is a clearly drawn line and a rigorous order. Do not threaten me again," he said, shaking his finger in her face, "or I will spank you for the spoiled child you are."

Elsa rose and edged between them, reminding Tora of her mother. "You may go now, Tora. But you are to report to Cook at five tomorrow morning."

"Cook?" Tora squeaked.

"Agree to the arrangement with Kristoffer and report to Astrid's cabin at seven, or to Cook at five. And you *will* be nothing but a gentle, courteous servant to whichever one you choose."

"I will do no such thing!" Tora shouted, grabbing her skirts and giving the two of them what she hoped was a murderous glance. "I have never heard of anything so unfair!" With that, she exited the cabin and slammed the door behind her. She rushed to the fo'c'sle and looked out across the starboard railing to America. Oh, America, America. The *Herald* couldn't reach her fast enough.

Peder had watched his wife in wonder during the scene with Tora. *She handles herself so well,* he thought. Already, she is a woman of substance. Yet as soon as Tora slammed the cabin door, she wilted on the love seat. He sat down beside her, gently urging her to relax and place her head in his lap. She did so, and he wordlessly unwove her chignon until her hair—the color of a morning moon—lay in waves over his knees and thighs. He ran his fingers through the silky strands, pausing at her scalp to massage her skin.

"You did your best," he said as she sighed heavily.

"Yes. But was it enough? How did I go from newlywed to parent in two days?" She smiled wearily up at him.

"What can I say? I am especially virile."

They laughed together softly, finding relief in humor.

"She looks at us with those doe eyes of hers and thinks she can get out of anything. It is time she finds out that she is responsible for her actions . . . before it's too late."

"I think she gathered that that was your stance," he said, slowly moving his fingers to trace the delicate lines of her sculpted jaw, chin, and nose. He moved on to her lips as she closed her eyes, obviously relishing his touch, visibly relaxing. "She will figure it out soon enough, sweetheart. Do not worry."

"It is difficult not to worry about Tora. I am afraid—"

He cut her off, pulling her into his arms, unable to keep from kissing her any longer.

She smiled up at him as he leaned back again. "I take it you have something on your mind other than my sister."

Peder nodded. "I have the fairest Anders sister on my mind."

"I like that about you," she said, giving him an impish grin. "Your distinct taste in women."

With that, Peder gently picked her up in his arms and stood. "It is difficult to focus on a captain's duties when one has honeymoon thoughts on his mind." And without another word, he carried her into their bedroom, shutting the door tightly behind them.

Karl took his turn at the wheel later that night when all was quiet above deck, the passengers sound asleep in their bunks, along with the sailors who were not on duty. Tonight there was a warm breeze that reminded Karl of a Polynesian island and a waxing moon that threw a bright trail on the shimmering waters of the North Atlantic.

Night was Karl's favorite time aboard ship, a time when he could almost imagine he was on the *Herald* alone, ready to conquer the world with such a vessel beneath his feet. Oh, to be captain! Everything in him yearned for it, and he knew it wasn't far off. By owning 40 percent of the Ramstad Yard, by rights, the next ship off the Ramstad ramp would be his.

The watch had rung four bells for ten o'clock when Peder joined him, standing silently behind and to his left, doing as Karl was, lifting his nose to the gentle headwind, enjoying the gentle pitch of the ship like a friend's welcome laughter. They stayed that way in companionable silence until Peder broke their private thoughts with words.

"It is good to be on our way."

"Yes. It is at moments like this that I long for my own ship."

Peder paused. "I understand."

"I still think that we should consider a steamship as the next project. Sail is on its way out. I know you love it, Peder, but we must be realistic. As your partner in Ramstad Yard, I must insist upon it."

Peder coughed and changed the subject. They had been over the same ground many times. "How are the ill faring?"

"Most have recovered from their seasickness," Karl said, glancing at him. "A few will suffer all the way to Boston. But the most worrisome are Kaatje and Astrid."

"Is it their condition?" Peder asked delicately.

"I suppose," Karl said with a nod.

"Does Cook have anything that could help them?" As was customary, Cook also served as doctor and carried a chest of supplies to help remedy a variety of ailments.

"He gave me a bottle of tonic tonight."

"Let me take over here," Peder said. "You go see to the women, if you don't mind."

"Not at all," Karl said amicably. He turned to leave.

"Karl," Peder said.

"Yes?"

"There's something I need to talk about with you."

A note in Peder's voice sent a chill of foreboding down Karl's back. Did he know about his feelings for Elsa? Had he seen the growing admiration that Karl had tried so valiantly to hide? Karl halted his wild concerns, willing himself to face whatever was at hand. "Yes?"

Peder looked down at the deck flooring, and after a moment of hemming and hawing, finally said, "It's nothing. We'll speak later."

"Are you sure?"

"Yes, yes. It can keep." He dismissed his friend with a look and Karl turned away, feeling ill at ease. Peder was not one to keep things back. What was he hiding? Something told Karl it was not Elsa.

He walked to the water barrel and poured fresh water into two tin cups for the women below. He knew it would be tough for them to get it down. He also knew that if they didn't start retaining some fluid soon, both mothers and their expected babes could die of dehydration. After days at sea, they were already perilously weak.

Karl entered the dark passageway that led to his cabin and the rest of the passenger hold. The thick, oily smell of the kerosene lamps that lit the passageway—as well as the stagnant, spoiling aroma that arose from the bilge—filled his nostrils. It made him feel a bit nauseous himself when he paused to think of it. Knocking twice, he entered the cabin after a feeble voice bid him welcome.

Kaatje and Astrid looked even worse than yesterday, if possible. Even in the warm light cast from the flame of the lantern, both women were ghastly gray. Karl pasted a smile on his face and found himself speaking loudly, as if by his voice's power he could infuse life into the women.

"Fresh water," Karl said, holding out the two cups.

Both women groaned, but sat up.

"You need to drink as much as possible, if not for you, then for your babies."

They nodded and accepted the tin cups as he offered them.

"Are you feeling any better?" he asked hopefully.

"I am afraid not," Kaatje said. "But thank you for inquiring." She reached out to touch his hand. "I am sorry that we have displaced you in your own cabin. We could move to our place in the hold now."

"No, no," Karl said in dismissal. "Just focus on feeling better. I am fine."

He looked at Astrid. "Are you at all better?" She simply shook her head.

"Well, I do not know if you're interested," Karl said, pulling a bottle from his back pocket, "but I have a bottle of Hostetter's Stomach Bitters, sent to you from Cook. He picked it up in New York." Karl leaned closer to the flame to read the label. *"Hostetter's Celebrated Stomach Bitters. A pure and powerful tonic, corrective, and alternative of wonderful efficacy in disease of the stomach, liver, and bowels . . ."*

"Please," Kaatje said, holding up her hand for him to stop. "It sounds terrible."

"It says here that it cures seasickness," he tried.

"I do not think we're interested," Astrid said wearily. "Thank you very much for thinking of us, though."

"I would fear for my child," Kaatje said, leaning back against her pillow.

I'm afraid your child is going to get hurt in other ways, Karl thought, but shrugged and nodded. "You women know best. I'm going to send

Cook down with more broth. You really do need to get something down very soon."

"Thank you, Mr. Martensen," Astrid said. She closed her eyes. Yes, she was undoubtedly in bad shape. His eyes raced to Kaatje. She too was fading.

"I will leave you two to rest, then. Good night."

Both women mumbled a soft good-bye.

He tiptoed out of the cabin and shut the door with as light a touch as possible. He was making his way up the passageway when he almost ran into Elsa. He reached out to steady her and had to remind himself to remove his hands.

"I'm sorry, Elsa. I did not see you."

She laughed, her smile shining in her eyes. Karl dragged his own eyes away, concentrating on the bottle in his hand. "I just brought them fresh water. Tried to give them this. They'd have none of it."

Elsa took the bottle from his hand, lifting it to the light to read the label. Karl stole the moment to study her. What would it be like to hold her? His body ached from the effort of restraint. What if he lifted her chin right then and brought his lips to hers? *Dear Jesus, God, help me!* he cried silently.

"I must go," he said briefly, determined to get this madness under control. "I'm going to send Cook with some broth. Try to get them to drink. As much as possible. Their lives and their babies are in grave danger."

She nodded up at him with an earnestness in her eyes that drew him like iron to true north. He wrenched his eyes from hers and fairly ran down the passageway and into the cleansing, cool air of the Atlantic night.

s i x

lsa took up her position on the deck above the captain's cabin, as she had for the past week, and sat down with a contented sigh. On her first day aboard, Stefan, the steward, had placed a wooden chair there for her after pointing out that the spot had one of the finest views on the *Herald.* She wished for the ease of a hammock, but knew that Peder would frown upon such an unladylike seat. Still, this was quite nice.

Below her, she could see passengers walking the perimeter of the deck, the ladies' parasols bouncing in the wind. Little Knut, hiding from Mikkel Thompson's wife, Ola, ducked behind a barrel. Elsa watched as Ola called for him, obviously concerned. He laughed and she grabbed for him, but he ran away, apparently thinking that she was playing with him. Ola, a rather straitlaced woman in her sixties, did not appreciate his antics as Nora or Elsa might—or as Tora could, if she would cease her pouting and help care for the child. Elsa looked beyond them to her sister. Having refused Kristoffer's offer like a petulant child herself, Tora leaned over a rail, peeling potatoes for Cook.

Elsa turned her attention to more pleasant matters. Even ten days out to sea, the excitement aboard ship was palpable. Everyone hoped they were going to something better, and they were not yet far enough away from Bergen to be homesick. She thought of the towering mountains of Bergen, picturing the seven snowy peaks above granite hills, which, in turn, shot up from the deep fjord below. Yes, Bergen was beautiful. But the sea . . . the sea was an incredible vista itself. Miles and miles of water stretched before them. Yesterday Europe had faded from view, leaving her feeling like a gnat on an elephant, tiny aboard a moving, breathing giant. Yet there was something exhilarating in riding the wind and the water. It felt as if in some small way they had tamed the elephant just by being a part of it.

As she pulled out her sketch pad, she thought of the story Riley had told her yesterday about what the gold miners had called seeing the elephant.

"It was an ol' joke, ya see," he had said in his characteristic Cockney accent. "When a farmer heard the circus was comin', he loaded his farm wagon with produce and hurried to town. On the way, he met the circus parade, led by an elephant. His horses bolted at the strange sight, tipping over the wagon and spilling vegetables all over the road. 'I don't give a hang,' the farmer said, 'for I have seen the elephant.'"

Elsa looked up at the wizened sailor who had once been a forty-niner, still fit at what she supposed was well over fifty years of age. "What does that mean, Riley?"

"It means ya go for the seeing of it as much as the doin' of it, ma'am. Least to me, anyway. I come up short when it came to gold, but I was never sorry to have gone. That's why I'm a seaman now. I've been a miner and a shop clerk. A man of the fields. But the sea. The sea is where I will spend the rest o' my days."

"I understand," she said, nodding. And she did. The ocean all about her was magical; thousands of nautical miles stretched beside them, before them, beyond them. It reminded her of what the desert might feel like, with a whole lot more water. "Is this what you felt like, Moses?" she whispered, facing the wind and feeling it caress her face. "I like it now, but forty years of wandering at sea might seem as intolerable as your own decades in the desert."

She looked up into the burgeoning sails and spotted a sailor in the crow's nest. Yancey, she thought he was called. The wind billowed his shirt as fiercely as it ripped at the sails, but he looked happy. His eyes scanned the horizon, and occasionally he would shout an announcement like "Bark on the port quarter!" to indicate another vessel was in sight and its location.

"Bark ho!" Karl would answer from his station at the wheel.

Shifting her chair and taking up her pencil, Elsa sketched the man in the crow's nest from her point of view. She got lost in her drawing and it was two hours before she looked aside again. When she did, Peder was behind her and stole a quick kiss before looking at the sketch in her lap.

"What is this?" he asked, taking the pad from her fingers. "Why, Elsa, this is very good." He looked from the pad to Yancey and back again. "I never knew you were such a talented artist."

She felt shy under his scrutiny and praise. "It is merely a hobby."

"It is more than that," he said, leveling his mossy green eyes at her. He was clearly delighted with his discovery. "It is much more than that. Do you paint too?"

Elsa shrugged and squirmed under his penetrating gaze. "I have never attempted it."

"You should. This is a gift. We should nurture it."

She smiled. She loved the way he embraced life. Another man might find a woman's talent something to deride, but not her Peder. There was her husband, encouraging her to take it on and better her skills. "I used to want to be a shipwright."

His eyebrows rose in surprise. "You did? I never knew that."

"Papa frowned upon it. Said I should just focus on a woman's duties of being a wife and a mother."

Peder laughed. "Well, I appreciate my father-in-law's aspirations for you. But I do not take so much time to care for, do I?"

"No. Especially since Stefan cleans up after you in the cabin and washes your clothes." She waved at a clothesline that was quickly drying several of Peder's white shirts. Their underclothes were pinned demurely on a line inside their cabin.

"And what of your desire to be a shipwright?"

Elsa raised an eyebrow and looked at him. Did he think it was all right to have such aspirations? Suddenly Ola emerged at the ladder that scaled the captain's cabin, looking for Knut. "Have you seen the little urchin?" she asked in exasperation.

"Let me dispatch a couple of sailors to help flush him out, Mrs. Thompson," Peder intervened.

As the woman nodded once and disappeared down the ladder, Peder turned back to Elsa. He leaned over and raised her chin, drawing her eyes to meet his gaze. "I appreciate you and all you will be, Elsa," he said in a low voice. "I should have married you years ago."

His intensity embarrassed her. "When I was all of Tora's age?"

"Perhaps. You were a different young woman than Tora. But I wanted to be captain before I returned for you."

Elsa nodded and glanced over the ship. Peder's mention of his role drew her attention to Karl. "Have you told him yet?" she asked.

Peder followed her glance and frowned slightly. "No." He paused, changing the subject. "There is an artist in New York I want you to meet," he said. With that, he departed, obviously not wanting to discuss further the secret he still held from his best friend.

Kaatje was getting better, and she was able to manage a brief trip around the deck, leaning on Soren's arm. The fresh salt air felt wonderful against her skin and seemed to clear her head. She returned to the cabin reluctantly, but eager to check on Astrid. She seemed to be better too and had been able to hold down a cup of broth yesterday and again today, giving her hope. Soren set down the pail of fresh water near the bunks and left Kaatje with a tender smile and a pat to her stomach. Kaatje, feeling happier and more content than she had in the last year, pulled up the one chair in the cabin and sat down beside Astrid's bed.

She took her friend's hand. "Still feeling all right?"

"It comes and it goes," Astrid said wearily. "One moment I think I am past it, the next I worry that things have gotten worse. The good news is that this baby is soon due. I think it will be all right if she's born early."

"You think it is a girl?"

"I hope so. Can you imagine living with three men?"

Kaatje giggled, happy to hear Astrid attempt a joke. Her smile soon faded though as Astrid wearily closed her eyes. "Kaatje."

"Yes?"

"Can you bring Knut to see me today? Kristoffer keeps him away. He worries that he'll tire me. But I miss him. It would do me good to feel his small arms about my neck."

"Yes. Certainly. Should I go see to it now?"

"Perhaps in a while. Just after I take a brief nap. I should have the strength for the little terror then."

"You're a good mother, Astrid. I hope I do as well as you have."

Astrid waved away her praise. "It is a natural thing, to love your child. I would do anything for Knut. You will do anything for yours. It is a God-love you come to understand. Suddenly, you realize how God feels about you when you look at your baby. I look at Knut and there's such love . . . ah, look at me," she said in disgust, wiping away sudden tears. "Just thinking about him makes me cry like a baby."

Kaatje smiled at her friend. She was so delicate, so thin . . . and such a good mother. *Please, God,* she prayed silently. *Please let her get well.*

"Tell me a story, Kaatje," Astrid said. "Tell me how you and Soren fell in love." She moved her pillow, settling in.

"There is not much to tell. I had been in love with Soren for years.

Since I was twelve years old, I think, when he used to come to our farm to milk the cows for my father. Later, when my parents died of the influenza and I stayed with an aunt on her farm, he would leave a flower on the doorstep each morning. I got up very early one morning and caught him. When I asked him about it, he said, 'I thought you might be sad. Flowers seem to make girls happy.' Oh, how he stole my heart!" she said with wide eyes and a big smile, remembering.

Astrid opened her eyes and smiled gently back at Kaatje. She took her hand and said softly, "I understand that he steals the hearts of many."

Kaatje withdrew her hand, feeling her face fall to a frown. "That is behind us."

"I hope so, my friend. It must pain your heart."

Kaatje searched Astrid's eyes. There was nothing but compassion in them. Kaatje had not spoken of Soren's indiscretions to anyone but Elsa, and even to her in limited fashion. Obviously, her secret was known to others. She nodded, quick tears welling at the corners of her eyes. "It does."

Suddenly, Astrid took her hand again, closed her eyes, and began praying. "Father God, we pray that thou wilt take Soren in hand. That thou wilt give him eyes for no one but his wife. And, Father, we also pray for Kaatje. That she can find forgiveness in her heart and trust in thy ways. Be a lamp to her feet, Father God, as she tries to find thy path."

"Amen," Kaatje whispered.

"Amen," Astrid echoed. "Kaatje, would you get down my Bible and read some verses to me?"

"Certainly." She rose and took the old black leather Bible from the shelf above Astrid's head.

"Do you have a Bible?" Astrid asked.

"No. I always love hearing from the Good Book, but I never have owned one. There never seems to be enough money."

"We must remedy that situation. Once in America, I'll see to it."

Kaatje widened her eyes in surprise. "That is very generous, but—"

"No, do not argue with me, Kaatje," Astrid said gently. "Every believer needs a Bible. It is how we get to know God."

Kaatje wondered again at how close Astrid sounded to the Lord. How did she get to that point? Kaatje longed for the comfort the other woman seemed to take from her faith. "Where do I begin?" she asked.

"Let's see, a good one for us who will soon labor . . . go about two-thirds of the way back through the Bible to the book of Matthew and find chapter eleven, verses twenty-eight through thirty."

After searching for a few moments, Kaatje finally found the verses and began to read, listening to her own voice spill out words of hope. "Come unto me, all ye that labour and are heavy laden, and I will give you rest. Take my yoke upon you, and learn of me; for I am meek and lowly in heart; and ye shall find rest unto your souls. For my yoke is easy, and my burden is light."

Tora was furious. She could not believe that her own sister would allow this unfair, this barbaric situation to continue. The Queen, as she had taken to calling Elsa with derision, had sat above in her chair all afternoon while Tora peeled potato after potato with an old knife. Her fingers, nicked here and there, burned as she washed them with salt water. Cook, who never said a word—merely pointed at her next task and then ignored her—seemed to even resent her presence in the cramped galley.

She wiped her forehead with the back of her hand. Then, feeling suffocated and woozy from the heat as another batch of bread came out of the giant cast-iron, wood-burning oven, Tora sank down on a stool. Cook was immediately at her side, motioning to the carrots that she had been chopping.

Mopping her forehead with a wrinkled, damp handkerchief, she glared up at the old man. "I am tired," she said loudly.

He took her upper arm in his surprisingly powerful hand and, with a grip that was painful, pulled her upright. "You. Work." It was more than she had ever heard him say.

She placed her hands on her hips and looked defiantly down at him. At five feet, eight inches tall, Tora towered over the man, and she felt her chest fill with redefined power. Who was he to order her around? She was an Anders! Back home, she had had to do few chores, leaving most of the work to the maid and groomsman. And here, she was being treated like a common slave by this little, sweaty Chinaman. "I will not have you order me around, you small, meaningless man!"

His eyes narrowed and Tora's confidence suddenly faltered. "You. Work," he said, his voice dangerously low.

Tora inhaled through her nose and lifted her chin. "No. I've done enough—"

His slap astounded her, cutting off her speech. She could feel the imprint of his hand on her cheek, and she was sure the little heathen had left a mark. Holding her stinging face, she narrowed her own eyes. "You will pay for that."

With that, she trounced out of the tiny galley and into the welcome cool breeze of late afternoon. Tears welled in her eyes at the injustice of it all. Surely Peder would not allow this to continue! Perhaps if she played it right, she could even get out of serving the rest of her prescribed punishment.

She turned toward the helm, where Peder usually stood, and ran into Soren Janssen. He held her away from him by the arms and looked from her tear-filled eyes to the red mark she knew must be visible by the way his eyes narrowed. She thought about what a sight she must be, suddenly embarrassed under his handsome gaze. *Yes,* she thought, *I can see why Laila let you kiss her.* Unaccustomed to nervousness around men, she reached back to her neck, wicking away the moisture and freeing the damp tendrils.

"Please," she said prettily, "I need to see the captain immediately."

"Yes. Of course." He took her arm and escorted her to Peder, who stood at the wheel.

Looking casually from one to the other, Peder said to Soren, "Leave us."

With one look from her brother-in-law, Soren did as he was bid.

Tora worked up some more tears, hoping the handprint was still visible. "Do you see what Cook has done? The little man dared to slap me!" She wrung her hands, trying to look as desperate as she sounded. Most men would rise to such an occasion.

"Why?" Peder asked, his voice still casual, his eyes shifting back to the sea and then to the sails above him.

"Wh-what?" she asked, hating that her voice faltered.

"I asked you why he slapped you."

Her eyes left his face and searched the horizon, as though she would find the right words there. "I don't know."

"Tell me the truth, Tora."

She tossed her head. "I needed a rest. I felt faint. He demanded that I keep working. I refused. For the sake of my health, of course."

Peder studied her until she looked down, in spite of herself. "You never challenged his authority?" he said.

"I don't know what you mean."

"Yes, you do," replied Peder. "Will he confirm your story?"

Tora lifted her nose to the air. "In so many words."

She stood there in silence as Peder appeared to mull it over.

"So? What is your decision? Will you end this mad punishment now?"

Peder smiled and shook his head at her. "You really don't understand the ways of the world, Tora, for all you pretend to do so. I am concerned for your welfare. That is the only reason we have assigned you this *punishment*. You have made a grown woman's decision to go to America. I expect you to grow quickly into your woman's shoes and make further decisions that are befitting a mature woman." He studied her for a moment longer. "While I don't subscribe to the idea that women should be manhandled, I do believe that Cook saw you acting like the pouting child that you still are. He treated you as he would anyone on the ship who does not pull his—or her—weight. Grow up, Tora."

With that he looked back out to sea and ignored her.

Oh, the fury! Such anger built within Tora that she could swear the world was colored red. How dare he! How on earth had Elsa deigned to marry such a man! Even with all his faults, her father had never ever treated her with such disrespect. She took a deep breath and tried once more. "I think you owe me some respect as your sister-in-law."

Peder glanced at her briefly, then down at the wheel in his hands. "I take no pride in our familial relationship, Tora. Perhaps someday you will earn my respect. But not now. You have too far to go."

Tora left him without another word, fuming. Peder would pay for his unkind, rude ways. Respect, indeed! And what did he mean? Too far to go? Well, he would see. He would see how far she would go. Maybe someday she would marry a man who would take over his measly shipyard and turn him and Elsa out on the streets. Yes, she smiled grimly, that would be a fitting end.

The thought of going back to work with Cook was unbearable. Anything was better than that. Where was that Kristoffer Swenson? Surely she could use the situation to her advantage. There he was, farther forward. She ducked around a mast pole and pulled one large strand of dark hair from its knot, leaving her bun in disarray. There was nothing like a woman in crisis to bring a man to the rescue, she thought, allowing a tiny smile before she worked up the tears again.

Crying, she ran across the deck toward Kristoffer. Several sailors stopped to stare, their faces a mask of concern. When she reached his side, Kristoffer cocked his head and leaned toward her, placing a gentle hand on her forearm. "Miss Anders, what happened?"

"Oh! It was awful! That mean Cook dared to slap me! For taking a brief rest!"

Kristoffer searched her eyes and patted her arm. "I am sorry."

Real tears welled up at the relief of finding someone who commiserated with her at last. "I am the one who is sorry, Kristoffer. I should have agreed to your generous offer: to help you with your son in exchange for my passage." She lifted up her eyes to meet his, hoping they looked alluring.

Kristoffer firmly set her apart from him. He glanced up at the sailors lingering about. "Get back to work," he commanded, and the men obediently scattered. Tora felt the stirrings of respect for his understated power, even as a second mate.

Kristoffer turned back to her and said sternly, "Please do not look at me that way. I am looking for care for my child and wife only. Do you understand?"

Tora sighed. "I do not know of what you speak."

"I think you do. But I need your help." As if on cue, Knut popped up from a huge coil of rope on deck and giggled merrily at their surprise. "Mrs. Ramstad, Mrs. Thompson, and Miss Paulson have done more than enough already. But I cannot care for him and carry out my duties aboard the *Herald* adequately."

Tora nodded.

"I promise, I will not ever lift a hand to you. But you must fulfill your end of the bargain. For now, you must feed and clothe and care for Knut. Later, you will also help my wife when our new child is born. In exchange for six months of work, I will pay the price of your passage."

Tora nodded again, accepting his terms.

"Good. I will go tell Peder. See to it that Knut is washed before supper and in bed by seven." With that, he walked off.

It mattered little to Tora that Kristoffer had rebuffed her. Although he was tall and lanky and strong from his years aboard ship, he was rather homely with that long face, his only really fine physical attributes being nice hazel eyes with a certain intensity about them and rich, brown hair. Her eyes roamed over the deck as Knut ducked down in the ropes, avoiding her hands. Now *there* was an attractive man, she thought, her eyes flirting with Soren again as he boldly studied her. There was a very attractive man.

Peder entered the hot, smoky galley and briefly sympathized with Tora. Being tough on her did not come easy, but he knew he had little choice. If she was to make her way in America, she needed to find the right path now. With her girlish flirtation and womanly wiles, she was both dangerous and in danger. She felt she had power, but Peder was concerned that if she continued down this road, someone, at some point, might show her how little she truly had. And he would not be around to protect her. He thought of Burgitte, and was glad that his sister and Tora had parted ways years before. Tora Anders was not a good influence. How could she be so different from her sisters?

"Cook," he said, "Tora will be serving Kristoffer from here on out. Thank you for your patient diligence in dealing with her." He paused briefly. "My wife would like dinner served at six o'clock."

Cook looked him in the eye and nodded once, acknowledging his silent pardoning.

Later at dinner, Peder still couldn't shake the foreboding he felt over his headstrong young sister-in-law. What could he do to straighten her path? *Dear Father in heaven,* he prayed. *Give me the wisdom for the task.*

Elsa leaned over and placed a hand on his arm while their dinner guests, Pastor Lien and his wife, along with Bjorn and Ebba Erikson, chatted among themselves. "Are you all right?" she asked.

"I am fine," he said, working up a smile for her. "But you and I must talk about Tora. Something happened today," he said under his breath.

Elsa nodded. After taking a bite of chicken that Cook had butchered for their dinner, she said, "For now, we need to think of good things. Let's see, there's Nora and Einar's upcoming wedding, and Maine." Then she added, loudly enough for all to hear, "Tell us about Maine, Peder."

Peder smiled and began the familiar litany that Elsa never tired of hearing. "Maine is beautiful country," he said, wiping his mouth with the linen napkin. "Her coast winds back and forth, creating many harbors behind a wall of islands, perfect for shipbuilding."

Karl stood at the helm, trying to keep his eyes off Peder and Elsa as they strolled arm in arm, Elsa's head resting against his shoulder. Karl had prayed without ceasing for practically two days' time, beseeching Christ to lift this burden from his heart. But still he found himself repeatedly spying on the woman, watching as she sketched this and that about the ship, unknowingly providing a perfect opportunity for anyone to observe her.

He was not the only one to take advantage of the opportunity. Yesterday he had noticed Rees, a sailor of questionable integrity, shirking his duties and openly staring at Elsa. Inside, a rage of jealousy stole over Karl's heart. When Rees noted Karl's presence but continued staring, Karl had walked with long strides to the man and slammed him up against the cabin wall.

The man stared with big eyes at his first mate. "What—"

"Do not speak," Karl said quietly, his voice a menacing growl. "Do not look at the captain's wife in such a way again. Do you understand me?"

Rees nodded quickly, clearly afraid in the face of such fury.

"Do not get near her. If she approaches you, go the other way. I do not want to catch you looking at her again. Do you understand me?" he repeated.

Again Rees nodded, desperate to escape Karl's murderous hold. With disgust, Karl threw him to the deck. "Get out of my sight. Report to the second mate immediately for a new assignment. You obviously have time on your hands, and we have an entire ship to care for."

The man scrambled away, and Karl glanced up to see Nora and Einar looking at him in dismay. He ignored them and gazed out at the sea, bracing himself with his arms on the port railing.

When he felt a hand on his shoulder, he turned, raising his fists in natural defense. He let his hands fall when he saw it was Peder.

"What was that all about?"

"Nothing, Captain," he said, shaking off his friend's hand. "Sailor needed straightening out. I took care of it."

Peder looked him in the eye for a prolonged moment, then nodded slightly. "Very well. Carry on."

As Peder walked away, Karl mocked himself. *I am no better than the English Lancelot,* he thought. *In love with Guinevere, indebted to King Arthur.*

seven

*E*ncouraged by Peder's interest, Elsa had begun to draw the *Herald* in different situations: with her sails ghostly still in the calms; "between wind and water" as the sailors called it—when she began to roll with a stiff breeze, exposing the hull beneath the waterline; and from her imagination, tossing about in a fearsome storm.

It was with some surprise that Elsa found herself enjoying sketching ships in action more than their skeletons, as her father had done on his design board. Still, the knowledge of a ship's inner workings made her drawings more realistic, believable, immediate. Perhaps it was because Peder had warned them that a storm was brewing on their seventeenth day at sea that she visualized the *Herald* cresting giant waves on her pad that day.

The sailors had nodded at their captain's words, looking around at the calm seas that had plagued them all day, blocking their progress across the Atlantic.

"It's flatterin' weather, it is," Riley said, casting a distrustful eye to the skies.

"Gets ya all comfortable before the squall," Stefan added.

The men scattered as Kristoffer and Karl set them to work, preparing for the worst.

Throughout the day, Elsa searched the horizon for the menacing clouds the men obviously expected to make an appearance at any moment, but nothing happened until nightfall. Then as they ate their dinner, the ship began to rock violently. They could all hear Karl shouting orders to the sailors. "Furl the sails! Man your posts!"

Peder ignored the building winds and sounds outside the cozy cabin as he calmly ate his meal. The mahogany dinner table was outfitted with small silver ledges that kept plates and cups from sliding in weather such as this. Despite that, Elsa was amazed that the dinnerware kept its place as the *Herald* tilted so far that the liquid in their cups was at a forty-five-degree angle. Finally though, as the storm gathered strength, Peder calmly set down his fork and knife and told their dinner guests that he had better see them to their quarters.

He returned to their cabin soaked from his venture out, despite the oilskin coat he wore, and Elsa could swear that he was enjoying himself. "Nothing like a good storm to remember why you appreciate life," he confirmed. "Now to bed with you."

"I do not wish to go to bed," she said, placing her hands on her hips. "I want to see this storm firsthand. For my drawings."

"Not a chance," he said, shaking his head. "It's only going to get worse. And it's too dangerous for you on deck. You will stay in here."

Elsa scowled at him as he backed her up against the wall. In spite of herself, she had to laugh in the face of his sudden amorousness. He kissed her soundly, and then said, "Now get into our bed or I'll have to carry you there myself. And then Karl will not have my help on deck because I won't be able to resist my wife's feminine wiles."

"I will go, husband," she said with resignation. "See to your ship."

Peder pulled her into another brief, warm embrace and bent his head for a deep, searching kiss. "I love you, Elsa Anders Ramstad. Now promise me that you will stay put. It's dangerous out there."

"I will," she said, suddenly irritated. He spoke to her as he might speak to a child. "I already told you that."

"Good enough." With that, he opened the door and exited, leaving her to shut it against the powerful wind. She grabbed a cloth napkin off the dinner table and mopped the wet wood floor before going back to their room to undress.

Hours later, she lay awake as the storm threatened to toss her out of bed. It had been bad before, but now Elsa was truly frightened. Where was Peder? What if something had happened to him? She made her way to the tiny cabin window that looked out onto the deck and with shaking hands pushed aside the curtains. Her eyes widened in alarm. Huge waves were sweeping across the deck. What if Peder had been washed overboard?

Just then a giant wave rose beneath the *Herald* and her bow swooped upward. Too late, Elsa reached out to secure herself, and when the ship came crashing down as the wave passed, she went crashing with it. Her head hit a corner of the table in the sitting room as she careened to the floor, and she flinched at the pain. Elsa reached for the gash on her forehead and felt the dampness of blood on her fingers.

Elsa derided herself for her carelessness, lit a cabin lantern, and went to find a bandage for her cut. She was worried about her towns-people, who were undoubtedly terrified belowdecks. And what of Astrid? Kaatje was well now, but what was happening to her horribly ill cabin mate? If she could not help the sailors that battled to keep the *Herald* above water, she could certainly make herself useful with the *Herald*'s passengers. If nothing else, to spread calm and a little false cheer.

She fell again as the *Herald* crossed another mountainous wave. Outside, the wind sounded ferocious, taking on a low keening that spooked Elsa. Grasping one handhold and then another, she made her way to Peder's trunk. By the light of the sputtering lamp, she pulled out an old pair of pants and a shirt. She laughed mirthlessly, feeling slightly hysterical about her plans.

In minutes she was dressed, and using a sash from a pretty party dress in her own trunk, she secured the waist of Peder's pants by cinching them up. His shirt was huge on her, billowing out even though she had tucked as much of it in as possible. She looked through the tiny English armoire that was bolted to the bedroom wall, but could not find another oilskin coat. She would just have to brave the elements and dry off later.

Elsa looked out the window, waiting for the next huge wave to slam across the deck; after that she would have a few moments to cross the deck safely. Peder would not be pleased with her if he caught her on deck. But if he found her in the morning, caring for the passengers, he might be proud of her. She steeled herself for the rain and the wind and said a brief prayer as the next wave's momentum pulled at her, threatening to send her flying again. She held steady.

"It's now or never," Elsa muttered. She turned the knob of the door, and the power of the wind took her breath away. It took all her strength to close the door behind her, and in seconds she was soaked. She blinked through the rain, trying to see across the deck, but between the howling wind that drove the stinging seawater into her eyes and the rain itself, she found herself momentarily blinded. Panicked, she realized that her time was running short. She had to cross the ten feet of deck now or be swept overboard by the next wave.

It was too late. Blindly, she tried to open the cabin door, thinking she would make an alternate plan. But try as she might, Elsa could not pry open the door against the fierce wind. Her heart sank. Squinting against the spray, she moved left, searching for a handhold on the mizzenmast nearby. When she found it, she held on tight, trying to catch her breath. It seemed as if the wind sucked the air from her lungs then threatened to blow her about since it could not rip at the furled sails above her. She looked up and was able to see rigging flying straight out from the stays. Sails ripped at weak seams and blew horizontally with the rain.

Sailors madly made their way about her, each uselessly shouting in the muffling winds. As the *Herald* climbed the next watery hill, she braced herself against the mast, holding onto the brass mast band. Were the men bracing for impact too? She could see little in the driving rain.

As the *Herald* climbed and climbed, Elsa felt weak and exposed. She would never make it standing there, she decided. She could barely hold on as it was. She needed to get to the passenger hatch. Immediately. Grasping at anything she could get hold of, Elsa clambered toward the door not ten feet from where she stood. Everything was wet and slippery, but she was almost there.

Suddenly the ship paused agonizingly on the crest of the wave. Then Elsa almost took a breath of relief as the wave came sweeping over the ship.

The power of it astounded her. Its watery tendrils ripped at her handholds until she could hold on no longer. Salt water rushed into her mouth and nostrils as she slid over the deck like a skater on ice. She coughed and sputtered and flailed about, trying to grab onto something . . . anything. The water was carrying her to the railing. Would it wash her overboard? A scream for Peder lodged in her throat, strangled by her lack of breath. On and on she went, sliding along the deck, caught in the wave's mad dash back to the sea.

Elsa managed to grip the railing as the full weight of the wave pressed against her, threatening to drown her as it passed. *Please!* she cried out silently to God. *I don't want to die!*

A strong hand gripped her arm and pulled against the sea, like David against Goliath. Elsa emerged, gasping for air, half-expecting to see Peder pulling her from her watery grave. She blinked as the man pulled her the rest of the way out and to her feet. It was Karl.

He stared at her incredulously, looking her up and down. His barely visible Adam's apple bobbed above his coat collar as he swallowed hard then pulled her into a protective, wet embrace. She succumbed, glad to feel safe for a moment after her perilous slide. Her chest heaved for breath. Karl's body shielded her from the worst of the wind and rain.

"Come on!" he yelled over the wind's unearthly howl. Taking her wrist firmly, he led her across the deck and to the passenger hatch she had originally sought, even as the *Herald* tilted upward again. He wrenched open the door and practically shoved her inside, then followed her.

"Grab hold!" he shouted as the *Herald* began her fall.

The ship careened to the bottom of the next watery valley and Elsa's hands threatened to give way, but Karl reached out with one hand and grabbed her waistband, taking the brunt of her weight. When they were upright once more, he asked, "What were you doing out there, Elsa?" His exasperation was clear.

She raised her chin. "Trying to get here. I thought I could help the others."

Karl scowled, looking her up and down again, leaving her with little dignity in Peder's soaked, clinging clothes. "Good intentions will not keep you alive in the midst of a storm. You could have been killed! If I hadn't seen you go with the wave, no one would have been there to pull you out. In another moment you would have been over the side."

"Enough with the lecture, Karl. Do you not have something better to do?" Her face burned with embarrassment. She had risked his life as well as her own with her foolishness.

The muscles in his lower cheeks worked, as if physically holding back his fury. "I was coming for you to help Astrid. Her time has come. Eira's been hurt in a fall." He raised his hand toward her forehead then pulled it back before touching her. "Looks like you managed to hurt yourself too."

"I am fine."

Karl searched her eyes for a moment then said, "I'll wait until you check on her and then go with a report to Kristoffer."

Elsa reached out and took his large hand in her own. "Karl, thank you—"

He shook off her hand as if her touch burned him. "Go see to Astrid," he said gruffly. "I did what any man aboard this ship would do for you." His gray eyes did not meet hers again.

Kaatje was relieved to see Elsa arrive. "New American fashion?" she found the strength to joke at the sight of her friend's garb. "You look like a street waif drowned in a rainstorm."

Elsa gave her a brief smile and accepted the cloth she offered. She soaked up the worst of the moisture, then moved to Astrid's side. "How are you faring?" she asked gently.

Astrid winced as another contraction swept through her body. The woman was so weak, she could barely speak.

"How long has she been in labor?" Elsa asked Kaatje.

"Since this afternoon, she says. It has worsened with the storm, it seems. I'd say eight, nine hours." Kaatje's eyes conveyed the concern she felt for Astrid. Elsa nodded her understanding, then braced herself as another wave swept the *Herald* up its banks. She glanced fearfully at Astrid, but was relieved when she noticed the ingenious cloth stays that Kaatje had rigged for the laboring woman. Even on the steepest incline, Astrid stayed put, able to reserve her energy for the task at hand.

Astrid's eyes opened wide as another contraction racked her body. She shook her head after it passed. "I will not make it," she muttered.

"Nonsense!" Kaatje said, going to the side of the cot. "You must. For Knut. For your new child about to be born. For Kristoffer."

"I am so weak," Astrid said, weary tears running down the side of her face.

"You are strong," Kaatje urged. "The strongest I've ever met."

Astrid turned terror-filled eyes to her friend. "Pray with me,

Kaatje. You, too, Elsa. I need the Lord if I am to make it." Before they could begin, however, Astrid let out a low, keening cry as another contraction swept over her bulbous womb. "The baby is coming," she whispered.

Kaatje glanced beneath the sheets and nodded her confirmation to Elsa. Her aunt had been a midwife, and for once, Kaatje was glad for all the trips in the middle of the night to attend laboring mothers. She looked at her friend with concern. Few women looked well at this stage, but Astrid looked deathly ill.

"Send word to Kristoffer," Kaatje said to Elsa, who obediently dashed to the door. After speaking with Karl, she returned, bracing against another wave.

In an hour, Astrid's child was making its way out, despite its mother's weary, poor attempts at pushing. Kaatje worried for the babe's life, lingering so long between womb and world, but she was more concerned about Astrid. The sheets were soaked with blood. Something was dreadfully wrong.

"If the child is not born soon, they both will die," she whispered to Elsa, feeling frantic. Never had she seen a mother in such ill condition.

Elsa put a hand on Kaatje's shoulder, letting her know she was not alone.

Kristoffer arrived just as Astrid made one final attempt at pushing with the next contraction, and the welcome, tiny cry of their child was heard. With one glance Kaatje knew Astrid would not live. Astrid's face was a mask of relief, but also resignation. As if she had one foot in heaven, as Kaatje's aunt used to say.

Kaatje finished cleaning up Astrid as best as she could, wrapping her tightly in a second sheet, then looked up at Kristoffer. He was laughing and crying, gazing at his new son with joy and pride. "It is good for a boy to arrive in the midst of a storm!" he said boldly, smiling down at his tiny child. "We will call you Lars, for a brave man I knew once."

He looked over to Astrid, obviously expecting the glowing mother to smile over at the newest addition to their family. His face fell. "Where is Knut?" he asked dazedly. "His mother needs to see Knut."

"I will go for him," Elsa said. She hurried from the room, as aware as Kaatje that Astrid's time was short.

Kaatje watched as Kristoffer made his way to his wife, securing the child in her arms with a cloth sling. He grunted as another wave racked the ship. The child quieted, as if he, too, knew his time with his mother was short.

"You have done well, Astrid," Kristoffer whispered. He kissed her forehead. "You will get well, and we will make a new life in Maine." He spoke in a monotone, as if voicing his wishes would make them come true.

A small smile stole over her face. "Prop me up," she managed to whisper.

Kaatje grabbed her pillow from the top bunk and handed it to Kristoffer, who did as his wife asked. They had just gotten her settled when Knut and Tora arrived with Elsa.

"Mama!" Knut cried, running to the bunk.

They all braced against the next wave. After it passed, Astrid raised a shaking hand to stroke Knut's hair. "I love you," she whispered in Norwegian. "Never forget that, my sweet little *nisse.*"

Kristoffer placed his hand over hers, tears running down his cheeks. Knut looked up at his father in surprise. "He won't forget, Astrid. You'll be there to tell him."

Her eyes drifted up to meet his, and Kaatje fought off a feeling of panic, helplessness. Her friend was drifting away. *Lord!* she cried out silently. *Help us!*

Astrid's shaking hand left Knut's head and went to Kristoffer's face. Her voice suddenly gained strength, her last effort. "Take close care of our children, dear heart. I have loved you with all I have in me."

"I know, Astrid," he said. "I have loved you with all I have in me too."

Kaatje glanced at Elsa, then both gave in to tears at the sound of resignation in Kristoffer's voice.

Astrid closed her eyes, and they all held their breath, thinking that she had left them. Once more, her lids rose. This time her blue eyes were bright with life, and Kaatje found new hope that she would make it.

"Oh, Kris, Kris," Astrid breathed. "It is so beautiful here. Come with me, dear heart. Come with me."

Kristoffer let out a small sob. "I cannot, sweetheart. I need to stay here with the children. Wait for me. Wait for me."

"I'll be waiting, Kris. On the . . . other side." And with that, Astrid closed her eyes forever.

The morning after the storm broke bright and clear with a freshening breeze. Tora welcomed the morning—even knowing she awakened to the burden of two children. She had been terrified throughout the night, certain that the *Herald* would be ripped apart piece by piece, sending them all to the bottom of the sea. She had gained a healthy respect for the sailors who braved the sea out on the decks, even, begrudgingly, for her brother-in-law. He had, after all, seen them through the worst.

But the night had dealt them a second blow, she thought, as she numbly walked about the deck, cradling Kristoffer's newborn son. She was still unable to quite believe that his mother would never ask for him. And how was she going to manage? She was too young for such a burden! Why, it was practically like being *married* to Kristoffer, *and* saddled with two small children. At least the tiny infant was asleep. Little Lars had wailed throughout the night until Cook arrived with a bottle of goat's milk. After taking a tiny bit, the child slept as if he wanted to awake to a better world.

Despite her misgivings, Tora sensed the tiniest feeling of love beginning to grow. Lars and Knut had lost their mother, after all, and needed her. Where would she have been without her own mother?

Who would have protected her from her father? They would never have lived in peace without Mama as intermediary.

Tora found a seat on the deck and watched the sailors as they attended to the wounded ship. Here and there were groups of men working on a splintered mast, bringing up reserves of rope from the hold or mending a sail. Extra sails had been brought up and mounted early that morning when the storm broke. They worked feverishly, energetic with a new lease on life, tending to the ship's worst needs first, in case another storm hit.

Cook approached and wordlessly handed her another bottle of goat's milk. Knut watched the sailors, leaning close to Tora for once, as if seeking comfort from her presence. She wondered if he truly realized that his mother was gone.

Nearby, some of the men began singing as they pulled strong twine through a sail, like women at a quilting bee.

Long time was a very good time,
Bully blow, blow, blow, boys,
Long time in Mobile Bay,
Bully long time ago.

The song seemed to have endless verses, but Tora grew tired of translating their nonsensical English to Norwegian so she could understand it. One could respect their bravery, yes. But there was no understanding men such as these. They signed on to serve a captain to the death, facing fierce storms, boring doldrums, awful food, and terrible sleeping conditions. For what? She could make about as much sense of it as she could their songs.

"Tora," Elsa said, suddenly at her elbow.

"Elsa," Tora said dully, nodding.

"Kristoffer has finally left Astrid's side. He wants to hold Lars. And you need a rest."

Tora rose instantly, honest tired tears forming in her eyes. "Thank you. A nap would be wonderful right now."

"I'll come and wake you for the noon meal," Elsa said. She looked tired and sad. It *was* sad. It seemed almost unreal to Tora. Could Astrid really be gone? So fast? The poor woman had made it so far. Almost to America.

"He's probably wet," Tora said as the baby began to fuss. Her sudden concern for the baby's well-being took her aback. Why should she care?

"I'll find something to diaper him with," Elsa said. "Go. To bed with you."

As she left Elsa, something akin to love began to rise for her sister again. Elsa wasn't all bad, Tora supposed. If she were truly a tyrant, her sister would never have come to help her with the boys.

"Stay with Elsa," she said to Knut sternly. "Don't wander. The sailors are very busy and don't need *nisse* about."

"An elf!" Elsa said with a weary laugh. "That's exactly right! Come, my little elf," she said to Knut, reaching out to him. "Let's go and see your papa."

Burying a passenger was the most dreaded of captain's duties, thought Peder. Thankfully, with Pastor Lien on board, he would be spared this particular funeral. In the past year, Peder had buried five sailors at sea, three at once from a bout of cholera that had swept through the ship. But a woman. A woman as dear as Astrid Swenson. The thought tore at his heart. What if it had been Elsa instead? He needed to get her ashore in Maine soon. There she would be safe. No, the rigors of sea were no place for a woman.

He sighed and stood, suddenly feeling much older than his twenty-four years. Peder glanced out the cabin window and saw that everyone had gathered on the main deck for the burial. Earlier, Nora had prepared the body, then Karl had wrapped it in a tarp and weighted it with ballast to sink. It was a proud way to leave one world and enter the afterlife, Peder thought. Nothing could be better than burial at sea. But not for a woman.

Peder opened the cabin door, straightened his cap and tightened his belt over his coat, then walked with all the confidence he could muster to the heart of the group. He stood beside Elsa, who was weeping, and placed his arm about her. Directly across from them, Kristoffer stood with Knut in his arms, his chin high, his eyes red. Tora stood beside him, cradling the sleeping Lars in her arms. Peder bowed his head in silence for a long moment, hearing only the waves washing alongside the ship and the wind in the sails.

"On a voyage such as this," Pastor Lien began, "we do not expect tragedy to enter our ranks. After all, we are going to a new life, with new hope. To encounter death is a shock and most unwelcome. Yet yesterday our dear friend Astrid gave birth to a beautiful new child, and in turn she was reborn. She entered a place the Scriptures tell us we can be confident in because of what our Lord sacrificed for us. Her many weeks of pain and suffering are over, and she is whole and happy and at peace because she has met her Savior face to face."

His face brightened. "Let us concentrate on that! Yes, we all feel the pain of her loss, especially for Kris and Knut and little Lars. But we will meet this sister in Christ again, and we will rejoice together in the light of the Lord."

He paused, then opened his prayer book and read, "In the Name of the Father, and of the Son, and of the Holy Ghost. Amen. Our Lord Jesus Christ saith: The hour is coming in which all that are in the graves shall hear the voice of the Son of God, and shall come forth; they that have done good, unto the resurrection of life; and they that have done evil, unto the resurrection of damnation."

Pastor Lien stepped forward and placed his hand on Astrid's swaddled head; he gazed down at it as if staring at her lovely face in sorrow. "Out of dust art thou taken. Unto dust shalt thou return. Out of the dust shalt thou rise again. Blessed be the God and Father of our Lord Jesus Christ, who according to his abundant mercy hath given us a lively hope by the resurrection of Jesus Christ from the dead."

Together, they all prayed the Lord's Prayer, then Pastor Lien spoke again. "This is from Psalm 130," he said, reading from his

Bible. "Out of the depths have I cried unto thee, O Lord. Lord, hear my voice; let thine ears be attentive to the voice of my supplications. If thou, Lord, shouldest mark iniquities, O Lord, who shall stand? But there is forgiveness with thee. . . . I wait for the Lord, my soul doth wait, and in his word do I hope. My soul waiteth for the Lord more than they that watch for the morning: I say, more than they that watch for the morning. Let Israel hope in the Lord; for with the Lord there is mercy, and with him is plenteous redemption."

Pastor Lien looked at all of them and said unashamedly, "Beloved, our Lord came so that each of us might have eternal life. Let us serve him always and never falter in our belief that he is the resurrection and the life. Our sister Astrid was a good and true servant. She goes before us as an example we all could follow. And we will meet her again in glory. Amen."

With tears streaming down his face, the pastor stepped away. Peder nodded to two grim-faced sailors. They stepped forward, picked up Astrid's wrapped body, and carried it to the railing. Kristoffer went to her head, placed his big hand upon it in silent farewell then looked away as tears coursed down his cheeks.

Peder swallowed hard, pushing away unwanted visions of saying good-bye to his own dear bride. "On the third day the Lord created land and seas," he said. "Father God, we give back to you your own dear child, Astrid Swenson. We thank you for her time with us, for she was truly a godly example." Then he nodded, swallowing hard again against the lump that was forming in his throat.

The sailors lifted Astrid's body over the rail, and after a soft word from Peder, dropped it into the swirling seas. Her tarp-bound body floated for but a moment in the bubbly waves, then promptly sank.

At that moment, Kris let out an animal-like cry of pain and sank to his knees crying, "*Hvorfor?* Why, Lord? Why?"

The man's visible weakness took Peder aback, but he could not allow his own feelings to show, though his second mate's distress threatened to bring him to tears. He was captain of this ship, and the sailors would not appreciate such weakness in their leader. He set his mouth in a grim line and went to Kristoffer, placing his hand on the weeping man's shoulder. Knut, frightened by his father's crying, started to sob too. Peder nodded to the people, allowing them to disperse from the uncomfortable scene. The sailors left first, then the others. Only Kaatje, Tora, Elsa, and Karl remained.

It was Kaatje who finally went to Kristoffer and gently encouraged him to rise. She looked up at him with tender eyes and spoke quietly. "She was a gift, Kris. I'll always treasure her memory. You do so too."

The others also found words of comfort for him, but Peder's mind was blank. All he could think of was being in Kristoffer's position and losing Elsa. It left his mouth dry and his mind grimly determined. No, the sea was no place for a woman.

eight

Elsa struggled with her skirts as she made her way up the ladder to what had become her daily perch on top of the captain's cabin. Her heart pounded with excitement. Today she had a special subject for her sketching: the *Massachusetts,* racing the *Herald* to America, now just ten days away. An old clipper ship, the *Massachusetts* was a grand lady and about the weight of the *Herald.* She sailed broad on their starboard beam, her sails unfurled. The *Herald* was faster, but Peder stayed alongside, enjoying the sudden company in the midst of the Atlantic. Sailors climbed the rigging above Elsa, waving to their counterparts across the water, who were doing the same.

She loved this. The sea—and the surprises it offered. She understood the sailors who signed on for a lifetime. Oh, to have the freedom to go from one ship to another, traveling the world! Elsa sketched madly, frantic to catch the energy, the light, the excitement of the *Massachusetts* before the *Herald* finally outdistanced her and left her behind.

"Hello," Peder said at her shoulder, startling her since she had not heard the ladder's creak. He leaned down and looked over her shoulder, his breath a welcome small gust on her neck.

She shied away with a smile, pulling the sketch to her chest. "Not yet. You cannot see it until it is done. So go away!" she demanded firmly. "I need to work fast and will brook no husbandly distractions."

"Certainly," Peder said, shrugging his shoulders and turning away. "I guess you do not wish to hear her story."

Elsa turned in her chair. "You know of that ship?"

"Aye. She is captained by a good man, Clark Smith. It's most likely that she's carrying tea from London. It is his most frequent cargo."

"I saw a woman wave awhile ago. Is that Captain Smith's wife?"

Peder's smile diminished to some extent. "Yes. Emma frequently travels with him."

Elsa seized the opportunity. *Never mind the sketch,* she thought. "What a wonderful idea. Oh, Peder. I love this!" she waved out to the sea and above her to the men in the rigging. "I can see why you love it too. I feel more alive than I have in years! I love the adventure, the wonder of it all." She reached out to take his hand and brought it to her cheek, looking up at him with all the love in her heart. "Please, husband. I want you to consider something."

He waited, caressing her cheek slightly, but seemingly unable to ask what she wanted. It was as if he knew what was coming and feared it.

Elsa pressed on. It was now or never. "I have heard that many wives travel with their husbands." Peder's hand fell from her face. "I so want to see the world with you, Peder. I would like to travel with you."

Peder grimaced and looked across to the *Massachusetts.* "I don't know who has filled your head with such foolishness. I disagree with Smith. I think it is foolhardy to take women along on voyages when they're better off safely tucked at home."

She rose. "Safely tucked? You speak of women as if they are children. And there is no such place as a safe place. Why, I could die in a carriage wreck or from a disease that sweeps through our tidy Maine village."

He turned to her, his face stern, color rising from his neckline. "Elsa, I . . ." He stopped himself, obviously thinking twice about what he had to say. He took her hand and gathered a deep breath. "Sweetheart, you know I want nothing more than to be with you day and night. In a few years, after Ramstad Yard is in full swing, I will. Until then, I do not think it is a good idea. There are many dangers for a woman at sea. It could be a rogue sailor when I'm not around to protect you. And you speak of disease—but we encounter many more diseases in port than you ever would in Camden, to say nothing of the storms."

Elsa turned away from him, battling the urge to argue. He was her husband, after all. Her mother had spent years ingraining in Elsa and her sisters to trust in their chosen mate's judgment, to abide by his decisions. But still, this was much more difficult than she had anticipated. How could what Peder wanted be so different from her own desires? Did he not wish to be with her as much as she desired to be with him?

She glanced up at him quickly. He was staring at her intently, his face a mask of concern. They had never argued. Would this be their first?

"Tell me about Maine again," Elsa said, changing the subject. Maybe with time Peder would come to see her side and agree to take her with him. For now peace was more important. He had a whole ship full of people he had to worry over. She would not be one of them.

Peder gave her a tentative smile and began the familiar refrain. As he did, he gestured toward her chair, encouraging her to sit. As soon as her head was against the backrest, his work-roughened hands were on her forehead, gently, lightly sliding downward, closing her eyes. She smiled. By closing them, she could imagine her new home.

"Her coast winds back and forth," he was saying, "providing harbor after harbor in which to build my beautiful ships. But on a picturesque harbor sits a town called Camden-by-the-Sea. Her coast is sheltered by a massive island called Vinalhaven. It is not far from Portland, where you can go to buy dresses and such. But you won't want to leave. Our land stretches up a wide, treeless hillside, perfect for the shipyard, and at the top, the trees begin. Just inside that forest is our home. We'll leave a strip of land clear for the front yard. Imagine! Our yard stretches straight into the Atlantic!"

"And the house?" she asked, feeling calmer by the minute.

"The house?"

Elsa opened her eyes. "The house. What does it look like?"

Peder frowned and placed his chin in his hand. "The house. A good question. But I can't seem to remember."

Elsa gave him a sardonic smile, catching on to the fact that he was toying with her. "Draw it. Maybe it will help you remember."

"Yes, a good idea." He motioned for her to move her legs aside and sat on the end of the chair. He immediately began to sketch. In the distance, from the fo'c'sle, Elsa could hear the sailors singing a somber song as they worked.

> *Just one year ago tonight, Love*
> *I became your blushing bride*
> *You promised I'd be happy*
> *But no happiness I find*
> *For tonight I am a widow*
> *In the cottage by the sea.*

Elsa stared at Peder as she listened to the words. He was holding out his sketch of a cartoonish shack, obviously a joke, but his grin fell fast as he too heard the words. He knew what was coming.

"I'll not sit in some cottage awaiting news of your death, Peder Ramstad. I could not stand it. I'd rather die beside you than slowly die alone."

Peder took her hand. "I understand. But I swore to your father that I would take care of you, protect you. I don't think taking you along on my voyages would be living up to my promise."

"I am a grown woman, Peder—and I am your wife. I want to be with you. My father would understand that."

Peder sighed. "I will think it over. All right?"

Elsa nodded, thankful that he was at least listening to her. Her heart soared with hope. "Yes. Think on it."

It was only after he left her side that she remembered Peder had never sketched their real home.

Kaatje walked the perimeter of the ship, enjoying the sight of the *Massachusetts* beside them as they slowly passed her. It reassured her to remember that they were not all alone out here in the great Atlantic. She looked down at the silvery-blue waters racing by, thinking of Astrid somewhere beneath the waves. Oh, how she missed her friend! Elsa was still dear to her, but her mind was on her new husband, not Kaatje's ongoing troubles.

She frowned as she thought of Soren. Even in such cramped quarters, he had managed to make himself scarce, telling her that the small cabin made him feel claustrophobic. He often left her for hours at a time, helping sailors tar the ropes or carry out other duties, he said. But Kaatje couldn't help but wonder. *No,* she told herself, *do not allow yourself such thoughts.* Surely he could not be with another woman. Where would they go? She laughed out loud then turned in embarrassment, afraid she had been overheard.

No matter. No one was near her. Up ahead, she spotted Tora with Knut and Lars. Knut played with Tora's parasol, running around and around it, while she looked on with a bored expression and shifted Lars to her other shoulder. Even with two small children in tow, Tora looked glamorous. Her shiny, dark hair was tied up in a chignon and anchored with an elegant ivory comb. She was dressed in a charming blue princesse dress, made of silk, and over it, she wore a sleeveless polonaise of ivory. It fell gracefully over the short train, emphasizing the girl's slim figure. Oh, to come from money like the Anderses, Kaatje thought. Never had she owned a dress such as that.

Putting her envy aside, Kaatje smiled and approached Tora. Perhaps some time with Astrid's children would bring back memories of her friend in a tender way.

"Tora!" she called as the girl turned to walk aft with the children.

Tora turned to see who called and then immediately glanced away. *That is odd,* Kaatje thought. Still, the girl stopped and waited for Kaatje.

"I thought I'd spell you with the children," said Kaatje. "Why don't you rest for a bit?"

Tora looked at her, and Kaatje thought she saw a hint of derision in her eyes. She ignored the troublesome feeling. The girl was just difficult, that was all. She was probably still resenting her position with Kris, especially now with two children. In Kaatje's mind, though, Tora's consistently petulant demeanor spoiled her beauty.

"That would be fine," Tora said with a graciousness that sounded a bit forced. "I'll return in an hour if that is all right with you."

"Fine, fine. Go enjoy yourself."

Tora left her side with no further word.

"Hmm," Kaatje said to Lars, who seemed to be flourishing on goat's milk. "At least you're a content little baby," she said, kissing his forehead. "She could have it much worse." She looked over to Knut, who looked bereft without the parasol. "Come, son, let's go find my husband. He'll throw you high into the air and catch you at the last minute. That should cast away your doldrums."

Knut looked hopeful and placed his tiny hand in hers. "Where is he?"

"I do not know. Shall we play a game of cat and mouse? Let us pretend we're the *katt,* and he's the *mus.* Now be very quiet," she said with her finger to her lips. "We're on the hunt and must sneak up on him before we pounce!"

A smile spread across Knut's face. "Let's go!" he screeched in Norwegian.

Kaatje smiled as the boy pulled her along. Somewhere she knew Astrid would be smiling at her son's delighted grin.

Tora was on her way to her bunk to take a brief nap when she met up with Soren in the passageway to the hold. He smiled lazily at her as he held the door, and she edged past him, allowing her body to touch his. It was a subtle movement, but unmistakable. Soren let the door shut behind them, and they were alone in the darkened hall.

"In there," Soren said in a low voice, eyeing her hungrily.

"In Kaatje's room? What if she comes in?"

"She is out on—"

Just then, Nora Paulson came through the narrow passageway, studying them both before passing. She turned at the door. "Since you're apparently free from your duties, Tora, perhaps we should have your English lesson now."

Tora looked at her, hoping the woman could see the daggers in her eyes. But her voice was innocent. "Oh, thank you, Nora. But I'm afraid I have just a moment to myself before I have to get back to Kaatje and the boys."

"To Kaatje?" Nora said pointedly. "Where *is* your wife, Soren?"

"On deck," he said. "I thought I'd just grab her shawl."

"Ah," she said, apparently mollified with the thought that he was getting back to his wife shortly. When she was gone, they smiled at one another like naughty schoolchildren.

Then, before anyone else could come upon them, Soren pushed Tora into the small cabin that he had shared with Kaatje since Astrid's death. His lips were upon her neck, sending delightful shivers down her spine before the lock clicked in place.

"Soren, I do not think we should continue to do this," she protested lightly.

"You say that every time," he purred in her ear. "Tell me you do not like this."

Oh, he was thrilling. And Kaatje was such a fool to let a man like this stray. *Just one more time,* Tora thought, dismissing a niggling thought. Surely this could not be wrong. Surely something wrong could not feel so . . . so right.

Peder drew a line on his chart and then wrote in his logbook, constantly scratching out his mistakes and moving on. Keeping the log was typically a job for the mate, but Peder enjoyed it. Today, however, his mind was elsewhere, for although they were making great time, the approaching coast brought forward issues he had to face. First there was Elsa and her clear desire to sail with him. And then there was Karl. He had to be forthright with his friend about Ramstad Yard and the financing his father had offered him.

Deciding not to tarry any longer, Peder invited Karl to lunch. "Come," he said, "it will be good for Kris to have his turn at the wheel. Nothing like a ship at his fingertips to remind a man of the goodness of life."

Karl paused, as if searching for a reason to say no, but then shrugged. When Peder stopped to think of it, his best friend had not sat at his dinner table in over a week. Peder had taken to his suggestion of entertaining others, but now felt poorly about it. Karl probably felt ousted, his rightful place occupied by others. Karl's cabin had even been taken over by the Janssens after Astrid's death! Never mind that his first mate had insisted that the pregnant Kaatje remain in a comfortable berth; Peder should have intervened. Kaatje was well now. And the first mate deserved preferential treatment.

As soon as they were seated, Cook brought two steaming platefuls of *farikal,* a slow-cooked dish of cabbage, mutton, and black peppercorns.

"Elsa is not joining us?" Karl asked after Peder had blessed the food.

"No. She ate earlier at my request."

Karl's eyes darted to his.

"I need to talk over something with you."

Peder took a few bites, then looked over at Karl, who was eating slowly, studying his friend's face for clues to what this was about.

"I am afraid I have a confession to make and wished to do it in privacy, Karl."

His first mate waited, placing his fork on his plate and wiping his mouth.

"You see, I've dreaded doing this because I was afraid of your reaction. I am afraid it will upset the applecart, as our new countrymen say."

"Just say it, Peder. Out with it."

Peder looked him steadily in the eye. "On our wedding day, my father gave us a gift."

"And?"

"He told me that he would finance Ramstad Yard, top to bottom."

Karl searched Peder's eyes for several seconds as if to see if he was joking. When Peder merely returned his stare, waiting, he shoved his chair back with a loud scrape and stood abruptly, his face flushing in anger. "And you told him no, right? That we had obtained our own financing? That we had an agreement, sixty-forty?"

Peder lost his nerve and dropped his gaze. Karl's response was everything he had feared. "No," he said softly. "I accepted his gift."

"And you waited until now to tell me? Why so late, Peder?"

"This is difficult, obviously. I knew you'd take it hard."

"Take it hard? Take it hard! I'd say I have just reason to take issue," he said, pacing. "Peder, I've worked alongside you for years. I've scrimped and saved to get my 40 percent. For what? You're telling me Ramstad-Martensen Yard is a thing of the past. Oh, yes, stand aside for the mighty Ramstads! I should've known old Leif couldn't keep his sticky fingers out of his son's business."

"Now just a minute—"

"So that's it? I am out?"

"No, no! Karl, I want you as my number one man. I need you there."

"Your number one man? But not your partner—"

"It will almost be like having a partner."

"But my dreams of building steamships? No, no. You will set them aside for *sometime later,* in favor of your romantic sailing ships. It's over, Peder." Karl raked his hands through his hair. "It's 1880 and sail is on its way out. Steam is our ticket to the future."

"There is still room for sail, Karl. These ships are cheaper to build, more reliable in many ways—"

"There you go! You'll never admit sail is dying. Sure, there's room for some new schooners. I can see that there might be some money in hauling cargo in the big old tubs. But steam, Peder. That is where we would make our yard successful. You hold on to sail because your father loves it. And with his money, I'd wager that we will never see a steamship leave Ramstad Yard."

"I will make sure of it. Karl, I respect your views—"

"Aye, but not enough to hold to the dreams we forged as boys, eh? No, I guess friendship comes after finances in the Ramstad family." He strode to the door.

"Karl, wait. Truly, I want to work this out with you."

"You have made your decision, man. Now I have to make mine." He left without another word, closing the door soundly.

n i n e

or the third day in a row, Elsa ate lunch with Peder in silence.
Ever since his blowup with Karl, her husband had been mo-
rose, and Elsa had been forced to cancel their nightly dinner parties. He had made their guests so uncomfortable that she had begun
making excuses to the various passengers, begging off for one night
and then the next. Not that Peder seemed to notice. He didn't even
seem to notice her. Or had she done something wrong too?

Tonight she had dressed in one of her finest dresses, hoping to
catch his attention. Her mother had ordered three new gowns from
Copenhagen for her as a going away present, and she had been saving them until they got to America and were in more gracious surroundings. The one she wore tonight was an evening dress with a
shorter skirt, or what they called a quarter train. The bodice and skirt,
however, were still the long and sleek look—an unfortunate, confin-
ing feature in Elsa's mind—and were made of a beautifully shaded
turquoise lampas, trimmed with turquoise blue satin and pale, straw-
colored surah. The sleeves were quite daring and short, and she wore
matching straw-colored gloves. Still, Peder had not commented.

Perhaps it was her lack of a decent bath in the last month. She was used to bathing at least twice a week and did her best with the basin of water, but oh, how she longed for a steaming copper tub!

Elsa placed her napkin by her plate and sat back in her chair to study her husband. He leaned over his plate, shoveling in the food. His eyes were ringed as if he had suffered from loss of sleep in the last ten days. Elsa concluded that it was not that he lacked interest in her, it was that he could not stop thinking about his friend and the breach between them.

"You know, you could just say no to your father," she began.

He looked up and scowled at her. "Say no to the most assured road to success? He's promised me twice the money that Karl and I could raise together."

"But is what Karl said true? Will you feel like the American Ramstad Yard is truly run by your father? Wouldn't there be joy in building something totally your own?"

"This will be more my own than what I would share with Karl."

"But you made a promise, Peder."

"Enough!" The anger in his voice and the pulsing veins at his neck unnerved her. Never had he raised his voice to her. Seeing her surprise, his voice softened. "Forgive me. I did not mean to yell. But I am making what I think is the best decision. Karl will come around. He can still own 20 percent of a much bigger, promising shipyard."

"But at what cost? You said yourself that you would make all the decisions." Elsa rose and went around the table to kneel by his side. "Peder, he is your best friend. Since boyhood. Do not let it fall aside as you move forward."

Peder grimaced and shook his head. "I do this for you, Elsa."

"I have what is important to me," she protested. "I appreciate that you wish to honor me, but turning away friends will not make my gold seem more shiny. I'd rather wait. Build the business slowly. And keep our dear friends."

Peder stood, his face a mask of iron. "I have decided. It is my business, not yours."

Elsa swallowed hard, willing back her quick anger. She had been trained to think about what she said before saying it, something Tora never seemed to grasp. By the time she felt all right about her retort, Peder was gone, slamming the cabin door behind him.

"O Lord, Lord," she prayed out loud, holding her head in her hands. "Be with those two prideful, stubborn men. For I know this is not your way. Teach them to honor one another and love one another, and give them words to heal the wound that has opened between them."

Sighing, she stood and went to the china cabinet, where she pulled out two old, amateurish but clear drawings of steamships. Secretly she agreed with Karl. While sailing ships were classically beautiful, steam was part of their future. It was just a matter of time before she would find the courage to tell Peder.

Kaatje rounded the corner of the deck, soaking in the fresh air and warm sun on her skin. She felt wonderful now that her seasickness had gone, and she caressed her burgeoning belly when no one was looking. Soren had gone missing yet again, and she wondered briefly where he could be hiding himself. She shielded her eyes and looked to the crow's nest, where he often claimed to go. There was but one sailor up there now. Ever since she and Knut had been unable to find him when they had played cat and mouse the week before, Kaatje had been vaguely uneasy. But she banished away the doubts, wanting to focus on good and upright hopes and dreams, rather than the sordid memories that seemed to plague her.

Pushing them away, she thought instead of his soft kisses that morning, his warm hands and earnest voice telling her that he was so glad she was his. *Thank you, Father,* she prayed, looking out to sea. The sun glittered on the water as if echoing her praise, tiny mirrors of flickering, shimmering light against the dark sea. The sky was a light blue, and the sun hot on her face. It would be a warm one, judging from the early afternoon heat. Possibly the hottest yet. She owned a parasol, dilapidated as it was, but she could never seem to remember to carry it with her on deck. It was just as well. Soren claimed to like her freckles and sun-rosied cheeks, regardless of the fashion. And for a farmer's wife, there was little fashion to worry over anyway.

Kaatje resolved to see what Elsa was up to and started toward the captain's quarters, knowing she would probably be sketching up top, as usual. She wanted to be nearby if her friend wished to talk about whatever was going on between Karl and Peder. The whole ship was rife with gossip, covering the topic ad nauseam, as far as Kaatje was concerned. Kaatje's elderly aunt had always said, "Live by what you know, not what you believe." Apparently, a lot of people on the ship wished to believe the worst.

The most troubling rumor involved Elsa and Karl and unchaste glances. Not wanting to listen to such folderol, Kaatje had dismissed the idea out of hand. But she could not stop herself from remembering the two times she had caught Karl eyeing her friend—the way Soren had eyed other women. It troubled her. But those instances had been prior to the wedding. And Karl had been Elsa's friend for as long as Peder had. Surely an upright man such as Karl would never . . .

Enough, she told herself. *Go and be a friend.* Reaching the ladder, she called out, not wanting to disturb Elsa if she was with another. "Hello, up there. Any room for a fat friend with child?"

Elsa's face peeked over the edge. "You're hardly what I would call fat. Yes, if you can safely make your way up here, do so. I'd appreciate your company right now."

Kaatje climbed up and sat beside her on the bottom portion of the chaise lounge. "The only good news about my getting fat is that my corset is a thing of the past," she whispered. She smoothed her wide maternity skirt beside her. It was thin, gray wool, itchy under the best of circumstances and torturous under the sun, but it was the most comfortable of her dresses in terms of size. And Soren claimed to love it because it brought out her gray eyes.

"Lucky you," Elsa returned conspiratorially. "I'd give an arm to the people who set the styles if they would call for the worldwide burning of all corsets."

"And give up that tiny waist? I bet Peder can circle it with his hands!"

"Still, I wouldn't be sorry to give up these miserable stays."

They sat together in companionable silence for a moment, looking out to sea.

"If I keep getting visitors," said Elsa, "I'll have to make the ship's carpenter build another chair."

"Oh, that would be delightful. This is the best view on the ship, you know, barring the crow's nest."

"I know. Then consider it done. I'll get another chair made, and you can rest here beside me while I draw."

"Sounds heavenly. What are you working on now?"

Elsa turned her pad so Kaatje could see, and she caught her breath. "Elsa, that's amazing! It's almost frightening to look at—it brings back that terrible night."

Elsa's face grew sorrowful. "I know. I'm sorry to remind you of the night Astrid died. But there's something magnificent in thinking about the *Herald* cresting those horrible waves and living to see a peaceful sea the next morning. In fact, it reminds me of Astrid in a way, making it through this life and going on to the next. In comparison, this life must seem like a storm, and heaven . . . well, like *heaven*. So peaceful."

Kaatje nodded, smiling as tears edged her eyes. "I like that. You are right." She studied the drawing again. "Peder is right. You have a gift."

"Ah yes. Peder. My husband seems to have left the ship and appointed someone else in his stead. I gather by your visit and those concerned gray eyes that you've noticed."

Kaatje met her gaze. "I have."

"He is so driven that he does not pause to look at the damage in his wake."

"I take it you mean Karl."

"I do. He . . . Peder . . . he's just so . . . so stubborn."

Kaatje laughed. "He can't possibly be more stubborn than your father, Amund."

"Possibly," Elsa said with a smile, and the two settled back for a heart-to-heart talk.

"He does it all for you, you know," Kaatje said.

"I suppose. But I have told him that I have all I need. If only . . ."

"What?"

"Well, you see, I believe I would like to travel with him . . . sail with him."

"And he does not want that?"

"He is afraid." She looked at Kaatje's confused expression. "Afraid I would be hurt. Astrid's death only seemed to hasten his decision against it. And now with Karl possibly leaving, I think he feels adrift, unsettled. To his way of thinking, having me along would only be another burden to bear."

"Surely," Kaatje said carefully, "it is not as bad as all that."

"Almost," Elsa said glumly. "All I can think of is watching as Peder sails out of port and being left all alone."

"With Tora," Kaatje said, compassion evident on her face.

"With *Tora*," Elsa repeated.

Tora sighed in relief. The two boys were asleep at last, with Knut curled up beside the baby in what once had been Astrid's cot. Knut had insisted on napping there of late, and Kaatje had been quick to encourage Tora to allow it. The cabin held, after all, Knut's last memories of his mother. Generally he seemed to be coping well, but at night if she wasn't up with Lars, she was comforting Knut, soothing away his nightmares. She was exhausted and ready to nap herself.

Tora eyed the upper bunk. Never mind that Soren slept there. She'd do anything for a rest.

She stepped on her skirts and made several false starts, but finally made it up into the creaky old cot above the sleeping boys. Within seconds, her eyes were closed, and she fell deeply into sleep. It seemed like only minutes later that warm hands were roaming her. Tora opened her eyes to see Soren's face close to her own and felt his warm breath on her neck.

"What a delightful surprise," he whispered, his eyes alight. "I come back to my room for a moment, and I find you in my bed." He moved to kiss her, but she pushed him away.

"No. No more, Soren. We will wake the boys."

"We have been quiet before," he grinned. He moved toward her again. "Come on, kitten. No one will hear."

"No!" she whispered fiercely. She shoved against his chest and turned her cheek to him to avoid his kiss. "We are done, Soren. No more. Get off of me or I will scream."

Soren frowned and moved away from her. Then he gave her a half-smile. "Is this a game? You want to be chased?"

Tora sat up and shook her head. She swung her legs over the side and hopped down off the bed. Miraculously, the boys still slept.

Soren tried reaching for her again, but she stepped aside, avoiding his hand. "Outside," she mouthed and walked out the door with an air of confidence.

Soren closed the door behind him, looking down one side of the dim passageway then the other. He was handsome, undoubtedly, but stupid. And she was tired of him and his growing number of comments that revealed his supposed possession of her. Men were such simpletons. Offer your body and they believed they controlled your soul.

"It's over, Soren," she said, lifting her chin.

"No, don't say that, kitten. It's just begun," he urged, moving toward her.

"No," she said, cocking one eyebrow and placing a small hand on his muscular chest. "I said it's over. Done with. I was napping, not enticing you."

"That's what you say, but—"

"No, Soren." She slowly enunciated each syllable. "We are finished. I have bigger plans in mind than an ongoing affair with a poor dirt farmer."

Outraged, Soren acted. Tora did not see it coming, and the force of his blow sent her reeling. She struck the wall and immediately bled from a scrape at her temple. Tears of surprise and anger fell as she leaned against the wall, glaring up at him.

"You will pay for that," she threatened. Then, "Help!" she screamed, without waiting a moment longer. "*Help!*"

Peder was on deck when he heard a woman's cry. In an instant, he had the door open and was taking in the scene of an angry Soren hovering over Tora, who was cowering and bleeding. In a fury, he charged Soren and, holding him against a wall, yelled, "What is going on here?"

The man was mute. Peder glanced from Soren to Tora, and back to Soren. The guilt on Soren's face and the defiance on Tora's told Peder everything he needed to know. This was not a case of transgression against an innocent woman. This was the heart of an indecent affair.

"No! No!" He gripped Soren's neck in his two powerful hands and struggled with the desire to choke the man. "Have you no respect for your wife, man?" he asked incredulously. "She sits up there on the roof with my wife, probably telling her of your new life together and the children that will follow this one. And where are you?" Peder shook, he was so furious. He had to get some air before he tore them both apart.

From the other side of the wall, they heard Knut's frightened wail. Peder glanced at Tora. There was a hint of fear in her face now.

"You! Get back in there to the children. And Soren, you will come with me." He backed off from the man as Soren massaged his throat. Peder straightened his own coat and cap. "With me," he said again, firmly.

Tora opened the cabin door quietly, trying to slink inside. "And Tora. You may not leave that cabin until either Elsa or I come for you."

"But the boys—"

"Not until one of us comes for you."

She closed the door without further argument.

Silently seething, Peder escorted Soren to his sitting room. He then ordered Stefan to guard the door, with clear instructions not to let Soren out.

Furious, despairing, and unwilling to place this on Elsa's shoulders, Peder went to Karl. His friend looked up at him in surprise, for they had been tacitly avoiding one another for days now. His look of surprise melted to one of consternation at the sight of Peder's drawn face.

Peder reached out to him. "I need my first mate. Are you available to advise me?"

Karl took his hand and gave it a firm shake. "Certainly. Where shall we go?"

"The fo'c'sle."

Giving Peder advice on Soren Janssen's extramarital affair burned Karl to the core, consumed as he was by his own guilty thoughts of Elsa. Still, he managed to give his old friend what he thought was solid advice: "Stay out of it." To punish Soren publicly would mean punishing the innocent Kaatje. What was meant to stay behind closed doors was meant to stay behind closed doors. "But we will give Soren a private, firm warning, no?" Karl said.

"And I will speak with Tora."

"Let us go to Soren. The man has been begging for a lesson for years now. Perhaps we can persuade him to find the happiness that God intended him to find with his wife."

Manhandling Soren would release much of the tension that had built within Karl for weeks. His fists had begged to punch the man, but Peder had forbidden it, only wanting to threaten him seriously enough to keep his path straight for the remaining five days on the *Herald.*

Inside, however, Karl fought his own war. For was he not as guilty as the man they threatened? If Karl was half a man, he would confess his sin to Peder. He had accepted Peder's apology and told him that he did not know what was the right next step in their business relationship. But in the meantime, he would stay. What a hypocrite! Accepting Peder's apology while knowing that he had done the man a greater wrong. If the Scriptures were right, his only hope was to tear his eyes from their sockets.

As much as the thought of breaking with Peder pained him, he could see no other route. He had to leave. Perhaps Leif's gift had been providential . . . God's method of keeping Karl out of temptation's way by removing him from the picture entirely. Yes, that had to be it, he told himself as he breathed in the deep salty air that he had come to love along with Peder. Embracing the sea had cemented their friendship. Loving the same woman would end it. But Peder must never know the truth. He might blame Elsa, who was innocent of any of this. No, Karl would never take that chance.

Karl bowed his head. *I feel some peace over this, Lord,* he prayed silently. *This is your path for me, is it not? Perhaps it is better for us both, Peder and me, to part ways. I am thankful that you are walking ever beside this humble sinner, Lord. And keep my walk as pure as can be.*

Much later, Karl stood alone in the shadow of the captain's cabin, chewing on the stem of a long-empty pipe and listening as the port watch rang seven bells. It was nearly midnight, the full moon almost at its zenith, but he was not tired. Too many thoughts raced through his head.

He took one last look at the moon and turned to round the corner. He stifled a gasp. There on the other side of the cabin beside the starboard rail was Elsa, a vision in her white cotton dressing gown. Her hair was long and loose, waving down her back. She was looking north, and as Karl leaned back into the shadows, unable to tear his eyes away, he saw why. Faintly, in the distance, red and green lights waved on the far horizon. The northern lights.

Karl took another step back as Peder joined her at the rail.

"Oh, Peder," she said softly, leaning her head on his shoulder. "Isn't it grand? Father told me it was God whispering to me and to always think of him when I saw them."

"A good image," Peder agreed. "Someday you'll need to see the southern lights too. Sweetheart, I owe you an apology. Since my argument with Karl, I fear I've been a bear to live with."

Karl eased backward, making his way around the cabin. He had done a lot of things he wasn't proud of, but he would not eavesdrop on his friends.

Before going below to his sleeping quarters, Karl glanced back to the north. "If that is you whispering, Father, thank you. I'll learn to praise your name, regardless of how I feel about what you are doing in my life. For I trust you."

t e n

*E*lsa helped Cook bring out platters of food for their elaborate, celebratory *koldt bord,* a picnic dinner on deck for all, including the sailors. It was a dual celebration: Peder had just married Nora and Einar, and tomorrow they would all be in America. As on Elsa's own wedding day, most of the passengers were dressed in the traditional *bunad* of Bergen, with Nora wearing the same gorgeous headdress that she herself had worn . . . when was it? Almost a month and a half ago, she calculated. So much had happened, so much had changed, and they had not even reached America's shores!

All day the ship had been electrified by the people's palpable excitement. Tomorrow they would be in America, land of promise. *Tomorrow I shall have a proper bath,* Elsa mused, thinking that fact almost equally as exciting. She still loved the sea and wanted to travel with Peder; she would simply need to convince him of the necessity of proper bathing rituals, even at sea. She went back to the galley, planning all the while. Would she like Boston? What would Maine really be like? Were her imaginings on track?

Cook silently handed her a steaming platter of pressed cod and poached salmon. Kaatje passed her with a pot of cabbage in sour cream. It was the last of the feast to be served, and the guests on deck hovered nearby hungrily, like sharks around a wounded sea lion, Elsa thought. Before them was a makeshift table that looked very much like Elsa's own wedding feast, minus the lamb dishes. As was befitting a remarkable repast at sea, they served a great variety of fish, including herring, flounder, sardines, and a lobster for each person. Peder had brought on a cask full of salt water and live lobsters before they set sail, anticipating this celebratory night before landing. In addition, there were meat loaves, cheeses of four varieties, hard salami, and carefully hoarded fruit.

"All right! It is all here!" Elsa announced, and the ship gave up a unified cheer at the news. Never had food looked so good. For most of the passengers, dinner fare had been a dull repast of hardtack and salt beef and fish, with the occasional respite when invited to the captain's table. Seeing their hungry faces, Elsa felt a pang of guilt for feasting as they had. But such was life for the captain and his wife, she supposed. Perhaps she would not be as excited about traveling with him if she too were reduced to such dull fare.

Pastor Lien blessed the food, going on much longer than most wanted him to, Elsa imagined, then Nora and Einar started off the line of diners. Dressed in costume and celebrating a wedding, Elsa felt at home and wondered if she would ever feel so again. In America her neighbors would likely be from many places, Peder said. They came from Germany and China, Italy and Mauritania. From all over the world people came to the United States. For freedom, for justice, for a new chance in life. And she was one of them.

Dinner was followed by dancing. Two passengers brought out a fiddle and an accordion, and Peder opened a small wine keg, which was strictly monitored by the stern-faced Kristoffer. Still, there was little need for alcohol to achieve the high mood. They danced until late in the evening, even after the little ones gave in to sleep and the adults' feet ached. They all felt it: the need to express their jubilation, the need to laugh and sing and be free after their long voyage.

In one of the last folk dances of the night, Elsa left Peder's side as the couples switched partners and found herself side by side with Karl. She flashed him a smile. She owed him so much. For standing by Peder's side all these years. For apparently forgiving him his change in plans for Ramstad Yard. He was a fine friend. A brother, really.

"You are a tremendous friend, Karl," she said, as he held on to her elbow and waist and hustled her around their small circle.

"Yes? Why do you say that?" he asked, remaining face forward. His neck was flushed. From the exertion, she assumed.

"You know why." They finished the dance and bowed to the others in their group then to one another. When they came up, they bumped heads lightly. Elsa giggled. "Now that was graceful. I'm sorry. Are you all right?" They walked to the railing as the music paused for a moment and many went for refreshments.

"Fine. It was probably me. I'm a better sailor than a dancer."

"Nonsense." She smiled up at him. "Thanks for standing by my Peder all these years. For bringing him safely home each time." Impulsively, she stood on tiptoe and kissed Karl's cheek, which was rough with a day's growth of beard.

He looked at her, suddenly serious and intent. Elsa, confused by the look in his eye, took a step backward. Silently, Karl turned on his heel and left her, making his way through the crowd until she could not see him anymore.

Elsa whirled back to the railing. What had just happened? Never had she seen him look at her that way . . . the way Peder looked at her.

Kaatje, having observed the two, joined Elsa at the rail. "So you finally see what has been before you all this time."

Elsa looked over at her with a bewildered expression. "What are you speaking of?"

"Karl. You have seen what he feels."

"Karl? He is my friend. He feels nothing more."

Kaatje stared at Elsa until she met her gaze.

"He feels nothing more, right?" Elsa asked in a soft, faraway voice.

Once again Kaatje said nothing, waiting for her to come to her own conclusions.

"Father in heaven, please let her be wrong," Elsa said, staring upward, then back at Kaatje and then out to sea.

Kaatje studied her friend, taking in the vision she made. Soft tendrils of golden hair had escaped her cap and curled around her neck. With her hair pulled back, her eyes were all the more luminous, her curvy lips all the more apparent. To Karl, she undoubtedly looked fetching.

Kaatje's mind leaped to Soren and his indiscretions. She knew now where he had been all those missing hours, during all those days. The long strands of dark chestnut hair in her bed . . . the afternoons when Tora would emerge, looking slightly mussed. Soren had taken to staying in their cabin of late—to study his English, he said—but Kaatje had overheard Peder and Karl talking. He had been caught with Tora, and thinking they would spare Kaatje the embarrassment, they had confined the man to his cabin and Tora to new quarters at the opposite end of the ship.

The revelation came not as a surprise, but as something to which one nodded, and agreed that yes, that was about what was expected. *O dear God,* she had prayed, *make North Dakota a land of men.* But her prayer brought her little comfort. For Soren was ill in a way, seemingly destined to seek his healing in women. It was like a disease. And she was powerless to stop it.

"Kaatje," Elsa said forcefully. She brought her head up, suddenly aware that Elsa had been speaking to her. "How long have you known about Karl?"

"I suspected for weeks," Kaatje said curtly. She felt overwhelmingly tired and irritated at Elsa's naiveté. Could she not see? And what did she have to worry about anyway? It was not her husband who lusted after another woman. She simply had another man in love with her. Oh, for Elsa's problems!

"What is the matter? Are you feeling poorly?" Elsa asked, peering at Kaatje in the looming darkness.

There were few lanterns about, and Kaatje was glad because she felt very close to weeping. This was supposed to be the happiest night of her life! Tomorrow they would be in America, in a week they'd be in North Dakota, a month after that, in their new soddy on their own land. In five months they would welcome a child! And where was her husband? Confined to quarters like a common criminal. Suddenly a rush of anger left her furious with Peder and his sanctimonious ways. What did he know? Perhaps his case was all conjecture. Perhaps Soren was innocent!

"I am tired," she said irritably to Elsa. "I am going to bed."

She turned away and almost ran into Tora, who looked resplendent in her own Bergen costume. After searching the girl's narrowed eyes for a moment, Kaatje left, angry tears cresting her lids and sliding down her cheeks. No, she had seen Soren glance at Tora herself. Inside, she knew the truth.

The dancing had ended, and most of the passengers had turned in for the night. Only a few remained on deck, enjoying the warm summer night. Several sailors hunched around one of the lanterns, playing an ill-tuned accordion and singing together softly in the afterglow of the party. Some of the Camden group huddled around another lantern, talking, planning how things would go.

Peder clapped Karl on the shoulder, feeling weary but very

satisfied. They were nearing land and were close to bringing all these people to the land of their dreams. Their way would be hard, undoubtedly, but once there, they had the chance to make something of themselves, *for* themselves, instead of for a landowner or boss. In America, *they* could be the landowners, the bosses. It was the Great Promise.

He pulled Karl close, in an old, familiar gesture of friendship. "Thank you for staying on for a while, Karl. I know it is difficult for you."

"In many ways," Karl said softly, cryptically. "I'll say again that I don't know how long I will remain."

Peder nodded as if he understood, not wanting to bring up anything negative that might harm their friendship again. For theirs was a partnership forged on the iron of many years, a true partnership.

"I will show you, my friend, that you can prosper in our business too," Peder promised. "I will build a steamship directly after this first schooner, and you can take as much financial interest in her as you care."

Karl looked at him in surprise. "You are quite serious?"

"Yes. Of course. I want you to succeed too. After that, we can build a steamer for every two sailers."

Karl smiled. "You're serious?" he repeated. "And I might buy shares for those also, all that I can afford?"

"As many shares as you wish," Peder said, feeling magnanimous and glad that he was able to please his friend again. "See? You get to share in all the profits of your dream ships without the pressures of financing the yard. You're free to build your own fleet."

Karl nodded, obviously thinking it through. "I had not thought of it in that way. To be honest, I had thought you would just never get to a steamer."

Peder scowled at him. "You know me better than that. You are my friend, my partner. I would not overlook our friendship for the sake of business."

Karl looked at him steadily. "You already did. You took your father's loan without discussing it with me."

Peder shifted uncomfortably. "Well, yes. But I'd like to think of it as a providential change in direction. Perhaps over time we'll both be more successful—me with my yard, you with your fleet."

Karl nodded. "Perhaps. I'm willing to give it a try."

"*Gud,*" Peder said, sticking out his hand.

Karl shook it firmly.

Peder smiled broadly, feeling as if all was right with the world. "Elsa!" he called to his wife, who stood at the railing looking out at the sea. "There are no northern lights tonight, *elskling*. Come join us!"

Karl watched Elsa come toward them tentatively, her eyes lowered.

"We have good news!" Peder said to her. "Bring us some refreshments, will you, wife? We have to have a toast."

She left, obviously glad to escape Karl's presence. He knew she had recognized his feelings toward her. He had seen it in her eyes at the end of their dance together. Her discomfort made him feel miserable. Perhaps she would forget—or think she had misread him. Perhaps they could put this nonsense behind them when they got to Camden-by-the-Sea and get on with the business of building a shipyard. Yes. That was it. It was just a phase. Like a moon reaching its zenith, surely these feelings would crest then fade away. Karl clung to that thought as he mumbled his thanks when she handed him a crystal goblet.

"Karl has agreed to stay on," Peder informed her. "After our first schooner, we'll build his beloved steamer. And it can be all his, if he wishes."

"Oh, Peder, that's a wonderful solution."

Karl nodded. "But I won't make the first one all mine. Perhaps 60 percent. Who, after all, is foolish enough to invest all his money in one ship? And I might want a part of the schooner."

Peder laughed and raised his glass. "To our new partnership."

Karl clinked his glass against Peder's. "To our new partnership," he said.

Inwardly, however, he hoped that his own path to success would eventually take him far from Peder and Elsa—for their sakes as well as his.

eleven

Boston
July 22, 1880

*E*lsa studied her reflection in the mirror. Looped in a braid, her hair was smooth and silky, giving her a mature, sophisticated look worthy of a captain's wife. As did her new, pale green walking suit. The bottom was trimmed with a deep-pleated flounce and the polonaise with a darker green trim. At hip, sleeve, and bust were luscious, wide bows in the same color. To top it off, she wore a straw hat adorned with green ribbons and silk roses.

"That'll do for the Americans," she whispered, smiling. A surge of energy sent her scurrying to the door. She did not want to be late for the first sighting of her new homeland!

She was barely out the door when the sailor in the crow's nest shouted, "Land ho!" pointing to the southwest. "Land ho!"

Despite the late-night celebration, all passengers were up and dressed in their best finery. Now, as one, the group *hurrahed* and pushed to the railing, peering toward the horizon. They were silent for several long moments, every eye scanning for the first glimpse. Elsa was willing to wager that every person itched to climb the rigging and join the sailor in the crow's nest.

"There she is!" Einar shouted.

"Land ho!" another man echoed.

Moments later they could all see the slim sliver of land, and they laughed and hugged and slapped one another on the back. They were home, or close to it, anyway.

"Boston, Massachusetts, United States of America," Elsa whispered to herself, staring at the hazy outline in the distance.

Peder had arranged for his passengers to disembark in Boston, rather than New York, to avoid the mess at Castle Garden. In Boston, they processed several hundred people each day, compared to Castle Garden's three or four thousand, and oftentimes immigrants passed more smoothly through Boston's immigration house.

Peder relinquished the helm to Karl and came to Elsa. They smiled at one another and shared a quick hug.

"She is beautiful, no?"

"What I can see of her."

"Don't worry," he said, patting her hand. "You will love our new home."

Elsa loved the sound of it: *Our new home.* It felt as if they were truly beginning their life together.

Kaatje found herself continually glancing at her husband, wondering at the change in him. Ever since the *Herald* had docked, late in the afternoon, he had been very protective and solicitous of her, helping her down the gangplank, asking Einar to watch over her while he went after their luggage, staying close to her side as they moved into the immigration lines. She felt safe and cherished, once again able to believe that this truly was a new beginning for them. From here on out, all things would be new, including her trust and love for Soren. He was her husband, and despite everything, she could not imagine life without him. Last night when she had confronted him about Tora, once again he had begged for forgiveness, and though her heart was broken, she had granted it. Today, however, her hope was renewed. For Soren would be a new man in North Dakota. They just had to get there.

It would take a while, though. A customs agent gave them each several sheets to fill out and kept an eye on them until they had all completed the task. Then, with a translator in tow to make sure all understood his directions, he led them to a government-sponsored hotel in which they would stay the night. Tomorrow they would begin their process to citizenship. The hotel was not grand, but even the creaky beds felt luxurious to the sea-weary passengers. Most could not sleep anyway, so excited were they to be in America.

Their high countenance ebbed the next day, Kaatje noticed, as for hours the Bergen group wound through the immigration house assembly line. Like the cattle at home, Kaatje thought, simply following the cow in front to the feedlot. The immigrants wore chalk marks on their clothing, indicating their country of origin and date of arrival. They went in and out of booths, up and down stairs, waiting in line after line. "It is this way for a purpose," Soren said. "See the officials? They watch your breathing as you climb the stairs to find out if you have lung disease. They make you carry your own luggage to make sure you're not hiding a limp or other ailment."

Kaatje looked at him admiringly. How had he learned so much? His knowledge and confidence reassured her, and she was glad he stayed close to her, especially when they encountered uniformed officials asking quick questions in their American-accented English. Nora had learned her English from a woman in Britain, and the Bergensers from Nora, so their new tongue suddenly sounded foreign on the lips of impatient American officials. "What's your name?" the first fired at her. "Where are you from? Where are you going? Do you have any education? Do you have any skills? Who paid for your ticket?" On and on went the questions, thirty-two in all. Kaatje held her breath at the end as the official looked over the paper then stamped it.

She was in. At least she was almost in. With trembling fingers she handed the doctor at the end of the line her paperwork as Soren looked on. She had heard horror stories of people being turned back for medical reasons, forced to return to their homeland on the next outgoing ship. "What's your name?" the doctor asked, matching her response to the slip. "Are you suffering from any special diseases?" he asked.

"Only pregnancy," she said, smiling.

He did not return her smile. "How far along?"

"Four months," she said, growing serious. Did they not allow pregnant women to enter? she wondered, feeling the beginnings of hysteria.

"Any difficulties?"

"Only at sea, when I was ill."

He looked up sharply. "Ill?"

Soren stepped to her side and placed his arm around her. "She was seasick."

"Step aside, sir. The lady will answer for herself, please."

"He is right. It was only the seasickness. I was soon well and up on deck."

The doctor nodded once and wrote something on her sheet. He stepped forward and checked one of her eyes, then the other, then scrawled something more.

"You may pass," he said.

Kaatje and Soren emerged from the hall holding hands, feeling like pardoned prisoners.

Tora trailed behind Kristoffer, Elsa, and Peder, daydreaming about her future *without* the two children in her arms. Lars was soaked and desperately needed a new diaper; Knut refused to walk or let his father carry him. "I want Tora!" he insisted. Finally Peder coerced him to ride on his shoulders, and she was free of at least one burden. Why would anyone willingly choose motherhood? she wondered, bouncing Lars in an effort to quiet the child.

"I'll go for a diaper," Elsa said finally. "I'll catch up with you."

"Fine," Tora said. Elsa looked a bit irked that she did not lavish praise and thanks, but Tora ignored her. She was in the land of opportunity. And just as soon as she could make her escape, she would be on her way. Surely Peder and Elsa would not make her serve Kristoffer for the prescribed six months. He would just have to find another nanny for his children. Maybe Elsa herself could care for them.

Tora gave the next uniformed official a long, steady gaze, flustering him a bit.

"What's your name?" he asked, staring at his sheet of paper as if he could not look up again.

"Tora. Tora Anders," she said softly, giving her voice a musical lilt.

He looked up, his eyes warming to her tone. Oh, this was going to be easy, she thought. *America is mine.* But she had eyes on someone bigger and better than a callow immigration official. She wanted someone with true power, someone who could make her powerful as well. Then Elsa would see what—

"Miss?" he was asking.

"I am sorry. I was daydreaming about this lovely new country of mine and thinking that I am all alone in it."

The young official looked confused as he glanced from Tora to the children. Obviously he thought them a family. "Oh, I am just caring for the children," she said.

He brightened, obviously hoping that her flirtation might mean she was interested in him. But as soon as he leaned forward, looking her in the eye, Tora's interest waned. The thrill of conquest was gone.

"Come on, Tora," Peder said gruffly, pulling her along toward the next station.

"Ouch. You're hurting me."

"You need to stop that."

"Stop what?" she asked innocently.

"Batting your big blue eyes at every man who steps in your path.

It will work against you someday, Tora. And I won't be around to step in," he added, obviously referring to that night on the *Herald* with Soren.

"I do not need you to step in," she said indignantly, wrenching away her arm. "I am a grown woman."

"With a little girl's idea of a just world."

"Well, I don't know what you mean by that, Peder Ramstad, but I'll thank you to keep your opinions to yourself."

"I will be happy to do so just as soon as you are someone else's responsibility."

"Like mine?" Kristoffer asked, stepping up behind them and taking the restless Lars from her arms.

Tora let out a sound of disgust. "I'm my own responsibility. No one owns me."

"But you owe me five and a half more months."

"Surely you do not intend to hold me to that bargain," Tora said, looking at Kristoffer with what she hoped looked like righteous indignation.

"I surely do. You are indebted to me for the passage I've paid to your brother-in-law. Since you are penniless, you will repay me, Tora." His eyes were gentle, but determined.

Little did he know that she was not penniless. Sewn in the hems of her skirts was money "borrowed" from her father against her future dowry. That dowry was rightfully hers. But she would not use it to buy passage. She needed it to establish herself somewhere and lure the right man—a wealthy man—to her side. If it took five more months to work off the passage, she could wait. She would use the time to study her alternatives. *I must move wisely,* she thought. Yes, let them think what they wanted of her. They'd soon see she was no mere girl.

Peder left Elsa and Tora at the final station in line, confident after a word with James, an official he knew, that there would be no problem. Besides, Kristoffer remained with them, partly to see Knut through—everyone over two years of age was documented—and partly to help with Lars. He also knew Kris saw in Tora's eyes what Peder himself saw: the urge to bolt. If they didn't keep a close eye on her, she was liable to run for the next train to New York.

He left the brick hall and breathed deeply, smelling the hot summer city smells of dust, flowers, and horse dung. The ground felt curiously solid under his feet, as it always did after a voyage, and he walked as if each leg held a ten-pound weight. What was it about the sea that made a man feel lighter? Peder turned the corner, and after narrowly avoiding a coach, spotted Karl. He walked behind him for a while, thinking about catching up to him, when his friend turned and entered a saloon. Peder frowned. In all the years he had traveled with Karl, he had seldom seen him enter such an establishment.

He followed him and ambled up to the bar, taking the stool beside Karl. "It must be bad, to bring you in here."

Karl looked over at him in surprise. "The heat," he said, by way of answering. "Are you so bored that you must follow me?"

Peder shook his head as the bartender looked at him after taking Karl's order. The man was back in an instant with a tall glass mug of frothy beer, and for a moment Peder lamented his decision. But it was poor practice to set such an example for his men, if any came by.

"Listen, Karl," he said, "I have to leave. You know why. But is there something . . . Look, is something the matter? Are you having second thoughts about the business?"

Karl shook his head, staring at the beer. "No, I am fine. It's the heat. I'll just have one and be out. Now get on with your business, man."

"All right. See you tonight?"

Karl nodded. "At the Oasis, right?"

"I hope so. I'm going there now to try and secure the rooms. If it doesn't work out, I'll leave word at the *Herald* where we can be found."

"Good enough."

Peder left the dark establishment, ignoring the lingering glances of the working girls and hoping Karl would do the same. No good could come from such a place, and he hoped Karl was serious when he said he'd be out after his one beer. *Listen to me,* he said to himself, *I sound like a clucking mother hen.* Such was the life of a sea captain, he decided. Always looking out for the lives of his crew.

Karl watched as Peder walked past the dusty saloon window. What did he know of troubles? The world was at his feet with Ramstad Yard coming together and Elsa at his side. Sure things between them were temporarily bridged, but how long could it last? God had granted him a reprieve, it seemed, after a night of fervent prayer. But he felt distant and sad, removed from all about him, trying to find the grace to praise the Lord for the respite. Perhaps after a while his life would feel good again, right again, he thought. Perhaps this path could work. Just to be sure, he would steer clear of Elsa. *That was it,* he coached himself. *Steer clear of Elsa and get your steamer built. After that, captain her while others are built in Camden. Reevaluate your life then.*

He sighed in relief at the thought. That's what he needed. A new ship beneath his feet, a tropical island in the distance, and an all-male crew. Danger avoided. Righteousness upheld.

Suddenly he felt as free as when he successfully negotiated a threatening reef and the men on board cheered his expertise. Yes, even as Peder's right-hand man and without the girl of his dreams, Karl Martensen would make something of himself.

t w e l v e

*E*lsa stood amid the throngs of people and the multitude of languages in the Boston train station, struggling to hold back her tears. Only two days ago they had disembarked from the *Herald*, laughing as many of the immigrants kissed the ground; now, suddenly, they were parting ways—some to the West and some to the North. She had been so caught up with the voyage itself, then the joy of their arrival and acceptance in America, that she had avoided the thought of parting with Kaatje and the others—especially Kaatje.

She knew she was being ridiculous as she clung to her dear friend, but she could not help herself. It was if she were leaving Bergen again.

"Please write," she begged of Kaatje, pulling away.

"You know I will," Kaatje said, reaching out to give her one more embrace.

Elsa turned to Soren and gave him a fierce look. She lowered her voice. "Promise me you will take care of her," she demanded.

Soren laughed, embarrassed at such a command. "Of course. She's my wife."

Elsa leaned nearer to him, looking him dead in the eye. "No, Soren. I mean it. Promise me you will take care of her."

"Of course," he repeated, clearly irritated by now. He took Kaatje's arm and picked up her bag. "Come, Kaatje. They're boarding."

"All aboard!" yelled the conductor as the train's bell clanged. "All aboard!"

Kaatje stood on tiptoe and hugged Elsa once again, their tears mingling on Elsa's cheeks. Then they parted, and in so doing, Elsa felt as if she were being ripped in half. She said good-bye to the others, wishing them all well and whispering advice until they were all on the Baltimore and Ohio train, waving their hats and handkerchiefs.

"Last call for the Baltimore and Ohio! Washington! Pittsburgh! Chicago!" yelled the conductor. "Last call for the B&O!"

"Good-bye!" Elsa called, wondering at the sorrow in her heart. It was always easier to leave than to be left, she reminded herself, and wondered if this was how her parents had felt as the *Herald* sailed out of sight.

Kaatje leaned out the window as the conductor blew the horn and the *ch-chuh* sound of the wheels gathered speed. She watched as Elsa and the others grew smaller in the distance and the train track gently swooped away. Would she ever see her beloved friend again? She hoped so. Kaatje felt sorrow at leaving a loved one behind, but it was good to be en route to their final destination. Soren took her hand as they settled back in their dilapidated, maroon, upholstered seats. One look at him and she knew he was already in North Dakota, sowing the seed, harvesting the crop.

Coal smoke drifted in the window, but with it came a gentle, blessed breeze that cut the awful humid air. Sweat trickled down under Kaatje's corset, and she squirmed to get a better position to catch the breeze. She should have worn her cotton work dress, she thought, not this awful wool gown. But pride had urged her to don her best, stifling though it was. Her fellow Bergensers had done the same, and for a lot of poor farmers, they looked fairly nice, making their economy class coach car look nearly like first class.

Behind Kaatje and Soren sat Birger and Eira Nelson. Eira had a way with herbs and the healing arts; perhaps she would help Kaatje deliver her child when the time came. Behind them were the two bachelors: Nels, who exulted at the thought of all that land for his future sheep, and Mathias, the future cattle rancher who had been rechristened Matthew at the immigration hall. She smiled as she listened to him retell the story.

"So in front of me was a German Jew who was so flustered and confused when they asked his name, that he replied, *'Ich vergessen—'*"

"Which means 'I have forgotten,'" Nora chimed in, as well versed in German as she was in English.

"To which the inspector said, 'Welcome to America, Ike Fergusson. Next!'"

The whole train car laughed as one, enjoying the story again.

"And when I got up there, I did not argue either when I told him my name was Mathias, and he renamed me Matthew! I like having an American name," he said proudly, fist to chest. "It makes me more at home already!"

Across the aisle from the rechristened Matthew sat Pastor Lien, his wife, Amalia, and their five-year-old daughter, Klara. Kaatje marveled at how good the little girl had been aboard the ship. She had played quietly and listened intently to her teacher, learning English much more quickly than many of the adults. In front of her sat her teacher, Nora, and Einar, the newlyweds, holding hands and talking softly, their heads close together. Kaatje was happy for their union. Nora had waited so long for Einar to propose. She shot a smile over at Nora. No, traveling with nine fellow Bergensers was better than none. Together, they could still be a community for one another until they found community with others.

Nora reached across the aisle and handed Kaatje her fan.

"No, I couldn't," Kaatje protested. She knew Einar had purchased it from a vendor in Boston as a wedding gift for Nora, an uncommon extravagance for such a simple man.

"You take it," urged Nora. "It is the blessing of all expectant mothers that others treat them with a little extra kindness."

"Thank you," Kaatje said, reluctantly taking the luxurious fan. Its handles were made of ivory and the linen covering nearly matched it in color. On it was a delicately painted picture of a Japanese woman in her native kimono, sitting beside a tiny, strange-looking tree with a curved trunk. In her hands was a fan like the one Kaatje held.

"An exotic fan for a Bergen farm girl, is it not?" she asked Soren.

"A befitting fan for my wife," he said, tenderly touching her cheek. "I should have purchased one, too, that day with Einar."

She looked down, embarrassed by his praise. Was that not evidence in itself that he had recommitted himself to their marriage? He loved her. First, best, and always. The gentle rocking of the train and Soren's hand in hers reassured Kaatje that all was right in her world, especially now that they had left Soren's dark-haired temptress behind. Surely in a land where they gave away one hundred and sixty acres to every person who sought it, there would be few women and far between. On their land, they would form their own little country, a hundred and sixty acres of safety. Yes. In the Dakotas, she and Soren would find their way.

Tora sighed in relief as the train slid out of sight. Soren was at last out of her hair, one more step accomplished in her path to a bright future. She grimaced as Lars screamed at the top of his lungs and Kristoffer glanced eagerly around for her, but then steeling herself, she went to the man. In spite of herself, there was something in the baby's cry that tugged at her heartstrings, urging her to move. And after all, she mused, she needed to convince them all that she'd embraced her lot if she was ever to escape it.

As she walked across the stifling platform, Tora placed a hand on her stomach. Ever since that awful, heavy breakfast at the inn, she had felt queasy. The sensation brought tears to her eyes.

Kristoffer glanced at her, misreading her misty eyes. "You are sorry to see them go?"

She stifled a smile, ready to take advantage of his concern. "Yes. It makes me feel just that much farther from home," she said prettily.

"You will like Camden-by-the-Sea," he said, taking her arm as Lars nestled underneath her chin, despite the heat, and soon quieted. "I have sailed there many times with Peder. There are shops and a bookstore that will keep you busy when you need a distraction from the boys."

"I hope so," she said. Together they left the station, and Kris hailed a cab, a black coach with one horse. Someday, she would have her own George IV phaeton like those she saw on the streets of Boston. The elegant coaches were slipper-shaped and open so that a lady's fine dress might be seen. Yes, that, and a matched span of golden horses to lead it. She would go fast, everywhere, for time was of the essence. They all wasted so much time! Five more months would seem like an eternity.

Tora glanced over her shoulder as she heard the whistle of another train leaving the station. What she wouldn't give to be on it, going to someplace exciting, where things *happened*. Instead she was destined to board that cursed ship again and be carted off to some sleepy town to the north. Such was her life. But her time would soon come.

Peder breathed a sigh of relief as he and Elsa hailed a hackney, a coach for public hire. He felt as if half his responsibility had departed on that train after five long years of planning. He wished them the best. He and Karl had told the men all they knew about the rough country to which they were headed, hoping to impart a sense of realism. But he knew that they remained hopeful that their land would be all the railroads promised, an Eden in a world of deserts. "Father, be with them," he prayed quietly as he settled into the coach beside Elsa.

She bowed her head beside him, joining in. "Yes, Father. We ask that thou wilt watch over them. Help them to make good decisions and avoid harm. Help them find fertile land in which to settle and build. And go before them always."

"Amen," Peder said, placing his arm around her. "And now on to *our* new land. Are you excited?"

"Terribly. But I am glad so many of our people go with us. If they all had departed on that train, I am afraid I would be horribly sad."

"This from the woman who says she'd like to set sail with me!" Peder said, making a point. "I can just see us in Hong Kong and you begging me to leave because you are homesick. No, it's obvious to me that a woman needs a village, a community to which she belongs."

Elsa was silent, looking down at her hands as a muscle in her jaw worked. When she spoke, her words were measured. "A woman's place is beside her husband. Yes, I might be lonely without friends and neighbors aboard, but I would be much more lonely without you."

Peder glanced at her. How were they to resolve this? He had hoped that her comment meant that she had at last come to agreement with him. "I was pleased to see Tora go to Kris this afternoon," he said, tactfully avoiding the subject that got them both so upset. "She seems to be coming around. Perhaps with time, she and Kris will become . . . attached."

"I think that is far-fetched," Elsa said gently.

"You never know."

"No, I suppose not. But I'm certain Tora has something else in mind. This time in Camden is like a prison sentence to her, and she'll look for any opportunity to dig a tunnel to what she considers freedom."

"And if she escapes?"

"So be it. I cannot be her keeper. And I would only lament placing such a burden on Kris."

"You will take in his children if she abandons them while we are at sea," Peder stated.

"I will take them in if we are at home," she corrected, with no note of aggression in her voice. "And I will speak to Ebba Erikson or Ola Thompson about it when we sail."

Peder thought about setting her straight, then elected not to press the issue. There was time enough to convince her. Once they were in Camden and she had the task of settling her new home, Elsa would be so busy she probably wouldn't notice when he sailed without her. What they needed were a few children of their own, he thought, warming to the idea.

Yes, with a few children, Elsa would be happy to stay at home.

bitter truths

September 1880–April 1881

t h i r t e e n

Elsa absently wandered around their Camden cottage, missing her husband for the fifth time that day. He had been at sea for six weeks, leaving after a terrible argument in which he forbade her to come and commanded her to stay.

"Please, Peder. Don't you see? It is because I love you that I want to be with you."

"No, Elsa. I've made my decision. You must abide by it."

"Just like that? What if I do not think you have given it the consideration it warrants?"

He had stood there, glowering. *"Do not second-guess me."*

"Do not dictate to me."

"It is finished. Done. I have decided."

With all these thoughts crowding in on her, she needed air. She stepped outside onto the verandah. The beauty of the autumn day caught her eye and momentarily eased her anguished thoughts. The leaves were turning, the sky was a bright blue, and Elsa felt the urge to paint the scene. Seizing any idea that might afford some distraction, she hurried to her supplies and brought out a fresh canvas, a pencil, and her newest adventure in media, oil paints. She would illustrate their home on a small canvas so that she might mount and frame it for Peder's cabin on the *Herald*.

Our cabin, she corrected herself. As beautiful as her new home was, she was determined to be on the next outbound ship with Peder.

Elsa left her supplies in the dry, tall grasses in front of her home and went back for easel and chair. Five minutes later she was settled and sketching the house. This view of it still took her breath away. Somehow inside she forgot its simple, forthright beauty. From here it all came back. The Atlantic breathed a fresh gust up the hill from the water, and Elsa smiled. This was a good idea. How many letters could she write Kaatje, anyway?

She concentrated on the elements before her, warming to her task. She had been overwhelmed at her first sight of Ramstad Yard and even more by the quaint cottage beside it. She had been overcome as Peder led her through their home. Only the first floor and the outside were complete. "The rest will have to wait for the success of Ramstad Yard," he said, smiling and exultant as she shared in his joy over their home. As much as Peder infuriated her, at the moment Elsa longed to see that smile again.

She studied the contrast between the narrow first-floor clapboards and the intricate second-floor shingle patterns. The gables were steep, and the encircling verandah had spindle-like ornaments often found on homes built by architects influenced by the Queen Anne master, Richard Shaw. But her favorite part of the house was the turret on the north side, a towering lookout in which she could watch for Peder as she had from the hills bordering Bergen. Many windows let in as much light as possible, and a giant, medieval-type chimney boasted of the warm fires that would kindle come winter.

As the sun sank lower in the sky, Elsa completed the rough sketch and began to paint, using her tiniest brushes for detail. A house had none of the action that ships did, but she was inspired. For she knew that it was with love and sacrifice that Peder had built this home for her. If only he were with her right now, she mused.

A thought came to her. Peder loved this growing talent of hers, nurtured it, in fact. Perhaps she could argue that she needed to travel with him for research. How else could she insert the sense of realism, combined with the romanticism, that made artists successful? If that did not convince him, she would argue until she was blue in the face. Why be married if only to be continually separated?

She glanced over her shoulder. Down below in Ramstad Yard, they were completing the caulker's shed where men would soon twist and prepare rope, and the long house, a single-story mold loft where others would craft models or set out the ribs for the new schooner. All of the men from Bergen were gone, however, off to sea on the *Herald* to make some more cash before winter settled in. Kristoffer was the only one who remained behind, left to oversee construction at Ramstad Yard and the care of his home and children. The workers at the yard had made good progress in the last six weeks, and things were taking shape. Elsa returned her gaze to the house, wanting to capture the colors of the autumn leaves before putting away her paints for the day. It had been a wet year, she was told, so the colors were more muted; in dry years they would be brilliant gold, gaudy orange, and vermilion. But Elsa preferred the more subtle hues of ocher, russet, umber, and mustard—they held a depth that captivated her and her brush as she mixed the oils to get just the right shade. She was excited to try her hand at painting. Ramstad House looked warm and welcoming, and she wanted to remember this day forever on canvas.

❧

Peder looked out at the turquoise sea and longed for his wife. Had he been wrong to leave her in Camden? These last weeks had been agony as he rehashed their argument and agonized over his wisdom in leaving her. He could not find any peace about it.

Peder wanted Elsa with him. Their short runs to the West Indies for sugar and pineapples were nearing an end. Once the schooner was built, he would go to Australia for wool and to China for silk, competing with the medium clippers that now dominated the sea lanes to those countries—and beating them with his faster ship. On those voyages in which he would be gone for months, he wanted Elsa along.

But how could he do so? Had he not promised God to love, honor, and protect her? And had he not promised Amund that he would keep her safe?

He had not anticipated missing her as he had. Peder shook his head and returned to his charts, measuring the distance to Camden. At this rate, they would be home soon. He smiled. It would be good to see Elsa. They would resolve their differences somehow. He would hold her in his arms and take her to their bed. He swung his fist in the air as a surge of energy exploded through him. They would make better time than ever, if he was worthy to be called captain of this ship.

Laughing at himself, he left the cabin and strode to the helm. Karl looked at him, surprised by his quick gait. Peder studied the wind and the sails for a moment then looked back to Karl. "Set all sails," he commanded, his voice jubilant. "We're going to get home to Camden as fast as we can!"

"But Captain," Karl protested, low enough so none of the men would hear, "we're almost between wind and water now. Setting the other sails might have us turn turtle."

Peder sobered and reevaluated his command. Karl was right to question him; they were speeding along at quite a nice clip. But no, there was still room for a bit more speed. "My command holds," he said, and turned back to his cabin.

"All sails set!" shouted Karl without hesitation.

"All sails set!" rejoined the crew, acknowledging the command.

"Cap'n?" Karl called.

Peder turned.

"I assume you're thinking of home."

"Aye."

"Once we arrive, I'd like to take care of the *Herald*'s chandlery needs. I could accompany some of our cargo to New York via railroad and get those supplies for the shipyard we discussed. I want to do some research on our steamship anyway."

Peder smiled broadly. Not only was he getting home sooner, but his first mate would see to the errands that would have taken him away from Elsa again right after returning. "I'd appreciate that, Karl."

"Consider it done," Karl said. He glanced up to check the set of the sails. The sailors working high in the rigging and those down below at the capstan were hauling up the remaining canvas.

Peder watched for a moment, thinking about his friend's offer. It seemed incredible that anyone would want to leave home as soon as he returned, but then Karl did not have Elsa. Did Karl offer this kindness as a friend? Perhaps he had noticed Peder's distraction, his penchant for standing on the bow, looking northwest toward Maine. Whatever his reasoning, Peder was glad. To him, it felt like an answer to prayer.

Tora lay on her narrow bed while Knut played on the floor beside her with six blocks that Kristoffer had carved for him. Lars, thankfully, was sleeping, and Knut seemed to sense that once again Tora wanted peace and quiet. She closed her eyes wearily. Taking care of the boys without Kristoffer was not easy. Keeping up with the house—even one as small as their three-bedroom, Federal-style cottage—was tiring. How did one live without a maid? But worse was this plague that had come over her body, this siren's call to sleep for an hour twice a day. It was the worst part of her pregnancy.

She figured she was more than two months along. *God's wrath* was how she referred to it in her private musings. Well, she'd show him. Even God would not rule her life. Elsa, up on her hill in Ramstad House, had said she longed for a child. Soon enough Tora would birth the baby and be done with it, leaving it on its aunt's doorstep for her to raise. She had the means. She had the interest.

And Tora had bigger and better places to go. A child was not part of the picture, and certainly Kristoffer's children were not a part of it.

Tora rolled her head to the side and watched as Knut built a tower out of his blocks then tore it down, over and over. She had grown reasonably fond of the boys these last weeks, but was merely serving her time. She felt none of the feelings that mothers did for their own—or what she had witnessed in self-sacrifice and generosity from her own mother. To Tora this was a job, a job thankfully over in another four months. Three months following that, the baby would be born. Would she be able to leave her own child as easily as Kristoffer's children? What would become of them?

She dismissed the niggling questions as she ran a hand over her abdomen. Not only did pregnancy make one exhausted, it made one fat. Was there anything less fair in the world than to saddle women, the weaker sex, with childbirth? It was all that nasty Soren Janssen's fault. He, after all, did not have to bear the burden she did for their torrid affair. What was his price? Nothing, she thought with a mirthless laugh. He had probably already found someone else in North Dakota to take her place, God help the poor soul.

Tora giggled suddenly. The only good part about her situation was that she would have the chance to shake up Elsa's orderly life. She sat up. "Get your coat, Knut. Auntie Elsa invited us for dinner. And I have news I need to share with her."

The boy scrambled to his feet and ran for his coat while Tora fussed with her hair and put on her hat. She studied her reflection in the mirror. She looked ghastly, and it brought her high mood crashing down. Her flesh was peaked and her eyes sunken.

What was happening to her? She was Tora Anders! This would not be her end. She would not drown in this dreary little town, nor care for these boys until she was old and ugly. She would leave! Soon . . . or all her dreams would be sucked into the mire of Camden-by-the-Sea. She was born for something higher than a three-room cottage on the shores of a forsaken land. She wanted money and all that it could buy.

She wanted expensive clothing and beautiful things around her. She wanted to be a powerful man's bride. And that man was not Kristoffer.

"I am ready," Knut said, taking her hand and pulling.

"Very well," Tora said, giving herself one last determined glance. "Let me get Lars and we will be off." She bundled up the baby in a soft wool blanket that Kris had purchased in Australia on one of his voyages, then followed the bouncing Knut out the door. The three-year-old was happy to escape the house, and Tora had to agree with him. He ran ahead, knowing the way to Ramstad House, just a five-minute walk away. There was practically a path worn through the tall, dying field grass, for Knut had grown quite fond of his Auntie Elsa.

It was all very fitting, Tora thought, for them to grow close. Perhaps Elsa would take Knut and Lars in with Tora's own child when it came. Or maybe Kris would find someone else to slave away and shoulder his burdens while he supervised the yard or was away at sea. She tripped over a rock and almost fell, then frowned at her surroundings. This was a miserable, lonely place to live. And so dull. She wanted society, a dinner out, a ride in one of those high society carriages rather that a cross-country stroll to her sister's. She could have stayed in Bergen and fared better than this.

Up ahead Knut reached the house and ran into Elsa's outstretched arms. She hugged him and laughed as he said something, then rose and waited for Tora to reach them. Elsa was dressed for dinner in an elegant gown their mother had given her, and she looked quite lovely standing on the porch. Her smile faded as she saw Tora's own stern expression.

"Good evening, Tora," she said. "My goodness, you look tired. Are you all right?"

"I am fine," Tora said, climbing the steps and flashing a false smile at her sister as she passed. "Simply pregnant," she tossed over her shoulder, then winced as she heard Elsa suck in her breath. Why could she not curb her tongue? The last thing she needed was to have Elsa think she was proud of herself. Tora quickly composed her face and turned to seek sympathy.

"What—" Elsa began.

"It is awful, is it not?" Tora cried. "I don't know what I will do." A few tears crested her lower lids and slid down her cheeks. Tora didn't wipe them away.

Elsa's face was ashen. "Knut," she said, "I have some new blocks for you to play with in the kitchen." Tora followed behind them, sniffling. Knut looked up at her, concerned.

"Knut, Auntie Tora will be fine. We just need to speak for a moment. Could you please play by yourself like a big boy and watch your brother?" Elsa took Lars from Tora's arms and settled him in the wooden cradle she kept near the hearth for their visits.

"Yes ma'am," he said soberly. Elsa let the door swing shut and pulled Tora to a dining room chair.

"Tell me. Who was it? What happened? Oh, Tora, how on earth could you have let—"

"I did not *let* anyone," Tora said, raising her chin a bit. "I didn't. You must believe me! Oh, Elsa, you must help me figure out what I will do! You must!" Elsa held out her arms, and Tora leaned into her embrace.

"I am here," Elsa said soothingly, sounding as maternal as Tora desired her to be. "I do not wish to hear the sordid details. Let us focus on what you might do to recover."

"Recover?" Tora asked, hearing the hysteria in her own voice. She pulled away and wiped the tears from her cheeks. "This is not something from which one recovers." She got up from the chair and began to pace the length of the room, glancing at Elsa occasionally. "The only thing I can think of is to have this baby then give him to you and Peder to adopt."

Elsa shook her head. "Wait. You're moving much too quickly for me. I just found out that you are . . . expecting."

"But think of Mama! Such news would kill her!"

"Let us think of you first. We will deal with our parents later. Now sit. Tell me when you expect the child."

"April, I suppose."

"There are homes for young women—"

"You would send me away?" Tora cried.

"No, no," Elsa said, gesturing with her hands for Tora to settle down. "Of course not. I'm simply thinking of all our options."

Tora stifled the smile that threatened to curve her lips. Already her older sister was thinking of this as her own problem. Surely Elsa would help her figure a way out!

A rush of sisterly concern had flowed through Elsa at Tora's revelation. It was only later, as she mulled it over, that Elsa became angry. How, after all, was she sure that Tora had been drawn unwittingly into such a predicament? She had seen for herself how Tora used her feminine wiles to get what she wished. Elsa felt the heat of her embarrassing thoughts rise up her neck. Could Tora be wanton, not a victim?

The thought overwhelmed and saddened her. She felt such a responsibility for her sister! Should she not for the unborn child as well? Oh, to have her mother near! Surely Mama would know what to do! Did she not have enough to worry over without this too? There at her writing desk she bent her head in prayer, unable to do anything else. *Lord, Lord!* she cried out silently. *I feel so lost. So confused. What am I to do with her? With the child?*

It is not a trial for you to bear.

The clear answer to her prayer took Elsa aback. "But she is my sister!" she prayed aloud.

She is my child.

"But . . . but we are so far from home . . ."

You are in the world I gave you.

"I am so worried, Father . . ."

Be still.

"I cannot. I cannot turn my back on her."

Be still.

In his answer, Elsa knew what God wanted from her. He wanted her to trust him, to trust him with Tora. In his own time, in his own way, he would deal with Tora Anders and her child. Until then Elsa would trust him and know that he would guide her in her role with Tora. Wearily she said, "Into your hands, Father, I give my sister and her child." She opened her eyes and wiped them with a handkerchief, stared out the window for several minutes, then turned to the letter she had received from Kaatje that day.

> *It is difficult to believe that the baby is only a few months away. At least the exhaustion that accompanied my first months of pregnancy is gone. So too have my uglier memories of Soren in Bergen and on the Herald faded. Although our farm seems dismal now, I am glad for the dissimilarities. It affords me assurance as I thank God for my new life. Our new life, I correct myself. Oh, Elsa, I am happy, happier than I can ever remember being.*
>
> *Soren works from dawn to dusk at clearing and preparing the land. We have a burly, even-tempered Cleveland Bay who helps him. The horse ignores me when I haul coffee out for Soren. My husband does not. This land is rougher than we were promised, but we were warned. And the soil is rich and fertile. If we can only get some decent rainfall, we shall do well.*
>
> *Some immigrants have already come and gone, giving up on dry-land farming and its challenges. But we love it. We have broad vistas where you can see for miles. It reminds me of the sea. I feel as if I am on the verge of watching a miracle. It is our new beginning, Elsa. Nothing can destroy it. And surely nothing will impede our progress.*

Elsa paused and looked out to sea, hearing her friend's gay laughter in her words. At last God had smiled upon Kaatje and Soren!

f o u r t e e n

⁓

*E*lsa climbed the stairs of the turret, noting as she exited to the open, unfinished second floor that the air had turned decidedly crisp. She glanced at the brown oaks and red maples that bordered the yard; many of their leaves were gone, and what remained were a pale reminder of autumn. Peder had missed it all, she thought sadly. Her painting, while it had turned out well, held none of the awe-inspiring *motion* that the trees had once carried. That was the only way she could think of describing their colors in the crisp autumn breeze. She had worked and worked on the colors, getting the shading almost dead-on, but they still seemed flat to her.

That was why she preferred ships. It was easier to show life in a moving ship than in a dying leaf. She could not wait to be at sea again. Surely Peder had missed her as much as she had him. This would work to help her in her arguments when he came home. The *Herald* was due any day now, but it was likely that it would be later in the week. Still, Elsa could not keep herself from the turret, as if a sixth sense was telling her that he was near. It was as it had been in

Bergen. She had waited for days on the hills, looking for the *Herald,* knowing, even though he hadn't written, that Peder was coming soon.

She scanned the horizon. It was about ten in the morning, and after her morning routine of reading a chapter of the Bible and praying, then writing a bit to Kaatje, Elsa found little to do. Ever since Tora had shared her devastating news, Elsa had sought release in furious housecleaning or an absorbing painting. Now the house was in immaculate order, and she had completed three paintings: one of the house; two of ships in the harbor below.

It was no longer enough to distract her from worrying over Tora and the forthcoming child, or the aching distance she felt from her husband, compounded by the sour note on which they had parted. She looked north to the dark, foreboding clouds that had gathered close to the shore and were moving steadily toward Ramstad Yard. Had Peder encountered another storm? The thought left her sick with worry.

Elsa turned her face from the clouds, choosing to focus on the hope that would come from the south, and there, on the horizon, was a wisp of a ship. The *Herald?* Her heart leaped. There was no telling for sure, but something within her knew. He was coming. He would be home soon. She let out a little shriek of glee and rushed back downstairs for Peder's telescope. Returning to the top floor of the turret, she focused the glass with shaking hands, and her feeling was confirmed. It was Peder!

"Thank you, Father!" she cried, clasping her hands and looking heavenward. Then she rushed downstairs again. Suddenly, a multitude of things clamored for her attention, things she wanted to accomplish before Peder came home, most notably preparations for a fine dinner. She needed to find the roving fishmonger and his cart, stop by the butcher's, then afterward, the baker's. She hoped he had some fine flatbread left! She would make Peder's favorite, corned trout, if the vendor had any fresh fish. If not, she'd make his second favorite, pork roast with brown onion sauce.

She would not go to the wharf to meet him; however, it might be unseemly for the captain's wife to behave so. And Peder seemed overly aware of such social niceties, to the point of coming across as priggish at times. Take, for instance, his refusal to allow her to wear dungarees aboard the ship, despite their practicality.

Besides, it would do Peder good to make him come looking for her. She was still a bit angry at the way he had left her after their argument, commanding her like a king in his castle. But she would make their home seem like paradise, coercing him never to leave again—or at least to take her with him when he did. She would put Cook to shame!

Elsa grabbed her purse and left the house for the stables behind it. There was no time to summon the neighbor, who had agreed to help her with tasks such as this. She could harness the horse herself and be on her way in the time it would take to fetch him. The horses stomped and nodded their heads as if in greeting when she opened the door, making her laugh then coo her hello. She chose her favorite, Muskatnøtt, named for his nutmeg color, and whistled to him. She readied the buggy and was out on the road in no time at all.

Peder was concerned when Elsa did not turn up at the wharf as they docked. Surely word had reached her by now. Was she still so angry at him? He was mollified by the fact that it seemed childish and unseemly to run into one another's arms in front of others, but it did not take away the sting. Surely her absence was meant as a barb.

He sighed, happy to hand over the responsibility of the cargo to Karl. He had only one thing more to do before he headed home to Elsa; he needed to speak to the harbor master about docking the *Herald* for a few days. Peder intended to make one quick run to Bangor for lumber and get it to New York before the winter weather settled in. He shook the rain from his coat and looked to the gray sky as it continued its soaking mist. All right, before the *real* winter weather settled in, he amended. He and Karl wanted a bit more cash in the bank before they turned full-time to shipbuilding. It would allow them to buy more shares in their own ships and thus a greater share in the cargo profits.

"After a while," he called to Karl, taking his leave.

"After a while," Karl said, crossing the bridge to shake his hand.

"Godspeed, friend. I hope all goes well in New York this week. Get the top price you can for the sugar."

"As always."

"And do not gather so much information on steam that you come home and pester me to build your ship first."

Karl smiled with him. "Off with you, man. I will send you a cable when I reach the city in two days."

"Good enough." He waved over his shoulder, eager to get home to Elsa and know where they stood. He hoped there wasn't too deep a chasm between them. He ached to hold her close and kiss her as never before.

Kristoffer nodded and smiled at Peder in greeting as he walked down the plank. They gripped hands fiercely. "Got the mold loft done, Cap'n."

"Very good," Peder cried, clapping him on the shoulder. "And the caulker's shed?"

"All set. We even have the ship ramp complete. Need a ride home?"

"No, thank you, Kris, I think I'll get my land legs and walk."

"Very well. See you tomorrow then."

Peder bid him farewell and walked through the wharf, into the small town, and down its curvy, cobblestoned main street. By the time he stopped to speak with the harbor master and arranged to dock the *Herald* for a few days, the rain had quit. He reached the end of Main Street within five minutes and smiled as Ramstad Yard came into view. The mold loft had shiny new shingles on its roof. The young pine siding looked yellow and fresh, and when he raised his nose to the air, the ocean breeze carried to him the smell of new construction.

Down lower, closer to the water, was the caulker's shed, or rope house. And even farther down the slope was the completed ramp on which the Ramstad ships would be crafted, a long, sloping slide that angled at the prescribed five-eighths of an inch per foot. This angle did not lend too much pressure to a growing ship, but allowed it to slide into the water once it was fully crafted and released.

Peder grinned. Yes, Ramstad Yard, America. All his dreams were coming to pass.

He turned and looked toward the house. From the chimney came a small, wavy tendril of smoke, making his home look all the more inviting. In the window burned the soft light of a kerosene lamp. So she had seen him arrive. Surely this was a form of greeting. With renewed vigor, he walked toward his home and wife, and, hopefully, dinner. His stomach rumbled in response, and his body tingled at the thought of holding Elsa at long last.

At that moment she opened the door, a vision in her violet gown, and it sent him running. It was as if the world and its cares faded at the sight of her and her smile. All that mattered was holding her in his arms. He raced up the front steps two at a time and rushed to her. Before she could speak, he bent his head and kissed her, crushing her body to his.

When he could finally bear to release her, he hastened to speak first. "Forgive me, Elsa. I'm sorry I left with harsh words between us. After our argument, we should have come to some resolution. It was terrible to be gone from you all these weeks, fearing that you were still angry."

"Oh, Peder. Of course I was angry. But I was sorry, too, that we parted in such a manner. It was horrible, these weeks apart . . . not knowing if . . . let's never do that again."

"Agreed." He pulled her into his arms for another fierce embrace then gazed into her eyes. "I never knew I could feel this way, Elsa. I never knew it would be so good to see someone."

"It's glorious, isn't it?" she asked, smiling up at him.

"It is." He sniffed the air. "Is that what I think it is?"

"Yes. The fishmonger had no trout, so I had to settle on pork in brown onion sauce."

"Oh, the sacrifices I have to make! Come, wife, let's go into our home, eat our dinner soon, and retire early."

"You are tired?" Elsa asked in consternation.

"Not at all," he said with a grin.

When no one came to the door at her knock, Tora entered the house and smiled at the sound of the Ramstads arguing. *Well, well.* And the *Herald* had only just docked the day before. "Hello?" she called half-heartedly, really wanting to find out the cause of the commotion before she presented herself. Perhaps they were arguing about her, in which case she wanted to be forewarned. She crept toward the open library doors. Elsa had no house servants as yet, so Peder obviously assumed that they were discussing something in private. Tora could see Peder's back as he sat at his desk and glimpsed Elsa as she paced before him.

"Surely on such a short run, it would make sense for me to accompany you," Elsa was saying.

"On the contrary," Peder retorted. "For such a short time, it is wiser that you stay at home. I'll be home within two weeks, Elsa!"

"And I told you that I am tired of being at home. Alone."

"That is unfortunate." He looked down, as if carefully constructing what he had to say before speaking. "What exactly did you anticipate when you married a sea captain?"

"I don't know. Not this. Your homecomings are lovely, but what sort of a marriage is that? After the winter, I'll see you . . . what? Three weeks of the year?" Her voice was high and tight.

"Only for a short time, Elsa," Peder said, speaking as if she were a child.

"For three years, you said!"

"For three *short* years," he reiterated. "Then I'll be home with you and our children, watching over Ramstad Yard."

Tora leaned back against the wood-paneled wall. So darling Elsa didn't have everything she wanted. That was a first. She chastised herself for being so malicious; her sister, after all, had not yet agreed to care for her unborn child. She needed Elsa, so she would play the dutiful, good sister and win her over. She'd play the victim with Peder. Her only hope was surprise. They must suspect nothing about her plans for escape, or she would be trapped in dreary Camden for the rest of her life.

"And when you launch each ship?" Elsa was saying, beginning to sound hysterical. Tora peeked in again. "Somehow I cannot see you sitting on the porch with me while a new ship takes her baptismal trip. Nor do I want you to!" She sighed. "Peder, you were born for the sea. I don't wish for you to be shackled to our home."

"This is hardly a home in which I'd feel shackled," he said irritably.

"Of course not!" Elsa said, wringing her hands. "You misunderstand me. Ramstad House is lovely. But my heart is not here." She rushed over to him, knelt, and placed her cheek to his thigh. "My heart is with you. Please, Peder, please. I want to travel with you. I want to make a life with you—at Ramstad House when we are at home, on the sea when we are not." She looked up at him, her face wet with tears. "Do you not miss me when you're gone?"

Tora chose that moment to enter. She backed up, coughed, and called "Hello" as if she had already done so several times. She entered the library and came up short, as if surprised by the scene before her. "Oh! Pardon me! I called," she said, pointing over her shoulder. "Kristoffer is home with the boys, and I thought I would come say hello to my dear brother-in-law." She looked from one stricken face to the other. "I am intruding. Forgive me. I will return later."

"No, Tora," Elsa said, rising and wiping her cheeks. She studied Peder's stoic face and looked away, clearly miserable. Her voice was tight, as if on the verge of crying. "You may stay. I would say we are at a standstill in this discussion. Pardon me while I go get some air." She stopped at Tora's side and looked back at Peder. "Greet my husband. Stay for dinner." She lowered her voice. "But hold your news until I return."

"Very well," Tora said with a shrug, moving to settle into a library chair.

"Elsa—" Peder called.

"I need some air, Peder," she said from the hallway. "I'll return in an hour. I want to take Muskatnøtt out for a ride."

Peder allowed her to go then began looking over some paperwork. Tora could tell he wasn't reading, just holding the papers to cover his distress. "What is your news, Tora?" Peder said wearily, setting down the paper and rubbing his eyebrows with one hand. The front door slammed.

"She asked me to wait—"

"What news?" Peder roared, rising and leaning over the desk.

Tora's hand flew to her throat. How dare he take such a threatening tone and pose with her! She had to stay the anger that begged her to respond with, "Temper, temper. She's merely referring to my pregnancy." That would put the overbearing man in his place! But she knew it would also work against her. Instead, she used the rush of emotion to work up some tears.

Peder sat down, narrowing his eyes at her with a suspicious expression.

"Really, Peder, my nerves cannot take such violence."

He sighed and pursed his lips. "I'm sorry. I'm not angry with you, just . . . Perhaps you should wait for your sister."

"No," she said, wiping a fat tear from her cheek. "It is all right.

We are family now, right?" She took a deep breath. "What I must tell you is that I am in a delicate condition."

"You mean—" Peder began, his face coloring.

"Yes," she nodded. "I'm afraid Soren Janssen took advantage of me one night on the ship. I was horrified, of course, and wanted nothing more than to forget it ever happened. I never told anyone because I did not wish to hurt Kaatje. That day you found us in the passageway, he was trying to force himself on me again." She warmed to the story as it came closer to the truth, and she could *feel* the righteous indignation she knew would sway Peder.

"I had narrowly escaped him. He came on me in the cabin as I napped. Can you imagine?" She fanned herself, as if wanting to waft away bad memories and push back her tears. "I made it to the hallway and told him to never get near me again, when he slapped me. It was then that I called for help." Tora looked down quickly, wanting Peder's image to be of a young girl wronged, a victim in his presence.

He did not speak for a long minute, then said, "This is the truth, Tora? Look at me."

She raised her eyes to his, knowing her future hung in the balance. It was difficult, but she managed to hold his gaze. "Yes," she said, nodding then looking steadily back at him. She blinked rapidly. "Every word."

Karl rode his rented mount high into the hills above Camden, following a faint path with fresh tracks. It was no wonder that someone else rode here. It was beautiful and haunting amid the tree skeletons and their autumn crop on the forest floor, a thick blanket of faded fall colors. He turned at a switchback and climbed higher, hoping to eventually reach the top of this hill and find some place to contemplate his future. By tonight, the *Herald*'s cargo would be unloaded and ready for the train. He would leave for New York tomorrow. His departure could not come too soon. In Camden he could think of nothing but Elsa. It threatened to drive him mad as he paced his hotel room in town, until he had finally settled upon the idea of an afternoon ride.

It had been a good idea. The air refreshed him, cleansed him of his obsessive thoughts. Time and again he turned wandering romantic notions to the business at hand—building the schooner then his steamer. He had his work cut out for him in research, for none of the Bergensers had worked on a steamship, and few in Camden knew much more.

Karl's mare raised her head and whinnied as they walked, and he could detect an increased energy in her gait, as if she smelled a pile of grain in her stall and was hurrying toward home. It was soon clear what had inspired her. Up ahead was a brown mare, the color of nutmeg. His heart skipped a beat. Surely, this was not Peder's horse. The last thing he needed was to come across Peder and Elsa in such a romantic setting. He didn't think his heart could bear it.

But his heart would have to bear much worse. For as he neared, he could hear a woman weeping, and his brow furrowed in concern. Was it Elsa? Was she injured? He made a sound low in his throat, urging his mount to a stop, and leaped to the ground. He scrambled up the hill, following the sorrowful sounds, slipping on damp leaves. At last he reached the top and emerged to find a clearing of granite that looked over the forest below and the harbor beyond it. The vista was glorious. But it was not the view that stopped his heart. It was Elsa. She was alone, sitting on a huge, flat boulder, her arms on her knees, her head on her arms. Her body shook as she wept, and the sight and sound of her distress tore him apart.

"Elsa?" he asked tentatively. He wiped his sweaty hands on his pants.

She looked up, and a sob caught in her throat. Quickly she tried to wipe away the tears and make herself presentable. "Karl," she managed. "What are you doing here?"

"I was out for a ride . . . I came across Muskatnøtt—"

"And you heard me," she finished for him.

"Are you all right? I will leave you in peace, but I wanted to make sure." He reached into his pocket and handed her his handkerchief.

The act of kindness seemed to tip her over the edge, and she began to cry again. Haltingly, he sat down beside her. He swallowed hard. "Elsa, what is it? What is the matter?"

She stood suddenly, wiping her cheeks with his handkerchief. "It is that Peder," she spat out. "He is so obstinate; he refuses to take me with you on this next voyage. You'll only be gone two weeks! It is an easy voyage, but even so, he refuses to allow me along!"

She paced angrily back and forth along the edge of the boulder, and Karl held his breath, wondering at the image of her against the view beyond. Even disheveled from her ride and weeping, she was worthy of a portrait. He wanted to pull her into his arms. But a still, small voice told him his role was that of a brotherly friend, no more. She was not his to take. Nor would she ever be. The thought of it threatened to make him weep himself.

Elsa stopped suddenly and studied him. "What do you think of that, Karl? Is he not being overly protective? If I were your wife, would you not take me along?"

Dear God, Karl prayed silently, running his hand through his hair. *Does she know what she asks? Is this of you, Lord? Or is this sweet torture of the devil?* He dared to look up at her. "Do not ask me that," Karl said.

"Why not? You are first mate, are you not? His dearest friend. Perhaps if you agree with me, you could persuade—"

"Elsa!" he said, a bit louder than he had intended. "Stop," he said, lowering his voice and coming to his feet. "You do not want me in the middle of this. It is your marriage. A private matter. And it is up to you and Peder to determine the right thing."

She whirled away from him, her skirt and long braid flying. He had hurt her by not joining forces, and his heart ached knowing it. "I am sorry, Elsa."

She raised her hand, as if to halt his words. "No, Karl. It is I who

am sorry. Forgive me for bringing you into this. You are a good friend
and a wise man to stay out of it."

Karl swallowed. So that was it. Their encounter was at an end.
The voice within him commanded him to leave. His own desire com-
manded him to stay. Would he tear in half if he turned to go? "May
I see you home?" he managed to ask.

"No, thank you. I'll be along shortly." She turned and gave him
a half smile. "Don't worry about us, Karl. Peder and I will resolve our
differences in time."

Karl nodded then willed his body to turn and climb down from
the boulder. Yet he felt as if he remained behind, watching another
man leave. Oh, that it were so. He reached his horse and mounted
swiftly, whirling the mare around and back toward town like a man
chased by a demon.

"What, God?" he cried once he was out of earshot from Elsa.
"What would you have me do with these feelings?" He pulled the
mare to a stop and shook his fist at the heavens. "What?" he
screamed. His question echoed off the nearby cliffs. "Is this my trial?"
he asked miserably. "Is this your way of proving whether I am a worthy servant?"

Karl resumed his ride, feeling spent, helpless, and weak. How on
earth could this all be resolved in a way befitting a man of faith? And
how could it be resolved when he felt himself so miserably distant
from his Savior? Perhaps he had been abandoned entirely, he thought.
Only one idea sustained him: Tomorrow he would board a train for
New York, leaving Camden and temptation behind.

Kaatje winced as she rose from bed, feeling the taut ligaments sup-
porting her abdomen stretch at the effort. How could her body ex-
pand to accommodate another two months of the baby's growth? She
felt bloated and round, and her ankles were horribly swollen, but all
in all, life was tremendous. Kaatje smiled as she padded over the dirt
floor to the bucket of water at the door. It was warmer than usual this

morning, more like late summer than fall. For the first time in weeks, she didn't shiver as she left her warm bed. But as she drew the blanket aside—their makeshift front door—there was no doubt about it; the crisp edge to the breeze outside warned of winter.

This morning was typical of their routine of late. Soren rose with the sun, eager to get to his work, and built a fire in the yard to brew a pot of coffee. Then he walked over a quarter mile to their neighbor's well to draw a fresh bucketful of water for Kaatje's use. By the time the coffee boiled, Kaatje would rise and sleepily make her way to the bucket at the door to wash her face.

Kaatje dried her face with an old rag. Then crossing her arms, she studied Soren as he worked without his shirt, digging a well. Powerful shoulders topped a lean torso that led to a svelte waist. Sweat trickled down his face and chest in tiny streams over dusty skin, even as his breath showed up as clouds in the early morning light. On and on he worked, determined that they would have their own well by first snow.

Kaatje grabbed a shawl from her cedar chest and wrapped it about her, feeling a shiver of excitement run down her back to be able to brazenly walk out into the yard half-dressed. Their farm sat a quarter mile from their nearest neighbor. Old Lady Engvold, as everyone called her, had acquired over 460 acres of land, having homesteaded 160 of them herself and purchased the others. Her land bordered theirs to the west and south. Fred and Claire Marquardt, whose farmhouse sat about a half mile away, owned to the north of them, and on the east was a dear Dutch man named Walter Van Der Roos.

Walter had come to introduce himself soon after they arrived, blushing as he offered Kaatje a pair of wooden clogs, beautifully carved with an intricate pattern, that his dead wife had once worn. Kaatje had taken them without hesitation, thinking of the large holes in her boots that had been patched and repatched over the years. The clogs were a bit large, but comfortable enough. She put them on now and padded out to the campfire, thinking about silly superstitions.

Soren had been able to settle on this prime piece of land because an old cemetery stood on the southeast corner and no one else wanted it. What was all the fuss about? Kaatje had spent many a day wandering about the withered crosses and faded tombstones, tending to the neglected graves. There was something fascinating about the place. It was a reminder that she was very much alive despite being so near death, she decided.

Crouching by the fire, Kaatje poured herself coffee in the tin cup Soren had left beside it. Still her husband did not see her. She watched him in silence, viewing him through the steam of her bitter coffee as if he were a vision. After a while Soren set down his shovel and wiped his face with a rag. He looked to the horizon then toward the soddy. At last he spied her. "Aha! My wife finally rises!"

"I have been up for a while," she defended with a smile.

"And how long have you been watching me like a prairie dog?"

Kaatje laughed. The prairie dogs were their constant companions, sitting on their haunches and watching their every move. "Long enough to appreciate your work."

Soren cocked his head to the side. "It is a man's work."

"And I appreciate that my man works as he does to make a home for me."

Soren climbed out of the hole and walked over to her. She rose and offered him her coffee cup. He drank, then handed it back to her, studying her closely. "It is better here, isn't it, Kaatje?"

Kaatje nodded. Soren took a step closer and placed his hands on her hips. "And I like it that you can go about in your night shift and shawl." He raised his hands and twisted about like a dust devil. "Freedom! Privacy! A place to call our own! America!" He said "America" with relish, enunciating each syllable. He grinned and pulled her close once more. "It is a fine, fine thing that we've done."

"It is," Kaatje said, feeling utterly satisfied. She shook her head and stepped away from Soren. "Now I must tend to breakfast. Can you hold out for another hour? I hoped to send a letter to town with Mr. Marquardt this morning. He said he'd be by about nine."

"Sure," Soren said. "Go write your letter to Elsa. Tell her I'm taking care of you," he added with a grin. "Tell her I was afraid not to after her fierce warning."

"I'll tell her." She stood up on tiptoe and kissed her husband. "You are taking fine care of me."

Soren pulled her in as close as possible, resting his chin on her head. "I hope so, *elske*. I want everything to be right for you here."

"And I for you."

f i f t e e n

⁂

*N*ow that they were together again—with no immediate
threat of separation—the urgency was gone, and Elsa relaxed
as they settled into the routine of life in Camden. Each morning Peder rose, ate breakfast with her, then headed to the yard. On the
ramp stood the white oak frames of the *Sunrise,* Ramstad Yard's first
ship, looking like the bleached ribs of a giant beached whale. But no
one would work on her today. Today was their first American holiday,
Thanksgiving, and Elsa had enlisted the help of an American neighbor to prepare a traditional feast.

She grinned again as she caught a whiff of the turkey roasting in
her cast-iron stove in the kitchen. Elsa mentally listed what remained
to be done as she searched for her drop pearl earrings. They must
"whup" the potatoes, as her new southern friend, Bessie Walters,
called it, and boil the yams. Bessie said she always added something
special—a family secret—to the candied yams, and Elsa hoped to
catch her at it.

It was good to be surrounded by friends, she mused, old and new,
on a day such as this. Tonight they would host Karl, Kristoffer and

his boys, Tora, Bjorn and Ebba, Mikkel and Ola, Bessie and her husband, Richard, and their two daughters.

Elsa looked at her reflection once more. Peder had chosen wisely for her. The gown was made of fine, golden silk at the bodice, and the skirt was of white silk that gave way to three tiers of delicate lace. The sleeves were slightly gathered at the shoulder, and at the wrist, tiers of lace matched the skirt. The neckline was high, and at her throat, she wore her grandmother's brooch. The trim fit of the gown complemented her form, and Elsa wondered what she would do when she became pregnant. Let out all these dresses? Buy new ones? Peder spent money on her clothes as if he had an endless supply, when she knew the reality of their situation. But she would worry about it later. It was a concern for another day, not Thanksgiving.

A knock at the door brought Peder out of the parlor as she left the bedroom. He made a fashionable figure himself in a new, double-breasted coat with velvet collar and cuffs, and striped wool trousers. "I'll get it," he said, stopping to give her a kiss on the cheek. "You look lovely."

"Thank you," Elsa said, as he went to answer the door. She followed behind, wanting to welcome their first guest alongside her husband.

Karl shifted his weight from one leg to the other and looked up, a new bowler hat in hand, as Peder opened the door. He too looked handsome in a new, short-fitted jacket and matching trousers. The cool gray wool of his suit brought out the color of his eyes. He shook Peder's hand firmly then bent to kiss Elsa on the cheek, the perfect gentleman. For some reason, her thoughts flew back to that afternoon on the peak above Ramstad House. Feeling foolish and a bit guilty for telling Karl about her argument with Peder, she had not told her husband of their meeting.

It was an answer to prayer that she had not destroyed the balance of things with her childish ways. If anything, in the three or four times that Elsa had seen him since that day, Karl had been more aloof.

Perhaps her foolishness had turned him aside. In any case their relationship was still warm, but now properly distant. Anything that she had observed—or others, for that matter—had clearly been dealt with, or altogether a figment of their imaginations. Karl Martensen was obsessed with his steamship, not her.

"Come in, Karl," she said warmly. "I see you went shopping with Peder. May I take your coat?"

"Certainly," he said, handing it to her. "It seems that I have done my share in fattening the shopkeepers' wallets of late. I must stay away from New York! The people there are of a different breed and fill my head with folderol."

"Like steamships," Peder quipped.

"I was speaking of an unreasonable need for more clothing," Karl returned, raising one eyebrow.

Elsa laughed, glad to hear the banter between the two, and followed them to the parlor.

Before long the other guests arrived, and the house was alive with conversation and laughter as they gathered around the dining room table with Peder at the head and Elsa at the foot. Bjorn was debating with Kristoffer about the wisdom of the yard's new schooner design. "We should simply build another clipper," the bearlike man said quietly, obviously hoping to avoid Peder's ears. Peder smiled. The man had never whispered in his life.

"You will see, Bjorn," he said loudly. "Our schooner will have your heart soon enough."

"And if she doesn't," enjoined Karl, "our steamship will."

The men laughed, and Peder raised his crystal glass after Elsa had refilled them all. "To the American holiday . . . to our holiday . . . Thanksgiving. We have much, indeed, to be thankful for this year."

"Hear, hear," called the men, and as one the company lifted their glasses.

Over the rim of her goblet, Elsa watched Tora. The girl barely looked pregnant, defying the fact that she was four months along. Elsa wondered if her sister had told Kristoffer about her condition and watched as Tora leaned over and whispered in his ear. The man's lean, tanned face broke into a smile, and he winked at her. Once again Elsa wondered what was transpiring in that three-bedroom cottage down below. It had been five months since Astrid's death, and as much as the two had loved one another, Kristoffer was in dire need of a wife. He could not mourn forever.

Elsa frowned. It wasn't entirely proper for a young, pretty girl like Tora to be living in an unmarried man's home, regardless of her station and duties or the fact that the man slept in the Ramstad Yard long house. Elsa looked down the table at Peder. She knew from experience what the intimacies of living together brought forth, and Kristoffer's cottage was small. Kristoffer and Tora laughed together again, and Elsa found herself hoping that her sister wouldn't hurt the man. Kris was still wounded; he didn't need more heartbreak.

Bessie bustled off to the kitchen again, and Peder leaned over toward Mikkel, who sat stiffly beside his wife Ola, watching the goings-on as if he were tolerating the shenanigans of toddlers.

"We will eat well tonight, eh, Mikkel?" said Peder.

"Well enough," Mikkel allowed. The old bird was somber, but solid. Peder said there were few men at Ramstad Yard that he could count on more than Mikkel Thompson. He and Ola postured themselves like the elders in Bergen, often coming across as superior, but served as a wealth of knowledge on a variety of subjects. They were true friends. And no one could run a crew like Mikkel. The old man could get men to work longer hours and be more efficient than anyone Peder knew. Bjorn was a good worker, too, and his wife, Ebba, lived up to her name, which meant "as strong as a boar."

All in all, they were a good mix, this hearty crowd of Bergensers, and a fine beginning for Ramstad Yard, thought Elsa. Together these people would build Peder a business. As she looked around the table, never in her life had Elsa been more thankful.

Tora assisted Bessie and Elsa in getting the food to the table, although she was feeling terribly tired again. The charade was wearing, and Tora wondered how long she could keep it up. Perhaps she shouldn't. Her dresses, after all, could not be let out much more. Surely Kristoffer would know before long. It would be better to tell him herself, perhaps soften the blow.

She smiled as she approached the table, placing a delicate hand on Kristoffer's shoulder as she leaned over to set the dish of stuffing before him. "Pardon me," she said demurely.

"It's quite all right," he said, smiling up at her. His hazel eyes were still sad, and Tora felt both a twinge of guilt and a strange desire to erase his pain. She immediately dismissed both inclinations. This pregnancy was simply playing havoc with her emotions. She could not rely on them as real. Surely she did not feel anything for Kristoffer. He was nothing, a worthless second mate to her brother-in-law. There was someone greater out there waiting for her. And she would find him.

Knut ran up to her and tugged on her skirts. "I'm hungry," he whined.

"Your dinner is in the kitchen," she said. "Go and join the other children at the kitchen table."

"I want turkey!" he said, running toward the kitchen.

"You'll have it soon enough."

Lars was in the master bedroom, sound asleep on Peder and Elsa's bed, surrounded by pillows. Tora felt another odd heart palpitation. Who would care for the boys when she left? She knew now that she could not last the duration of her pregnancy. She would find a suitable home for her child wherever she landed, but she had to leave Camden. She had to. Kristoffer would just have to find another nanny. Surely someone in the village . . .

"Tora?" Elsa said in irritation, holding out a heavy bowl of mashed potatoes. "Take these to the table."

Tora used one hand to wipe perspiration from her brow. The kitchen was stifling from the heat of the stove. Like Camden, she thought, as she took the bowl from her sister. Escape or wither.

At the table the men were talking once again about boring ship industry news, with Richard Walters, Bessie's husband, sharing the latest gossip. Richard owned a small yard of his own next to Peder's, and the two had become fast friends. This time Tora carefully avoided touching Kris as she set the bowl on the table, but he immediately stood to pull out her chair.

Elsa entered with the turkey, and everyone oohed and ahhed, their mouths watering at the golden bird's aroma. There was a veritable feast before them. Tora tried to smile as Kristoffer made a comment in her ear about getting her share. So he had noticed her increased appetite. Tora seemed unable to eat enough these days. It was showing and not only through her stomach. She had agonized over arms and thighs that were plumping up, but still could not seem to stay her hunger.

Kristoffer was not being mean. He obviously meant it as a compliment when he called her healthy. He was nice in many ways, but he was not, and would never be, one of Tora's conquests. She knew she could have him if she wanted him. He was in the palm of her hand already. But she didn't want him now. Or ever. She was leaving Camden. Just as soon as she could manage it.

When Tora excused herself, saying she wanted to get the children home to bed, Karl excused himself as well. He had watched Tora and Kristoffer throughout the evening, and what he saw concerned him. He walked behind her and the boys for a while. The lantern she carried cast her form in sharp silhouette. Karl observed the new curves she'd gained with some added pounds and distantly decided it made her all the more alluring and dangerous. Did Kris see her as the vixen she was? He trotted to catch up with her, suddenly angry at the memory of her hand on Kristoffer's shoulder.

"He cannot take a broken heart again," he said without preamble. The memory of Kristoffer's agonized cry as the sailors dropped Astrid's body overboard still awakened him at night.

Tora turned, Lars asleep in a sling over her shoulder. The lantern swung in one hand, Knut's hand in the other. "Karl! You scared me to death!"

"Forgive me," he said, momentarily taken aback. But he charged on, wanting to have his say. "I just do not want you to hurt him. It would be better for you to leave now than to win his heart and then leave him."

"I do not know of what you speak," Tora said, pivoting and walking away from him with her nose in the air.

He caught up with her easily. "You do. You know what he's been through. Good grief, woman, you were there when she died." Karl looked quickly down at Knut, who seemed to be so sleepy he did not care what the adults spoke of. "Losing Astrid almost killed him. It is only the boys that keep him going. And he doesn't need you in the middle of his life, messing with his heart. A man can only tolerate so much, Tora."

She stared back at him silently. "You speak from experience?" she asked, smiling thinly as if she knew.

"Of course not," he said, flustered.

"You do. So there it is. You know my secrets, and I know yours, Karl Martensen." She leaned closer. "Or at least you think you know my mind."

"Ah no," he said. "I would never claim to get inside the labyrinth that is your mind."

"Stay out of my life, Karl. You've said your piece, now be gone with you. Off to your lonely rented cottage to sadly dream of my sister."

Why had he gone after her? Concern and care for a friend had opened him up to attack. He did not want a skirmish with Tora Anders. He simply wanted her to leave Kristoffer alone. He raised his hands, feeling the muscles in his jaw work. She was infuriating.

"I don't know what you are talking about," he said, "nor do I care to. As you said, I've said my piece. But I want to say one more thing. If you will not tread lightly for Kristoffer's sake, do it at least for the boys. Think what you are doing to them."

He turned on his heel and left the circle of lantern light before she could respond. The cool darkness welcomed him, and he breathed deeply for the first time since entering Ramstad House earlier that evening.

lsa awakened with the sun, thinking of Kaatje and Soren and how desperate her friend must feel. Even when Peder left her for the sea, she remained in a comfortable home with neighbors close at hand. Kaatje was all alone. Elsa rose, built up a fire, then sat in her bedroom window seat. She picked up Kaatje's letter and read it yet again.

> *25 November 1880*
> *Dear Friend,*
>
> *I thought of you several times tonight, missing your company and wondering when and if we might some-day celebrate this American Thanksgiving together. I hope you spent the day surrounded by dear ones as I had hoped to do. Soren insisted that we spend the day with our new neighbors, Fred and Claire Marquardt, Mrs. Engvold, and Walter Van Der Roos, since we see the Bergensers every Sunday, and I agreed. It was a most awful day.*
>
> *We were just sitting down to the table in our tiny*

house when some other neighbors stopped by. We quickly made room for the four of them, although there was hardly enough of the tykmelksuppe and ham and potatoes to go around as it was. They are a nice but terribly poor Norwegian family who have been on this Dakota land for four years. They are moving away to Montana Territory, where they have relatives. This is a terrible time to move, but they appear to be desperate, unable, I suppose, to even last the winter. I wish them Godspeed. Snow is just around the corner, and they have quite a few miles to cover before reaching a warm home and a welcome.

But that is not the worst of it. Soren has it in his mind that we should apply to homestead their land. Can you imagine? What is one man to do with 320 acres? I am told that one man can only manage thirty acres. Yet I try to remain silent. It is a man's place to make such decisions. Soren has grand ideas, and I do not have the heart to stop him. But what if this wide, vast land overwhelms him? What if, in trying to manage too much, he cannot manage any? It frightens me so! The only bright spot of the day was that Soren got so excited about this idea that he scarcely noticed our pretty neighbor, Mrs. Marquardt.

I am sorry to delve into such personal matters. I beg your pardon if this offends you. Soren would think that speaking of it to our Bergen loved ones was most rude and unforgivable, but I needed to speak of it to someone, so I turned to you, my friend. I will look for a letter from you, Elsa. As always, I send a kiss and a hug.

Your loving friend,
Kaatje

Elsa walked over to her desk and dipped her pen in the inkwell to respond.

15 December 1880
Dear Kaatje,

Thank you for your letter. I too find myself afraid over some of the decisions that Peder makes about Ramstad Yard, consequently putting us on shaky ground. I console myself that people do not get ahead by not taking risks. Does that help you at all? It is a risky thing, this life. And the only way through it is forward. I pray that Soren's decision will later prove wise and that you find peace.

Elsa crumpled up the paper, smudging the ink. She rose and threw it into the fire. Her words seemed trite, too light for what Kaatje was obviously experiencing. Did she herself not know a similar angst? Peder continued to insist on sailing without her, and the thought of it made her feel lost. And she hoped he would consider Karl's plans for a steamer shortly. She sighed, feeling helpless so far from Kaatje. *I commit this to your hands, Father,* she prayed silently, staring up at the ceiling of their bedroom. *Please, Jesus, take care of Kaatje. And be with Soren. Help him to be a wise and caring husband.* She turned to stare at Peder, still asleep in their large four-poster bed. *Help him to watch out for Kaatje as Peder does for me.*

Elsa felt guilty for her continued desire to travel with Peder. After all, it could be her out on the Dakota plains, living in a dismal soddy with a husband whose dreams were bigger than the state could hold. Peder had put his dream into action, and as a result, she had a beautiful home with loving neighbors. But she could not help herself. She loved Peder with all she had in her and wanted to be with him always. "As long as ye both shall live," she whispered, repeating her vows to honor him. Yet this had little to do with honoring Peder; he was being unreasonable, fearing for her so.

She got up from the desk and walked over to the bed. She sank down on her side and, with a delicate hand, reached out and traced Peder's profile, a hair's breadth away from his skin. His nose was long and straight—aristocratic, as some would call it. His chin was strong, and the stubble of his beard glistened in the dim light of dawn. A brown curl of hair lay against his forehead, and the rest of his hair was tousled this way and that. She often struggled not to laugh aloud when he rose, looking so silly with his hair mashed in places and on end in others.

He blinked and smiled at her hand so near his face. He took her hand in his own warm one, kissed the palm softly, and turned to her sleepily. "Good morning."

"Good morning, love," she said.

"What has you up so early?"

"Thoughts."

"Of what?" he asked, opening his eyes again.

"Kaatje. Soren. Tora. Us." She lay back and looked up at the ceiling, visualizing each face as she mentioned the names.

"There is little you can do for Kaatje and Soren. They must make their own way."

"I know, but she is due soon and so far away. And Tora…what will she do? She has not even spoken to Kris yet about her . . . indisposition. Who will care for her and the children? It won't be me. But how can I turn away? Unless . . ."

"What?"

"Unless I take her babe to sea with me." She sat up again and studied him intently. "I still want to go with you come spring, Peder."

Peder frowned and pulled his hand away. He swung his legs over the side of the bed and ran his hand through his unruly hair. "It is only December, Elsa," he said tiredly. "All of this is conjecture. Let's cross our bridges when we get to them, eh?" He glanced over his shoulder at her.

She sighed and looked back at him. "All right. When we get to them. But hear me when I say this, Peder. You will not order me to stay at home again. If we come to that decision mutually, all right. But I will not be commanded like a sailor on your ship."

Peder rose, angered at Elsa's open defiance. But when he looked at her, his heart softened. She was beautiful in her simple night shift, looking more like a girl than a grown woman. Her hair fell down over each breast in golden waves, and her eyes were larger than usual as she dared to meet his gaze. His heart nearly tore in two at the thought of leaving her again. And she did really love the sea and was doing more and more painting. Getting quite good at it, in his opinion. Other captains brought their entire families with them, but taking Tora's child was a whole other matter. His thoughts flew to the father. Peder dearly desired the chance to beat Soren Janssen to a pulp. It would kill Elsa if she knew.

"She hasn't told Kristoffer yet?" he asked.

Elsa sighed. "I told her she had to tell him within the month or I would do so myself. Honestly, dealing with her is like dealing with a child. I feel like a parent."

"A mischievous child with child."

"Yes. She is not equipped to raise her own son or daughter. It would be a travesty to turn our heads."

"But you've said yourself that the only way Tora will learn will be to face the consequences of her actions."

"But then I wonder if that is fair, considering her allegations against whoever . . . forced himself upon her."

"I vacillate over the decision as well," Peder said, pacing, "but truth be known, I doubt the girl's story."

"True . . ." Elsa muttered.

"Has she come right out and asked you to take the child?"

"In so many words. It's part of what irks me—she assumes I will,

absolving her of all her problems. She's acting quite odd. I don't know
if she'll even remain in Camden for the duration of her pregnancy if
I refuse the baby. Her obligation to Kristoffer is up this month."

"Where would she go?"

"I don't know. She has little or no money."

"I cannot imagine her here, Elsa."

"Peder, she is family."

He looked at her quickly. If Tora was in the house, then perhaps
it would be better for Elsa and him to leave together on the *Sunrise*.
Then the girl could find her own way, and they would be spared the
pain of watching her. But there was time enough to tell Elsa that he
might allow her to sail with him. For now, they would simply agree
to disagree until he felt some peace about the decision.

It was mid-December before Tora finally found the courage to tell
Kristoffer. With each passing day, it became clearer that Kris felt
something for her, and she knew he would not take the news well.
She chose to do it in the evening when the boys were in bed and
Kristoffer was preparing to leave for the mold loft where he slept.

"Kristoffer, wait. There's something I need to speak to you
about."

He turned to her, his eyes soft in the warm light cast by the fire.
He had a hopeful expression on his long face as he took two steps
toward her. In his hands he twisted his hat. "There is something I've
wanted to say to you, too, Tora."

"Wait," she said, holding up her hand and sitting on the edge of
the rocking chair by the fire. "Let me talk first. I don't believe you will
have much to say to me afterward."

Outside the rain began pounding on the roof in earnest, with
drops that sounded the size of marbles.

"If this is about you leaving at month's end—" he began, sitting
on a stool near her.

"No," she interrupted. "This is about you and me. These have been better months than I expected, Kris. You have been kind to me. But I will go at the end of the month."

"You don't have to. You could stay—"

"No. I will go," she rushed on. "You see, Kris . . . I'm expecting a baby."

His mouth dropped slightly, and even in the dim light, Tora could see him blanch. He shook his head then placed his head in his hands. "I have been so stupid," he said. "It was right in front of me all along."

Disbelief turned to anger, and he rose, pointing his finger at her. "I was beginning to care for you. But you are . . . You're nothing but a little . . ."

She jumped to her feet, immediately defensive in the face of his growing fury. "What? What were you going to call me, Kristoffer? Did you ever stop to think that I was wronged? Hurt? Taken without my consent?" Righteously indignant, Tora was beginning to believe her own story.

The words hung in the air between them for several moments. Then Kristoffer's brow furrowed further, and his eyes darkened. "Out," he said in a low voice. "Get out. Consider our deal done."

Tora shrank against her chair. He expected her to go out into that rain? Into the night?

"Out!" He stepped toward her and gripped her arm, painfully pulling her to her feet. He dragged her to the door and, grabbing a shawl from the peg by the door, shoved it into her hands. "You can come back for your things tomorrow, but you will not spend another night under my roof."

With that he cast her out, shutting the door behind her.

Tora scowled, enraged that he could treat her so after all she had done for him and the boys. And in the rain! Quickly she raised the shawl over her head, but she was soaked in seconds. She had not anticipated his reaction. She had not even had time to tell him her story, to win his support! If Elsa and Peder had believed her, surely she could have convinced Kris. But he had appointed himself judge and jury! And he called himself a Christian...

Fury and confusion soon brought her to tears. Pride kept her from pounding on his door or going to her sister. She needed time to think. But where?

A light at the top of the hill shone like a beacon to a lost ship. Karl. Maddening as he was, he would not turn away a hysterical, wet woman from his door. She looked over to Bessie and Richard's home to her left, and to the right, at Bjorn's and Mikkel's houses. All were dark. *Karl it is,* she decided.

Karl was sitting by the fire, sleepily reading *The American* by Henry James, when the knock sounded at his door. It so surprised him that he was instantly awake and on his feet. He had not anticipated Tora, but there she was, weeping, soaked, and hysterical. She looked up at him through her long lashes, and her blue eyes drew him in. If he stared at those eyes long enough, he could pretend she was Elsa. As if in a dream, she rushed into his arms, and he awkwardly embraced her.

Her cold, small body saturated his own clothes, and Karl backed away from her.

"Come in, Tora," he said grimly, gesturing toward the fire. "You're soaked."

"He threw me out! Out into the rain!" she sobbed, taking his chair by the fire.

It was so cold out, Karl had thought the rain might turn to snow by morning, and Tora only had a wet dress and shawl about her. She shook so fiercely that after a moment he grew concerned.

"You must get out of those wet clothes. Go into the bedroom, wrap yourself in the blanket from my bed, and come back to the fire. I'll pour you some tea."

"Thank you," she said, her voice shaking from the tremors that racked her body.

In a moment she returned, her bare neck and shoulders peeking out from the blanket. Karl averted his eyes. Whatever had pushed Kristoffer to do this to her must have been fierce, and Karl refused to be taken in by her.

"Why don't you tell me about it," he said, as if speaking to a child.

"There's nothing to tell! The man's a tyrant!" Her hand trembling, she raised the tin cup to her lips and sipped the hot tea.

"I don't believe you, Tora. Kris is one of the most levelheaded men I know. Now what did you do?"

Tora gave him a malevolent look and stared back at the fire. She raised her chin.

Here it comes, Karl thought, a bit amused by her antics. At least it provided some distraction from his long, lonely evening.

But she did not have the chance to say a word. A pounding at the door stopped her, and she looked fearfully over her shoulder.

"Kris?" Karl asked her calmly, raising one eyebrow. He sauntered over to the door and opened it. Kristoffer stood in the doorway, rain dripping off his soaked hat and onto his oilskin coat.

"Karl," he said with a brief nod. "I'm looking for Tora. We had an argument and . . ."

His voice trailed as Karl stepped aside, letting him view Tora before the fire. Too late, Karl realized what Kris would see: Tora's naked shoulders above a blanket. With a roar, Kristoffer charged him, tackling him to the ground and taking the wind out of him. Kris punched him before he could regain his equilibrium, but Karl caught Kris's next fist.

"Wait! It's not what you think!"

"It is! I've seen enough—"

"Kris! She came to me soaked and shivering. She had to get out of her wet clothes. We were only talking."

Kristoffer looked from him to Tora, who now stood by her chair watching them as if they were a stage show. "Is that true?"

She nodded, seemingly speechless for once.

Kris, obviously feeling like the village idiot, rose and helped Karl to his feet. "I . . . I am sorry," he said, clearly miserable.

"No worry," Karl said, massaging his sore jaw. "Tora just seems to bring out the best in people."

Together they looked at her, and she raised her nose in the air. "If you think I am going home with you, Kristoffer Swenson, you have another think coming."

"Tora, I . . . uh . . . I was unfair. I should have let you tell me how it happened."

"How what happened?" Karl asked.

"How she . . ." he began, but then, embarrassed, refused to say more.

"How I became pregnant," Tora said defiantly. She stared at Kris then at Karl. "A man took advantage of me aboard the *Herald.*" Her eyes filled with tears, and she looked away. "But my agony's not over, is it? I still have the trial of a situation like this to bear over and over again. How am I going to live? What will become of my child?"

Kristoffer's jaw worked as he made his way over to the sobbing girl, while Karl put two and two together. Tora pregnant. The *Herald.* Soren Janssen. It all figured, and Karl said a quick prayer for them all. God help them, this was a mess. And Kris believed her story.

Karl felt torn, not knowing what to do. Tora looked up at him with those big blue eyes that sent him careening back to thoughts of Elsa, clearly begging him not to say more. And Kris . . . well, Kristoffer needed her. He needed a wife and a mother for his children. And Tora, since Soren was another's husband, needed a father for her child. Maybe if they married, it would be the best solution for all. So he kept his mouth shut as the two spoke quietly by the fire.

They left together moments later after Tora had put on her wet dress in the bedroom while Kris once again made his apologies for jumping to conclusions. As Karl shut the door behind them, he said another prayer of thanks that it was not he who was mixed up with the girl.

But Karl knew he would not sleep that night, for he could not shake the feeling that he had sent a lamb off to pasture with the she-wolf.

Kaatje shivered under her quilt, wishing for her aunt's down comforter that she had left in Bergen. Her old feather bed and comforter might have had a chance against this bitter cold. She stared at the tallow candle that she kept burning by her bed, anxiously waiting for Soren to return from the barn. Kaatje had heard stories of men getting lost in the snow between house and barn, wandering until they froze to death, but Soren had been determined to go.

Outside the wind howled, and the poorly crafted shanty on their new land did little to stop it. She had to admit that the windows and wood floors felt more civilized than the soddy, but the walls had none of the insulation that the good old dirt had provided. Here and there were cracks that Kaatje had attempted to patch with rags, but still the cabin was drafty. And outside the first snow was beginning to fall. Oh, how she ached for Soren's arms! What if he never returned, leaving her alone on the Dakota prairie! If he would just get back to the house and climb into bed with her, she could relax, cozy and warm against his body in the midst of their first winter storm.

The front door blew open, swirling flakes coming in before a dark form. Kaatje rose to a sitting position, her hand at her throat, her heart banging against her ribs. "Soren! You startled me."

"These homesteads get awfully lonely, eh?"

Kaatje smiled and raised the covers. "Yes. Now undress and come to bed. I was just wishing you were here to cuddle with me."

In an instant he was beside her, cradling her in his arms. "Should I blow out the candle?" he asked.

"Not yet."

Through the window she watched the giant flakes swirl and fall, an entrancing, hypnotic display. They lay together for a long time before the baby moved. Soren drew away from her in surprise. "What was that?"

She smiled, feeling like Saint Nick, as the Americans called him. "Why, that's your child," she said.

Soren hooted and sat up. Kaatje sighed, missing his warmth already as he placed a hand on her swollen stomach and waited. After a moment the baby kicked again, then rolled.

Soren's mouth dropped. "You feel that every day?"

"Every day, all day."

"It's a miracle!" Soren shouted.

Kaatje laughed at his exuberance. "Yes. It is. Someday soon that baby will come and greet us." The thought sobered her. "I don't want to be alone on that day, Soren. You'll have to go for Eira."

"Just as soon as you tell me to," he said solemnly. Soren caressed her cheek. "Don't worry, *elskling.*" He leaned toward her belly. "And I'll watch over you too. Shall I tell you of the farms we will have someday, little man? The rain will fall, and the sun will shine, and you and I will establish a ranch here that will spread for miles. Your mama and I are just beginning."

seventeen

~~~

When Peder arrived home on Christmas Day with a letter from Elsa's parents, she thought it the best present of all. Elsa straightened the paper on her lap, treasuring each word before her like a hug from her distant mother, and began to read aloud. As she did so, Peder settled down to listen in a chair nearby.

> *15 November 1880*
> *Dearest Elsa and Peder,*
> *Christmas greetings to both of you and happy New Year as well. I should have gotten this letter off earlier, but I have found myself quite busy of late. I pray that the new year finds you settled and happy. We were so relieved to hear that Tora is well and with you. Thank you for sending word immediately. Amund and I had assumed that when she disappeared, it was on the Herald. I am sorry, dears, for any burden you must bear because of her impetuous decision. Thank you, in advance, for caring for her.*

Elsa shot Peder a glance. Her mother did not know, as yet, all that had transpired for Tora aboard the *Herald* and afterward. Would she be angry with her elder daughter for not taking Tora in herself? She continued reading.

> *My good tiding: Garth has begun courting Carina in earnest, and for the first time, she seems amicable to the idea. Perhaps you younger ones marrying caught their interest. In any case, I expect a proposal any day.*
>
> *I have poor tidings that I need to share with you as well. Your dear father is failing.*

Elsa let the letter fall to her lap. Papa! Failing. And so far away . . .

"Elsa, keep reading. Perhaps it is not as dire as it sounds," Peder said.

With shaking hands, Elsa picked up the letter again.

> *The doctor believes that it is heart trouble again. He has been in bed for weeks, feeling weak and suffering from numb toes and fingers. He cannot work, and lying in bed brings him to despair. But the worst happened three days ago. He suffered a fit and was left useless on his left side and has a difficult time forming words. I must spoon soup into his mouth and close his lips for him to swallow.*
>
> *Forgive me when I say this, dear ones, but I pray for his release if he cannot be healed. I pray that he will find peace in heaven and restoration at Jesus' side. For a man as proud as Amund cannot live on in such a state. It would be worse to watch him slowly waste away than to mourn his departure. Will you join me in my prayer? For healing or release.*
>
> *I am thankful for Carina, but miss my other two*

*daughters. Please encourage Tora to write. Young ones
must make their own way in life, and all is forgiven.
I long for a word from her. I send my love and a
prayer of bounty for each of you.*

*Your loving mother,
Gratia*

"Oh, Peder, I must get home! I must!"

Peder rose and came to her side, placing a hand on her shoulder. "I am sorry, dearest. There is no way. There are precious few ships that would dare a crossing in the midst of winter. Look outside."

Elsa's eyes flew to the gray, swirling waters then to her painting. She knew she was being irrational, but her heart ached at the thought of her father passing without one more kiss from her. She wanted to fly like the birds to Bergen, walk in the hills high above the fjord, watch the northern lights once more by his side.

"No," she said sadly, giving in to tears. "He cannot die yet. He cannot. There's so much I want to share with him! Perhaps Mama can bring him here in the spring. Perhaps you and I can go and get them!" She looked up at Peder, feeling as desperate as her voice sounded.

He knelt by her side, taking her hands in his. His face was sorrowful. "Love, I understand your pain. But they are far away. When you left on the *Herald,* you were essentially saying good-bye to them forever."

"But Karl said—"

"What?"

"He said that perhaps your ships would pass near Bergen one day. I had thought that I would see my parents again. At least once. And now Papa is dying." She could utter no more words, for she was choked by her tears. She felt so far away! So distant! So helpless!

"You know that I would see you home if I could. But it's impossible. Entirely too dangerous. We need to stay here and pray for your parents. Concentrate on the Lord, Elsa. He will see us all through."

"God! Where is he? Surely this cannot be of him."

"We all will reach the end of our days."

"But not Papa! He is too young!"

"He is nearing seventy. His own father passed at what? Sixty-five?"

His attempt at reasoning angered Elsa. Could he not see that she did not want practical assessment, but simply love and commiseration? What was it about men that they always had to whittle things down to their inevitable practicalities?

"I need to go and find Tora," she said coolly, rising and dropping his hands.

"Elsa—"

"I need to go find Tora!" she repeated, sweeping out of the room.

Peder went to their bedroom when Elsa did not rise for supper. He supposed he had botched his husbandly duties this afternoon when he had attempted to reason with her. She was obviously not in the mood for cold, hard facts. Would he ever understand the intricacies of marriage? In contrast, running a ship was simple. Men were men, and easily understood. Furthermore, as captain, what he said went on his ship, unlike at home. The same tactics, when employed here, tended to breed discontent rather than the idyllic home off the waters he had imagined. It was a whole new world, in which Peder felt like an explorer.

Elsa lay on the bed in the gloomy darkness. Peder lit a kerosene sconce above her head and placed a gentle hand on her side. At least her tears had stopped. He cast about for the right words to assuage her pain. "Love?" he dared.

"Yes," she answered. "I'm sorry, Peder. I have taken myself away from you all day, but I felt I needed some privacy."

"I do not blame you. I was a buffoon. You obviously needed a caring ear, not the captain at the helm."

She turned and smiled a little. "It is not your fault. You were simply trying to make me see the reality of my situation."

"At the cost of caring for you best."

She laughed, a mirthless sound. "We are both still learning. We have been apart as much as we have been together."

Peder took her hand and placed it over his heart. "It is something I have been rethinking of late. I have not decided for sure," he warned, "but I do agree it would be nice to have you along this spring."

Elsa nodded, obviously afraid to push it further at the moment. "I have a present for you."

"For me?" she asked, turning and sitting up.

"Well, yes. You do remember it's Christmas, don't you? As rotten as the day began, it should end on a better note." They had celebrated with many of their Camden friends the night before, reserving this day for themselves.

Peder left the bed and went to a huge, wrapped canvas by the door, then brought it to her. She had the string untied and the brown wrapper ripped off in seconds, looking like a child as her face lifted in excitement.

"Oh, Peder! A Long! A painting by Fergus Long!" She studied the painting before her in reverence then asked him to bring the lamp closer. It was a picture of three brigantines and a bark at dawn in Boston Harbor. "Look at the detail! There's such a calm feeling about his work, it's almost spiritual."

Peder smiled, glad she was so pleased, and happy to take her mind off her father. "He has agreed to take you on as a student."

"A student?" she asked in wonder, looking up at him as if the news did not quite register.

"Yes. I took the liberty of taking two of your paintings down to show him—"

"You did not! How horrifying! They are not suitable. Peder, you should have asked me—"

"And he was very impressed. He thinks you have a natural talent that should be cultivated. In fact, Long demanded that I bring you down to see him."

"You jest."

"No." Peder reached into his lapel pocket and drew out two train tickets. "We leave next week. We'll be in New York for a week or more, depending on how you fare with Mr. Long, and we'll stay at the Park Avenue Hotel. Merry Christmas, love."

"Oh, Peder!" she cried, pulling him down onto the bed for a quick embrace. "It's wonderful! You wonderful, wonderful man!"

He chuckled and leaned back. "It's amazing how one can go from cad to wonderful in one day, eh?"

Tora's way out arrived in the same mailbag as the awful letter from her mother. She felt more sorry for her mother than for her father. It would be horrible to watch someone waste away in front of your very eyes. Tora shook her head and waddled to the stove, removing the hot biscuits from the oven. In her six months of indenture, Tora had become somewhat of a cook. Thus, having read about the expanding railroads and the dire need for decent restaurants along the tracks, she had hatched her plan.

She would remain with Kristoffer and the boys beyond her required stay simply because she was still saving money and planning carefully. Kristoffer had begun paying her, and using that, along with the money she had pilfered from her father, she could get to Minnesota and still have a sizable amount to place in a savings account.

The letter that had just arrived was an answer to prayer, God smiling on her at long last. In it, Mr. Trent Storm, a railroad dinner house mogul, was requesting that she report for an interview in March. An opening had formed along the Northern Pacific line, and her bilingual status should serve her well.

Trent Storm had styled his business after the successful Fred

Harvey, creating restaurants along the railroad lines. These dining places had become so popular that the railroads promoted their tickets with "Storm meals en route."

Tora had read an article on the man soon after arriving in America and remembered that he liked to employ "attractive young women of good morals and pleasant disposition." The Storm restaurants never served canned food, and they coordinated their menus so that no customer ate the same meal twice en route to his destination. It was a vast improvement over the roadhouses of old, where travelers often found their meals to be meager, spoiled, or rife with vermin.

When she came across an advertisement in the newspaper, Tora considered it providential. Despite the fact that "Storm girls" were "carefully screened, closely supervised, and lived in a dormitory," they were also expected to live in the "wild and dangerous west." That sounded good to her, Tora thought with a laugh as she looked out a window at the sleepy little town to the south. It would be in the wild and dangerous west that she would find someone with the spirit and the entrepreneurial sense to win her.

"Duluth," she said, reading the letterhead again and again. Surely that was a bigger city than Camden. Maybe even bigger than Boston! And it would work perfectly. She would remain in Camden another few months, have her child, then leave the cursed town behind forever. There was but one hitch: Mr. Storm wanted to see her in March, and she wasn't due until April. Surely she could delay the interview until May.

"Dear Mr. Storm," she mentally formulated her response. "Due to a family emergency, I am afraid I cannot reach Duluth until May." Once in Minnesota, she would check into her options for the child. Surely in a big city she could find fitting adoptive parents! Elsa had tearfully informed her last week that the child was Tora's responsibility, regardless of how she had become pregnant. *She planned to travel with Peder . . . A child was too much . . . Tora and her child were welcome to stay at Ramstad House . . .*

She was heartless, Tora concluded, and refused to listen to another of her older sister's lectures. She would see! The least she could have done was take the child, her own flesh and blood, and claim it as her own to their parents. Instead she demanded that Tora write them with the news! Why, the very shock could kill their father!

Tora laughed hollowly, thinking again of her sister's unreasonable demands. There was no way she would write to her parents now. No, her family would all soon be behind her. She had a whole life before her. And it would all begin in a place called Minnesota.

eighteen

Karl leaned forward as the train came to a stop, brakes squealing. He rose as soon as the conductor called, "Announcing Saint Paul! All those en route to Minneapolis, next stop!"

As he made his way down the aisle, Karl smiled for the first time in what felt like weeks. He was miles away from Camden-by-the-Sea and from Elsa, with more than enough to occupy his mind. The fellows in New York had been quite helpful with his research last fall, but they had encouraged him to look up John J. Hall in Saint Paul. After he had sent a letter to Mr. Hall, an associate of Hall's had written him back, welcoming a visit. Americans were a wonderful lot, Karl concluded as he stepped down the steep passenger car stairs. Open and warm, for the most part, even in extending a hand to a potential competitor.

He looked about, straightening his new, long overcoat, which was double-breasted, and sported a shoulder cape, flap pockets, and wide cuffs. He touched the brim of his bowler hat as a young, attractive brunette looked his way, and he felt more alive than he had in months. If he could not have Elsa, perhaps another woman would win his heart. And in the meantime, he had more than enough to do looking after his business. He intended to be a business mogul himself one day, the head of a successful steamship company. Ramstad Yard would be the beginning, but Karl would not finish there. No, there was much more ahead.

As passengers gradually cleared the platform, a few waiting gentlemen became more obvious. Karl looked from one to the other, and finally found a gaze that welcomed him. "Martensen?" the man asked as he neared.

"Yes sir," Karl said, extending a hand. "You must be Mr. Bresley."

"That I am. But you may call me Bradford or Brad," he said, shaking Karl's hand firmly. Karl liked him immediately.

"Call me Karl," he returned, studying the man who looked about his own age and near his height, but with brown hair and eyes. Bradford Bresley reminded him a bit of Peder's elder brother, Garth.

"Where are you from, Karl?" Brad asked as they meandered through the luggage, looking for Karl's valise.

"Bergen, Norway. Lately of Camden-by-the-Sea, Maine."

"Ah," Brad said. "I thought I detected a Scandinavian accent."

"I'm an American now," Karl said. He pointed to his bag. "This is it."

"A man who travels light," Brad said. "I think we'll be friends," he added, clapping Karl on the shoulder.

Outside the railway station, he led Karl to a magnificent town coach. The four-wheeled carriage resembled the state coaches that carried the well-to-do, and Karl felt a bit conspicuous. It was John's private coach, Brad informed him. With one empathetic look at the driver and footman, who must sit outside exposed to the elements, he climbed in beside Bresley, glad to escape the giant, wet snowflakes that fell about him.

"Been to the Twin Cities before?" Brad asked.

When Karl shook his head, Brad said, "We'll do a quick tour

then. John would have welcomed you himself—he loves an entrepreneur—but he's in Canada, working on the Canadian Pacific Railway."

"Railroads? I thought the man was into shipping."

"The shipping company is coming along fine. Railroads have always been his passion though. He really built his steamship company to better serve the railroad. He worked for a freight-forwarding company until '66 then formed his own transportation and warehouse agency on property leased from the Saint Paul and Pacific Railroad. That was the beginning of it all. Since his firm was especially designed for easy transfer of cargo from steamboats to railroad cars, it was immediately successful. John won contract after contract."

"You admire the man," Karl said.

"I do." Brad paused briefly. "Just always work with John, not against him. As long as you keep that in mind, you can work well with him. Get in his way, and you'll be run over."

"I'll consider it fair warning. But I doubt I'll even meet the man. My business is bound to be complete before he returns from Canada."

"You never know," Brad said with an infectious smile. "John Hall cuts a wide swath. And he likes seamen. Says that a man of the seas is his kind of man. You're a captain?"

"First mate."

"Champing at the bit to be behind the wheel, eh?"

"Oh, I get my fair share of wheel duty. It is the idea that the ship would be mine that appeals."

"And you have your mind set on steam."

"I do. It is the wave of the future, is it not?"

"I think so. But the sailers . . ." Brad's eyes took on a faraway look. "I'd give my eyeteeth to sail on the open seas again."

"You captain a steamboat on the river?"

"Used to. Lately John has me working on some new business ventures."

"A promotion?"

"In some ways. Though I prefer the wheel to a desk. I'm considering asking for a demotion."

The two men laughed together and continued chatting amiably until they reached the docks.

Karl leaned out the window. There along the docks were five steamboats, fresh from the yard if the new paint was any indication. He glanced over at Brad, who smiled like a proud parent.

"Finest fleet on the Red River," he said. "Come meet the men. They can't wait to tell you all you want to know about steam."

After the fifth full day of work down at the steamboat yard, Karl bathed at the hotel in a deep copper tub, then dressed in the ridiculously fine clothing that Brad had insisted he buy the day before. There was a ball at a business associate of Hall's tonight, and Brad had finagled an invitation for Karl. The only stipulation, he said, was that his new friend would not embarrass him by wearing anything outdated. "We want to attract the women, Martensen," he had said, "not repel them."

Now Karl stood before the full-length looking glass, appreciating the tailor's work. The fine blue wool suit had a short jacket with a waist seam, covered buttons, and what the tailor called a ticket pocket. The cuffs were shaped and very stylish. With a laugh, he picked up the walking cane that Brad had insisted he purchase and shook his head at his folly. What had become of the sailor? He looked like a citified prig.

A knock at the door distracted him, and he went to welcome Brad. His friend wore a similar suit in a rich brown. "We will have no trouble attracting the ladies in this finery," Karl said. "But I warn you now, Brad. If I have to stay in this straitjacket for long, I'm likely to burst."

"The dancing will help with that. You'll be staring into some gorgeous debutante's eyes, and you'll think no more of your suit. But she will. It was a fine purchase, Martensen."

"Thank you," he said doubtfully. He followed Brad out of the room and down the hall to the small, elegant elevator with its open brass grillwork. As they rode down to the lobby, Karl marveled again at the city's technology.

In minutes the two were safely ensconced in a warm hackney en route to the ball. They drove along Third Street, and Karl watched as they passed the myriad shops. There was the Boston One Price clothing store and R. A. Lanpher men's furnishings, where he had purchased his suit that day. There was D. W. Ingersoll & Company and Mannheimer Brothers for dry goods, Griggs & Company for groceries, George Lamb's smoked meats—a fitting name, Karl mused—and the tropical fruit store of L. B. Smith. Yes, Saint Paul was a nice city. The weather was fairly inclement, but after years at sea, Karl could adapt to anything. *Perhaps I could live here,* he thought. *Perhaps this is where God would have me move.* Just as soon as Ramstad Yard was up and running strong.

"That's a fine hardware store," Brad said, pointing as they passed Adam Decker's. "We'll have to get there before you leave," he added.

Karl watched as a pharmacy, a tobacco shop, and a host of others went by before they turned the corner out of the business district of the lower town. Soon they were in a fine residential area, with homes that each took up one-quarter to one-half of a city block. The streets were lined with giant oaks and maple trees; the barren limbs would be handsome come spring. Glowing gaslights lined the street.

The hackney pulled to a stop behind a dozen other rented coaches not far from one of the mansions.

"We're waiting in line," Brad explained when he saw his friend's puzzled face. "Ever attended a ball such as this?"

Karl laughed. "I am a sailor from Bergen. What do you think?"

"No matter." Brad smiled. "I will walk you through it, old boy. Just stick with me."

When they reached the house, a footman opened their cab door, and the men climbed out. The Gutzian mansion was gorgeous, built in an ornate, French Second Empire style. It was constructed entirely of stone and featured magnificent, tall windows. A red carpet swooped down from the front entry over marble steps. At the door was a butler. "Invitations, gentlemen?" he asked formally.

Karl searched his ticket pocket and finally fished out his invitation. Brad had already handed the man his. Behind them, a couple climbed the steps. "You may go in, gentlemen," the butler said with a cool smile.

Once inside Karl could hear the music and laughter. They handed hats and overcoats to a steward, and Karl followed Brad up the sweeping grand staircase. He had never been in a house such as this. Even Ramstad House in Bergen or the best in Camden-by-the-Sea did not hold a candle to it. The ceiling rose twenty feet above them on the first and second floors. When they reached the third floor, Karl realized that the entire level was dedicated to the ballroom.

At the far end a small orchestra played sweeping, marvelous music. Countless stewards and maids moved among the guests, offering trays of tall crystal glasses of champagne and elaborate hors d'oeuvres. And the women . . . it seemed that there were hundreds of young women in elegant gowns, many of them looking his way. Perhaps his heart had not died with Elsa. Perhaps he could find a new love, a new life, here in Saint Paul.

He fingered his collar uncomfortably. It was twenty degrees warmer here than at the entry, and Karl was soon glad for the lightweight wool of his suit. Brad grabbed two glasses from a passing steward and handed one to Karl. "To tomorrow."

"To tonight," Karl returned, clinking his glass.

"I know what will drive the young ladies wild," Brad said, a glint in his eye.

Karl cocked an eyebrow. "Brad . . ." he warned.

"Trust me, mate." He turned to the couple nearest to them. "Clarence! Cassandra! Let me introduce you to my most fascinating new friend. He's a shipping baron of late, but once was a sailor who saw the world."

In minutes they were surrounded, and Karl was passed along from one group to another. The women seemed especially interested in his stories and listened with captive expressions as he told tale after tale. Karl enjoyed himself more and more, liking this feeling of being front and center for once, not just first mate. He felt attractive and witty as the girls laughed when he chose a funny turn of phrase. And then Brad introduced him to John Hall's daughter, Alicia.

She had listened to his last story of fighting off malaria and beating a storm with a limited crew when he finally caught her eye. His words slipped, and he had to concentrate to finish his sentence. For Alicia Hall was captivating. A mere wisp of a girl in height, she was all woman in form. Her hair was the color of chestnuts, and her eyes a bewitching green. Her skin was a pale ivory, and her dress was cut seductively low. He coughed and looked away, trying to regain his equilibrium, but his eyes dragged back to hers like a lead anchor to the sea's bottom.

Alicia smiled at him, parting the crowd as if she were a foot taller and twice as wide, then took his arm. "Captain Martensen," she said. "I insist that you take me out to the dance floor."

He did not bother to correct her on his true title, enjoying the notoriety and the thought, for once, that he *could* be captain. After all, his first steamboat would soon be done. If not this year, then next. As they whirled about, Karl felt happiness, true happiness, for the first time in months. He smiled down at Alicia, who brazenly held his gaze, and wondered at his desire to stare at her for hours and memorize each nuance of her face and hair and neck.

It happened that they did, indeed, spend the next several hours together, talking, dancing, laughing. Karl found Alicia to be an intriguing combination of forwardness and aloofness, which gradually, by the end of the evening, gave way to warmth and friendliness. She was delightful. She even stood on tiptoe at the end of the night, as they walked in from the foyer and through the shadows, to give him a quick kiss.

Karl felt reborn. This was his place . . . a new home. He would return to Saint Paul, Minnesota just as soon as he could manage it.

n i n e t e e n

⁓⚬⁓

*E*lsa sat on a stool, nervously painting on a large canvas while Fergus Long stood behind her, watching every move.

"You know, Mr. Long, it is difficult for me to do this with you watching me every second. Could you leave and come to check on me periodically?"

"Yes, yes. It is important, though, for me to watch your technique."

Elsa turned to look at the short, squat, aged man. He had a firm look on his face, but kind eyes. "I beg your pardon," she said contritely, feeling herself blush. "Of course you may watch if it will help you to instruct me."

Fergus studied the canvas for a moment then took two steps back, studying her with his head cocked. "You are a fine woman, Mrs. Ramstad," he said, ignoring her blush. "Perhaps we're going about this all wrong. Let's take the afternoon to get to know one another. We'll talk while I sketch your face, and you sketch mine. Good?"

Elsa raised an eyebrow in surprise. "Faces? But I want to become adept at ships, not people."

"It is all intertwined, my dear," he said, handing her a sketch pad and a thick lead pencil. He took a seat five paces from her and picked up his own pad and pencil. "Now," he said, beginning to sketch with a smile, "tell me about Bergen. Your family. Why you came to America."

So began their friendship on that day in late January. In a matter of hours, Elsa knew a great deal about the man and liked him immensely. She learned that he was about seventy years of age, had been educated in Paris, had lived in Stockholm, London, and Hong Kong, and that he remained single. And he knew her story as well.

Long was also modest, and in contrast to most of his contemporaries, he did not moralize or construct allegories through his work. "Normally, I just do ships and coastlines, not beautiful women," he said with a wink. They had laid aside their sketch pads, and he was showing her some of his work.

Elsa smiled and continued walking along his gallery, where painting after painting hung. His ships had an American spirit to them that appealed to her—a keen pragmatism, an inventive splendor of form. He combined scrupulous detail with a realistic edge. Most had been done in the '50s and '60s. Many artists had surpassed him in fame since then, but Elsa still thought him one of the best.

"There is a spiritual quality to your work that I would like to emulate," she dared.

He looked up at her in surprise. "What do you mean?"

"The stillness, the nuances of light," she said, nodding to a picture of Boston Harbor that resembled her own. "Your entire atmosphere seems ethereal. Somehow you're able to remove yourself so that you do not come between the artwork and the audience. It's a gift."

Fergus guffawed. "Some would say it's a curse."

Elsa smiled at him knowingly. "Unable to accept a compliment even after all these years, Mr. Long?"

"As you will come to know, Mrs. Ramstad, a work is never quite right in the artist's eye."

Peder sat in the men's lobby of the hotel, smoking a fine Cuban cigar and enjoying the conversation about him. He still felt like an interloper, a boy floating in men's circles, and had to convince himself that he belonged there among them. He was, after all, president of Ramstad Yard, Camden. It was his duty to make friends among the decision makers of New York and around the world. For it was they who would make his shipping line successful.

"I tell you, Seattle lumber is some of the finest around. And they have scads of it," said Henry Whitehall—of Whitehall Lumber Company fame—then took a sip of his Scotch whiskey. Peder glanced at the glass the man had ordered for him, which remained untouched and sweating on a cloth napkin. Whitehall was tall with black hair salted with gray and coal black eyes. His countenance was fearsome. "There's a future there, and I mean to be a part of it."

"You plan to take off for some forsaken corner of Northern America?" asked James Kingsley, himself an iron baron and an old friend of Whitehall's. In contrast, he was short and stocky with a closely trimmed, gray beard. "I can just see Augusta's face," he added with a wink toward Peder. "No, I think you will spend the rest of your days in New York. She's as firmly ensconced in society here as my own dear Hazel."

"Well, if I can't convince the old woman to take off to territory unknown, then perhaps I'll simply invest."

"Here, here," said Kingsley, raising his crystal glass. An alert waiter came and filled it again after he sipped, pouring from a crystal decanter. James looked over at Peder. "Perhaps our young friend Ramstad here has the perfect entrée into the northwestern lumber market, eh? See there? He does not even imbibe. A wise man, I'd wager." He raised his glass again in a silent salute. Peder found it ironic.

Henry pursed his lips, raised his eyebrows, and looked Peder over. It was the first he had looked his way since James had introduced them. After a moment he nodded a bit. "Well, what do you have to say for yourself, Ramstad? Where will you take your ships? To the Far East? Or would you be satisfied running lumber for my company?"

Peder drew on his cigar and slowly exhaled. He hoped he posed as dramatic a picture as he sought to portray and was not turning green from the foul tobacco. "I would be happy to supply your company with lumber," he returned, "with a fat slice of profit for myself."

Both men laughed at his audacity. "You'll do fine," Henry said, nodding with appreciation at the younger man. "And I like your spirit. Let's talk some business, shall we? Tell me why you're building a schooner instead of a steamboat."

"As a matter of fact, we're planning on building our first steamboat soon after the next schooner. My partner is in Saint Paul now, gathering more information and the last of his financing. But I'll play straight with you, gentlemen: I am a sailing man through and through. It's my partner, Karl Martensen, who has the passion for steam. I want to try my hand at sailing a schooner. They're faster than clippers and wider at the bottom, perfect for hauling cargo such as lumber."

"Will your steamboat not be more reliable? And faster?"

"At times." Peder paused to look directly at both men. "But I prefer to trust the winds that God sends me to power my way. I have been successful so far. We'll try our hand at a steamship, but they are temperamental and given to boiler explosions and other disasters. I much prefer nature's way of travel—wind."

"I admire your spirit," said Kingsley. "I wish I were younger. I'd like to travel with you to Washington Territory."

"You'd be welcome," Peder said. He hesitated. "After all, I'm considering taking my wife along on our next voyage."

Both men looked up at him to see if he jested, then at one another. Whitehall smiled first.

"I believe I saw your wife in the lobby this morning with you," he said. "If you will permit me, I'll tell you that she is admirable in her carriage."

"He means stunning," James translated.

"Yes, well," Henry said with a glint of humor in his eye, "I only mean to say that I can see why a man would not like to leave a young wife such as Mrs. Ramstad for long."

"Hear, hear," James said.

Peder smiled and nodded, enjoying the subtle confirmation of his decision. After all, captains frequently took their wives along these days. Fretting over Elsa's safety was old-fashioned. And these last months had only further convinced him that he wanted her near, twenty-four hours a day. He exhaled and watched the fragrant smoke dissipate into the air, visualizing her amidst it.

Tora noted that Kristoffer stayed at the house later than usual after dinner, long after the boys were in bed. Outside, the wind howled and the snow swirled. She wondered if he was aggravated at having to leave the cozy little home and warm fire for the Spartan boards and makeshift bed in the mold loft each night. It mattered little, really. In a few months she would be gone, and he could once again reside in his own home. Silly conventions, she thought. They had not even kissed, and yet society demanded they sleep in separate buildings.

The fire cracked and popped noisily, and she looked up from her book, a novel by an American upstart named Twain. She liked the writer's spirit. But thoughts of the author left her as she glanced at Kristoffer and found him staring intently at her. "What?" she asked nervously.

He looked uncommonly handsome in the flickering light of the fire, and Tora understood that tiny seeds of love might be sprouting in her heart for the man. She stood and nervously bid him good night, moving as fast as she could, given her advanced pregnancy.

"Tora."

She turned, not wanting to stay, unable to leave. "Yes?" she asked, feigning disinterest.

"I need to speak to you, Tora." He rose and came near her. She backed up a step. His hand went to his neck, rubbing hard as if to pull away an ache. "You see . . . I think we ought to get married."

Tora snorted and walked around him, back to her seat—as if her sole intention was to pick up her forgotten book. "What an idea!"

He followed her, turned her around, and placed a hand on her cheek. "You are a complex woman," he said, "but I think I'm beginning to love you."

She dropped her eyes as she brought her own hand up to gently pull his away from her face. "I do not need your charity, Kristoffer."

"You need somebody. Despite what you try to tell the world."

"I can take care of myself."

"And your baby?" he asked quietly.

"I have plans for her too."

"I would like to be the father to a daughter," he said, acknowledging her assumption that the child would be a girl.

Her eyes flew to his face. He was really so kind, so dear. And he represented all that she didn't want in life.

"I'm sorry, Kristoffer. I really am. But it cannot be."

Kaatje stared out the window, watching swirling snow that seemed endless. Already it was piled high against the shanty—almost to the window ledge—and the only blessing was that it sealed out the wind. "Like an Eskimo in an igloo," Kaatje whispered to her one-month-old baby, Christina. The child was fussy that morning, and Kaatje wished for the hundredth time that Soren was coming soon. He had a way with the infant. As soon as Christina was in his arms, she tended to quiet and giggle.

Soren had told her that morning that he would not come back to the house until dinner. He was busy patching their makeshift barn to protect their one horse, dun cow, and chickens from the winter wind. Kaatje knew the animals were vital for their survival and so kept quiet upon hearing about the plan. Perhaps Soren would bring eggs when he came in. She comforted herself with the thought as she kneaded bread and set it by the stove to rise.

Christina whimpered on the bed, pulling her knees to her chest as if in pain. When Kaatje went to check on her, she was shocked at the heat that emanated from the tiny body. The child was burning with fever.

"Oh no," Kaatje whispered. How could she be ill? Neither Kaatje nor Soren had had even a sniffle in the last months . . . Then an idea took hold, despite Kaatje's effort to push it away.

Fred Marquardt had stopped by the day before in his sled, wondering if she had mail to take to town or any other needs. He had taken four letters and brought back a sack of flour and some butter for her. Before he left, she inquired about his wife, Claire.

"Oh, she's gettin' along," the man had said, "although she has a rotten case of the influenza."

"That's a shame," Kaatje said. "I do hope she will feel better soon."

"Oh, you know Claire," Fred said. "She'll plug along and be up and about before we know it."

As Kaatje remembered this conversation, she thought about the quiet, petite, and too-attractive Claire Marquardt. How had such a stunning woman ended up with such a plain man as Fred? Thinking about it made her uneasy. Perhaps Claire was restless, and knowing Soren's weakness . . .

It was possible that during her brief contact with Fred, Kaatje had picked up the illness and passed it along to her child. But what if it hadn't been from Fred? What if while Fred was away in town, Soren went to visit Claire himself? Kaatje had not seen him until suppertime yesterday, and when he came in, he seemed cold and distracted, content only to hold the baby close and stare at the fire, He had said little to her all evening—and had barely eaten anything.

Kaatje pulled Christina into her arms and walked about the room as the child wailed. She bounced, she rocked, she sang, but the baby obviously was unwell. Was it the result of another of Soren's indiscretions? Or had he already been with Claire Marquardt before she was sick? Kaatje's mind whirled. Yesterday when he went to her, was he disheartened because of her illness? Was that why he was so down the night before? After all, it was a perfect time for a tryst, with Kaatje believing him at work in the barn, and Fred away at town. Her mind went wild. Her heart felt like a stone.

I am making myself crazy, she thought. "Believe the best," she mumbled, unable to hear her own words over Christina's wail. But it mattered little. "Believe we have begun anew. No more of the bad habits, Soren. Right?"

Kaatje sat down to feed Christina, but soon after eating, the baby vomited all over the bed and her mother. Kaatje fought off tears as she cleaned up the mess, changed her dress, and fretted over the child. Finally Christina drifted off to sleep.

O God, Kaatje prayed. She felt like breaking out into a sweat herself when she thought of the many children who died of influenza each year. She gazed at her perspiring daughter, limp with fever. *Please heal Christina. And let me be wrong about Soren.*

She watched over the dozing baby all afternoon as she baked bread and pulled out some salt pork and butter to accompany it. At last Soren arrived.

"Hello, sweetheart." He greeted her with a grin, but it faded fast when he saw her face. "What? What is it?"

"It is Christina," she said, hurriedly shutting the door behind him. "She is sick. The influenza, I think," Kaatje added, carefully watching his face.

But he turned from her before she could read his expression, crossing the few feet of floor to the bed and baby. He pulled off his gloves and placed a roughened hand on the tender infant skin, then drew back as if singed. "She is burning up! I will go for Eira. She will know what to do."

Kaatje nodded. "Eat a little supper first. You will need your strength if it continues to storm." She looked out the window. The night was dark, and still the snow cascaded down upon them. "I do not know, Soren. Perhaps it is not wise for you to go tonight. Look. It still snows. It might be too dangerous. You could get lost."

"I will be fine," he said, his mouth full. He swiped a chunk of bread through the soft butter on his plate. "The Marquardts gave me an old pair of skis yesterday."

Kaatje froze. Soren glanced up at her and held her gaze. "What?"

"The . . . the Marquardts?"

"Yes. What of it?"

"I did not know . . . I did not know you had been there lately."

"Yes, well, I went to borrow an ax from Fred two days ago."

Kaatje rose and walked toward the window, not wanting him to see her expression. "And you spoke to Fred? He was there to give you the ax?"

"No. He was off checking on Old Lady Engvold. Mrs. Marquardt was there though. She gave me the skis. They were her father's, apparently, and since they got the sled, they rarely use them."

"Did she give you anything else?" Kaatje asked, hearing a chill enter her voice.

"No." He looked her in the eye. "Kaatje, are you asking me what I think you are asking?"

"Should I be?" She turned to face him, her hands trembling.

Soren's lip clamped shut, and he glared at her.

"Did you get close to Claire?" she dared. "Close enough to get the influenza and give it to Christina? Fred came by yesterday and said she is ill with it."

"Of course not! I mean, we were close enough for her to hand me the skis, but no more."

"No more?" She stared at him, and he dropped his gaze.

A second later he stood suddenly, and his tin plate clattered to the floor. Christina awakened and screamed in fury.

Soren crossed the creaky floor to Kaatje and shook his finger in her face. "I will not be interrogated in my home, do you hear me? We have started fresh here, Kaatje, and I will not tolerate any disrespect from you."

"Soren, I—"

"No, I do not want to hear it. I will be back shortly. I'll fetch Eira to tend to the baby."

With that, he pulled on his coat with quick, angry moves and slammed the door behind him. Kaatje watched through the window as his dim form disappeared into the night. When she turned to wearily pick up her crying daughter, Kaatje joined her, rocking back and forth on the bed as sobs tore at her throat. Never had she felt more alone.

t w e n t y

March 14, 1881

They were moored in a picturesque harbor of the West Indies that afternoon, and Elsa was completely enthralled by the translucent turquoise of the water. It was unlike any water . . . any color . . . she had ever seen. The Caribbean Sea held such miraculous hues of greens and blues that she wondered if she could convince Peder to stay yet another day. Other grand ships were anchored nearby, and Elsa felt drawn to them, wanting to paint their graceful forms as they floated on the gentle waves of the harbor. She was certain Mr. Fergus Long could not have been dragged from the spot, even if life and limb were threatened. She also wanted to capture the colors of the villages leading down to white sand beaches and the strange trees they called palms—and knew it could take her weeks to accurately portray the glory.

But she could tell from Peder's continual worried glances to the bank of clouds in the distance that he was anxious to get the *Sunrise* under sail and on toward their goal, a distant place past the Horn called Washington Territory. They were loaded with supplies for the growing cities in the Northwest and, in exchange, were to return home loaded with lumber for a man named Whitehall. Peder informed her that the man had financed quite a few shares in the voyage and, in so doing, guaranteed Whitehall Lumber Company first pick of all cargo on their return.

The ship had sailed beautifully since they left Camden, and Elsa was so happy to be there to see the brand-new white sails against azure skies that the days melted away quickly. What joy to see Ramstad Yard's first ship launched! And what could be better than sailing on her maiden voyage? Karl had come home from Minnesota ready to sail on the *Sunrise,* but eager to begin work on Ramstad Yard's first steamer. Elsa smiled as she remembered watching Peder the night before, debating with Karl over designs, and still vacillating over the wisdom of moving forward in steam at all. But he was getting closer to being convinced, and she was happy for Karl and thankful for what the decision would mean for his friendship with Peder. It was an affirmation of their relationship—as partners and as friends.

Kristoffer had remained at home again, this time to oversee the construction of the new schooner—to be built simultaneously with Karl's steamer—and to care for his family. Stefan had been promoted from steward to second mate, and Riley from seaman to third mate. At her insistence, Elsa covered Stefan's previous duties in caring for the captain. Karl, as usual, served as first mate. Some new sailors had signed on for this voyage, but many of the men were those who had traveled with them from Bergen. Elsa had learned that Peder was gaining a reputation as a fair and good captain, consequently earning him a loyal crew.

She herself felt closer to Peder than ever, but tried to stay out of his way and keep her mouth shut. She wanted to fit in well and not be seen as a nuisance or a hindrance. She wanted him to forget that she was along, until he looked for her. Because this was the beginning of the rhythm of their new life: at home in Camden-by-the-Sea during the winters and on the water during the rest of the year.

Something seemed to have clicked for Peder while they stayed in New York in January. She wondered if the scales might have been tipped by the persuasiveness of Fergus Long, who had insisted after their week together, that squirreling Elsa away in some house would be strangling her artistic muse. "She needs fresh air, the song of the sails," he told her befuddled-looking husband. "If you will not take her with you, she will need to find some other method of inspiration for her work. Would it not be more advantageous to you both for her to simply travel along?"

Elsa had not put Long up to it, but was thrilled to hear him lecture Peder anyway. She had talked until she was blue in the face. Then she had left it up to God . . . and miracles transpired. Was this not a miracle? She leaned back on her chair above the captain's cabin, closing her eyes to the sun and feeling the rays warm her face. It was hot and humid, but the breeze off the water smelled fresh and invigorated her.

She wore a cap-sleeved shift of blue and white cotton with no stays or crinoline beneath. The neckline was teardrop-shaped, allowing some ventilation. It was blessedly comfortable, and due to the ninety-degree heat, Peder had nodded his approval over her girlish attire. Elsa was just settling back for a short nap when Karl's voice startled her awake.

"All hands!" He yelled. "All hands! On deck immediately for the captain's announcement!"

Elsa sneaked a peek at the first mate, wondering again, as she had several times in the past two months, what had happened to him in Minnesota. He had come home somehow changed; he was even more aloof, lost in his own dreams. Perhaps speaking with others who were as excited about the future of steam had taken him further from his Camden friends. Her own conversations with him had been short, and even then she felt as if he were looking through her. Maybe he had met a woman . . . Elsa smiled. That was it. She was sure of it. Karl Martensen was in love! The thought relieved her heart, and she wondered briefly over it until Peder's voice brought her back to the present.

"As you know," Peder was bellowing, his chest puffed out in what Elsa termed his captain stance. He paced as he talked, and Elsa smiled, enjoying the sight of her handsome husband lecturing the crew, his curly brown hair glinting in the sun. This voyage was different from their Atlantic crossing from Bergen. Coming from Norway, Peder had been as much host as captain. On this trip he was all captain, and Elsa thrilled to see him in command, his crew watching him with rapt respect. What she would have missed if she had remained at home in Camden!

"As you know," he repeated for effect, "I require that all able seamen on my ship be able to swim. Now all of you claim to be decent swimmers, but I want to see it for myself. So off with you. Over the side! Karl will go down in a longboat for those of you who tire easily," he said.

Several of the men grumbled, and some shifted their feet back and forth, but a full two-thirds of the crew clambered to the edge of the *Sunrise* and, with great whoops of glee, jumped, somersaulted, and dived off for the waterline twenty feet below. Their splashes and hollers made Elsa laugh, and she yearned to dive in after them. A swim would be a blessed reprieve from the heat! Without thinking, she climbed down the ladder to the main deck and climbed up onto the rail. She wavered there, her breath caught short by the height. Still, there was no time like the present, she told herself, dimly hearing Peder lecturing those who remained on deck that "swimming is vital if you barnacles hope to survive a shipwreck!"

Patiently, he was giving them a lesson on what to do, reassuring them that they could climb down the ropes to the sea and practice while holding on, when Elsa took a deep breath, eyes wide, and made a slow, graceful dive off the edge. The last thing she heard was Karl's astonished "Elsa!" and the swimming crew's shouts of affirmation when fingers met water, parted it, and allowed her to slip into the cool, refreshing depths.

When she emerged, feeling as free as the porpoises that frequently traveled alongside the *Sunrise,* Karl was turning the longboat toward her, and all the men still aboard were staring down openmouthed at her, Peder along with them. His expression soon turned grim, and Elsa looked away, feeling the first pang of dismay at her impulsive act and wanting to enjoy a moment more of this blessed freedom before returning to the ship. She looked toward the men in the water, who grinned at her, although the second mate, Stefan, stared at her a bit too long for her liking.

"Elsa!" Karl said over his shoulder, rowing toward her. "Hang on. I will be there in a moment."

"Do not be silly!" she called. She looked up at the ship again, consciously avoiding Peder's dark gaze. "Hey, you up there! Able seamen! If a woman can do that, can't you at least *climb* into the water?"

The challenge surprised the men, who still hung back on board. Within seconds, they were over the side, every one, and clambering down the ropes to the water below. Elsa smiled and dared to look at her husband. She laughed as he shook his head in wonder. She had been forgiven, apparently. But then his gaze left her, and his brow furrowed. She knew that look of concern and followed his line of vision.

Karl arrived with the longboat, blocking her view, but shortly another rowboat came alongside, carrying four strangers. The men stared at Elsa in wonder, and for the first time, she felt some embarrassment. She suddenly realized that her skirts were billowing up about her, and who knew how much of her legs was visible in the crystal waters. She felt naked facing their leers—particularly the man in the bow who appeared to be in command—and angry as they continued to look at her. Elsa glanced up at Karl, wanting to climb aboard and escape, but he was steadily studying the visitors.

"Well, well, well," said the man in the bow, his accent obviously

British. "What have we here? I come to extend my greetings to the *Sunrise,* and what do I find? An enchanting mermaid!" He bowed at the waist. "Captain Mason Dutton at your service, *madam.*" His eyes were merry, but derision lurked behind the laughter. He looked up toward Peder, standing at the rail of the *Herald.* "A female to service the crew?" he asked insolently.

Elsa noticed the crew had quieted, treading water to hear what transpired. They were all on alert. Just because of her? Her heart sank. Was this how she defined staying out of Peder's way?

"My wife," Peder said thinly, darkly, daring the man to say more.

"I beg your pardon," Captain Dutton said, obviously taken aback. "A most unfortunate assumption." He glanced over at Elsa. "If I were to have a wife as lovely, I too would encourage her to swim . . . but not so brazenly with the crew."

Karl stood, his hand shifting to the side arm at his waist. The boat rocked slightly. Elsa felt a blush rush up her neck. She wondered if she was turning purple from the embarrassment of the situation.

Peder raised one hand to his friend, while continuing to stare back at Dutton. "I am Captain Peder Ramstad. Did you come here to insult my wife and challenge me, Captain Dutton?"

Mason shook his head, smiling in regret. "Not at all, my good man. Forgive me if it sounded as such. What you do with your wife is your own concern." He looked down, sighed, and then looked back up at Peder. "Again, my apologies to you, and to you, Mrs. Ramstad." His glance toward Elsa this time was remote, polite. "Shall we start anew? My name is Mason Dutton, captain of my own merchant mariner, the *Lark,*" he said. "As you can see, I have become quite removed from social niceties and am starved for polite society. I wondered if I might impose and ask you to join me for dinner."

Karl slowly sat down again and watched Peder's face. Elsa did the same. As one, the crew waited too, still treading water or holding on to the lines against the ship.

Peder studied his visitor for a moment then spoke. "Thank you for the invitation, captain. But why don't you join us instead? We have a fine cook. Dinner will be served promptly at six. You may bring two men with you, no more."

Was he mad? Inviting the man to dinner? Elsa's eyes flew to Karl's, but his expression told her nothing. Then he glanced down at her. "Protocol," he whispered. Ah, so that was it. Some antiquated sense of seagoing chivalry demanded that Peder invite the man to dinner.

"Good enough," Mason said. "Until tonight," he said, glancing over at Elsa again. He tipped his short-billed cap toward her. "*Mrs. Ramstad.*"

Peder watched closely as Dutton's crewmen turned the longboat around and rowed back toward their own ship, an older clipper. Every nerve in his body seemed taut with energy. Then with a quick hand motion and without looking at Elsa, he directed Karl to bring her back aboard. Discreetly, Karl pulled Elsa into the boat then rowed over to the side of the *Sunrise*. A few of the men began to splash and dunk one another, but the festive mood was gone.

Four sailors heaved at the capstan, hauling the longboat with Karl and Elsa back aboard. The men averted their eyes as she climbed out, and after one tearful, sorrowful glance at Peder, Elsa hurried to their cabin.

Peder could tell that she was miserable. She had made a poor choice and was now paying for it. He would need to say little to her, perhaps simply caution her at a later date and make sure she had a chance for a private swim once in a while. The fact that he had overlooked one of her needs seemed obvious to him now. He himself had been excited at the thought of a refreshing swim. Thus a part of him could not fault his wife, who, sweltering in the heat, had moved on impulse.

After Karl had climbed out too, he joined Peder at the side. In the distance, they could see Dutton and his men climbing the ropes to board the *Lark*.

"What do you make of him?" Peder asked.

"I don't like it. The man reeks of piracy."

So he wasn't alone in his assumptions, Peder thought. Piracy had been largely eradicated since the first part of the century by British patrols, but merchant seamen could never be too careful. Indeed, Peder knew many captains who trained their men to fight and armed them in case of attack. In contrast, Peder chose men with strong builds, but did not purchase weapons for them. They were allowed to bring knives—the tool of the trade—and one side arm aboard, the latter to be kept in their sea chests.

"I agree," said Peder. "That's why I didn't want to leave the ship tonight."

"Perhaps I shall double the dogwatch," Karl said.

"See to it," Peder affirmed.

"Tell Cook to expect six for dinner," he added. "And I would appreciate it if you would join us." Peder and Elsa had eaten alone since they left Camden, wanting the time to themselves.

"Done."

Peder turned to go then looked back at Karl. "As a further precaution, let's station two armed men in our bedroom while we dine," he said. "Just in case."

"And two at the door?"

"No. We don't want to alarm him. Bring the men to me at quarter to six, and we'll hide them away in the bedroom. I want Dutton to think we are unsuspecting. There's no telling what he's after, but perhaps we'll find out tonight."

Peder left Karl's side and went to his cabin. Inside, Elsa was sitting on the bed, weeping quietly. He shut the door behind him, waiting for her to look up. When she did, it nearly rent his heart in two. "Elsa, Elsa," he said, no chastisement in his voice, just remorse at her decision.

"Oh, Peder, can you ever forgive me? It started so innocently, really . . ." She paused to search his face. "The men were diving in, and all I could think about was swimming as children . . . diving off the rocks into that wonderful, glacial water."

He knelt beside the bed and took her face in his hands. "I know it began innocently, sweetheart. I know your heart, and there isn't anything treacherous in it. But I need you to always stop and think before you act. The crew is generally trustworthy. Karl and I hand-picked them. But you never know. And with sharks like Dutton circling—"

"If he is a shark, why invite him for dinner?"

"I want a chance to see him again in a different light. Maybe I misjudged his intentions. But if they are evil, I want to get a handle on him before he attacks."

"Attacks?" Elsa's hand flew to her throat. "Is he . . . is he a pirate?"

"I hope not. Piracy is rare these days. But there still are a few merchant marines who pretend to be honest businessmen, but in fact make their living by stealing from others. The *Sunrise* could be in danger if we're not alert."

She stared down at her lap, disconsolate. "This is why you feared taking me along."

"Yes." His tone sounded as grim as he felt. Had he made a terrible decision by bringing her? Yet he had never known life could be so good, so full, until Elsa joined him. He felt at peace about it, even in the face of possible danger. They would simply have to trust that God would keep them safe.

Elsa suddenly stood. She sighed and straightened her shoulders. "I will make you proud of me, Peder. You will see. I will be the quintessential lady, a treasure as the captain's wife."

"I am already proud of you, Elsa," he said, touching her cheek gently. "I already treasure you."

She smiled and looked down at the floor. "If you will excuse me, I must prepare for dinner. We have guests coming, you know."

"So I heard," he said, watching as she moved away to pour water into a shallow bathtub.

❧

When Captain Mason Dutton arrived that evening with his first and second mate in tow, he was the consummate gentleman, displaying none of the rakish disregard for Elsa's feelings that he had shown earlier. Conversation was lighthearted and easy, and Peder began to wonder if he had misjudged the man. Dutton had a delightful sense of humor and seemed from all angles just another businessman. Perhaps they had gotten off on the wrong foot, Peder mused, smiling as Dutton cracked another joke. After all, there *were* captains who brought along women for their crews. None were his friends, of course, but it was not entirely unusual.

He glanced at Karl as Cook served dessert. His friend's eyes were still alert and his mouth tense, leaving Peder to fulfill the social niceties. Karl's job as first mate was to make sure the crew and ship were safe. Clearly he still wasn't convinced that Mason Dutton was not a threat.

Then Peder looked toward Elsa. She had been conspicuously quiet throughout dinner, obviously wanting the evening to be over despite Dutton's tacit disregard of her. She looked fetching in her violet gown, and if the man could ignore her in that, Peder thought, then he wasn't interested.

By the time the captain of the *Lark* rose to leave, taking his two men with him, Peder had decided that he had been all wrong about the man. Dutton had been nothing but polite and charming all evening. Peder was even a bit embarrassed at having to let his own men out of his bedroom after their guests rowed away. Maybe it was having Elsa along that put him on edge, he thought, his eyes flitting to her. Perhaps this was just one of many adjustments he would have to make in having her on board.

She looked over at him, her eyes sleepy. "I am glad that's over."

"Come now," he chided her. "Captain Dutton was nothing but charming."

"All I could think of was my humiliation this afternoon."

"Nonsense," he said, putting an arm around her shoulders as they stood on deck, looking across the harbor. "All that Captain Dutton will remember is a nymph in the waters and a lady at the dinner table. I will be the talk of the seas. All men will envy my good fortune in choosing a bride."

She looked up at him carefully. "So you are not horrified by me?"

"Horrified?" He leaned closer. "Come. I think we need to get you out of that stifling dress and corset. It will help you think more clearly."

She returned his mischievous smile then walked away, discreetly entering their cabin several minutes before him as had become their habit.

In the dim light of a sliver moon, Karl watched as the intruders climbed over the side, moving as subtly as serpents. He motioned to Stefan to wait for a moment—let them think they had gotten aboard without discovery—before his men were to open fire. Stefan nodded, and Karl crept forward on the deck, a gun in one hand and a knife in the other. Then without waiting another second, Karl shot the first man in his line of vision then another. With an unearthly shout, the men of the *Lark* cascaded over the side and onto the *Sunrise*'s deck, charging the sailors who defended her. Guns went off, one after the other, and Peder emerged from the cabin, half-dressed and armed with a revolver. The rest of the *Sunrise* crew poured from the companionway stairs, each carrying their own weapons. Karl was glad they had handpicked their crew. In a fight such as this, they would need every man.

He had only been in hand-to-hand battle once before, when he and Peder served as seamen to Captain Lehman, who had been as adamant about self-defense as Peder was about having a crew who could swim. Lehman had beaten them all in fistfights, going to great lengths to train them to defend themselves and prepare for the worst. That training had meant their survival in a fight such as this one off the coast of South Africa and later had saved their lives when he and Peder had been attacked on the streets of Seville.

The cabin door slammed shut behind Peder, and Karl took heart as he heard the lock crack into place. Elsa was safe in the cabin.

Just then a man charged at him, screaming, and Karl knifed him as he neared. With a gurgle, the man fell to the deck.

"Karl! Behind you!" Peder yelled, and Karl whirled as a sailor jumped him from the cabin roof. As they rolled, Karl shot him in the gut, and his assailant went limp. The smell of burning oil and light brought his eyes to the rail, where several sailors climbed in bearing torches in their teeth. Fire. If they were not careful, it would be the death of them all.

Karl had heard about pirates who burned ships to the waterline then pillaged their remains, paltry as they might be. He reloaded his gun and quickly shot the last man over the rail, who shouted in pain and fell back over the side. But he had missed the first two. Where were they?

Karl's heart stopped as he looked past Peder—who fought off one man then turned to face Captain Dutton—to the sailors with the torches. Running, they were touching their torches to anything flammable, including the cabin. *The cabin. Elsa!*

Karl shoved his gun into his belt, unable to take the time to reload. A man jumped him, pulling him backward in a stranglehold. Then flipping him to his stomach, his attacker landed on top of Karl, driving the wind from him. Karl was struggling, unable to free himself, when Riley charged his assailant with a rebel yell. Quickly the weight on his back was removed, and Karl struggled to his feet.

The ship was afire. Worse, the captain's cabin was in flames. Elsa opened the door, coughing and holding a club to her chest. She was clothed in her nightdress, her hair down, and looked like an angel emerging from Meshach, Shadrach, and Abednego's fiery grave. Karl's heart caught as a man stole around the corner and grabbed Elsa. She screamed when he grabbed her, flailing at him with the club. But he was behind her, rendering her blows useless.

Fury rose in Karl's chest at the sight. With a low growl, he followed the man to the stern, trying to focus on him and not Elsa, who continued to scream and beat his back and legs with her club. All about him, men were firing weapons, slicing with swords, gutting with knives, or punching with their fists. Groans and screams and moans filled the air. The acrid smoke of gunpowder stung his eyes, making them tear.

Elsa's kidnapper was nearing the railing when Karl caught up with them. He was just three feet behind when the large man set Elsa down on the deck, ripped the club from her hand, and threw it into the sea. He was laughing, holding her hair in one hand and pulling her head back for a kiss when Karl's knife caught him in the kidney.

The man sank to the ground, and Elsa covered her face with her hands as if she could hide from the frightening scene around her.

"Are you all right?" Karl asked her urgently, grabbing her by the arms. He had to yell to be heard over the noise behind them.

Elsa dropped her hands then her eyes widened. "Behind you!"

He whirled to face two swarthy men, advancing from either side. "We don't want you, man," one tried to convince Karl. "We got orders for the lady."

So they *were* after Elsa. She was a valuable commodity in these parts. A white woman with blond hair could fetch a nice price. Part of the cargo, Dutton probably thought.

"Never," Karl said. "Take a step closer, and you're dead men."

"He speaks bravely," said the second man with derision. "Don't worry, mate, we're prepared to meet our maker iffin it's time."

"It will not be your maker." He slashed forward and stabbed one with his knife, then whipped around to elbow the other in the face. With both assailants down, Karl looked at Elsa and motioned with his head. *Over the side,* he mouthed. He raised his eyebrows to hurry her along. If she would disappear and the *Sunrise* crew could put out the fires—as half of them were working at doing—then perhaps the intruders would retreat.

Suddenly strong arms gripped him from behind. Karl winced as the unseen assailant forcefully pulled his arms back. Another man came around in front of him and punched him in quick succession in the stomach then under the chin. His breath flew from him; his teeth rattled. Still he found the strength to raise his legs and kick away the man before him. Karl was gasping for breath when a shot rang in his ears, and the arms around him suddenly dropped away. He turned and saw that Peder had downed his attacker with a shot to the head. The sound still rang in Karl's ears, and he wondered if he would ever hear again.

He looked around. The fires were out, and the men were back to hand-to-hand combat. Their chances were better now, at least, and the *Sunrise* was all right for the moment. Peder tripped, and Dutton advanced on him with a sword. Karl tackled the intruding captain to the deck. He punched the man's perfect chin before he could rise. Dutton's first mate advanced on Karl, and he jumped away as the man slashed at him with a huge bowie knife. Distantly he felt the slash as it cut him across the chest, but felt no pain.

His attention was on two sailors, who pointed out toward the bay as if they had spotted something. *Elsa.* They had seen her in the light of the moon, he was sure of it. Ripping off their shoes, they dove in after her.

twenty-one

*D*esperately weary, Elsa was almost ashore when she felt a
hand on her calf. In terror, she dragged herself out of the water but was hampered by her clinging skirts. She focused on the
tree line not forty feet from her, thinking that if she could just make
it there, she could hide. But she would have to fight off the man who
held her first.

Large hands gripped her leg, and she heard heavy panting that
echoed hers from the effort of swimming so far. Desperately she cast
about as he dragged her back toward the sea. Her hands closed
around a large scallop shell as he turned her over. "Thought you were
gettin' away from me, missy?" Another man stood behind him, grinning in the moonlight.

She slashed at the immediate man's face, but only nicked his
shoulder, making him bellow in anger. Quick blood spotted the gash
as Elsa turned and ran, struggling to get up the beach. Terror gripped
her heart as the man caught up with her and pulled her to a stop.

Dear God, her heart cried out. *Deliver me!*

He shoved her to the ground, holding her by the hair. Before she could move, he was on top of her, reaching, pulling, forcing his mouth on hers. She bit and screamed and kicked, but the man was large and agile, easily fending off her blows. Elsa felt defeated and worn. What good would it do to resist? Even if she escaped, there was another nearby. Still, her heart told her to fight, and she made one last effort.

Suddenly, the man was pulled off of her. She distantly watched as Karl punched him until he was out cold. Dimly she realized she still screamed, but could not seem to stop herself.

Karl came toward her, arms outstretched as if trying to soothe a caged animal. "Elsa, it's all right. He can't hurt you."

"No! There's another one!" She looked about wildly, certain the other man would attack from the waters or tropical foliage behind them. Where had he gone?

"No, Elsa," Karl said in a low voice, his hair dripping onto his soaked shirt. "There were two. I got both of them."

"No, no! There will be more. We must hide!"

"Come," he said soothingly. "We'll go into the forest and hide."

She nodded and ran through the dense underbrush, ignoring thorns that lashed at her legs, and through a bank of palms that shielded them from the harbor. There in a tiny clearing, she felt safer. But she trembled so much that she wondered if she could remain standing a moment longer.

Karl reached her just in time. As soon as she was in his arms, she sank, and Karl crouched, lifted her in his arms then sat down with her. With his back against a palm tree, he held her against his chest. "Shhh," he said, stroking her wet hair. "You're safe now. The *Sunrise* crew will see to the rest of them."

"What about Peder?"

"He's fine. I saw him before I went in after you." He caressed her head, waiting for her to stop trembling. "It was awful, Elsa. But the worst is over. You're safe, sweetheart. You're safe."

For a moment it was as if no one else existed. In her relief and gratitude, Elsa wanted nothing more than to be close to this dear friend who had saved her. To concentrate on his loving eyes, not the evil beyond. He was her strength, her shield. She turned her head and looked up at him in the soft moonlight. "Thank you, Karl."

His eyes closed for a moment, then he opened them to look at her from under heavy lids. "Elsa, Elsa," he groaned. She frowned at his tone, wondering if he was hurt. Then, cradling her head in the crook of one arm, Karl laid her down on the forest floor and kissed her before she could say a word.

Peder sensed that the fight was waning. They were slowly gaining the upper hand over the marauders, and it was a good thing. Many of his crew were injured or dead, and the *Sunrise* had sustained damage from the fire and the melee. The thing that concerned him most, however, was that he had not seen Elsa since she emerged from the smoky cabin. He had tried to get to her, but was unable to free himself. After Karl had tackled Dutton, Peder had glimpsed his friend diving over the edge. Had Elsa escaped? Was Karl going after her? Was she all right? His hands grew damp with fear. It infuriated him that he could not free himself long enough to see to her safety himself.

When the fury evolved into energy and renewed vigor, he turned toward Dutton, who was once again on his feet. Peder picked up a saber from a fallen sailor and, although he was no fencer, went after the rogue captain like a madman on the warpath. Dutton backed off, warding off his clumsy blows with a surprised look on his face. He managed to hold Peder off at swords' points for a moment.

"You think you can eat my food, ogle my ship?" Peder said, tense with waiting for Dutton's next move. They each panted, chests heaving, worn from the effort of sustained battle. "You think you can burn her to the waterline and pillage my cargo?"

Dutton moved left, returning his gaze but saying nothing, breathing hard.

"But above all that, you think I will simply disregard the way you looked at my wife, the way you spoke to her?"

"I will make you a bargain."

"What?" Peder asked with a laugh. "What can you possibly offer me?"

"Let me go, and your wife will live."

Peder froze. "What are you talking about? Elsa is safely ashore, hidden from you and your scurvy crew."

"No. If they value their lives, my men have taken your Elsa and hauled her aboard the *Lark* for safekeeping. She is valuable, you know."

Peder gritted his teeth and, moving suddenly, shoved Dutton's rapier aside and broad-shouldered him to the ground. They ended up on the deck, Peder on top, his saber against Dutton's neck. He battled against the urge to slit the man's throat right then. He leaned closer to the pirate. "You had better pray that she is unhurt."

"Isn't that your prayer?" Dutton asked insolently.

In a rage, Peder hit him. Dutton quieted as he cradled his head.

Peder looked up to see several of his men surrounding them. "All clear?" he growled.

"They've turned tail and run, Cap'n," Stefan said.

"And the first mate?" he asked.

"Over the side, Cap'n," put in another. "He went after the two louts who were chasing Mrs. Ramstad."

Peder swallowed hard. So Elsa *had* gone overboard, chased by Dutton's men. Was she all right? Had Karl gotten to her in time?

"You there, tie up Dutton and make sure he does not leave," Peder ordered. "Stefan, come with me. You're unhurt?"

Stefan nodded. The second mate was not overly tall, but stocky and broad-shouldered. If Elsa and Karl were still in danger, Peder would need someone by his side. "You are an able swimmer?"

"Aye, Cap'n, one of the first in this afternoon."

"Good enough. Let's make sure my wife and first mate are safe and sound." Peder did not wait for Stefan's agreement. He picked up a large bowie knife from another fallen sailor, placed it in his clenched teeth, and dove overboard.

The salt water stung against Peder's cuts and grazes as he hit the surface and began swimming, but its sting served to revive him. *O God,* he prayed silently as his arms and legs propelled him smoothly and swiftly through the water. *Let them be all right. Please don't let me be too late.*

Two shots rang out from the *Sunrise,* and Peder grimaced as shouts carried over the water.

"Cap'n!" Stefan shouted. "It's Dutton and his men! They're getting away!"

"Let them go," Peder grumbled, treading water. "First things first." He had to see to his wife, then quickly get back to his ship.

Before long he and Stefan were stealthily walking ashore, wanting to gauge the situation before making their presence known. He nodded to the two bodies on the beach, and Stefan went to ascertain their condition. Looking one way then the other, Peder moved closer to the tropical forest. The *Lark* was a good quarter mile from shore. Were the two sailors lying prone on the sand the only marauders who had given chase? Maybe Karl had killed them and hidden Elsa away! He knelt as Stefan joined him, listening for anything more than the breeze in the palms. Nothing.

"Elsa!" he whispered loudly. Before him, visible in the moonlight, he could see where someone had trampled their way into the underbrush . . . or where someone had been chased . . .

"Elsa!" he tried a bit louder, his heart pounding in fear. "Karl!"

It was a long moment before Karl realized that Elsa was pushing him away. He was so convinced that her feelings were similar to his, so carried away by the closeness of the moment, the sensual pull of damp, cool fabric over warm bodies, that he ignored all else. All thoughts of Alicia Hall . . . of Peder . . . flew from his mind. When he came to his senses, he leaned back, and Elsa used the moment to push him away. Stunned, he watched as she stood and shook her head, as if to erase what had just transpired. Through the shadows and shafts of moonlight, Elsa backed away, looking at him as if he were one of the pirates.

He hopped to his feet, his hands out, beseeching her to understand. "Elsa, Elsa, forgive me! It was just too much! You could have been killed! I'm sorry I kissed you. I wasn't thinking. I was only so glad that you were alive, unhurt . . ." He shook his head and studied her. They were making no progress, just advancing across the small clearing in a desperate dance. Elsa still looked stunned. Surely she had suspected! Surely she had wanted the kiss as much as he had wanted to kiss her!

"Elsa, you must understand by now. Surely you've known. I've tried to forget it, to shove it away. But each time you come near, I can't, Elsa. I'm in love with you!"

"No—"

"Yes! I've been in love with you since we returned to Bergen last year and I saw you waiting high on the hill. But you never looked my way. It was always Peder, Peder. Why? Was it his money?"

She looked at him with an incredulous expression of outrage.

He ran his hand through his damp hair, feeling the grit of sand. "How can I make you understand?"

She kept shaking her head as if to awake herself from a bad dream.

"Please understand, Elsa. I did not want these feelings. I begged God to take them away. But I cannot rid myself of them. I've come to believe that God wants us together because—"

"Stop!" she commanded.

Karl froze, waiting.

"Don't say another word. You simply make it worse."

"But surely—"

"Elsa! Karl!" Peder burst into the clearing behind him, but Karl did not turn. He could only stare at Elsa and watch her expression turn to one of relief at Peder's arrival. It was as if he watched her being pulled away from him forever, like an iceberg out to sea.

"You're safe!" Peder rushed toward Elsa, and she ran into his arms, her face already turned away from Karl's.

Peder hugged her then held her away, seeing the dark stain of blood on her dress front. "Elsa, are you all right? Are you hurt?"

Elsa shook her head and looked toward Karl.

"Are you all right, man?" Peder asked in concern, looking at Karl's chest.

For the first time, Karl noticed the wound that bloodied his white shirt. But he knew that the worst wound he bore was deep inside him. At that moment Stefan arrived, but Karl barely looked at him.

"Thanks, brother, for protecting my wife," Peder said soberly, taking a step across the clearing to shake Karl's hand. But Karl stepped back from his friend's proffered hand, staring into Elsa's eyes.

It was over. It was all over.

There would be no going back.

His actions had changed everything.

<h1 style="text-align:center">t w e n t y - t w o</h1>

Elsa paused, her pen poised over the blank paper. For a moment she allowed herself to think of Karl. It had been over a month since the attack on the *Sunrise,* Dutton's escape on the *Lark,* and the revelation of Karl's feelings. Had she known all along, or had her own naiveté made her blind to the warning signs? Kaatje had even commented on it. Did she just not want to hear the truth? Had she hurt Karl more in being so stubbornly blind to the truth?

She agonized over it, but could resolve nothing in her own mind and heart. Perhaps writing would be cathartic, she thought, picking up her pen again and dipping it into the inkwell.

> *29 April 1881*
> *Dearest Kaatje,*
>
> *I pray this finds you well and nursing a healthy baby. Do I have an honorary niece or nephew? Mail has not caught up with us yet, though we hope to find a package awaiting us in San Francisco. Perhaps then I*

*shall discover your news. Let us see . . . The little
mite must be near to four months old by now? It
seems impossible that you could be a mother for as
long as that, and I have yet to meet the little man. Or
is it the little woman?*

Elsa paused and thought about Tora. Was she truly an aunt by
now? She felt a brief twinge of guilt for not remaining by her sister's
side, but then quickly repeated to herself why she had left: Innocent
or not, the girl had to learn, and it would be painful lessons that
might shape her into a woman. Then her thoughts naturally turned
to the recurring question of who the father could have been. Tora always refused to say, and Elsa, embarrassed over the whole mess, had
not pressed her. An image of Soren entered her head, but she dismissed it, feeling terribly sinful even imagining that such an affair had
transpired. No, better to forget recriminations and marry her sister to
someone respectable, someone who would care for her and her child.
Perhaps the whole experience would force Tora to grow up and marry
Kristoffer, as she should.

*I, on the other hand, am still without child, de-
spite my desperate hope for one—and not for want of
trying. I suppose that God has insight that I do not,
and the child will come when it is right. In the meantime, I am traveling with Peder to Washington
Territory, the first voyage on which he has allowed me
along.*

Once again Elsa thought about the attack, but decided not to
mention it. Kaatje would only fret if she thought Elsa in danger. And
the danger was long past. The *Sunrise* had been repaired and was
ready to face the Horn, just a month behind schedule.

*We were given the opportunity to remain here in
the West Indies this last month and a half, and I have*

completed a painting of which I feel sure Fergus Long would be proud. I love it because it will always re-mind me of this—Elsa paused, reflecting on word choice—*idyllic cove and the adventures encountered here. The only sadness in it is my memory that it is here that we parted ways with our dear friend Karl.*

Feeling claustrophobic as first mate, Karl has left us, unexpectedly opting to move to Saint Paul, Minnesota, to accept an offer to pursue his own steamboat enterprise with some railroad baron. This came as some surprise, as Peder had planned to build Karl's steamboat after this next schooner. But appar-ently he was decided and so eager, he could not finish our voyage west. Instead he hopped a merchant vessel heading toward New York. He should arrive in Saint Paul within a few weeks. I do hope that his new ven-ture goes well. I fear we will see precious little of him in the future.

"But that will be our saving grace," she whispered, staring at her words. What kept her from spilling all of the story onto the page? Why keep it a secret from her best friend? But Peder did not even know what had transpired, she concluded. He had looked at her with some suspicion after Karl had left in such a hurry. But he was simply casting about, trying to find some reason for Karl's irrational decision and behavior. Peder's countenance had turned from bewilderment to anger when they had returned to the ship and he discovered Karl's plan to leave. Elsa shivered as she remembered their heated argument in the sitting room. She had huddled on the edge of the bed in the next room, listening, unable to tear herself away, terrified by what was transpiring.

"What has happened to you?" Peder had roared in frustration. "Something monumental must've happened for you to behave so!"

"Nothing has happened. I simply feel I am on the wrong track. That God has a different path for me to follow. John Hall has offered me this opportunity—"

"As have I! Why not remain with friends and build your business alongside us?"

"You do not understand. There is more to it. John will have my steamboat done by the time I get there, not in another year. I can begin my own enterprise now." His tone sounded half sure.

Peder was silent for a moment. Elsa could almost picture his face. "I do not understand, man. In our yard, you will have your own vessel in a year, built to your specifications. Why do I get the feeling that you are running from something? Why come all this way just to turn around? Is it money?"

"No, no. How many times do I have to tell you? I wanted to make sure you were going to be all right, that the *Sunrise* was shipshape. Surely you won't encounter anything worse than the *Lark*'s attack. The *Sunrise* is almost repaired, and the injured or dead seamen replaced—"

"With men I doubt in some respects," Peder interrupted.

"They are sound. And so is the *Sunrise*. You will be fine without me."

Peder hesitated, then spoke. "Why do I feel like something has changed between us? You are . . . distant."

"I do not know what you're talking about. Look, the *William Jeffries* sets sail for the States at sunrise, and I intend to board her tonight if the captain will have me."

"Why are you running out on me?" Peder asked, his voice rising. "There is an aspect to this story that is hidden from me. Never in the ten years we've traveled together have I seen you act this way. Why are you not telling me all of it, Karl?" He sounded exasperated.

"My business is my own," Karl said sharply.

"Your business? Your business? Is not your business also mine? Aren't you intertwined with Ramstad Yard?"

"I was, once," Karl said, his voice rising to meet Peder's. He changed tactics. "Was it ever going to be ours, Peder? I mean, really *ours?* Were you ever really going to get to my steamboat, or would there always be another schooner you wanted to get into the works first? Were you just playing me along, using me?"

Peder sputtered, and from her bed, Elsa could imagine his enraged face. "Do not take this path, Karl," he warned. "You will regret it."

"I already regret it," Karl returned. "I regret ever planning a business with you. I'm leaving, Peder. It is better for both of us. I'm tired of living under the Ramstad umbrella like my father before me. I'm tired of competing with my best friend. Can we not part amicably?"

There was only silence in response.

"I wish you could see my side in this, Peder, I really do." From the other side of the wall, it sounded as if Karl was walking toward the door. "You may send my shares in the *Sunrise* to an address in Saint Paul that I will forward to you."

"Fine. If that's your stance," Peder said, "I am better off without you."

There was silence for a moment. Then Karl spoke one last time, his voice low. "Yes. You are better off without me. Good-bye, Peder. God be with you. Bid good-bye to Elsa too."

And with that he had gone. Elsa had not even glimpsed his face again, which left her feeling both relieved and uneasy. Was she supposed to go to him? Try and make amends? Find their footing in friendship again? She shook her head, staring blankly at the letter before her. There were no easy answers. And life seemed to just grow more and more complex. *Please, Father, show me your path,* she prayed, suddenly aware of her need.

Peder entered the cabin, glad to leave the glaring heat of the tropic sun. He found Elsa at the desk in the bedroom, her head in her hands, apparently in the midst of writing a letter.

"Hoping to get a letter off to Kaatje before we leave?" he asked, sitting on the bed. He closed his eyes for a moment. The dizziness was getting worse.

She turned in her chair to look at him, and he dimly registered the alarm on her face. "Apparently I look as bad as I feel," he mumbled.

"Goodness, Peder, how long have you been ill?" She rushed to his side and eased him to his back, then bent to take off his boots.

"Since yesterday. But we must get going, Elsa," he said, trying to rise.

She laughed. "Why now? We've been here well over a month. What's another few days?"

"Cargo. Every day we lose is less money we will earn for the year. The *Sunrise* will need several voyages to pay for herself." He wanted to moan with the effort of speech. "Of all the times for Karl to leave." Peder lifted his hand to his head. Silently Elsa followed suit.

"You have a fever. Are you dizzy?"

"Yes."

"What do you think it is?"

"Probably malaria. I've had it several times. That's what it feels like. I'll probably be indisposed for the next few days, love."

"How can we sail if you are ill?"

"We'll leave on the morrow with the first mate in command."

"You have not named a first mate. Or are you promoting Riley?"

"No. Stefan, as second mate, is the logical choice. He will be my first mate. I've come to find out," Peder managed, feeling the effort of every word, "that he is an accomplished sailor. He will see the *Sunrise* out of this harbor and to sea."

"Stefan? Is not Riley more promising?"

"Do not argue with me, Elsa. It is simply not done that way."

She stiffened beside him. "Do not treat me like one of your sailors."

Peder sighed. His head was beginning to throb. "It is my decision to make and my responsibility. Riley is a good man, but Stefan has rounded the Horn twice as many times."

Elsa, blessedly, was silent on the matter. "Get some rest," she said curtly, covering his shivering body with the blankets. Within seconds he slept.

Two weeks after leaving the West Indies, the *Sunrise* sailed into São Salvador, Brazil. It was a lively seaport town, but Elsa was in search of only one thing: a doctor. Peder grew more ill by the day, fading in and out of consciousness. She had done her best to tend to him, but knew he was in desperate straits.

As they left the ship, Stefan and Riley walked on either side of her. Two other sailors walked behind, and both were armed. In a town of olive or dark-complected people, the sight of a fair-haired woman caused quite a stir. People reached out to her hair, and though the men batted their hands away, some still touched her. By the time they reached the center of town, Elsa's chignon had come undone. Unable to pin it back up without the lost hairpins, she allowed her hair to fall over her shoulders.

"You should always wear it down, Elsa," Stefan said, looking at her boldly, open admiration on his face.

Elsa frowned at the first mate's familiarity. Riley scowled and stepped between them. "This way, *Missus* Ramstad."

They turned and walked down a narrow alleyway, led by a small, half-dressed boy who had been promised two bits if he would get them to a doctor. Peder was too ill to move, so they had no choice but to bring the doctor to him. Besides, who knew what other illnesses lurked in a poorly kept city such as this? Elsa refused to risk Peder getting a secondary infection.

The boy paused in front of a doorway covered by a bright-colored cloth. He turned and grinned, holding out a hand for his reward.

"Le' me go in first, ma'am," Riley said, stepping in front of her.

He emerged minutes later, looking grim. He spoke in broken Portuguese to the boy. The boy nodded. Riley looked back at Elsa. "Only doc in town, I'm afraid."

Elsa took a deep breath and walked through the curtained doorway. Inside, people moaned from benches that lined the small, dimly lit room, and there was an awful stench. An old woman waved them into an inner room, and as they passed through into an open courtyard, Elsa felt some hope. But her hopes were soon dashed as Riley introduced the doctor. The man grinned, showing his few remaining, stained teeth. His fingernails were rimmed with dirt, and as he took her hand to kiss it, she had to fight the urge to yank it away. She must try to be gracious, for this man might be Peder's only hope.

Then she looked around, examining the room closely. There were dead cockroaches in the corner and mud on the stucco floor. The examination table had dried blood on it, and there were rusty instruments on a nearby table. Elsa looked no farther. "We're leaving," she announced.

"Wait, Elsa," Stefan said. "Maybe it's not so bad if we remove the doctor from this place."

Elsa looked at Riley. "Ask him how he treats malaria."

The despicable doctor listened to Riley and reached for a mask and a rattling shaker then a jar of dried leaves.

"Why, he . . . he is a witch doctor," she said in disbelief. Suddenly the room felt closer, a sense of evil oppressing her heart. "We're leaving. Now." Without another word, she turned and walked out, hurrying, wanting to run.

The men caught up with her outside in the alleyway. She took deep breaths, wanting to claw at her high-necked collar. Her heart was pounding with fear. Everything in her warned against this nasty, evil place.

"He might be our only choice," Stefan said.

"He's not much of a choice at all, in my opinion," replied Riley, looking belligerently up at Stefan. "Let's abide by the lady's choice."

Stefan looked from Elsa's determined face to Riley then shrugged. "Fine. If the Cap'n dies, it's on your heads."

"Listen to me, Stefan," Elsa said, infuriated at his insolence. "If I thought that man could help my husband, I would be the first to drag him to the *Sunrise*. But he's a *witch* doctor. I can do better than that by simply looking at Cook's books on doctoring."

"Fine," Stefan said, offering his arm. "Now can we get you back to the ship?"

"Fine," Elsa said, ignoring his proffered arm and stepping forward.

Riley left them three blocks later to search for fresh fruit, cornmeal, and fresh water. They still had quite a bit in supply, but since they were already here, he thought it best to restock. Stefan agreed and sent him away.

As they resumed their walk, Stefan and the other two sailors again protecting Elsa from the crowd, Stefan looked at Elsa admiringly. "You're not afraid?"

"No," she said, swatting at a hand on her shoulder, wincing as someone tugged at a lock of hair. "They are simply curious."

"You realize that if we were not here, you'd be carried off?"

She glanced at him and bristled, not liking what she saw in his eyes. He was looking at her as if *he* would like to carry her off. Was this what Peder had feared? That he might not be around to protect her from wanton sailors? Well, she could stand up for herself. After all, his best friend had kissed her! If she could deal with that, she could certainly fend off a few misguided souls. With this thought, an idea took root. A little Bible reading would do the whole crew some good! That would put a damper on this sinful mate's wandering eyes!

Within minutes, they reached the docks and their longboat. As the sailors rowed them away from shore, Elsa breathed a sigh of relief. They had not found a doctor, but they had at least returned safely. The sailors would return for Riley later and board with fresh fruit, which Elsa could grind up and spoon into Peder's mouth. Also, she would reread Cook's doctoring books to see if there was any remedy she had missed.

Later that night, dressed in her nightgown, Elsa sat at the desk and struggled to read the dim letters on the yellowing pages of *The Contemporary Medical Journals of John B. White*. The flickering light of the kerosene lamp, the rocking of the boat, and Peder's loud, rhythmic breathing soon lulled her to sleep, her head resting on her arms over the book.

It was the creak of the door that awakened her. The lamp still burned, and she raised her head. Then she saw him. "Stefan! You frightened me! What is it?" she asked, pulling a shawl about her shoulders. "Is everything all right on the ship?"

"Fine," he said, closing the door behind him.

He walked over to Peder, touching his forehead and shaking his shoulders. Her husband didn't wake. "How long has he been unconscious?"

"All day," she said uncertainly. "What is it, Stefan? What do you want at this hour?"

He turned to her, a slow smile forming. "Why you, of course."

"Pardon me?" Her heart stepped up to a staccato beat as he took one step toward her then another. Elsa stood and backed away. She raised her chin, trying to portray all of the courage that she could not find in her heart.

"You were involved with our previous first mate, were you not? Why not be my companion?"

"I was not! I do not know of what you speak!"

He took another step toward her, and Elsa desperately thought of weapons she could reach to defend herself.

"The captain turned a blind eye on you two on that island, but I did not. Karl wanted you for himself. I could see it in his eyes. You must have spurned him. That's why he left."

"How dare you speak to me this way! I take offense at such

audacity! First Mate Martensen saved me from the pirates. That is all."

Stefan's angular face softened, and he raised his hands toward her in a conciliatory manner. His small eyes roamed over her then to Peder. "Come now, Elsa. We're friends, right? Your husband is out cold. I thought you might need some comfort."

Elsa bumped into the far wall and edged back toward the desk. On it was a sharp letter opener beside her pen. "Get out, Stefan. You have misinterpreted past events and have made a fateful decision tonight. I am removing you as first mate."

"You cannot do that," he said with derision. "You have no power."

She lunged toward the paper opener and quickly held it out like a knife. "I do. I am strong, not some waif waiting for you to take advantage of her. *Riley!*" she yelled at the top of her lungs.

In seconds, Riley and three others burst through the door. They studied Stefan and Elsa in wonder.

"Stefan has made inappropriate advances on the captain's wife," she said with shaking authority. "Put him in chains. I am removing him as first mate and taking charge of this ship. You, Riley, will be my first mate."

Riley paused for a moment, a slow smile taking over his face. He sheathed a knife that Elsa saw for the first time, then turned to the others. "You 'eard the cap'n! Put the man in chains."

Stefan looked at her with a combination of shock, dismay, and malice. "You will need me around the Horn. Nobody's done the Horn as many times as I. You'll need me!" he yelled as they led him away.

Trembling, Elsa sank into her chair. Riley watched respectfully from the door. "One adventure after another, eh missus?" he cajoled, as though trying to ease her fears.

"Yes, Riley. One adventure after another. Let's review our course first thing in the morning, all right? I want you to teach me more about charting. I think I'm getting rather good at it," she said.

"Aye, aye, Cap'n," he said jovially. Then softer he added, "Get some rest, eh missus?"

"Yes, Riley," she said. "And Riley?"

"Aye?"

"Thank you."

"Aye, Cap'n."

the sorrowing spirit sings

April–November 1881

twenty-three

With the early spring thaw came renewed health for Christina and an uneasy truce between Kaatje and Soren. Believing that they would make good money on their combined parcels of land, Soren had purchased a pair of oxen by paying down a little and securing a note for the rest. This debt made Kaatje nervous, but Soren seemed to know what he was doing and would tolerate little argument from her anyway. Wanting to live in peace, Kaatje elected to say nothing.

With Christina strapped to her chest in a sling, Kaatje hoed the soil to plant a garden. She enjoyed being outdoors, with the aroma of freshly tilled soil and the sight of Soren in the distance, clearing the land. He had insisted on tilling their new land first, and Kaatje agreed. If ultimately they could only hold on to one homestead or the other, she would prefer the new lot with the clapboard shack rather than their original quarter of land with the dirt-floored soddy. This section also had the creek nearby and the barn.

Old Lady Engvold had sniffed when she stopped by that morning, intoning that the previous Norwegian homesteaders had been driven out by their own greedy foolishness. "If they had started with a dugout or a soddy," she said, "They would still be here."

"It is my gain," Kaatje said, trying to maintain her jovial mood.

"Drafty, though, isn't it?"

"A bit more than the soddy. But it has a better roof—*and* a floor. I have much to be thankful for."

"To each his own," Old Lady Engvold said, flicking the reins over her horse's back. "Another day," she said.

"Another day," Kaatje mumbled, forcing herself to wave. Why did the old woman have to be so grim?

She thought back over the encounter as she hacked and pulled at the dark soil. Perhaps the old woman was lonely, bitterly lonely, after the winter. Still it was spring, time to leave winter's shadows behind. Kaatje looked across the field, shielding her eyes as the baby stirred against her. The late afternoon sun cast Soren's form in silhouette. She, too, would leave her winter shadows behind, Kaatje thought.

April had been an exhausting month. Blisters upon blisters swelled on Soren's hands even though he wrapped them in rags. Thirty acres had been cleared by fire, rocks had been stacked into neat piles at the corners of their property, and the land plowed. Tomorrow Soren would begin working the soil down with the disc and drag behind the oxen, while Kaatje followed behind with a sack of grain, broadcasting the seed.

When all the clearing and planting was finished, it would be time to begin the process of putting up hay. By fall they would have ten head of cattle, according to Soren's plans, and needed as much of the rich prairie grass as they could put up to feed them through the winter.

Despite this backbreaking, agonizing work, Soren still had the energy to pace after dinner. Most nights, he would take a lantern out to the barn, bring out their weary oxen, and plow until he could not stand. Tonight, however, Soren paced back and forth in their small house, too weary to plow, too agitated to sit. His steps made the floor-boards creak, making it difficult for Kaatje to concentrate on her *hardunger*. She looked up from her needlework to watch him, until he caught her gaze.

Tears threatened. It was happening again, just like in Bergen. Kaatje knew the signs: boredom, agitation, restlessness. Soren gradually would become short with her, pacing their home like a lion at the Bergen zoo.

"What?" he asked, obviously itching for an argument.

"Nothing." She returned to her needlework. Christina rustled in her cradle then settled down again. Beside Kaatje, a fire crackled in the stove, sending out a comforting heat, for the spring evenings were cool. Still Soren paced.

Kaatje was fearful, wondering who his next conquest would be. Claire Marquardt? She hoped not, for it might kill Fred to find out. Or maybe Fred was like Kaatje, so used to his spouse's indiscretions that it almost felt routine, this pattern of straying and remorse and forgiveness.

"I have to leave, Kaatje."

Her eyes flew up to meet his. "Wh-what?"

"I have to leave. I've been thinking. It is the only way. The rail-roads are paying so well that if I go and work for them for a few months, we'll have enough to *really* make our way at this."

"What are you talking about? We have enough seed, don't we?"

"Yes, but as I figure it, only for about forty acres."

"But you have only cleared thirty. One man can't be expected to do more than that."

He walked over and knelt beside her. "You are thinking small, *elske*. I want to be big, a grand farmer, not some two-bit immigrant. I want to show Old Lady Engvold that I'm not as foolish as the previous homesteaders. I want to pay off the oxen and buy you a matched span of geldings to pull a new carriage. I want to tear this cold house down and build you a snug log home. To do that I need better equipment and money to hire out some work. And I've been thinking—with the contacts I could make on the railroad, I could find a better deal on our cattle."

Kaatje felt as if the air had been driven from her. "Just what have you been told you could earn?"

"A good bit. Enough to hire out some work and put away some money for next year's crop. As I figure it, we could plant sixty acres next year and buy a cradle and scythe to cut hay. No more sickle. Who knows? Maybe I could even convince others to go in on a threshing machine. We would save so much if we didn't have to hire it out. Lots of farmers about these parts do it, Kaatje. It is the way they make it."

Rage built in Kaatje's chest, and when she stood, she was shaking. "We are finally home, Soren. Together. Alone. And you cannot stand it!"

"I never said such a thing!"

"You intend to leave me all summer?"

Soren was on his feet now, scowling at her. "It would not be all summer—"

"How long?"

"Just until July. I will be home for harvest."

"Well, that's a relief!" Kaatje said, tossing up her hands. She wondered at the tone of sarcasm in her voice. "I was worried you would leave that to me and Christina." Soren's face grew darker, but Kaatje could not curb her anger. "How do I know this is not a ruse?"

"A ruse?" Soren asked in a low voice.

"An excuse to find some other woman. How do I know you'll return?"

Soren's face grew red as the fury took over, "I intend to go and earn money so I can make a better life for you and my child, and what do I get? Not the respect and love and gratitude that I expect," he spat out, "but blind accusations and disrespect! Everything I have done," he said, shaking a finger at her, "I have done for you."

"Including Laila? And all the others? How about Claire Marquardt?" The words were out before she could stop them. Suddenly she felt empty, yet relieved of her burden.

Soren raised his hand, threatening to hit her, and Kaatje cowered. His own motion, and her reaction, seemed to anger him more. Without saying another word, he turned on his heel and left the house.

It was with some relief that Tora received a second letter from Storm Enterprises at the end of April. She reread the return address, repeating Trent Storm's name over and over. His writing was masculine, strong but clear, and Tora envisioned him as a savior from her desperate circumstances. Her baby, Jessica, for once was utterly at peace as she napped in the old pram. Tora ignored the maternal pride that swelled in her heart at caring for her own flesh and blood, concentrating on the fact that the child and the boys held her from what she wanted, truly wanted. She frowned down at the three of them.

Lars was on her hip, and Knut was teasing him, pinching his toes until he shrieked. She batted Knut's hands away. "Stop it," she told him firmly then looked up at the postmistress, Judy Gimball. Her hands had shaken as she accepted the letter from the nosy woman, who always looked at Tora as if she wore a scarlet *A* on her breast. Along with all the other townspeople. She was sick of Camden, sick of them. Tora quickly turned to leave.

Unable to walk all the way home and not know what Mr. Storm had to say, she stopped in front of the mercantile and sat on the front stair. "Go choose a candy for yourself and for Lars," she directed Knut, and with a whoop, he went dashing into the store. She opened the letter, which was written on fine stationery, giving the envelope to Lars to distract him, and wiped the perspiration from her forehead.

She scanned the salutations, whispering aloud the important parts. "Sorry to hear about your delay . . . unfortunately had to fill the position with another . . . good news is that there is another available . . . May. Report to my offices no later than the twentieth of May." She looked up from the letter, staring blankly at the horses and buggies that passed before her. What day was it? How long had she to get there? Her heart leaped at the thought that it might already be too late.

Knut came to the door. "To-ra," he whined, wanting her to come in and pay for his chosen treats.

"In a minute, Knut," she said in irritation over her shoulder. She scanned a well-to-do couple coming up the boardwalk and rose. "Excuse me, sir, may I ask the date?"

He looked at her with some disdain. "It is the twenty-ninth of April, young lady."

Tora smiled broadly. "The twenty-ninth! Thank you!" She turned toward Knut, and he smiled in shy surprise at her own rare grin. "Let's buy you that candy!" she said, taking his hand. "Today we will buy a whole pound!" she enthused.

They left the store minutes later, the boys enthralled with the candy, and Tora left alone to her dreams and aspirations. She remembered Karl's glowing words about Minnesota and the city of Saint Paul, and visualizing Duluth as much the same, she began to chart her escape. The boys could be left to their father's care, and Jessica could be weaned. But what to do with her?

As they passed the shipyard, thoughts of Soren and their times together on board the ship leaped to her mind. Yes. That was it. Would it not be sweet justice? After all, it was only fair that he live up to his responsibility in all this, she decided, looking down at Jessica. Kaatje was a good woman. She would raise Jessica well. And North Dakota wasn't far from Minnesota.

That settled it. She would deliver Soren's child into Kaatje's arms, along with the truth. Oh, he might try to deny it, but what could he do? If they refused the child, she would leave her on the porch, and as a good Christian, Kaatje would have no choice but to pick her up and raise her as their own. She'd only be a couple months younger than Kaatje's own child, Tora mused. And as the girl grew, there would be telltale signs of who her true father was. Already she favored the man, with tiny blond curls and a familiar set to her chin.

Tora felt like skipping. Yes, she would make her way to the Janssens' farm, deposit Jessica with her father, then leave for her new life.

"Thank you for the candy," Knut said, coming up beside her and taking her hand. Tora felt the levity of the moment slide into melancholy as she considered Knut, Lars, and her daughter. There were times when she enjoyed her life, when she relished the peace of it.

But she steeled herself against it, determined to move on to the world in which she belonged.

Society.

twenty-four

Kaatje watched as the buggy in the distance approached, kicking up a trail of dust that drifted across the green fields of spring wheat. Soren had been gone a month, working on the Northern Pacific Railroad, but was to return for harvest. Could this be him already? It was really too early to expect him, but still Kaatje found the courage to hope. Indeed, she battled against the fear that he was never returning, that she and Christina were truly on their own.

As the coach drew closer, however, Kaatje could see the figure of a woman. Why, it looked like Tora Anders! She smiled. Even though she did not care for the young woman, it would be good to see any of the Anders family. She missed Elsa so! But what on earth could bring Tora to North Dakota? Her heart sank. Perhaps Elsa was ill.

Tora pulled up in front of the house, calling out to the horse with a soft "whoa." She was dressed in a new riding suit of dark blue, and she flashed a smile as she stepped down, brushed the dust off herself, and walked toward Kaatje. Stunned, Kaatje opened her arms to the girl.

"Tora Anders, what on earth are you doing here?" she asked.

"I secured a job," Tora said simply, proudly. "Or I should say that I *expect* to secure a job. And there's someone I want you to meet." She turned back to the coach. "Is Soren not home?" she asked over her shoulder.

"No. He is away working on the Northern Pacific, trying to earn some more capital for the farm."

"Oh, that's a pity," Tora said as she reached into a large basket on the seat—no, it was a bassinet, Kaatje recognized—and pulled out an infant that was perhaps six weeks old.

"Oh! Tora! Congratulations! I had not heard that you had married! How could Elsa not have told me? I just got a letter from her last week." She reached for the child, cradling her in her arms with soft coos. "Why, she must only be a few months behind my own Christina." The child was gorgeous, perfectly formed, with soft blond curls peeking out beneath her frilled bonnet.

"I am not married."

Kaatje glanced at Tora quickly, searching for something to say. "The father . . ." she began lamely.

Tora met her gaze unwaveringly, waiting.

Kaatje frowned. Before she could stop herself, her thoughts went from Kristoffer to others who could be the babe's father. No. No, no, no! She glanced away from Tora's sapphire eyes to the surrounding fields. It was a beautiful early May day, with deep blue skies that met the fields of green. But her mind was not on the weather. She dared to look at Tora again, and she knew. Soren. The *Herald*. Her heart felt like stone, thudding away in a rib cage of steel.

"Her name is Jessica. She belongs here with you and Soren," Tora said matter-of-factly. "I simply am not prepared to be a mother. You were born to be nothing else," she added, her tone neutral. "Now I must be off. The four-forty leaves in an hour, and I must have this coach back." She broke off her businesslike monologue, came over to Kaatje—who felt like one of the stunned birds that occasionally hit her shanty window—and bent to kiss the child's forehead. "Please take good care of Jessie," she said with a brief crack in her voice. Eyes bright with tears, she turned on her heel and walked away.

Kaatje fought to find her own voice, hardly able to believe that all this was happening. A mother could not simply deposit a child like that and depart without a second glance. Could she?

Finally, she found the words her mind and heart were screaming. "*No!* Tora! What are you doing? What do you mean she belongs here? Tora! I will not take your child! Tora!" She ran after her. But Tora was already in the buggy and turning the mare around. She did not look back. The bassinet remained behind, left on its side in the middle of the road.

Dimly Kaatje was aware of Christina crying inside the house, awake from her nap. Yet all she could do was watch in numb disbelief as the black coach quickly wheeled back toward town, growing smaller and smaller in the distance. She felt the baby squirm in her arms and looked down. Sleepily the infant opened her eyes. They were not gray-blue like Christina's and her own, nor deep blue like Tora's. They were sky blue like Soren's—and her tiny chin was a miniature model of his. There was no doubt about it. The child she held belonged to her husband. And now, apparently, to her.

It was all too much. Her knees weak, Kaatje knelt on the hard-baked dirt, the child in her arms, the plains' breeze whipping about her, and wept.

Tora boarded the train in Bismarck, and as it pulled out toward Duluth, she felt freer than she had when she left Bergen. Her trial as a mother was over, and while her empty arms left her feeling a bit lost, she was overwhelmed by sensations of joy. Tora Anders was on her own at last, she thought, looking out at the endless plains. What a wondrous country America was! Why, Norway was only a small portion of the size! This land went on and on, and somewhere out there, she would find the right path that would lead her to her rightful position in society. She was sure of it.

Only one thing dampened her joy: a surprising concern for her daughter, which soon overtook her. But Jessica was better off with Kaatje. What future would the child have with Tora? If she took Jessie with her, Trent Storm would not employ her, and if she found another job, she would spend all her wages on a caretaker. That would not get either of them ahead in life. Soon enough Kaatje would fall in love with the child, in spite of the feelings she was bound to bring to the surface. And it served Soren right to have to deal with an enraged wife. It was only fair after what Tora had gone through.

Deciding that she needed a distraction, Tora pulled out the last letter from Trent Storm and the accompanying contract. To sign on with Storm Enterprises, she had to agree not to marry for a year—or forfeit half her wages. "No difficulty in that," she whispered to herself, giggling at the thought. It would take her time to find the right man and win him. There was no rush, for she wanted to choose wisely. She had to admit, Elsa had been right about one thing: If one chose poorly, one lived with the consequences. Being alone with Jessica and the boys had drilled that into her. So from here on out, Tora would choose wisely.

Karl had wired ahead from New York, telling Bradford Bresley of his plans and his train schedule. When he stepped onto the station platform in Saint Paul and saw the man waiting for him, Karl felt the first smile pull at his lips since he had left the *Sunrise* almost two months ago. It was impossible to look at Brad and not grin. The man's smile was so expansive, so joyous, that one could not help but join the fun. Perhaps he and Brad would eventually develop the kind of friendship and brotherly relationship he and Peder had forged—before he had ruined it all with his destructive infatuation with Elsa. If he had only prayed harder, been more devout in his beliefs, or been strong enough to leave before . . . No, he would not dwell on that now. He must put the past behind him. Saint Paul was a new beginning.

He reached out to grip Brad's hand, smiling in return.

"How was your trip?" Bresley asked. "You're back sooner than I expected."

"It went well," Karl replied. "Although I am glad to be off that train after the last six days. Give me a ship any day."

"Lucky you got here that quickly. But you had better get used to it. Working with John J. Hall, we'll frequently travel by train."

"Yes," Karl said, pointing out his two trunks to a porter. "I guess my future holds many changes."

Brad searched his eyes quickly as if something in his tone made him suspect there was more to the story. "Yes, well, John will be happy to hear you've returned. Ever since you left, he's been grousing about the need to get us moving on a new project."

Karl picked up his valise and arranged with the porter to have the trunks delivered to his temporary residence at the hotel where he had stayed on his first trip to Saint Paul.

"I was hoping to get back out on the river," he said as he and Brad made their way out of the station. "I'd like to gain some more steam experience."

"I understand that," Brad said, pointing to one of the coaches waiting at the curb. "But I'd wager that John will make you an offer it will be difficult to refuse. He has his mind set on us partnering in the new waterway business project. He wants us, with our combined experience, to head out shortly and do some scouting."

"I don't know if I want to take that direction," Karl said, sitting down heavily on the seat inside the Hall coach.

Brad sat down across from him and took off his bowler hat, setting it beside him. "I understand. But, Karl, this is going to be big," he said, gesticulating excitedly. "Trent Storm is in on it. Together we could make a killing."

Karl sighed heavily. Suddenly the weariness from his weeks of travel seemed to catch up with him, making him feel it was all too much to take in. "Why me? Why not let me captain my own steamer on the Red River and find someone else?"

Brad shrugged. "Hall likes you. You're obviously an entrepreneur; you've traveled the world. He probably figures this venture is right on track with your skills." Brad leaned toward him. "Do you know how many men would kill to be in your shoes?"

"Perhaps I ought to let them," Karl mumbled to himself.

"What?"

"Nothing." Karl sighed. Why did he feel so hesitant? Brad had just said that it was an unbelievable opportunity. Why did his heart tell him to walk away when his brain was telling him to move forward and not look back? "Let me ask you something, Brad."

"Anything."

"Do you feel entirely comfortable with the way Hall operates his business?"

Brad looked out the window briefly then back at Karl. "Don't take that tack."

"What do you mean?"

"I mean it is dangerous to question a man like John J. Hall."

"What? Then why do business with him?"

Brad sighed. "My die was cast a long while back. Once John wants a man in his corral, he gets him. I was like you—young, untried. Few would give me the time of day. John took me under his wing, and bang, three years later I have a coveted position with John J. Hall Incorporated, a fine home, and prestige. I couldn't leave if I wanted to."

"But surely—"

"No."

"Even if—"

"No." Brad sighed again, looking more serious than Karl had ever seen him. "As I said, my die was cast. So is yours, my friend." A smile grew on his lips but didn't reach his eyes. "Fortune smiled on you though. It looks like yours came up sixes."

Karl swallowed hard, suddenly feeling his mouth go dry.

twenty-five

Lugging two water buckets, Kaatje walked from the creek to water the newly planted elms. It was uncommonly hot for mid-May and worse with two babies strapped to her chest. Christina and Jessica seemed sleepier in the heat, napping for an extra hour, their bodies intertwined. Sweat trickled down Kaatje's neck and back, and she longed for the cool mountain pools of Norway. For that matter, she was ready to climb into the meager creek or at least place her feet in one of the wooden water buckets. She shaded her eyes and looked all about her. From this location, there was not another farmhouse in sight, just miles and miles of sprouting wheat and prairie grass. How long had it been since she had seen the mountains? Her heart ached for home . . . for Soren, as angry as she was with him.

How could he make her love him so, when he took others to his bed . . . fathered other women's children? She hated herself. Hated that she still cared for him. Kaatje paused and thought back to how he had looked the day he left, what he had said that last day. As her heart was splitting in two, he had taken her face between his hands and said, "Your job until I come home is to pray for rain and care for the livestock. I'll be home soon, *elskling*. I promise."

Kaatje, unable to say anything, only nodded and watched him go, walking to town on foot. From there he was to hop a train for Montana Territory, where the Northern Pacific was reportedly making its way toward the Rocky Mountains. He had not included in her list of duties that she would take care of his lover's child. Kaatje cringed at the thought of what others would call the child as she grew up. She never wanted little Jessica to feel the anger of such a title. Over and over she had cast about, trying to figure out a way to explain the child's arrival to the neighbors and to her Bergen friends at church. Whatever would she say? As a result she had not attended worship services last week, the day after Jessica had arrived, nor had she done so that morning. It was only a matter of days before Pastor Lien or one of the others would come to check on her.

She scanned the horizon again, her eyes landing on the waving prairie grass, soon ready for haying. How on earth would she do it alone if Soren did not return as promised? And with two small babies to care for? Kaatje felt panic rise in her chest at the thought. Not waiting another moment, she sank to her knees and looked down at her babies. Christina had an arm around Jessica, and Kaatje realized that she was growing to love the child, as much as she threatened to destroy her marriage. Jessie was the innocent, after all, and a child was a gift. Ducking her neck, she kissed one damp head then the other. Both slept on.

The prairie grass came up to her shoulders and waved about her in the gentle breeze. The soil was dry, but cool in the shade of the thin stalks, and Kaatje took a deep breath. "Father God," she prayed aloud, "I need you. I am here alone with two children who are counting on me and an absent husband. Help me to find the way out of this. Help me." A lump rose in her throat, and slow, fat tears welled in her eyes. She looked up at the sky, bleary through her tears, and cried out, "Father! You've gotten me this far! See me through. Dear God, see me through."

When she finished an hour later, having confessed her darkest anger and the sinful desires that seeped into her soul, Kaatje felt spent but relieved. The image of letting the trees die, the livestock wither, and the desire to fill Soren's half-completed well with rock had ebbed and died within her, the burden of her fury assuaged by the Savior. Kaatje would not destroy what was good in an effort to kill what was evil. She would carry on, for she was strong. And she was loved. Not through Soren's inept attempts, but with an everlasting, ever-true love of Christ. Nothing could get in the way of that. And never had Kaatje felt closer to him.

Tora entered the handsome two-story wood building that housed Storm Enterprises and made her way to the front desk. A young man looked up at her and smiled appreciatively, taking in the Tuscan straw bonnet, the cream-colored sateen dress in the latest style, and the delicate ladies' walking boots peeking from the bottom.

"I am here to see Mr. Trent Storm," she said confidently, watching his eyes return to her own.

"Certainly, Miss . . ."

"Miss Anders. Tora Anders. I have an appointment."

"I see. Please have a seat. Mr. Storm's secretary will be out directly to fetch you."

"Very well." She made her way to a wooden bench and settled into it. She was pleased with her new purchase and hoped that Mr. Storm would be also. He had advertised for young, attractive girls, after all, and she wanted him to be impressed. If the man at the front desk was any indication, she should do well. It had taken her a week to find just the right things and seriously depleted her savings to purchase dress, hat, and shoes, but she knew it was vital to present a suitable image. Tora took a deep breath to steady her nerves. This was the key to her future; she was sure of it.

Within moments a pretty young woman came to fetch her, and Tora rose to follow her to Mr. Storm's office. The secretary was dressed in a simple, dull gray dress, and for a moment, Tora fretted that she had overdone her costume. Perhaps Mr. Storm preferred the simplicity of a frontier dress to the society ensemble she had selected! Had she not read that he was conservative, providing chaperones for his employees as well as carefully guarded dormitories?

Her worries were laid to rest, however, as she saw his eyes light up. Perhaps her own eyes did the same, for Trent Storm was an unexpectedly handsome man in his late thirties. As he rose from the chair behind his desk, Tora noted his distinguished carriage. *What a relief to be in the company of a gentleman of substance!* she thought.

"Miss Anders, I presume?" he asked, coming around the desk and reaching for her hand. He was about five foot eight in height, not overly tall, but his lean, masculine form must delight his tailor. The perfect shape to drape, she thought. His hair was jet black with a premature sprinkling of gray, making him look all the more distinguished.

She extended her hand, hoping he would kiss it. Instead, he gave it a gentle but businesslike shake. His eyes were startling, a light green or hazel. On his right cheek was a long scar that intrigued her. She fought off the desire to touch it, to ask him how he got it.

Tora pulled her hand back delicately and flashed him a smile. "Why, Mr. Storm. I had pictured you as a bent-over old man."

He laughed, a great belly laugh, and the crow's-feet at his eyes crinkled in a merry look. Trent gestured toward the chair in front of his desk. "Sometimes I feel old and bent over. Please, Miss Anders. Have a seat." She did as he bid, then watched him return to his own chair, where he folded his hands and studied her briefly.

"Tell me, Miss Anders, why do you wish to work for Storm Enterprises?"

Tora folded her hands and studied him in return. What did he want to hear? "I read your advertisements," she said simply. "Escaping to the wild west sounded exciting, exactly what I needed."

"And from what are you escaping?"

Tora faltered for a moment. "From dying of boredom in a tiny town called Camden-by-the-Sea."

"Ah yes, boredom. You don't seem the type to abide by such nuisances as a dull life. So you seek adventure. Are you also expecting wealth?" he asked, clearly adding up the small fortune she wore. "Or are you independently wealthy?"

"If only that were true," she said, enjoying the chance to spar with someone of intelligence. She fingered the flounce of her skirt, which cascaded to the floor in three tiers. "I enjoy finery, but I am not afraid to work for it."

"I see. Well, I must say, you look delightful in the best our town's dressmaker can turn out." He leaned back in his chair, his eyes still not wavering from hers.

"Why, Mr. Trent!" Tora said, acting a bit shocked. "What would your wife say?"

His eyes lost some of their levity, and his mouth turned downward. "My wife died three years ago."

"Oh, forgive me," she said, genuinely remorseful that she had taken such an uncomfortable tack. "That must be very painful for you."

His eyes searched hers again, and she did not let her own gaze fall. "You are a cook?" he asked, suddenly rifling through the papers on his desk until he found her letter in the stack.

"Yes. I am quite good, actually."

"Yes, well, that is convenient. But I think you actually would serve Storm Enterprises best as a serving girl. I need attractive faces up front. It helps me win customers. I presume you are a good worker."

"When I set my mind to it."

"Is your mind set on it?"

"It is."

Trent sat back again and studied her for a moment before speaking. "I'll give you a trial run, Miss Anders. Tomorrow you will serve in my private dining car. I'm entertaining some important railroad executives who mean a lot to my business. If you do well, we'll see to a permanent position for you in one of the roadhouses. My secretary will give you all the pertinent details. Good enough?" He stood, dismissing her.

"Very well, Mr. Storm," she affirmed, trying not to gush. He was giving her a chance in his very own railroad car! "Good day, sir."

"Good day, Miss Anders."

Karl followed Brad through the monstrous Hall house, trying not to gape openly as they passed ornate furniture and elaborate stained glass windows. Brad smiled wryly at him. "You haven't seen anything yet, friend. Wait until you get a look at John's plans for his new mansion on Summit Avenue." Karl could not quite grasp anything more grand than this. And then he caught sight of Alicia. She stood at the foot of the broad staircase, and she looked as lovely as he had remembered.

"You forgot to write, Captain Martensen," she said, lowering her head and looking at him coquettishly.

"Forgive me, Miss Hall. I have no excuse. I have seen the error of my ways," he added, studying her. She truly was a treat to behold, and her flirtatious eyes belied a quick mind. "I have come to settle in Saint Paul. Chalk up my departure to wanting to see the oceans once more before settling on the river ways of your fine state."

She let the comment hang for a moment, then said, "Welcome home, Mr. Martensen. Be advised that I am not the type of woman who pines for a man."

"Of course not. I would not presume—"

"There are others who have been more bold," she said quietly as she passed him. "Good day. Good day, Mr. Bresley."

The two men watched as she walked down the long hallway

toward the back of the house, most likely well aware that they continued to watch her in admiration. When she was out of sight, Brad slapped him on the back. "Good grief, man, I'll be sorry you were ever invited to Minnesota. First you catch John's eye, and now his daughter's. I smell the scent of something great on the wind. Or is it just your meteoric rise that I smell? The singe as I get burned as you pass me by?"

His face held none of the caustic bite of his words, however, and Karl knew he was jesting. With just a hint of envy perhaps. For there was no denying that John Hall had taken a liking to Karl. He had handed over the captaincy of the *Merriweather* and allowed Karl to purchase 51 percent of the shares in the vessel, giving him true control and a hefty portion of the profits once she began her work on the river ways. And now, according to Brad, Hall had another promising business proposition for him.

As they resumed their walk to Hall's office, Karl's mind drifted toward some of the questions that continued to plague him. What was the man after? Why make such magnanimous overtures to someone he barely knew? Hall was not a man given to folly. Each move was one of careful design. It felt like a trap to Karl in some ways, yet he had little choice. His money was committed, already safely ensconced in Hall's bank account. Besides, why should he worry? If he wanted out later, he would simply ask John to buy him out. Looking around the grand hallway, he had no doubt that the wealthy businessman could come up with the cash at any time.

It was what Hall had said when they sealed their business agreement that haunted Karl the most, reminding him again of his father's charges of hypocrisy. "Sometimes an upright man has to make decisions in a gray zone, son," John had said, lighting a cigar. Karl had just handed over a cashier's check and signed the contract, sealing their deal on the *Merriweather*. "For it's a gray, gray world out there. If you must work in black and white, you'll never get anywhere. Learn to deal with the gray, and I'll make you a small fortune."

t w e n t y - s i x

Elsa sighed deeply as she sketched the eastern coast of Argentina, not far from the *Sunrise*'s starboard side. The wind was steady, reaching them on the port quarter; thus Riley sailed on a broad reach, seeking to make the best time. This took them away from the coast a bit, but as they neared the Horn, he said, they would have to tack back and forth repeatedly to make the best of wind and water.

The fresh breezes that day already had built swells of eight feet. What would the reportedly terrible winds of the Horn do? Elsa shoved away the fear that clamped down about her heart. If only Peder would recover his strength soon. By his own admission, Riley had much less experience than Stefan, having become a sailor later in life. And having sent the first mate down to the hold in chains, Elsa was now at a loss. The men looked at her with a mixture of admiration and concern, wondering if her decisions would send them all to the bottom of the deep.

Her sketch reflected the unease she felt inside, and she tore the paper from the pad and crumpled it in her hand. Surely if they could survive the Horn with the first mate in chains, Peder would accept that Elsa was strong enough to consistently travel at his side. She sobered. What if he did not get better? He had rallied with Cook's treatment of chinchona bark, yet still was so weak that he could not get out of bed.

The thought of losing him choked her. She loved him. If only they had been able to find a doctor! There was no getting past it. She would need to pray, on her knees, three times a day for protection for them all. "No time like the present," she whispered.

Unable to do anything else, she got out of her chair and knelt beside it. She prayed aloud, albeit quietly. "Dearest Jesus, we are heading into winds and water that you created, though they frighten us. I pray that you will be with each of my sailors, that you will give them wisdom and strength for what lies ahead. Help me to trust that you are with us, even during our darkest hour. And please, Father, please heal your son Peder soon. It is in Christ's name I pray. Amen."

When she opened her eyes, she saw that five sailors below her had stopped their work of sanding the deck with a holystone and wet sand and knelt with heads bowed. They had not been able to hear her, though they obviously were with her in spirit. Elsa smiled, tears quickly coming forth. Gradually the men raised their heads, one by one.

"We're with ya, Missus," said Yancey.

"The Cap'n will come out of it, you'll see," said another.

Elsa could only nod, too choked up to say a word, as the men returned to their work.

Five days later, Elsa knew full well why Peder wanted the most experienced men on deck when they encountered the fearsome storms off the Cape Horn of South America. The wind howled as if alive, a growling giant threatening to crush the *Sunrise* with claws formed of giant waves. Elsa was soaked and scared as she tried to maintain her footing at Riley's side. The man was struggling to lash the wheel, unable to control it any longer, as the waves began to sweep over the deck.

"Go inside!" Riley shouted. His voice was barely discernible against the roaring wind, but Elsa knew what he was after. Regardless of her claim on the captain's title, she had no experience in rounding the Horn, and with a jump to her heartbeat, she remembered the last time she had remained on deck in a storm. Karl Martensen was not here to fish her out this time, and Peder remained too weak to leave his bed.

Elsa resigned herself to leaving the ship to the capable sailors on deck. She also didn't want to distract them by unnecessarily putting herself in danger. She tried to pry open the cabin door, but the wind buffeted it closed. With all she had in her, she braced one foot against the doorjamb and gripped the brass knob with both hands, prying it open and flinging herself inside. The door slammed shut behind her. She panted in the darkness, wondering if Peder was awake.

"Peder?" she asked out loud. The noise of the wind made hearing difficult, but at least it wasn't the deafening scream of the deck. "Peder?" she tried again, reaching about to find the kerosene lamp.

"I am awake," he said wearily from the bed. His voice grew concerned. "What's happening? Where are we?"

"We are rounding the Horn," she said, lighting the wick. As the flame grew, the light spread its presence about the room. There was something comforting in the light amid the storm. Like God, she thought with a smile. Suddenly she felt irrationally reassured that all was well.

"The Horn! Who's on deck?" His tone erased any reassurance in Elsa's heart.

"Riley. He's at the wheel. It seems as if he's faring all right," she said, dropping her dripping oilskin coat to the floor and bracing herself for the next wave's impact.

"Where's Stefan?" he asked wearily, rubbing his eyes. He tried to sit up, and Elsa made her way to him, taking one handhold then another to avoid careening across the room. She sat down beside him on the bed, holding onto the headboard as the ship crashed to the bottom of a watery gully.

Peder winced as the *Sunrise* shuddered and rocked. "Where's Stefan?" he repeated.

Elsa hesitated. "In the hold. In chains."

"In chains? Why on earth would my first mate be in chains?"

"Because he made inappropriate advances toward me. I had to take charge."

Peder's white face took on a gray hue. "What have I done? Why didn't I leave you at home where you'd be safe?" He sank back down into the bed, his eyes closing in weariness. This was the longest conversation they had had in weeks, and he was clearly exhausted from the effort.

"I am safe, Peder," she said, pulling the covers to his neck.

"Right," he mumbled. "My first mate is in chains, my ill-experienced second has become first and is at the wheel, and my wife has become captain. I don't think that shapes up to an ideal world. We are in danger, Elsa." He opened his eyes. "Many, many ships sink off the Horn. You need every available hand on deck, especially those with experience. Riley is good, but he has not dealt with seas like these enough to be at the helm." He sighed and closed his eyes again. He spoke without opening them. "I want you to release him."

"What?"

"Release Stefan. He'll know how to get the *Sunrise* through this. You lock yourself in here. When we're to port and I'm well, I'll see to his future myself." Peder gripped her hand weakly and managed to open his eyes once more. "Right now our future depends on that man and the others. Bring him out of the hold, Elsa. Promise me you will." He passed out before he could hear her promise.

Elsa stared at her husband—so thin after weeks of nothing but broth and water—torn between his desperate plea and her own counsel. They seemed to be faring all right, despite the fearsome storm and Stefan in chains. Peder had been ill so long, who knew how clearly he was thinking? On the other hand, Riley said that the storm was bound to get worse before it got better. And Peder had been at sea on the long side of ten years. *And* he was her husband.

"To love and honor," she muttered, pulling on the soaked oilskin again and leaving the relative sanctuary of the cabin.

Out on deck, the spray of a wave sent a jolt of adrenaline through her body. "Riley!" she screamed, trying to make her way to the mate at the wheel. "Riley!"

She was practically at his elbow before he heard her over the deafening wind. Elsa hesitated to interrupt him, so intent was he at holding the wheel and shouting out orders heard by none. "Riley!"

He turned and glanced at her. "Get back inside! This is no place for you!" They braced as another wave released the ship, and they went crashing downward.

"I spoke to Peder! Peder!" she repeated, seeing his puzzled expression. "He wants Stefan released! Until we pass the Horn!"

"And at the helm?"

"Stefan!" she said sorrowfully. "He wants him here until we pass!"

Riley did not pause at her words. "Yancey! *Yancey!* Release Stefan! Outfit him and get him up here!" He glanced at Elsa. "And get him some food first!" he yelled after Yancey. He turned back to her as another wave passed. "You, missus! Get back inside the captain's quarters and bar the door. I'll come and fetch you when the way is clear!"

"Thank you!" Elsa yelled, and did as he bid.

The knock in the morning puzzled Elsa, for she was in the middle of a spring meadow, staring up at fluffy white clouds . . . where was that confounded sound coming from? Dimly, she realized that she was aboard the *Sunrise,* and the ship was once more sailing on an even keel.

She opened her eyes and shook Peder. "Peder! Peder! We made it!"

He groaned and opened his eyes, smiling a bit like a proud parent. "Well, of course she did."

The knock sounded again. Elsa rose, donned a night robe, and peeked out. Riley.

"Wanted to let you know, ma'am, that the ship made it through all right," he said. "Stefan is back in chains." He paused and shuffled his feet. "It was a good thing he was on deck, ma'am. Thought you'd like to know that. He made some decisions that I wouldn't o' thought of. Probably saved us."

"Perhaps," Elsa said, choosing her words carefully. "Thanks to you, we made it as far as we did. You're a good man, Riley. I will be sure to tell Peder what you did."

"Good enough, ma'am," Riley said, fingers to hat in salutation. He was obviously eager to finish the conversation and get on with his routine. "Carry on?"

Suddenly she felt the warmth of Peder's body beside her. He opened the door a bit more and said, "Carry on, mate."

Riley grinned. "Good to see you up and about, Cap'n. As ordered, sir." He turned smartly and left them.

Elsa stood there in numb happiness, staring up at her husband. With Peder up and about, perhaps the storm was truly over.

twenty-seven

Early on the morning of Tora's first day with Storm Enterprises, Trent Storm helped her board his private railroad car. "Thank you, Mr. Storm," she said, flashing him her most winning smile. She felt a bit odd on the arm of her boss and clad in a maid's uniform, but she would carry it off with grace and flair. "It's a beautiful morning for a train excursion, isn't it?"

"It is," he agreed. They made their way into the elaborate Pullman car, and Tora admired the rich wood-paneled walls, velvet-covered seats, and Tiffany oil lamps. Trent's car was obviously brand-new, with the latest in equipment. It clearly rivaled Pullman's Hotel Express, which had made headlines way back in 1870 for crossing the country in seven days.

Storm led her to a bar in one corner, on which was a china platter filled with a variety of pastries and a sterling coffee urn beside china cups. "You will stand here, alert for the slightest indication that one of my guests needs attention. Think you can handle that?" he asked with a wink.

Tora swallowed her pride and her indignation at his tone. "I think I can," she said, chin up.

"Good girl," he said, winking again, then turned to greet his arriving guests.

A well-dressed, middle-aged man and woman entered first, and Tora stepped forward to take the woman's bag and light wrap. Trent smiled his approval. Tora turned to begin arranging coffee cups as he greeted the others. She listened to their conversation and learned that the first couple was Mr. and Mrs. John J. Hall, of John J. Hall Incorporated, whatever that was. She wished she were one of the finely dressed ladies being waited upon rather than the servant. With her back to the room as she set the cups on a silver serving tray, Tora listened as John Hall made his own introductions.

"Bradford Bresley, I'd like you to meet two friends of mine from the Saint Paul, Minneapolis, and Manitoba line, Anton Gagnon and Rupert Conley. Gentlemen, my associate Bradford Bresley. Ah, and here is my newest associate, Karl Martensen. And I think you know my lovely daughter, Alicia."

Karl! Karl Martensen? Tora swallowed hard. It could not be! Surely it was another man with the same name. But with a quick look over her shoulder, her heart sank. It *was* Karl. He was here. And he could undo everything, for Trent Storm would not employ the young mother of an abandoned infant.

Alicia Hall sat down on a velvet couch and pulled off her kid gloves. She shot Tora a look of irritation. "Girl, I need you to do something with these." Not wanting to attract Karl's attention, Tora ducked her head and hurried over to the young woman.

"Certainly," she said, her voice barely audible. "Would you care for some coffee, miss?"

"Tea, preferably. You do have tea for me, don't you, Trent?" she called out flirtatiously.

Tora ducked back toward the counter, hoping against hope that she could make it through this perilous predicament without Karl recognizing her and causing a scene.

"Of course! The maid will see to it," he called. It grated on her to be called a maid, but Tora was glad he had not used her name. Perhaps if the men became engrossed in conversation . . .

With a loud hoot of the whistle, the train began moving, and Alicia squealed in glee. "No matter how old I get, Mother, I never tire of a nice train excursion."

From the other side of the car, her father said, "A fine attribute in a daughter, I'd say. Now, gentlemen, you're probably wondering what I have on my mind. Can you believe it involves money?"

Thankfully, as the men settled into their conversation, Karl took a seat with his back to Tora, and somehow she managed to deliver Alicia Hall's tiny silver teapot and cup and Mrs. Hall's coffee without dropping them.

"Good heavens, girl. Are you all right?" Mrs. Hall asked her, observing Tora's shaking hands.

"Oh, fine, ma'am, fine. Thank you for asking." But the woman was already turned away from her, looking out the window. How many times had Tora dismissed a servant in similar fashion? Licking her lips nervously, she went back to the counter and poured coffee for the men. She counted it a minor miracle when all were served and none glanced up at her face, including Karl.

John Hall was deep into his plans, outlining how he intended to take the St. Paul, Minneapolis, and Manitoba line west, fulfilling a long-sought dream of making it a transcontinental line to Puget Sound. "I've already reached my goal of taking her to the Canadian border, and I don't need to tell you how well we're faring from that venture," he said, gesturing about them. "My friend Trent here saw the wisdom of my decision and cashed in. Now we head west. Minnesota and Dakota Territory will finance us as we haul the immigrants' grain to market in the cities. In addition, we'll sell off land from our grants as we pass, and Karl and Bradford here will set up steamboat operations on each waterway as we go, keeping our fingers in the pot as the towns behind us grow."

Tora noticed that they neared the bottoms of their cups but was hesitant to refill them. The thought of nearing Karl terrified her. Steeling herself and taking a deep breath, however, she filled the silver serving pot from the urn and walked with trembling steps to the men. Their attention remained on John Hall.

"You want to hear more?" he asked, grinning.

"Yes," they said as one.

Certainly this John J. Hall held the keys to more futures than anyone she had ever met, Tora thought. If she messed this up, her ascent to society would be done for good.

She took a step backward as Hall lifted his coffee cup in a toast, as if it were a flute of champagne, waiting for the others to join him.

"Gentlemen, I salute the future. Our future," he said, looking around closely at each man present. "I say here's to the future of the Manitoba Road. May she one day be called the Great Northern Railway when we reach the Puget Sound."

They all said "hear, hear," in agreement, following his lead in looking out to the prairies they rushed by, and continued their discussion in detail.

Hall set his coffee cup on the table and nodded for Tora to refill it. She watched as the hot, brown liquid cascaded out of the pot, pulling it up just as the coffee reached the proper level from the china rim. She moved toward Karl's cup and felt herself blush, sure that he was staring at her. As John Hall began speaking again, she dared to look at Karl. Her heart stopped as his eyes met hers.

Tora's wrist went limp. Slowly the coffee poured out the spout, onto the table, then splashed into John Hall's lap.

Hall cursed. Tora gasped. And Karl leaped to his feet, handing Hall his handkerchief.

"Oh, I'm sorry! So sorry!" Tora said, frightened by what she had done.

"Miss Anders!" Trent said in dismay. The women had stopped talking to watch the horrible spectacle.

"I don't know what happened!" Tora cried. "I'm afraid I'm not well." This was not a convenient lie; indeed, she did feel faint.

Karl took the silver pot from her hand and set it securely on the table, then turned Tora toward the back of the train. "I'll just see her to a seat. John, do you need anything?"

"A new suit," he said, managing to laugh. "I get all dressed up for our meeting, Trent, and what do you do? Bring in a girl to spill coffee all over me!"

"I'm very sorry, John. The girl is new and inexperienced, but I didn't know she was ill. We will see to the cleaning of your suit."

"Fine, fine. Martensen? Martensen!" Hall turned to look at Karl over his shoulder before he could say a private word to Tora. "The maid will be fine. Get over here and listen to my plans. Together we are going to own the Great Northern! And Trent will feed our customers!"

When the train returned to Duluth that afternoon with the Hall party aboard, Karl had to fight off the urge to drag Tora off by the hand and demand her story. Instead, he continued as he had throughout the trip, steadily ignoring her. Still there was no getting past Alicia's eagle eye. As much as he appreciated the attentions of the lovely Miss Hall, he felt as watched over as a goshawk. Sailor superstition maintained that a goshawk brought luck, but if hurt, would be the undoing of a ship. What would happen if he crossed Alicia?

At the station, he alighted from the Pullman, then reached up to help Alicia down the stairs. Once at his side, she entwined her arm in his. Since she was much shorter than he, Karl was careful to keep his stride short. He met her gaze and smiled. She was lovely and obviously very interested in him. He had to be the most blessed man in

America—a great new job and an attentive girl on his arm. After years of living in Peder's shadow, the future was his. This had to be of God, he told himself. A normal path did not twist to blessings as it had for him.

Alicia squeezed his arm and looked at him steadily as they walked through the station and outside to a hotel coach that awaited them on the street. "So, Mr. Martensen, are you going to tell me about the girl?"

"The girl?" he feigned ignorance.

"The girl," she said, narrowing her eyes. "Out with it. Who is she? An old love?"

"She's from Bergen too. I knew her a very long time ago." Karl did not know why he protected Tora; he just did. It irked him that he was not entirely honest with Alicia, but somehow he had the distinct understanding that if Alicia felt that someone was in her way, she would destroy her. Like her father before her, he mused, remembering Brad's warning. Tora was obviously trying to make a new start in life. Could he deny her a second chance?

"Well, I must say, Mr. Martensen, I am relieved you do not have feelings for her. She's obviously an incompetent servant, not worthy of your attentions."

"As opposed to you, Miss Hall?"

"Why, I would not even care to compete with the girl. It is obvious for all the world to see that you only have eyes for me. She would be hurt."

Karl grinned at her precocious words. "We cannot have that," he said.

Alicia was a very pleasant distraction indeed, he thought. Given enough time, and with her on his arm, Elsa would recede completely from his thoughts, becoming a dim shadow in the bright light of his future.

twenty-eight

By June, Peder had improved remarkably. In the last week, he had even taken to standing at the helm for an hour a day. Not his usual six, but thrilling for Elsa to see anyway. The crew relaxed, again under the supervision of their well-respected captain instead of his bride—and Elsa relaxed too. She began a new painting, of the *Sunrise* battling to pass the Horn, interrupting it occasionally to sketch rare seabirds that she had never seen before.

She and Peder greeted each morning side by side on deck, the crew about them. Peder had taken to leading them in a brief morning prayer, and it gladdened Elsa's heart. Apparently their adventures in the West Indies, Karl's sudden departure, and Peder's illness had brought him closer to the Lord than ever. *You see,* she mused silently, *all things do work together for good.* If only *she* felt closer to him. It was more than his illness and the responsibility of his captaincy. Peder had grown distant, aloof. She must find out what was troubling him, for something obviously was.

She raised her nose to smell the cool breezes that coaxed the sails high above them to a full loft. They traveled in a northeasterly direction now, the sails close-hauled to make the most of the wind. Soon they would reach the equatorial calms, or doldrums. They'd had little trouble at that latitude in the Atlantic. Would they have a more difficult time in the Pacific? She hoped not. Suddenly Elsa ached for land. For a good meal at a fine restaurant. To discover a new city. San Francisco promised to be grand.

As the crew dispersed that morning, Elsa drew Peder aside. "May I speak to you in private?"

Peder raised one eyebrow. "Certainly. Our cabin?"

"No. Up here. Follow me." She hoped he would smile, but he did not.

"What is so important that you must pull me away like this?" She ignored his irritable tone and led him forward to the bow, pulling him close when they were behind the foremast. How good it felt to be in her husband's arms again! She stared up into his eyes, noting that the malarial yellow was beginning to recede in favor of the bright white of health. There was even some color in his cheeks now. If she could just get him to eat more . . .

"Elsa?" Peder asked in irritation. His hands dropped from her side.

She looked at him quickly. Yes, something was definitely bothering him. It was more than his illness, the Horn, and his mate again in chains below.

"Peder, please," she begged, growing more alarmed. She took his hand in hers. "Tell me. What is bothering you? What is it?"

"What do you mean?"

"It's you. Us. What has happened? There is a wall between us."

"I do not know of what you speak." His jaw was tight, clenched.

"You do," Elsa said softly. "Please tell me."

"Not now, Elsa. I have a ship to tend to." He turned to walk away, paused, then looked over his shoulder at her. "If that makes you un-happy, you need to rethink your course of action."

Elsa frowned, wanting to weep in frustration. What was he talking about? Of course he had to tend ship! But why not talk to her? What was wrong?

Elsa felt her heart sink. If they could not even discuss it, how would they ever resolve it?

It was the third time that week that Trent Storm had come to call on Tora, and the girls in the dormitory were in a frenzy.

"He's in love! The man's in love!" Missy Alexander said from the doorway, enviously watching Tora brush out her hair and wind it into a graceful chignon.

Tora picked up the beautiful pearl comb that Trent had given her the day before and thought about Missy's words. The girl was an idiot in most cases, but perhaps she was right. If so, it was a minor miracle, Tora thought, remembering that horrible day over a month ago on the Manitoba train.

She had left the Pullman car last, barely able to hold back her tears. To begin again would take weeks, and her resources could not handle such a setback. Why, she would have to sell her gowns just to pay the hotel manager!

A hand reached out to her, and she glanced up. Trent Storm stood on the platform below, waiting to help her down the stairs.

"There is no need to fire me, Mr. Storm," she said as she took his hand. "I know I failed you. I . . . I don't know what happened. Suddenly I felt so faint."

His eyes, instead of being angry, held compassion and concern. With a hint of doubt. "You knew him, didn't you?"

"Who?" she asked, feigning ignorance.

"That man. Karl Martensen."

"He looked familiar," she hedged. "It brought back bad memories that I'd rather not go into." Tora pulled out the stops on her feminine wiles, aware that Trent was opening an escape hatch. She fanned herself with her hand as if faint again, hoping to distract him. "If you'll excuse me," she gambled, "I'll get out of your way, Mr. Storm. Surely you have many girls more suitable to apply for this job. Good day."

She walked away, her head high, her heart sinking with each step she took away from him. Her pace slowed to a dispirited trudge. Her ruse had not worked. She had talked herself out of the job, not secured it. Would she ever learn when to speak?

Two blocks away, she dared to look back to the station. Trent was nowhere to be seen. Her spirits dismal, she slowly walked back to her hotel. As she climbed the steps, however, her eyebrows lifted in surprise. Trent Storm sat in a chair on the porch, rocking as if he had all the time in the world. He was dreadfully handsome, she thought, and as dangerous-looking as a riverboat gambler she had seen en route to Minnesota.

"You'll have to move faster than that if you wish to work for me, Miss Anders."

"W-work for you?"

"Indeed. I don't know what you're hiding, but I find it amusing to think about."

Miffed at being a target of his amusement, Tora looked away, debating between her desire to tell him what he could do with his job and her dire need of employment. He smiled as if reading her thoughts.

"Are you seriously offering me the job, Mr. Storm?" she asked, unable to curb the insolence in her voice.

His smile turned into a grin, revealing even, white teeth. "Yes, you will be fascinating," he said.

"Are you quite finished being entertained?" She turned to go.

"One more thing. Miss Anders."

"Yes?"

"Is there someone I should speak to? You see, I would like to call upon you."

"Me?"

"You."

Tora's mind whirled. "Why, Mr. Storm, is that acceptable? What would your friends say?"

He laughed. "Miss Anders, I live to please myself alone. So is there someone I should speak to? Or will you turn me down here and now?"

Tora stuck her nose in the air. "You may call on anyone you wish. Good day, Mr. Storm."

His laughter followed her into the hotel. And then he called, "See you tomorrow at eight, Miss Anders!"

Thus their relationship had begun. It was a confusing mix of employer and employee, widower and young love. Love? Yes, she supposed it could be true. But what was love to feel like? And could the man of her dreams have popped up so soon, so easily on her path? It seemed odd to her that something would come without striving. Surely it was a sign that something better was around the next corner. Perhaps Trent Storm was only her entrée to society. From there, she might meet another.

She frowned into the mirror. Why was it so difficult to envision herself with another? He had only been courting her for what, a month? Yet somehow he had seeped into her life so thoroughly that she could not remove him from her mind.

"Missy," she said, deciding to take control. "Please send word down to Mr. Storm. I am not well and wish to lie down. Make my apologies for me." She turned the pearl comb over in her hand. He was so *sure* he had her. Well, no one had Tora Anders until she wanted to be had. It was high time that Trent Storm learned she would not be at his beck and call.

Karl made his way out of the stuffy cabin crowded with people and perfume, glad for the fresh air off the Saint Croix River. The Halls frequently hosted parties aboard their steamboats, chugging for hours along the riverbanks as their guests drank themselves into oblivion. Karl had had his share that night and was feeling a bit woozy by the time he reached the railing. He had been with John J. Hall Incorporated for over a month, and his skyrocketing career had made him numb to his surroundings.

He leaned over the rail and watched the ice clink in his crystal glass. In the dim light from the cabin, the glass reflected a rainbow of colors, suddenly reminding him of watching Elsa on board the *Herald* and seeing the northern lights. Almost a year ago, he thought. How life had changed in such a short period of time! Without another thought, Karl dropped the glass, watching as it fell away from him and into the black, churning wake of the ship.

He turned away from the rail, rubbing his eyes as if to rid himself of the vision. He didn't want to think of Elsa. Nor of Peder. He had arranged for his Ramstad Yard checks to come to an accountant in town so that he himself need not correspond directly with the Ramstads. He wanted them to remain a part of his past while he actively sought his future. But would the future always feel this desperately lonely? Was he following the right path? Was it normal in the Christian walk to feel this distant from the Lord?

Or was he the hypocrite his father had called him? He had not respected his best friend's marriage by removing himself before his infatuation with Elsa got out of hand. He had remained in their presence, aware that destruction was imminent, unable to extract himself in time. If he had acted wisely, he could have stayed in Camden, overseeing the Ramstad business while Elsa sailed with Peder, rather than dance with the devil he suspected John J. Hall to be.

"I am unworthy, Father," he whispered. "I am unworthy to be called your son. Forgive me. Release me from this burden. Release me!"

But as he stared out at the dark water, no answer soothed his heart, no voice stilled the anguish in his soul. Would he ever get beyond these memories that tortured him? For when he was truly honest with himself, he knew that if Elsa had not stopped his kiss, he would not have stopped himself.

Forgive me, Lord . . . forgive me, he prayed silently.

A feminine hand startled him, drawing his hands away from his face. He had not heard Alicia join him on the deck. "Are you all right, darling?" she asked softly, her voice solicitous.

"Fine. Just a bit of a headache. Sorry I ran out on you."

"It's no surprise if you're suffering. The noise and heat probably got to you." She slipped her arms around his waist, looking up at him. "Is something else bothering you?"

Karl looked down at her. In the soft light, she was even more attractive, her auburn hair even darker, but softly reflecting like burnished copper here and there. He studied her eyes, so different from Elsa's but equally as beautiful. Alicia clearly loved him. Was he beginning to love her? Or was it just mutual attraction, a welcome diversion from Elsa Ramstad? Inside, all he could feel was emptiness, despair. In her eyes, he saw hope, the future. And he knew John hoped they would marry. Why on earth would he not want this lovely creature in his arms?

"No," he finally responded. "Everything is all right. It has taken me a bit by surprise."

"Surprise?"

"All my life I've struggled to reach my goals. Then I step off the train in Saint Paul, and suddenly all is right before me. My career, my home, my . . . wife." The word slipped out, and Karl was glad to find he did not regret it. It was obvious, after all, what was right. Elsa belonged to another. Alicia was in love with him. And in time, he would grow to love her too.

"Karl Martensen, are you proposing?"

As if in a dream, Karl knelt before her, taking her small hand in his own. "Alicia Hall, if your father will give us his blessing, will you do me the honor of becoming my wife?"

"Gladly, Captain Martensen," she said, sitting down on his knee and kissing him tenderly. She drew back slightly, smiling with delight in her eyes. "I know our courtship has been fast, but I thought you'd never ask."

twenty-nine

As the tugboat brought the *Sunrise* alongside a pier in the San Francisco harbor, Elsa sighed in relief. Even from the wharf she could see towering buildings clinging to the steep hillsides, testimony to the city's prosperity. Here in this bustling, civilized place, they could resupply and find a suitable physician for Peder. He had refused to stop farther south, wanting to push closer to their goal. They would winter here if necessary, but she hoped that, since it was only mid-July, they could get to Washington Territory then back home to Maine before winter. It all depended on Peder's health.

Riley looked at her in question, and Elsa nodded. They were releasing Stefan without pressing charges. She was eager to be done with the man and did not want to haggle with the harbor master or police. Sighing, she approached Stefan, but stayed slightly behind Peder's shoulder, despite the fact that the former first mate still wore chains. He looked miserably gray after his weeks in the hold and blinked in the bright sunlight.

"You helped us past the Horn," she said simply. "I will not press charges. But go from here and never come near a Ramstad ship again."

Stefan looked her in the eye as Yancey released him, rubbing his wrists where the manacles had chafed.

"You heard the woman," Peder said. "Be glad I did not whip your back to shreds for making such advances toward my wife."

Stefan did not say a word, just smiled insolently, turned, and walked down the gangplank to the pier and melted into the crowd. Her eyes followed him until she caught sight of Riley, speaking to a man who was writing furiously on a pad of paper. Once in a while, the man would look up to the ship rail and stare at Elsa as he listened. What was Riley telling him?

Peder broke into her reverie. "Are you all right, sweetheart?"

"I am fine," she said, placing her hands on her hips. "But you are going to a hospital for a thorough examination, and that is that. I want to be certain you are completely recovered."

Peder guffawed and met her look. "Elsa, I am fine. A sailor often grapples with malaria. It is part of the trade." She remained there, simply staring back at him, until he sighed. "If it will make you feel better to have some city doctors fuss over me, I'll get it over with. But we leave here within the week. Understood? I need to get to Washington Territory to pick up that load, or Henry Whitehall will telegraph someone else to do it."

"From what I hear, there is more than enough lumber to go around. If Henry's shipment is gone, we'll simply load another and sell it ourselves."

Peder smiled in open admiration. "Well, listen to the captain's bride," he said to the sailors around them. "She sounds more sure of herself than your captain."

"You married well, sir," Riley said, joining them aboard the ship and shaking Peder's hand. "Good to see ya ready to go ashore on your own two legs, Cap'n."

"Good to be out. Now will you kindly show us the way to this harbor's hospital?"

"This way, Cap'n. Oh, and the missus, of course."

"Riley," Elsa said, following him down the gangplank, "who was that man you were speaking to? He looked at me strangely."

"Aw, jest some reporter. From *The Chronicle*. By next week, yer name'll be known all over, ma'am."

They stepped onto the pier, and Elsa reached out to touch his arm. "What did you say?"

"It ain't every day a lady takes a ship most of the way 'round the Horn. Oh, and you'll be a-wantin' this, missus," he said with a cheeky grin. He handed her a fat packet of mail secured from the harbor master. Knowing she was being distracted, Elsa looked anyway. She was so hungry for news from her loved ones! She opened letter after letter as they walked, scanning them for pertinent news, looking up once in a while to make sure she did not lose the men.

There were two letters, forwarded overland from Maine, from her mother. She opened them according to postmark date.

"Papa is rallying!" she said to Peder, almost tripping over a barrel in her excitement. She mumbled an "excuse me" as she bumped one sailor's shoulder and a "pardon me" as she brushed past another. Peder pulled her closer to his side as Riley parted the crowd before them.

"And Carina and Garth are engaged, due to marry in the fall." She grinned at her husband. "Peder, can you believe it? Carina and Garth—*married*. We simply must find a way to go . . ." Her voice trailed as she buried her nose in the next letter, searching for news. "This one is from dear Kristoffer. A girl! Tora had a girl and named her . . . She left! Oh, I *knew* she wouldn't stay. But what about Jessica? . . . Oh, Judy Gimball's helping out with the boys . . . And here's some news for you about the yard."

"Elsa!" Peder said in frustration. "You are driving me crazy with these snippets. Slow down! How about if we wait until we reach the hospital, then you can read me every letter to the word?"

Chastised and a bit miffed, Elsa folded the letters away and followed her husband and Riley to the closest thoroughfare. There they hailed a cab and set off at a brisk clip.

"May I read as we ride?" Elsa asked stiffly.

"Well, of course," Peder said with a sigh. He scowled at Riley, who was hiding a smile, clearly enjoying the tiff. "I'm sorry if I hurt your feelings," he said in a low voice. "I am as anxious for news as you, but it is maddening to hear mere selections of what is bound to be an opera. Just read me the whole letter if you're going to share any of the news."

"Fine." She sighed. "Forgive me. I'm being silly. Here," she said, stretching her arm out to him. "Another one from Kristoffer, addressed to you. Probably about the yard."

Instead of opening another to read for herself, she hugged the letters to her chest and watched as Peder read his. It would take her all evening to read and savor all the mail! For now she was content to enjoy her happy anticipation since the letters, with both their good and bad tidings, felt like gentle hugs from faraway friends and family.

She stared at her husband as he read Kristoffer's letter. Was she being overly sensitive to his brusque manner and irritation? He was, after all, still battling to get well. Yet Elsa could not get over the idea that something was deeply wrong between them. At some point Peder had become dissatisfied with her, and soon, very soon, Elsa intended to discover why.

When Peder awakened the next morning, he felt better than he had in weeks. A long night's restful sleep between cool, crisp, clean sheets, and the care of physicians and nurses, had restored his spirit. It still bothered him to be fussed over, and he had remained in the hospital mostly for Elsa's sake. When he'd thought it through, however, he realized that if Elsa had been the one taken ill, he would have insisted on the same. And despite himself, he'd enjoyed the best night of sleep he'd had in a long while.

As he opened his eyes and looked around, he was pleased to discover Elsa by his side, with the curtains drawn about his bed, closing them off from the other patients in the ward. Then he noticed the tears in her eyes and on her cheeks.

"Elsa? What is it?"

"Papa. He died," she said, choking on the words. "Last spring."

"What? I thought you told me your mother wrote he was rallying!"

"That was the first letter." She sobbed and tried to get her tears under control. Peder waited patiently. "In the second, she told me he had passed on." Her voice cracked again. "She said he rallied just for her. He even got well enough to walk outside. Then he kissed her that night and was gone by morning."

Peder sat up and swung his legs over the side of the bed. "I'm sorry, love. So sorry. I know how close you were to your father." He pulled her from the chair to the bed and into his arms, trying to think of something to comfort her. "Perhaps your mother will consider coming to America now."

Elsa simply sobbed in response. Feeling helpless, Peder said nothing more.

Nearly an hour later, Elsa was quiet, yet remained in his arms. "At least *you* are well," she said softly. "I was so frightened, Peder. So afraid that you might die."

Peder smiled ruefully. "I'm sorry you had to go through that."

He leaned back against the pillows and studied her. He was suddenly weary again, so weary, and wondered about the woman he had married, thinking back to the feminine, inexperienced girl on the cliffs of Bergen in comparison to the capable woman at his side, seasoned by the past year. If he had died at sea, what would she have done? Contacted Karl? He pushed aside the thoughts that had plagued him for months, memories that had drifted through his fever-ridden torment.

She was his wife, and he liked the way she was changing, growing. "I feel I'm just beginning to know you," he told her. "To understand the woman I only knew as a girl."

She took his hand. "Thank you for bringing me along on the *Sunrise*, Peder. I know you have had doubts about the wisdom of having a woman—your wife—on board. And matters were not helped by Mason Dutton, Karl's departure, Stefan, the Horn . . . I know those incidents probably made you think twice about it. But this is right, Peder. It is right for me to be by your side. And I would like you to look back at all those events and think as I do: that God has smiled on us. He has shown us that we can weather all that and still be safe in his arms. Isn't our arrival here evidence of that?"

"I am still not convinced, Elsa. I do not know if I am being selfish and stupid for bringing you along or wise and gracious. But since you raised the matter, there's something I need to discuss with you, love." He paused to choose his words carefully as his thoughts went again from Elsa to Karl's departure. He lowered his voice, conscious of other patients nearby. "Something that has eaten at my insides since the West Indies, and it is high time I get it off my chest."

Elsa grew a shade paler. "Yes?"

Peder took a deep breath and plunged on. It was time he knew. "Did something transpire between you and Karl that I should know of?"

Elsa's eyes met his and narrowed, her brow furrowed in a deep frown. She shook her head. "What do you mean?"

Peder shifted, uncomfortable in phrasing such a difficult question. "I mean something . . . of a base nature. Did Karl . . . Do you know why . . . That night on the island, did he hold you? What I mean to say is . . . was he ungentlemanly in any way?"

Slowly she took his hand, and Peder prepared himself for the worst. "Peder Ramstad, I have never been unfaithful to you. Never. You have to believe that."

"But that night," Peder insisted. "Karl had that chest wound, and there was blood all over your dress, yet you were unharmed."

Elsa looked down at the sheets across his chest as if visualizing that night. She licked her lips and spoke. "Karl Martensen saved my life. More than once." She looked into Peder's eyes. "I think you're aware that he felt something for me. I . . . I realized it too late." Her eyes begged him to understand. "We were trying to find our equilibrium after the fight. He kissed me, Peder, nothing more, then you arrived at the clearing. I think that's why he felt he had to leave. I'm sorry. I should have—"

"You let him kiss you?"

Elsa looked up, embarrassed by his loud, personal question. "Please, keep your voice down. No. Yes. I mean, I did not intend—"

"What did you intend, Elsa?" He felt his face flush with rage. "I told myself that it could not happen. Certainly my best friend was faithful to me, and certainly my wife—"

"Peder, you must understand. I did not realize in time. Karl saved my life. I was shaking so badly I could not stand. He picked me up just before I fainted, then I was in his arms and . . . Oh, please, Peder!" Tears slipped down her cheeks. "You must believe me. I did not know it was coming. Surely you understand that had I known, I would not have let him near."

Peder pulled his arm from her hands. "Go away, Elsa. Leave me for a moment. I must think this through."

Swallowing hard and wiping the tears from her face, Elsa rose with as much dignity as she could muster. She had chalked up Peder's emotional distance to the malaria, but all along there had been something more. He had suspected the truth that night but said nothing.

"I never intended to come between you and Karl," she said quietly, then turned and swept out of the room as six other patients covertly watched her departure. Her husband did not.

❧

Tora studied her reflection in the dormitory mirror as she waited for Trent to arrive. She wrung her hands nervously. They were taking a train to Saint Paul that afternoon to attend the wedding of Alicia Hall's older sister. And she was certain that the one man who could destroy her would be there. Karl Martensen. Now Alicia Hall's fiancée. He knew her secrets yet had said nothing that day on the train. But she also knew that Alicia Hall had taken note of Karl's attention to her. The girl had watched her with catlike eyes, and Tora knew the look. It was one she could picture on her own face.

She did not want to mess with Alicia Hall. No, she and Trent would attend this wedding, and she would do her best to blend into the crowd. Surely a society wedding like this would be crowded with people. Tora had even taken care to wear the simpler of her two ball gowns, choosing the silver over the red. "Get in and get out," she coached herself.

It was the giggling that tipped her off that Trent had arrived downstairs. "He's here," Missy Alexander said, ducking her head in the door, her face covered with a silly grin. "Oooh, you look lovely!"

"You think so?" Tora fretted, for once in her life wishing she did not. Not because she did not wish to attract Trent, but so she would not be noticed by Karl or his fiancée. Alicia and Karl could destroy her chances with Trent Storm: Karl through his knowledge of her past, and Alicia through a well-placed word with her father. John J. Hall's business was much too important to Trent for him to ignore the man's wishes. No, Tora did not want to invoke the ire of either Alicia or Karl.

"Tora?" Missy asked from the doorway. "Are you going down? Mr. Storm's waitin' on ya."

"I *know*. I'll be down shortly."

Missy backed away as if stung. Served her right for meddling, Tora thought. She paced back and forth. Perhaps she should not wear the silver dress. Maybe a plain Sunday dress would be a better choice. But that would never work, not for such an important social occasion. Besides, such a modest costume might arouse Trent's suspicions. A knock at her half-open door made her jump. It was Trent, hat in hand.

"Excuse me, Tora," he said apologetically. "If we do not leave right away, I am afraid we will miss our train. I asked Missy to come back up and get you, but she refused." He looked puzzled.

"Yes, yes, Trent. I am so sorry," Tora said, rushing to the door and opening it all the way. "Forgive me. I was searching for a . . . a hand-kerchief."

"Will this do?" he asked, pulling a rich silk square from his pocket.

"Yes, yes. That will do." She took his arm and forced herself to smile. "I always cry at weddings."

He looked at her with a grin as he led her down the stairs. "Now why do I doubt that?"

Karl moved as if in a dream, dressing for the wedding while thinking of the last nuptials he had attended. Where were Peder and Elsa? Were they all right? He dismissed the thoughts. Undoubtedly, the Ramstads were better off without him. That self-reassurance still did not keep him from missing his best friends or the other Bergensers. He felt so far from what he had once considered home; Bergen was a lifetime ago, and memories of Camden faded in the distance. It seemed his whole life had been changed. For the better, he reminded himself. Today Alicia's sister would wed. And soon—as soon as Alicia got around to setting the date—they would wed. The reality of it sent a charge through his body that made his heart beat double-time.

An image of Elsa flashed through his mind before he could stop it. Curiously it was an image from their childhood. He could not peg the exact location, but he remembered her musical laughter and the color high in her cheeks as they raced barefoot across a grassy knoll to a mountain swimming hole. It was there that the boys typically dived recklessly into the icy waters, and Elsa followed suit. He could vaguely picture Carina sitting demurely on the edge, dipping her toes in. Tora was probably too young to keep up. But Elsa was right there with them, diving in, drawing the admiration of all.

Perhaps it was her swan dive from the *Sunrise* that had awakened the memory. Thankfully the memory only evoked tender feelings, not the longing of days past. Had the healing begun? He had prayed for hours at a time, often on his knees in the middle of the night, beseeching his Lord for relief. It was a good thing that his prayer seemed to be answered of late. For he was marrying another in a matter of months. Perhaps his own marital happiness would drive away the last vestiges of his mad pursuit of Elsa Ramstad. Maybe one day they could all be friends. The thought brought him some comfort.

"Thinking of your own future bride?" Brad asked, brushing his jacket and pinning a rose boutonniere to his lapel.

Karl shifted uncomfortably. "And other things."

Brad looked him in the eye. He was quiet for an instant before speaking. "You do love her, Karl, right?"

Karl blinked. "I think so."

Brad laughed and slapped him on the back. "Well, it's a good thing, old boy because if you back out now, the boss will have your hide. It's one thing for Alicia to leave a man—and believe me, there have been plenty—but quite the opposite to think of a man leaving Alicia."

An image of John hunting him down to mount his skin in his trophy room brought a sardonic smile to Karl's lips. "Shall we go?"

"She's a prize, you know," Brad said over his shoulder, leading him out the door.

He had a cabby waiting, who opened the door ceremoniously. Karl hopped in, smiling. Brad climbed in behind him and hit the roof twice with his cane to indicate they were ready. The cab lurched off, the horses' hooves clop-clopping on the cobblestone street.

"As I was saying, Alicia is a prize. But wait until you catch sight of my lady tonight." Brad sighed dramatically. "Virginia Louise Parker." He sighed again, and Karl kicked him.

"I do not jest, my friend," Brad said, sitting up and reaching out his hands to trace an hourglass shape. "If this feeling keeps up, I'm bound to be in your shoes."

"What? Engaged? Well, it is time I meet the lady, then," Karl said. "She's probably an old maid if she's taken up with the likes of you."

"Ha! Well, I might not have John Hall's ear at the moment—like some I might mention—but I'm poised to make something of myself. No sir, Virginia is not some old maid. She's a peach, and I aim to pluck her."

Karl frowned at him.

"Nothing ungentlemanly, mind you. I intend to do the honorable thing. I just do not intend to wait long enough for another man to get any ideas."

The cabby pulled to a stop in front of a Saint Paul mansion. "I see you intend to marry well," Karl said dryly.

Brad hopped out then turned back to waggle his eyebrows once at him. Karl chuckled and watched as his friend hurried up the front steps, spoke briefly to a butler, then disappeared inside the house. In a few moments, he emerged, proud as a peacock, a pretty brunette on his arm. When they reached the cab, Karl held out a hand to assist her.

"Thank you, sir," she said quietly, confidently, looking into his eyes for a moment. "I assume you are Mr. Martensen?"

"I am. And you are Miss Parker?"

"Indeed." She nodded once. Pretty, but not gorgeous. Sensible. He liked her immediately. It fit, that a rapscallion like Brad would find a woman like her to keep him in line. *Yes, it could work,* he mused.

"You are meeting Alicia?"

Karl nodded. "At the church. She is attending her sister. Do you know her?"

"A bit. I am an acquaintance of the Halls, but have never quite been accepted into their inner social circle."

Karl frowned, a bit uncomfortable at her frankness.

"My father and Mr. Hall had a parting of ways some years ago. The invitation to this wedding came as some surprise."

"Oh. I see." He could not help but feel that the Halls' ways were now his own responsibility. After all, at some point he would be kin. "Perhaps in time your father and Mr. Hall will mend—"

"No, no. Forgive me if I made you uncomfortable, Mr. Martensen. I simply felt that since Alicia is your fiancée, you should know that some water has passed under the bridge between our families. If you did not know, it might prove . . . uncomfortable."

Silence descended upon them, and all three listened to the creak of the coach and the rhythm of horseshoes until Brad broke in. "Trust my date to lay her cards on the table. See why I am crazy about her?"

Virginia smiled and swatted him with her purse. She looked over at Karl. "He makes me laugh. I make him be serious. A lovely arrangement, don't you agree?"

Karl smiled, the mood restored. "I am happy for you both," he said quietly.

Soon the cab pulled to a stop outside a huge Roman Catholic basilica, and Brad reached up to pay the driver as they exited. At least fifty carriages stretched out on both sides of the street, their drivers and doormen idling about in the sweltering July humidity, awaiting the return of their passengers. Karl followed Brad and Virginia as they climbed the grand, wide steps and entered the church.

He paused to gape at the entry while Brad took their hats and canes and disappeared. Almost every seat was already filled, even in the balcony. The sanctuary temperature must have risen ten degrees purely from the bodies that packed the pews.

"What's this?" he whispered to Brad upon his return. "A wedding ceremony or a business function for John?"

"Both," Brad said, stepping out to follow an usher who had Virginia on his arm. Karl had no choice but to follow. "The Halls practically financed this entire building," Brad muttered under his breath as they walked side by side down the aisle. "Your future mother-in-law is much more devout than John. He did it to please her."

Karl fought the urge to whistle. "I hope she was mollified," he whispered as they sat down.

The ceremony, which included a High Mass, went on for over two hours, with the priest speaking in Latin and the crowd fanning themselves or dabbing at foreheads with handkerchiefs. At one point Virginia leaned toward Karl and whispered, "I hope no one faints up there," nodding toward the wedding party. It was with some relief on everyone's part that bride and groom were pronounced man and wife, and the organ played the recessional.

Not until the reception at a luxurious downtown hotel did Karl see Tora, who gestured to him from the coatroom. Her presence hit him with all the warmth of a Bering Strait iceberg. His smile fading, he walked toward her quickly, wanting them to have their words and get it over with.

"Since I've seen no evidence of your child, I assume you've dumped it on someone else," he said without preamble. "With whom? Elsa?"

"Shhh," she said, scowling and pulling him into the small room, where she partially closed the door. "I found a suitable home for her."

"And Kristoffer's boys?"

"I fulfilled my duty to him. The deal was six months for passage to America. I stayed for eight."

"Because you were pregnant. Do you not realize that Kris was in love with you?"

"Never mind about all that," she said, waving her hand in dismissal. "That is past. You know about the past, don't you, Karl?" she asked slyly. She gestured about her. "We have both entered a new world. All I want is your promise that you will not say a word to Trent about knowing me. We will pretend that we simply have never met."

"Why? Will it not be a bit odd since we're both from Bergen? It will only be a matter of time before someone puts two and two together. Then our duplicity will only seem worse." It dawned on him why she was so anxious. "Oh, I understand. Trent's your new conquest. And you will present yourself as a virgin bride."

"And why not? I was taken advantage of—"

"Advantage, my foot. You cannot fool me, Tora Anders. No one has ever taken advantage of you in your life." Through the half-open door he caught a glimpse of Alicia in the hotel lobby, looking for him so they could make their entrance into the ballroom. "I have to go, Tora."

"Not before I have your promise."

"I will not promise you that."

"Yes, you will," she said, crossing her arms. "You will, or I'll have your fiancée thinking your intentions were not entirely honorable with me here in the coatroom."

Karl glared at her. "Like you did with Soren Janssen, right?"

"Promise me."

"Fine. Just stay out of my life, Tora Anders," he said, shaking a finger in her face. "Stay clear."

He turned to leave, paused, then said over his shoulder, "And wait five minutes to leave this room so there is no suspicion."

"Agreed," she said, obviously pleased.

How in the world had Tora Anders drawn him into her falsehoods? he wondered moments later, forcing a smile and taking Alicia's arm.

"May I present Mr. Karl Martensen and Miss Alicia Hall!" the doorman cried.

The ballroom erupted in applause as if they were royalty.

thirty

July 25, 1881

lsa stood at the bow of the *Sunrise,* her nose lifted to the wind. She could smell the fresh tang of pine and the loamy scent of the fertile ground not a half mile from the ship's deck. Her father would have loved this place. The thought pained her heart, for she longed to share her new life with her father. At least she still had her mother, and perhaps someday soon Gratia would come to live with them. If only Peder would come and stand beside her—come and wrap his arms around her! To some extent, that might help relieve her grieving heart. Instead he had anchored his anger deep within, holding onto his resentment, refusing to let it out with the tide.

She chastised herself for dwelling on this matter yet again. Peder would have to find his own way to deal with his feelings and whatever else was troubling him. In the meantime, a new land stretched before her, and Elsa intended to relish each moment. Seattle was a tiny town of mud and few civilized attributes, but she loved its spirit already. The dense conifer forests reminded her of Bergen, and with the many rushing river ways that dumped into Puget Sound, the territory was ripe for a healthy logging business. Elsa had decided that

Henry Whitehall knew what he was doing. Washington Territory would make many wealthy, and the Ramstads should share in the bounty.

As Peder approached, she turned and watched a steamboat leaving a nearby river and entering Puget Sound, hauling freshly harvested pine behind in a great net.

"You see her?" she said, pointing across the Sound. If she could not reach him on a personal level, perhaps she could approach him through talk of work.

"I do."

"You realize that we could build our own?"

"Of course." His tone indicated he didn't follow her train of thought.

"Think of it, Peder. If we built a couple more schooners and a steamboat like that one, we could have our own lumber business."

"I have enough on my mind without building a second business on top of the first."

He turned away, and she followed, echoing his slow gait.

"But what is to learn? You have been around Ramstad Yard in Bergen all your life. The *Sunrise* is testimony that you can build ships." She reached out to touch his arm, then waved at the coastline before them. "Does this not feel right to you somehow?" She shook her head. "I cannot shake it. It's like God is nodding and smiling. I can *feel* it."

Peder looked at her as if she had lost her mind. "So what? You want us to leave Camden? The house I've built you?" He shook his head. "No. We have enough to handle without moving to a town in an area that has not yet even claimed her statehood. Tend to your painting, Elsa. Leave the business to me."

His tone stung, and Elsa set her mouth in a grim line. "I would appreciate if you would not just dismiss—"

"I am the head of this family. I would appreciate if you did not challenge me."

She sighed in frustration. "And I would appreciate if you were not so imperious that I cannot even discuss our future—my future—with you."

Peder ran his hand through his hair, leaving a curl resting on his forehead. "I am willing to discuss with you any wise options, Elsa. I simply do not think this place is good for us—for any reason other than to load and leave."

She looked at him and back to the coast. It was beautiful. The towering, snow-capped mountain ranges were awe-inspiring, and the hills, with their thick evergreens, appeared more verdant and fresh than Maine. It was rough and yet inviting at the same time. It was so . . . *new.* Rough and untamed, ready to be made into anything they wanted.

"So you feel nothing?" she asked, waving toward it. How could he *not* feel what she did for this new land? "You do not feel any tugging at your heart?"

"You speak nonsense, Elsa," he said in dismissal. "If you think it is so beautiful, why not break out your oils and canvas and paint it?"

She swallowed her anger. Sometimes Peder could be fearfully pigheaded. No wonder Karl had been frustrated with him! She turned away and stared at the steamboat pulling away into the distance. No, she was sure of it. Steam and Seattle were in their future whether Peder liked it or not. It would just take him a while to discover the truth of it.

Peder left Elsa on deck and went into his study. The room was crowded with a table holding the standard seaman's charting equipment—an hourglass, sextant, his logbook, nautical maps—as well as a huge roll-top desk he had purchased in China, which had miraculously escaped damage from the fire. He sat down heavily at the desk, thinking about Elsa and Karl for the thousandth time. The island . . . the kiss . . . In a rage he stood, knocking over his chair. He clenched his teeth and swept the table clean with one arm, feeling some satisfaction as everything fell to the floor with a crash and *whoosh* of papers. He glanced back at the desk . . . and the envelope lying on it.

It was the letter that finally broke him. Addressed to him, clearly identifiable as Karl's handwriting. Crumpled and unfolded again and again, yet unopened since he had received it in San Francisco. Sinking to his knees on the hard pine flooring, he began to weep.

"Why?" he cried, looking upward as if able to see God in the wooden moldings. "How could you let this happen? He was like a brother to me. He was like a brother . . ."

He still is. The voice of God was discernible to Peder, regardless of the fact that he had shut out the Savior for months.

"No. A brother does not act as Karl has."

Leave his judgment to me.

"That's fine with me. You can send him where he deserves," Peder spat out. "But what am I to do with her?" he raged, standing and gesturing toward the door. He began pacing the cabin.

Be her husband.

"I was her husband, and I obviously was not enough, was I?" His words rang hollow, even to him. He heard no answer. "Lord, Lord, I cannot deal with it."

You are strong.

"Not this strong. She has not even asked my forgiveness!"

Forgive.

"Me? She has wronged *me*! She was not faithful! She let him kiss her! She should have seen it coming!" He was indignant. His tears dried on his hot face. He no longer felt God's presence, just the chilly dampness of the cabin.

"What is fidelity? What does it mean to be faithful?" he mumbled as he righted his chair and sat at the desk again. "Friendship . . ."

After a moment he picked up the letter and stared at it then beyond to his Chinese desk. He studied the ornately carved dragons and lotus blossoms and exotic diving birds along the top. Beneath was a more pastoral scene of inlaid pearl, depicting gently climbing hills, drooping trees, and gay birds.

He looked back at the letter. "Were you a dragon after my lotus blossom, Karl?" he ground out. He dropped the letter then rubbed his face in exhaustion.

Peder knew he had to deal with his anger, his jealousy, his harbored bitterness . . . to get beyond it. He *knew* that. But how could Karl have kissed his wife? How could Karl have endangered his best friend's marriage . . . their friendship . . . and his own future as well? Surely his prospects in Saint Paul were less sure than in Camden-by-the-Sea, regardless of how their plans for the yard had changed. Peder would have made him successful, even though *Ramstad* was the only name on the sign. Peder knew what loyalty, what friendship meant. Apparently Karl did not.

Sudden guilt struck him a devastating blow as he remembered his own sin. He had not been entirely forthright with Karl, after all. He had been disingenuous for months, hiding his father's financial gift from his friend and partner. Had he made the right decision? Would it not have been a better choice, would he not have been a better man, to gently refuse his father's money and follow through with the plans he had made with Karl? They would have made slower progress . . . the *Sunrise* would not yet have been launched . . . there would have been no voyage with Elsa along. No Mason Dutton. No island. No reason for Karl's defenses to be down, nor Elsa's.

"O God," he muttered. "I have been as guilty as they. Forgive me."

Forgive them.

Peder nodded once, knowing the truth yet unable to act upon it.

Was it memories of similar conversations with Karl about steamboats that had made Peder react as he had earlier to Elsa? Her suggestions and careful tone irritated him, chafing at his mind. He swallowed back the suspicion, the disastrous assumption that Elsa had spoken privately with Karl, agreeing to side with him, to work on Peder from the inside. The image of them together, kissing, threatened to swallow him, like a sea monster dragging them all down to the bottom.

She was innocent. Time and again Peder came to the same conclusion, chastising himself for thinking her capable of anything else. She was kind and loving to all and undoubtedly, one of the most beautiful women he had ever seen. Karl, who had also known Elsa since childhood, became infatuated with her from afar. The life-threatening drama played out in the West Indies had brought it all to the surface, tempting Karl to reveal his feelings.

God has a purpose for all things, he told himself. "And there had better be a good one for this," he muttered, anger building again.

With renewed resolve, he opened the letter to see what Karl had to say.

> *23 June 1881*
> *Dear Peder,*
>
> *By this time, I assume that you know the truth of why I had to leave the Sunrise and your side. I have betrayed you, my friend, and I will be eternally sorry for my actions. Please know that the love I felt for Elsa is old, as much a part of me as my right arm. As I think about it, I suppose I fell in love with her right along with you. It does not excuse my rash actions, nor ease the anger you undoubtedly feel toward me. After that night on the island when my body took control of my soul, I knew I had no other choice. I had to leave. To get far away from Elsa. For as much as she is completely devoted to you, I doubted myself. Forgive me, Peder. Please forgive me. In time, I hope that both you and Elsa will find room in your hearts to forgive me.*

*Things have progressed well in Saint Paul. John J.
Hall has taken me under his wing, and as a result, I
have been given unprecedented business opportunities.
In that regard, I am hoping you might be able to buy
out my investment in the Sunrise upon your return to
Camden, essentially ending our business involvement
for good. I trust that the ship is continuing to sail
beautifully and that your voyage will pay off handsomely. I will use my portion of the bounty to invest
here. For my future is here. You see, last night I pro-
posed to Hall's daughter Alicia.*

Peder let the letter fall to his desk. How could Karl have gone so
far? Henry Whitehall and James Kingsley, when gently probed, had
had little good to say about John J. Hall. The man was known for
shady business practices and ruthless ways. Now Karl was about to
marry the man's daughter? Or already had . . . And invest in his business? Peder shook his head. Karl was headed on a dangerous path. But
he was getting ahead of himself, Peder thought. Perhaps what
Whitehall and Kingsley had shared was merely hearsay.

*I believe that this will be a wise move, Peder.
Separating completely might allow us both to heal so
that at some point we may reunite as old friends. It is
not the way of our faith to allow such bitter feelings
to fester, and I do not want to be guilty of throwing
salt on the wound. I pray that you will forgive me. It
is my hope that later we will come back together as
the brothers we have always been.*
*You should also know that I have seen Tora. She
has moved to Minnesota and is reportedly being
courted by Trent Storm, the famous dinner-house
mogul. She seems well and happy, although she made
it quite clear she does not want anyone to know of*

our past association. She is trying to begin anew here, and apparently figures any knowledge of her past would inhibit her progress. I am sorry to say I do not know what became of her child. I pray that you do.

Wish all my old friends well from me, and if you find a moment to do so, pray that my own bride-to-be and I forge a marriage as solid as your own.

Sincerely,
Karl Martensen

⤜✺⤏

Tora opened her fan and closed her eyes as a wave of warm, humid air swept over her. Dressed for dinner and riding in Trent's carriage, she felt as if she would suffocate in the heat.

"Warm?" Trent asked mildly from the bench seat across from her.

"It is stifling. Never in my life have I felt such heat."

"Bergen was never this warm?"

"Warm, yes, but not so hot that one perspires. It is not even ladylike to shine like this."

"But hardly avoidable. The East Coast is similar once you leave the ocean." Trent frowned slightly. "Which reminds me, Tora, I would appreciate hearing how you came to live in Camden-by-the-Sea. If it is not prying, of course."

Tora licked her lips. "Not at all. I've told you of that terrible night when my ship and loved ones went down to the bottom." She frowned, working up some tears.

"If it is too much—"

"No," she said, raising a hand. "It is only that when I think of my dear parents and sisters drowning, and that I am all alone in this world, it overwhelms me."

Trent nodded, his look compassionate, yet a bit wary. She had not yet hooked him, but he was intrigued. Tora was sure of it. Perhaps this evening would be the clincher.

She shook out a handkerchief and dabbed at her face and neck.

"Papa was quite wealthy and bound for America to increase his re-sources. We were all excited to come to the new frontier."

"What did you say your father's business was?"

"Mining, of some sort," she said vaguely. "Papa never did want us girls to meddle the business. He thought it was thoroughly men's work."

Trent nodded, apparently accepting her explanation. "Unfortu-nately, all he owned was sold and carried aboard that ship in gold," she said.

Trent frowned, and Tora immediately understood that such a move would have been a poor decision for a good businessman to make. "I will never understand why he did things the way he did." A tear crested one lid and slowly rolled down her cheek. She smiled bravely. "He was a stubborn old man, and we never did see eye to eye. Nevertheless, I loved him and my family."

"Of course. It is a miracle that you survived."

"By the grace of God and a floating, broken mast to which I clung."

"What a horrible thing to have gone through." Trent sat back and studied her as the coach came to a stop in front of the restaurant. "It is interesting that I did not read of such a disaster. Shipwrecks almost always make the headlines."

Tora had not thought of that angle. "It was an old clipper ship, mostly used for cargo. We were practically the only passengers aboard. Perhaps it was not newsworthy. Or perhaps you missed the newspaper that day." She leaned forward. "But enough of sad memories. Really, Trent, I would prefer not to speak of it again. It is simply too painful. Should we not go in and eat? Hopefully it will be cooler indoors. And you will make me laugh like you always do, dear Trent, rather than bring a poor girl to tears."

"Indeed," Trent said.

She could feel his eyes upon her as she exited the coach, clinging to his hand. But she did not dare to meet his gaze.

❧

Karl stared at himself in the mirror as he wearily dressed for dinner. Alicia, proclaiming dining at home to be dreary, demanded they eat elsewhere each evening. Feeling inadequate and guilty for being unable to treat Alicia in the manner to which she was accustomed, Karl had procured a small loan from his future father-in-law to afford such niceties as dining in a restaurant each evening. Soon enough his own investments would begin to pay out, and he would find himself in a more affluent position. Until then he would simply have to swallow his pride.

What continued to puzzle him . . . nay, trouble him . . . was the fact that Hall must have seen this predicament coming. Indeed, there was little doubt in Karl's mind that John had thoroughly checked him out before hiring him. So why had he allowed such a poor Bergenser close to his daughter when his promising future still lay far off? Alicia had had far more prosperous suitors, but for some reason, she and her father both had favored Karl from the beginning. He knew that Alicia was given to frivolous ways, and her devotion could be attributed to love. But what was Hall's motive? The question plagued Karl.

Certainly John appreciated the stature it gave him to have what he called a swashbuckling, prosperous sea captain for a future son-in-law, regardless of the fact that Karl had not captained his own ship prior to reaching Saint Paul. But why bet his daughter's future on the promise of Karl's until it was a sure thing? Instead, John had moved as he always did, making quick, sure decisions and never looking back.

"Just never prove him wrong," Brad had said when Karl voiced his qualms. "Never *ever* prove him wrong."

Karl had laughed uneasily, nodding as if he understood. But what would transpire if his future did not unfold as golden as they all anticipated?

He wondered about this as he climbed into the Halls' coach and tapped the roof with his cane. Alicia was lovely, and in her arms, he was able to push Elsa out of his mind. She was a delight, often making him laugh at her antics. How long had it been since he had laughed as he had these last weeks? Not to mention her powerful feminine wiles, which made him long for the physical pleasures of a married man. He had sailed long enough to hear many a bawdy story from the sailors aboard ship. He had even been tempted more than once by the women who worked the docks, but had abstained, conscious of the purity the Christian life demanded. Now the few kisses and embraces Alicia had allowed him were enough to drive him mad with anticipation.

At the Hall mansion, where he waited for Alicia in the front parlor, Karl retied his ascot, watching his long fingers in the Tiffany-wrought mirror. His hands were getting soft, the calluses fading away. He thought of Elsa and the island as if they were a half-world and a lifetime away. Memories of Peder saddened him. For he knew that if his best friend dared to kiss his Alicia as he had Elsa, his own fury would burn bright. Why had he been so foolish? So weak? He shook his head at the madness of that night. He closed his eyes for a moment, searching for God in his heart. Why did he still feel so distant? Karl could make little sense of it.

Alicia swept into the room, looking glorious in a deep green gown. She smiled brightly. "I thought we would try Chez Pierre tonight, darling. It's all the rage about town. Janice said the food is unlike anything you have ever eaten in your life."

"Well, we cannot pass that up, can we?" Karl asked indulgently, glancing carefully around before taking her into his arms. She finished tying his ascot for him. "Unless of course I can persuade you to stay home and cook for a change." He grinned as her expression turned to exasperation.

She straightened to her full, petite height. "I am afraid it will be a long wait before I ever make you a meal. You can, however, join the family for breakfast or luncheon any day you wish."

"I figured as much."

"And that means?"

"That I am better off eating all the crazy nonsense at Chez Pierre than daring to eat a meal you would cook."

Alicia giggled and relaxed. "Why, Karl, I believe you are developing a sense of humor."

"I thought it time to do so. Shall we go?"

"Indeed," she said. She tucked her hand into the crook of his arm as they strolled out to the foyer. "Mother?" she called.

Mrs. Hall appeared at the top of the stairs. "Going?"

"To Chez Pierre."

"Have a good time. Good night, Karl."

"Good night, Mrs. Hall," he said with a nod.

After they entered the coach and the driver had pulled out into traffic, Karl turned to his fiancée and asked, "Alicia, what can you tell me about the Parkers?"

"The Parkers? Not much. Mr. Parker and Daddy once worked together."

"And now?"

"They had a parting of ways. Daddy wants nothing to do with him. I hear," she said carefully, looking Karl in the eye, "that Bradford has been seeing Virginia."

Karl nodded slightly. "Is that a problem?"

"No." She shrugged. "Why ever would it be a problem?"

"I wondered how the association might affect your father, since Brad works for him."

"I cannot say. Yet I would not be surprised if Mr. Bresley is soon called upon to demonstrate his loyalty to Daddy."

"In what fashion?"

"How should I know? Really, Karl, can we not speak of something more interesting than business? It's all I hear from Daddy." She reached into her beaded purse, and for the first time, he noticed how her hands trembled. He looked at her more closely. Her face was pale.

"Alicia? Are you well? Should we return to the house?"

"No, no. I am fine." She unlatched her purse and fumbled in it. "I simply need some smelling sal—" Suddenly she slumped forward in a faint. Karl knelt and caught her, laying her gently on the seat as he yelled for the driver to stop.

Alicia's open purse spilled its contents on the floor. Face paint, a handkerchief, smelling salts. As he reached for the smelling salts, the coach came to a halt . . . and so did his hand. There, peeking out of the purse, was a small vial labeled *Laudanum.*

thirty-one

By August the *Sunrise* was on her way home—"loaded to the gills," as Riley put it—with rough-hewn lumber. The cargo cast such a sweet scent about the ship that Elsa had a hard time smelling the ocean's briny odor she had come to know so well. Happily it reminded her of Seattle and her dreams of one day settling there.

In her usual place on deck, she leaned against her chair back and sighed at the blank canvas before her. Her heart was unsettled, her spirits down. She and Peder were still not getting along. Ever since she had made one small comment about the potential of a lumber business, Peder had avoided her like a mosquito carrying malaria. Suddenly her painting was not expression; it was bondage. He wanted to confine her with it and to it, and preferably at Camden-by-the-Sea. Her painting was neat. Orderly. It worked well with his own vision of how life was to be.

Elsa took her brush in hand and smeared a big, black streak of oil across the canvas, feeling better as each stroke of paint left her brush. Smiling for the first time in days, she took a swipe at the red and let that go. Then the green and yellow—although yellow was not nearly as satisfying as deep black.

Peder climbed up the stairs toward her, and Elsa was eager for him to see her work. Perhaps it would be the catalyst to end their ongoing strife. He stood behind her silently, obviously taking in the canvas before them.

"A new direction?" he tried after a bit.

"An artistic expression," she said, her voice clipped.

"Of?"

"I think you know, Peder."

"I do? Perhaps you could remind me."

She sighed and stood to face him. "I am frustrated. I am sorry I feel that way, but I do. We are in a partnership, you and I. You are not some king, and I am certainly not a servant."

"When have I ever—"

"I know that I am a fortunate woman, Peder. Truly. And I appreciate it. But you move forward so often without talking with me first. Camden-by-the-Sea is lovely, but not necessarily where I want to live forever, especially alone. Continuing to build sailers rather than steam is your dream, but not necessarily what I think is wise. Still," she said, putting up her hands as Peder stuttered in fury and grew red at the neck, "I understand that it is your business. So I go along with it. But when I come up with an idea, I do not wish for you to dismiss it summarily. I simply ask for the respect I deserve."

Peder groaned. "You do not think I respect you? What I have given you, provided for you, isn't enough? Our home? Your painting lessons? Bringing you along?" He looked at her as if she were a spoiled child.

"You have given me a great deal, Peder. That is not what I mean. What I speak of is what we have, what we do, together—our future. What we work on, work toward, together. I want it to be *our* dream, Peder." She reached out to touch his hand, and it seemed to steady him, calm him. "I want to be your partner in those dreams, too, your friend. Your best friend. I know you miss Karl. And I know you still struggle to forgive me. Can I do anything about that?"

Peder sighed and looked out to sea. "You are my wife, not my business partner. A woman's place is at home, minding the house and children. You see what my decision to bring you along has already brought us? More discontent. Not to mention almost getting you killed."

Elsa swallowed the quick words that jumped to her tongue. "A woman's place, Peder, is at her husband's side. Why label it as discontent? Perhaps it's vision."

"We cannot chase two dreams, Elsa."

"No," she said, tentatively placing an arm around his waist. "But we can pursue *our* dream."

Peder pulled away. "I have given you all there is to give. If it is not enough, so be it."

Elsa watched as her husband climbed down the steps and went to rant at some poor sailor who had tied a square knot instead of a bowline. Biting her lower lip, she picked up her brush again and painted a big, black stripe over the first.

Days later, Peder's argument with Elsa still lingered. He could not rid himself of the bile that rose in his throat each time he thought of saying he was sorry. He was torn between the honest belief that his path was the right one for Ramstad Yard and his devotion to his wife—between forgiving and holding on to his righteous anger. He was beginning to feel that there would be no end to her suggestions, her requests, which aggravated him. Was this married life? Or perhaps he had been a captain for too long.

He walked the deck from bow to stern, thinking about what Elsa had said, reflecting on how the oppressive doldrums they were experiencing echoed his own feelings. It was deadly still, as it had been for days, and incredibly hot and humid. Not a breath of wind was on the air, and the sails slumped like sad, dirty sheets waiting for the laundress. These were the days that Peder hated being a sailor. He was always in a hurry to get to his next destination. Karl would tell him, "Just enjoy the ride, my friend. Enjoy every day for the day it was created to be for you." From the start, Karl had seemed to have a deeper, more intense relationship with God than he, though Peder was witness and Karl the convert. It was as though when Christ entered Karl's heart, he moved closer to Karl than he ever did with Peder. Or maybe it was simply that Karl was better able to recognize God in the everyday.

It was difficult for Peder to see God in this day. It was a soulless afternoon, in his opinion, and only antagonized him, making him feel worse about life than he already did. He wiped the sweat from his brow and billowed out his damp shirt to relieve his perspiring chest. He looked out to sea, where the only ripple was from the dorsal fins of fish beneath the surface. Would this never end? They were already late, desperate to make time to get home, unload their cargo, and bring the *Sunrise* in for the winter. He fought the urge to scream in frustration. Surely if he could just get Elsa home, she would settle into their cottage and prepare for a baby.

Yes! A baby was the answer. It would resolve all of this, for Elsa would be too busy with the child to think of business. He would be free to do as he wished. Yet as exasperating as Elsa was at times—and despite the strife her presence had caused—had Peder ever known greater joy than with her traveling by his side? He thought not.

It is time for a new day. A new horizon.

It was time for forgiveness. *It holds me back,* he thought. *It's been holding me back for months, eh, Father?*

Be renewed, child. Renew.

Without stopping to think, he barked out the order. "Drop the lines! Starboard!"

Sleepy sailors hastened to obey him, a bit befuddled at such a command, but nonetheless following orders.

Peder stripped off his shirt and climbed to the starboard rail.

"Last one in peels potatoes for a year!" He sailed through the air, fighting off the giddy desire to laugh, knowing he would need his breath for his time below the waterline. Just before hitting the water, he heard shouts of glee and men scurrying to the side.

The water parted for his fingertips, and Peder slid through the aquamarine liquid, relishing the relief from the heat. It was no wonder that few fish jumped. It was too wonderful beneath the seas to leave. Conscious of the sounds of impact as other men jumped into the water, Peder relaxed and let his inflated lungs raise his inert body to the surface. It felt as if he were flying . . . going ten, fifteen feet upward until his face met air and he inhaled deeply. Feeling released at last from all the angst of recent days, weeks, months, he rubbed his eyes and hooted a call that all with him echoed.

When he opened his eyes, he spotted Elsa nearby, looking at him like a naughty, caught child. She actually looked frightened, obviously anticipating a sharp reprimand after what had happened the last time she went in the water. "Well, I did not wish to peel potatoes for a year," she said primly, chin up, as she continued to tread water.

Peder laughed. Laughed deeply. Was he such a fool to waste precious days with this wonderful woman beside him? Any days? Regardless of disagreements, life was too short. He wasted no more time. "I have been a fool, Elsa. Forgive me for being a stubborn old sea captain. Forgive me for not being your husband. Forgive me for not being your friend."

She smiled in surprise, her eyebrows tenting to the center as if she wanted to cry. "Oh, Peder," was all she whispered, pulling him underwater for a long kiss. They could hear the men's muted hoots and hollers and cheers. But the impropriety of it mattered little to Peder. He had his wife back. Moreover, he felt like a husband again.

That night Peder and Elsa sat over cold dinner dishes for hours, talking. Every time Cook came in to clear, Peder scowled at the poor man, letting him know he was intruding. Finally the man knocked and entered once more. With a quick bow, he stepped forward and took the dishes, not waiting for Peder's permission.

Peder smiled. "Anxious for your bunk, Cook?"

Cook ignored him.

"Forgive us for loitering," Elsa said. "Please. Leave them until morning."

Cook ignored her.

"I've never known the man to leave dirty dishes until morning," Peder explained.

"New day. New dish," Cook said at last, closing the door behind him.

Peder and Elsa laughed. "A good way to live," she said, looking at Peder meaningfully.

"A good way indeed," Peder said, steadily returning her glance.

How grand it was to again be on an even keel with her husband! Elsa felt dizzy with relief. "Peder, I must ask," she began, reaching across the table to take his hand in hers. "What made you forgive me at last?"

"It was eating at me. Time and again I'd go to the Lord and beg him to show me justice. I got the only justice I was owed. My stomach was in knots. I have not slept more than five hours at a time for months. And I could find no peace in the situation since I felt that I was wronged. But then I saw that you were innocent, my love. That I was punishing you for a sin never committed. It was I who held the sin and built upon it until it was bigger than both of us."

Elsa looked down. "I am sorry, Peder," she whispered.

His hand left hers to lift her chin. "For what?"

"For not seeing the road ahead. Maybe I could have—"

"I understand your heart, love," he interrupted. "Say no more. New day . . ."

"I beg your pardon?"

"New day . . ." he led again.

"New dish," she said.

Several days later the *Sunrise* left the doldrums behind and raced toward the Horn. Fall was coming on quickly, and they had fewer than forty days to get home safely. Anything beyond that was bound to endanger the *Sunrise,* her cargo and crew, when they got into the northern latitudes. So it was with some reluctance that when a brigantine trailing behind hailed them, Peder ordered a number of the sails furled to allow her approach. By that afternoon the *Connor's Day* drew alongside and ran up a flag signaling the request to speak to the captain.

It was rare for a merchant marine to pause mid-voyage for a visit with another. While the whalers commonly did this, being at sea for months at a time, merchants were eager to get their cargo to port and collect their funds. Peder eyed the ship and flag with some skepticism. Was it a trick? His experience with the *Lark* had made him leery. Still, through his scope he could plainly see a woman roaming the deck, and there was little doubt that Elsa would appreciate some female companionship. They had waited this long for *Connor's Day* to approach. What was another two hours?

"Furl all sails!" he directed Riley.

"Furl all sails!" his first mate relayed.

The crew repeated the command in unison.

"Run up the welcome flag," he said, then turned to Elsa. "We're about to have some company, Elsa. Perhaps you should set Cook to some refreshments."

"Run up the come ahead flag!" Riley shouted.

Elsa nodded once and was off, while Peder turned back to watch the *Connor's Day.* A longboat was lowered over the side, carrying what he assumed was the ship's captain, wife, and four crew members. The crewmen each wielded a long oar, rowing in sweet precision, and reached the *Sunrise* in minutes.

"Ahoy!" the captain hailed from the longboat, peering up at Peder. "Permission to board your fine vessel, sir."

"Ahoy!" he greeted. "Come ahead." They climbed up the netting to the rail, and Peder himself leaned to help the woman over the edge.

"Welcome to the *Sunrise*. I am Captain Peder Ramstad." Elsa joined him. "This is my wife, Elsa."

"Pleased to meet you!" the woman squealed. "You don't know how long we've been chasing you people. I told my Otto—this is my husband, Otto Keller—we simply *must* catch up with them. 'The woman's got letters,' I said. Didn't I say that, Otto? And I know what letters mean to a woman at sea." She stretched out her hand, offering Elsa a thick packet of envelopes. "They were in San Francisco. Harbor master said you had already come and gone and weren't anticipated back. Since you were headin' the same way we were, I figured I'd shanghai them for ya."

"Thank you," Elsa said. "Thank you, Mrs. Keller."

"Oh, please. Call me Emma. Short for Emmaline. Too much name for me, though. Everyone calls me Emma."

"Emma," Elsa said, smiling at her new friend.

With one glance at her face, Peder knew the Kellers would stay for dinner.

Long afterward when they had finished dinner and both ships were once more underway, Peder sat down with Elsa to read the letters. Most were for her from Kaatje, with one from Tora and another from Kristoffer to Peder. Peder read his own letter, mumbling about what Kris had to say about the status of his next schooner, problems with laborers, and weather delays. Meanwhile, Elsa read through Kaatje's letters, most of them seeming too personal to read aloud.

"Elsa . . . Kris writes with news of Tora—" his voice broke off as he studied her face. "You have bad news?"

"I do," she said. "That lout Soren left her to work on the railroad. Left her alone on all that land with a baby—or babies, as she says, although I cannot fathom of what she speaks. They could not have had another already!"

334

"Maybe one seems like two to a woman alone on the prairie."

"Indeed. If it hadn't been for her neighbors and the Bergensers, she would not have brought in their first crop."

"He did not return to help her?"

Elsa scanned through the letters again, looking for an answer. "No. He has not returned at all."

"You think he has left her?"

"She says little of him in the last letter. The only good thing about it all is that she says, 'I have been forced to my knees, and somehow I feel taller. The grace of God is an amazing thing, Elsa. For he lives within me. I had forgotten that for a time. But remembering has made me strong.' No, she says it here: 'Pray for me and my daughters. The Lord is mighty, but this world is harsh. Your ever-loving friend, Kaatje.' She says 'daughters'! Another! So soon! And that rat Soren has left them high and dry."

"Perhaps he'll return."

"Perhaps. Why do I doubt him?" she asked, hating the sarcasm she heard in her voice but unable to curb it. "Peder, we must send her some help. Might we wire her some funds? A little something to get her through the winter?"

"Indeed. Consider it done. We shall do it in New York when we unload the Whitehall cargo. It will get to her faster."

"You are so good, Peder. Thank you." She picked up the last letter, a note from Tora. Perhaps her sister had better news. The brief letter was not dated, but covered in her sister's distinctive scroll-like script.

"Her penmanship was always far grander than she," Elsa muttered.

Dear Sister,

By now Kristoffer has undoubtedly shared with you the happy news. You have a niece named Jessica. The greater news is that I have placed her with a loving mother and have gone on to chase my dream. I think I have found it. I am in love with a wonderful man!

His name is Trent Storm, and I intend to finagle a proposal from him someday soon. He is very well-off. Please be happy for me. Please do not be too angry that I have placed my child elsewhere. I admit it was more difficult than anticipated, but better for both of us. Kaatje will take close care of Jessie . . .

Elsa gasped and swallowed hard, feeling sick to her stomach.

Peder looked up from his own letter in concern. "What? What is it?"

"Tora," she said, numbly.

"What has she done now?"

"She left her baby with Kaatje. That is the second child to whom Kaatje refers."

"Kaatje? Why on earth—"

"Soren. Soren is the child's father."

Peder slammed his fist down on the table and swore under his breath. "How could she? How could she do that to Kaatje? She was the innocent among them!"

"She was the means to an end," said Elsa. "Tora wanted Soren to be punished. So she left her child. Her dear, sweet baby . . ." Elsa turned away from the letter, miserable at the grief her sister had brought into Kaatje's life and home.

Peder picked up the letter and read on.

Kaatje will take close care of Jessie, and Jessie will be with her father. I was not cut out to be a mother, Elsa. It was more difficult than expected, but at least it is finished. What is done is done, as they say, and it is doubtful that anyone could be a better mother than your beloved Kaatje. Tell Mama I am well. I will write her when I have reached the station for which I was born. —Tora.

thirty-two

Trent Storm had been dawdling in his courtship of late, Tora decided. The only way to make a man act was to force his hand.

And she thought she knew just the way to do it. As usual, she swept past his secretary and into his office without awaiting permission.

"Miss Anders!" the secretary said loudly, clearly irked at being ignored again. "Miss Anders! He is taking a meeting!"

"Don't worry, dear," she said. "He will not mind, since it's me."

She opened the massive wooden double doors and smiled sweetly as Trent rose and said, "Miss Anders, I'm sorry. I am in the middle of an interview." Tora looked over the sad woman in the chair before his desk and immediately knew she would be placed in the kitchen of some dreary train-stop restaurant.

"I need to speak to you, Mr. Storm. As soon as you are done here?"

The young woman rose. "If you wish, I could come back . . ."

"No, no," said Trent, irritated. "We will only be a minute." He turned to Tora and took her firmly by the arm. "You must stop doing this. You are important to me, but this is rude."

Tora raised her chin in the air and cocked one brow. "I am sorry if I intruded, *Mr.* Storm. It is simply imperative that we speak right away."

"All right, all right." He ran one hand through his elegantly graying hair. "Give me five minutes, and I will meet you for lunch down the street."

"Five minutes," she repeated meaningfully. It felt delicious to have such a hold on a man like Trent Storm! She swept out of the room and down the stairs, again plotting just what she would say and the tone of voice she would use. The next step had to be carefully orchestrated, and it had to be done quickly. Tora had received an invitation from Alicia Hall to attend a ball the following week. She intended to be gone before the woman could figure out the truth. When Trent's ring was on her finger, she could face anyone.

True to form, Trent arrived at the restaurant five minutes later. He sat down and steadily gazed at her across the table. "What do you have up your sleeve?"

"Whatever do you mean?"

"You know exactly what I mean. Tora, you never make a move without thinking about it twice. Why the drama? Why the grand entrance and hush-hush of urgency in your voice?" He leaned back and methodically unfolded his cloth napkin across his lap. The waitress emerged and took their order.

She chose to ignore his questions. "I have been thinking a lot about us of late, Trent. While I enjoy your company, I still have not done what I wanted to do when I first came to Storm Enterprises."

"And what is that?"

"See the wild west. You keep me working here under your eye during the day and on your arm in the evenings. I believe if you and I are to have more than a passing relationship, I need to go on and discover who Tora Anders is . . . what she's made of."

"And you need to go west to do that? All along, I thought you knew exactly who you are."

Tora fidgeted. This was not going as planned. "Of course. Perhaps I misspoke. I suppose I am looking for more. In me and in my life. You offer me the best here in Duluth. But I want adventure. I want to be on my own, prove to the world that Tora Anders is strong and independent."

"I see," Trent said, looking at the plate of food the waitress set before him. "And I hold you back from that?"

"Well, yes. While I have enjoyed your company immensely, Trent," she said, "and it is difficult for me to leave, I feel I must. Send me to the end of the line on whatever railroad John Hall is building currently. I want to set up with the town at the end and roll with the train as we move on. I want to be *first,* Trent. I want to be there. I have a certain business acumen. I could be your representative and get things set up just as you would have them. I know you better than most," she added.

"Indeed. And what if I said I was sorry to see you go?"

Tora smiled. "Do not be silly, Trent. Could you not come to see me anytime you wished? Besides, you have not shared your intentions with me."

"Is that what this is about? Forcing my hand?"

Alarm bells sounded in Tora's head. She needed to douse that fire immediately. "Certainly not," she said with a frown. "I am simply stating the facts. And the facts are that I was promised a position in the West, but then you began to court me. I know not what you intend. I am a woman alone in the world, Trent. And I must look out for my best interests."

"And why is it not in your best interest to remain here and be courted by one of the wealthiest men in Duluth? Do you wish to be rid of me, Miss Anders? For if so, simply say the word. Do not fear for your position. I am a man of honor and would allow you to keep working for Storm Enterprises."

Tora sighed and reached across the table to take his long fingers in her own. "That is not at all what I am saying. Will you not let me go away for a while, Trent? You can determine your intentions, I can have some adventure, and then we will reunite and discuss our future, should there be one."

"So forthright, so businesslike."

Tora winced. "I feel I have little choice. People are beginning to talk. It is unseemly for an employer to see an employee socially. Surely you realize that. I must go. And if you will not send me, I will go see Fred Harvey."

Trent raised an eyebrow. "Resorting to threats, Tora? You must really feel as if your back is against the wall."

"I feel I have few choices."

"I'll send you, my dear. But I will send you where I can keep a close eye on you."

"I do not need a father's eye, Trent."

"You need someone."

"And you, Trent? Do you need anyone?"

He smiled. "I do. Don't we all?"

They finished their noon meal while discussing the places Tora could go and the potential of various sites for a new Storm Restaurant.

"Do you have the time?" Tora asked as the waitress cleared away their plates.

Trent took out his pocket watch. "It's a bit after one o'clock."

"I must go. I do not want to be late for work," she said with a wink. "The boss is liable to fire me."

"Or take you out for dinner. Tonight? Eight?"

"I am sorry. I do not get off shift until nine, and that's a bit late for supper. Tomorrow?"

"Tomorrow, then. I would see you to work but I have business down the street."

"That's all right. Good day, Trent."

Trent Storm watched Tora Anders's trim form disappear through the hotel doors and past the wide windows. She was a fireball, that one, and planning something more than she would admit. When would she be honest with him? When would she tell him the truth? Tora Anders was hiding something. He was sure of it. It was both frustrating and intriguing.

Trent rose and threw some cash on the table, picked up his hat and cane, and departed. Looking east and west, he thought twice about what he was about to do. Seeing little choice, since she was ready to leave, he ambled down to a three-story brick building and climbed the stairs to the top. He knocked on a glass door painted with the words *Private Investigation* and entered without waiting.

"Mr. Storm!" the small man enthused as he rose from behind a giant wood desk. His walls were strewn with maps, many covered in red as if tracing a trail. "What can I do for you today?"

"Hello, Joseph. I want some family history on one of my employees. Make that everything you can learn about her."

"Giving you trouble, sir?"

"You could say that. I want everything. And soon."

"I'll do what I can, sir. What is her name?"

"It is Tora Anders. At least that's what she has told me." He tossed the man a piece of paper from his vest pocket. "That's her last known address."

"Camden-by-the-Sea, Maine, eh? Unlimited expense account as usual?"

"Whatever you need. Just get me the information as quickly as you can."

"Good enough, Mr. Storm. I'll get you everything I can as soon as I can."

Trent nodded and turned to go. He looked over his shoulder. "And Joseph?"

"Yes, sir?"

"It is imperative she not learn of your presence."

"Understood, sir. I'll be like a shadow in the dark. Yes sir, a shadow in the dark."

Karl wished he could blend back into the shadows of John Hall's library, to leave and not remember what he had just heard. Alicia had warned him . . . he had gotten hints of what Hall was capable of . . . but still, he was as flabbergasted as Brad at what his friend had been ordered to do.

"You heard me. I want you to go down to the docks and pay off every one of Parker's clients to end their business with him. Tell them that John J. Hall will keep them in business with his own shipments. In fact, he'll double their money for a year if they agree to it."

"You'll put him out of business, John," Brad tried again. "He has a family, employees—"

"As do I," Hall said, rising behind his desk. His eyes never left Brad's. "If Parker did not want a war, he should never have intruded on my territory. For years we've coexisted—until he went after the Sullivan warehouse business."

"One business, John? Is that enough to declare a war over?" Brad asked.

"Are you questioning my authority?" Hall asked. "Certainly you're smarter than that, regardless of the company you keep."

Brad's eyes narrowed. Karl fought off the urge to take a step back from the fray. Instead he said, "Why do we not focus on the new business at hand, John? You yourself said our future is out west along the railroads. Brad and I leave tomorrow for Montana Territory to begin siting waterways for potential business. Why obsess on one warehouse, here?"

Hall's eyes did not leave Brad. "This is about more than the future of business. This is about loyalty. This is about honor."

Brad guffawed. "You speak of a bribe as honorable? You're pushing me, John. You want me out because I'm seeing Virginia Parker?

342

Why are you so distrustful . . . so suspicious? I've been working for you what, eight, nine years? Isn't that enough proof of my devotion?"

"I think you've said enough," Hall said quietly. "Your decision is clear. You may empty your desk and turn in your key tonight. I want you out. Never return."

"Just like that?" Brad asked, incredulous.

"Just like that."

Karl swallowed hard, unable to believe what he was hearing. Surely John was bluffing. Brad had made him hundreds of thousands of dollars on deals.

"That's fine," Brad said sourly, striding toward the door. "I am tired of your gray areas and your almost-unethical, almost-illegal dealings. I wash my hands of you and John J. Hall Incorporated. Thank you for making my decision for me." He glanced back at Karl with a look that said *Are you coming?* then realized Karl was hopelessly entangled. "I'll see you later, Karl." He slammed the door behind him.

"I do not want you to see him again, son," John said, coming around the desk to place a hand on Karl's shoulder.

"You cannot ask that of me. Brad is my friend."

"He has betrayed us."

"Betrayal? He simply hesitated doing what you asked."

"You are soon to be family, Karl. You must behave like it."

Karl was sputtering, searching for words, when John reached inside his vest pocket and withdrew a fat envelope.

"Your first share in the steamboat enterprise, Captain Martensen," he said quietly, then turned and went to the other side of his desk.

Karl swallowed hard. The creditors were nipping at his heels. Striving to court Alicia in the manner to which she was accustomed was eating him alive. The cash in the envelope was certain to keep them at bay. He had no choice. He had to remain silent. Swallowing once more, he turned to go, ashamed of himself for not defending Brad, for not speaking up for what he believed to be right.

"Oh, Karl," Hall said, as if just thinking of something.

"Yes?" he managed to say in a civilized fashion.

John rose and came around the desk again. "I want you to visit the Parker accounts yourself. With Bradford out of the way, you've become my number one man. Congratulations. I'm making you my vice president. With an appropriate raise, of course." He reached out his hand.

Numb, Karl met it with his own cold, clammy fingers.

"Alicia will be thrilled, son," John said.

"Thrilled," Karl mumbled, and turned to flee the dark library before it swallowed him whole. He closed the double doors behind him, breathing hard as if he had just run the mountainous staircase before him. Upstairs, he could hear Alicia speaking with a maid, directing her. Had she taken her laudanum today? he thought bitterly. Was it purely for medicinal purposes as she maintained? He glanced over his shoulder. And who was John J. Hall, really? Was he in league with the devil? Just what had he gotten himself into?

He raised his hands to his face and rubbed hard. Suddenly he felt very alone and very lost. *Father,* he tried. *Father, are you with me?* But as usual of late, he felt very far from God. Why was it that when he needed his Savior most, he felt distant? What was blocking him from the comforting presence of Christ? He closed his eyes, resisting the urge to sink to the glossy parquet floor.

"Karl?" Alicia asked, suddenly standing before him. "Are you all right, darling?"

Karl opened his eyes and stared down at her. "I cannot speak with you now," he said. "I will see you later."

"But darling," Alicia said, staying him with her hand. "Isn't it wonderful? Daddy said he would tell you tonight."

"Tell me what?"

"About making you vice president, of course."

Karl frowned, his mind racing. "He knew? When did he tell you that?" He turned and gripped her arms, wanting to shake her.

She winced. "Ouch. Unhand me, Karl, that hurts!"

He immediately dropped his hands. "Forgive me. But please— when did he tell you?"

"This noon over luncheon. Why?" Her look was confused, innocent.

"He knew!" Karl swore under his breath. "Do you not see?" he asked Alicia. "He fired Brad to clear the way for me. He had it planned all along! He asked Brad—"

"It's only natural, Karl. He wants the best for you. For us."

"At what expense?" Karl asked in exasperation. He waved toward the library doors. "I did not ask for that."

"No. I did."

"What?"

"I did. I happen to know that you've had some financial difficulties of late and wanted to help."

"So you *asked* him to fire Bradford?"

"Of course not. I simply mentioned it to him and knew he would take care of it. I leave business to the men in my life."

Karl laughed mirthlessly. "Right. Look, Alicia, I have to leave. I need some time to think this through."

"I don't like it. Don't leave like this, Karl." She stepped toward him, her arms tightly encircling his waist.

He frowned down at her. She looked needy, desperate to hold on to him. He shook off her small arms and turned away.

"Karl!" she called. "Karl!"

But he did not turn back. He walked to the front door and outside, fighting the urge to run all the way. The air outside was blessedly cool, and Karl gasped for breath as if he had been wrestling with a shark underwater. *Maybe I have,* he mused silently. *Maybe I have.*

Kaatje sank to her knees on the hard floorboards in the small house and wept. It had been a fine harvest for the Janssens and a pretty decent one for her neighbors—even those on drier lands. She was to have taken the wheat to market along with the other Bergensers the next day. But it was not to be. The buzzing sounded at eight, and Kaatje had gone outside to see what it was. A great, black cloud of locusts raced toward the homestead, hungry jaws set for the dried grain. By the time they were done four hours later, they had eaten everything, including the wooden handle of the pitchfork Kaatje had flailed uselessly at them.

The girls wailed from their bassinets behind her.

What was she to do? It was all gone. She had no reserves, and it had been months since she had heard from Soren. They would starve. All three of them. Or throw themselves on the mercy of her neighbors.

On and on she wept, unable to hear anything besides her own grief. Soren was gone. Her friends had helped to bring in the crop, and now it was gone too. She would lose the farm. Where would they go? All the pain of the last months came rushing forward, and Kaatje felt lost in her sorrow. "Lord! Lord!" she cried over and over, incapable of anything more.

She did not know when she gave in to sleep, right there on the floor. But she was awakened when the door suddenly opened, and she squinted against the bright light of a setting sun. The girls whimpered from their bassinets, too exhausted to do more.

Nora Gustavson sighed and rushed in to help Kaatje to her feet. "Ah, Kaatje," she said. "It is the same everywhere. We have all lost what we worked so hard for. Here and there a farm was spared. But the Bergensers—we all lost everything. Poor Birger's sheep and goats will even have to struggle for food. But here," she said, leading Kaatje to the bed and going to tend to the children. Her own newborn baby was strapped in a sling to her ample body. She pulled a fresh bottle of milk from her basket and quickly filled the girls' bottles. "My Jersey cow will not have much more milk. It is a good thing our children are almost ready for solids, eh?"

"If we had solids to give them," Kaatje said miserably.

"Do not worry," Nora said sternly. "You have your Bergen family. Where we go, so will you." She handed one bottle to Jessica's eager hands and the other to Christina, then quickly changed their diapers and soaked blankets.

"Tonight we meet at Pastor Lien's home to decide our next step," she said. "The banker has already said no loans. A disaster area, he called it, as if we didn't know! None of us have enough funds to help support the others through the winter. Our men must go to work on the railroads. They intend to keep pushing the Northern Pacific west through the winter. And you will come with us."

"I do not wish to be a burden," Kaatje said miserably.

"Enough of that," Nora said firmly. "This disaster will prove to be the best thing that ever happened to us. You will see."

Kaatje snorted in disbelief. "How? Nora, we just lost everything! How can you be so cheerful?"

"If one does not look up, there is only down."

"Or ahead."

"Exactly. Look ahead or above. But do not look down any longer."

Kaatje looked away, still numbed by her loss. Her crop. Her husband. Her future. It was all gone.

"We will find a way to last through the winter. And in the spring the men will find us better land, not so picked over." Nora told her. "I hear in Washington Territory they never have to pray for rain! It is plentiful!"

"But Soren—"

"We will leave word where he can find you. We have no choice. You have no choice, Kaatje. You cannot waste away here, alone, with two small children. Come along tonight. Hear what the men plan to do."

Kaatje felt numb, uncaring. Nora was like the locusts, eating away at her until she agreed. "I will come and listen. Now leave me, Nora. Leave me be."

thirty-three

They had weathered one storm off the coast of Chile, and two and a half days later, Peder's crew was bracing for another. In between there had been calms—lulling Peder into hoping they might make it past the Horn without another—when the first blast of the Roaring Forties hit. Immediately, he sent his men to their quarters for oilskins. They lashed the oilskins at ankle, waist, wrist and neck, not in hopes of keeping dry, but rather to keep out some of the cold.

Elsa looked out their cabin window as Peder donned his own oilskins.

"Snow. What must winter be like down here?"

"I'd rather not stay to find out. Some captains would risk crew and ship to pass the Cape come winter, but I am not ready to take that risk." He looked at her without wavering. "You will stay put?"

"Please, Peder. I have been practicing—you've seen how I do on the rigging. Like a regular monkey, Riley says. You could use another set of hands."

"Believe me, it will be better if I do not have to worry over your safety. Please, Elsa." He cupped her cheek in his hand. "For me. Stay put. Tell me I do not have to worry over you."

"You will not have to worry over me. I will stay put." She grimaced at his look. "I promise. No adventures outside. Be careful, Peder."

"As always, love. I'll come and check on you as I can."

A knock at their door startled them both. Peder opened it to find Riley, holding on to the doorway as the ship lurched and rolled. "Cap'n! Anchor came right over the starboard side before we could lash 'er down! A couple a' men are injured!"

"Bring them in here!" Peder shouted over the wind. "Elsa will tend to them!" He turned back to her for a brief kiss, the spray of a giant wave filtering in around him, then ran toward the bowsprit where the men continued to wrestle with the huge anchor.

Within minutes, two sailors were unceremoniously dropped off, and Elsa set to work. One was unconscious, bleeding from a head wound; the other moaned over a broken arm. She shivered in the frigid air that blasted through the door and peeked outside. Thirty men were aloft, all working on furling the foresail, beating ice out of it as they did so. Fifteen others were on the starboard side, with body and soul lashings on—the lines that tied around their bodies and held them to the ship—and another fifteen on the port side. Elsa shuddered and wondered how they would all survive such fierce weather. Gritting her teeth, she slammed the door before more water could wash in.

She hoped the men had gotten the nets out above the bulwarks. They had saved four men during the last storm. Remembering her own terrifying slide down the decks, and Karl's saving presence, Elsa prayed as she grimly set to work. "Father God," she whispered. "Watch over my husband and these good men. Keep us all safe and see us through the storm." She looked from one man to the other, unsure of how to proceed. Cook, who usually looked after such matters, would be working madly to prepare food for the ravenous men, who would dash in for a quick bite whenever they could. Elsa had little medical knowledge, so she decided to simply do what was obvious.

Taking a clean blanket off her bed, she folded it once and laid it on the wood floor of the study. Then she unlashed the oilskins of the unconscious man, dumping out the water inside and patting his soaked clothing until it was damp. He was shivering uncontrollably. Deciding it was no time for decorum, she took off his shirt, hoping to bring up his frightening body temperature. With a heave, she dragged him into the study, right by the iron stove. After laying him on the blanket, she ripped a strip off an old cotton dress and wound it around the poor fellow's head wound. It was a nasty gash.

"Tobias!" she yelled to the other sailor, who was still moaning over his arm. "What's this man's name?" She almost had them all memorized. But this man was unknown to her, obviously a new recruit from the last harbor in Chile. He had jet black hair and bushy eyebrows, a nice chin and mouth. He was probably little older than sixteen years of age.

"Adolfo!" the other sailor returned.

"Well then, Adolfo," she said, settling him back onto the blanket, "I think that is all I can do for you." She swaddled him in another blanket, then placed a hand lightly on his forehead. "Father God, I ask that you bring your healing presence to this ship and keep Adolfo safe in your arms. Restore his health, Jesus. In your blessed name I pray. Amen."

"Amen," Tobias said from the doorway. He watched her with something akin to awe on his face. "Ain't nobody ever prayed over me like that, ma'am."

"Ever had such a nasty accident as Adolfo?" she asked, rising and coming over to examine his arm.

"No, ma'am. This is about as bad as I've had it."

She studied his arm, the awkward tilt of a bone in his forearm as it protruded at the break, making a huge lump under the skin. "I assume we must get that bone back in line in order to set it," she said to Tobias. The thought of it made her sick to her stomach.

"Yes ma'am."

"How do you want to go about it?"

"Any way you see fit, ma'am."

"All right. It would be better on a hard surface. Why don't you stretch out by Adolfo in the study? That way, if you pass out, I will not have to move you, and you'll be warm. Just a minute. I will get another blanket for the floor."

"You needn't—"

"Nonsense, Tobias. You deserve a little pampering," she said, giving him a sad smile. She felt like an executioner marching a prisoner toward the noose. She would soften the blow as much as possible. He followed behind her like an obedient child, lying down on the rough wool blanket when she waved toward it.

She knelt beside him, bracing herself as the swells outside built to new heights. "Let's get this over with before we cannot stay still long enough to do so."

"Whenever you're ready, ma'am."

Elsa studied his beefy arm, looking at it from all angles before deciding on a course of action. Tobias never took his eyes from her.

"If you'll permit me to say so, ma'am, it's an honor to be attended by you."

Elsa smiled at him. "Thank you, Tobias. But you may not say the same after I do what I must."

He was silent as she traced over his skin with her fingers, gently probing. Deciding, she took his forearm in both of her hands, pushing down on the top protruding portion while pulling upward from the other side, farther down. Tobias howled. Elsa felt dizzy. After a moment, he opened his eyes. "Sorry about that, ma'am," he ground out. "You did right. Cap'n got anything stronger in here than water?"

Elsa grimaced and shook her head. "Sorry."

"Then how 'bout one of your prayers?" he asked woozily. "I could use a little sleep. Might feel . . . better when I wake up."

"Certainly. Those I have in plentiful supply." She prayed all the while she wrapped his arm in dress strips and sterling serving utensils. When she was done, he raised his head a bit to see it.

"Fanciest splint I've ever laid eyes on," he mumbled, then passed out.

Peder had seen few storms as fierce as this one. He had passed the Horn twenty-two times in his years as a sailor, but this storm threatened his crew with plunging temperatures, frightening swells of sixty feet, and fearsome winds. All three hundred lines screamed like tortured animals, while the entire ship seemed to be bending, straining, groaning as it battled the heavy seas. He made his way toward the bow, wanting to make sure the anchor stayed lashed. In awe he watched as the bowsprit, normally fifty feet above the water, knifed through a rogue wave that caught them all unaware. The wave rose high above the deck, like a gigantic, angry grizzly on her hind feet.

Peder grabbed for the nearest lash and wrapped it around his waist, praying his frozen, stiff fingers could make fast the hitch knot before the wave enveloped him. He was just in time, sucking in a breath that held as much water as oxygen. He coughed violently, wondering if he would suffocate before the wave passed and he could again try for air.

After what seemed like minutes, his head emerged from the wave, his waist burning from the lash that held him fast to the mast against the wave's tremendous force. He looked around, certain the *Sunrise* had capsized from the force of the wave, but God bless her, she was still upright. Awash, but upright. He felt a surge of pride that she was a Ramstad ship. His high feeling was short-lived.

"Man overboard!" Yancey was less than a foot away from Peder, but he screamed over the wind to be heard. Peder nodded and followed him amidships. A frightened boy clung to the safety netting over the port side, too terrified to move. Riley was making his way to him. Peder blinked against the spray, desperate for the men, knowing there was little time before another wave came and pulled them both over the side.

It was the look on the boy's face that warned him another wave was upon them from behind, but it hit before he could brace himself again. He dived for the railing, holding on tightly, but the wave sucked him under, pulling him down the deck in a desperate rush past his own sailors.

Miraculously, two lashed-on sailors reached out from either side and clung to his jacket and waistband until the wave passed. With a low growl in his throat, he clambered to the edge and looked over the side. Riley hung by one leg from the netting. The boy was gone. Screaming his fury as if challenging the devil, Peder ran aft and, without another thought, jumped for the rigging above the net. Hand over hand, he made his way to the outermost part of the yard then hung like a circus acrobat on a swaying trapeze.

"Riley!" he screamed over the wind. "Riley!" He grabbed the lash hanging at his side, and unlooped it until it was full length, just barely reaching Riley's waist. Beyond the mate, the waves swelled and passed his head like circling, curious sharks on the hunt. It was like looking at a man with one foot in the grave, not wanting to die but unable to see any alternative.

"Riley!" Peder screamed, salty spray filling his mouth. As if hearing the voice of God, Riley wearily looked his way. His eyebrows shot up, and he stretched for the lash. Reaching it, he pulled himself upright and back onto the netting. He glanced at Peder, communicating with him silently. They had but one chance before they were both dead men. He jumped upward, catching Peder's hand.

The two swayed from the momentum and the force of gale winds. Sheer determination and brute strength kept them from letting go. Using Peder as a ladder, Riley pulled himself up over his captain, reached the yard and, hand over hand, made his way back to the ship. Peder followed him, and sailors handed them each a lash as yet another wave bombarded them.

When it was past, Riley leaned close. "I lost the boy!"

"But we did not lose you!" Peder returned.

"You abandoned ship!" Riley yelled, shaking his head in wonder. "I owe you my life!"

I could do little else, Peder thought grimly. What was he supposed to do? Sit there and watch as his first mate followed the boy into the swirling, deadly seas?

Peder ran astern, hoping to catch sight of the boy and throw him a line, but he saw nothing. The lad was gone and, in the cold waters and giant seas, as good as dead.

The next day the *Sunrise* sailed along at a good clip. About fourteen knots, if Elsa had counted them right as the sailors hauled the chip log aboard, measuring their speed. The storm was over, and once again the *Sunrise* had proven seaworthy. Unlike other captains, who considered a man overboard as yet another given of the trade to ignore, Peder led a short memorial service for Edmundo, the boy lost at sea. Elsa's heart swelled with pride over her husband and his methods. His devotion to his crewmen earned him nothing but respect and a love that would have any of them giving his life to save his captain's.

She supposed that that was why Riley had told her what Peder had done during the storm. Although Peder felt he had owed Riley a debt for saving the ship from the last storm and his wife from Stefan, Riley believed that Peder's saving act was twice the job. Peder had laid aside his one duty as captain: to never abandon ship. He had risked all that he had worked for. Sailors needed to believe that their captain would always be there for them. Much as she had impulsively dived into that harbor in the Indies, so had Peder acted. Yet his act held a hundred times the ramification. Everyone on the ship knew it.

Prior to the memorial service earlier that morning after the storm was beaten and the *Sunrise* was on safe waters, Riley had thanked Peder. Elsa, bundled up, was at last allowed on deck and witnessed it all.

"Cap'n," Riley said, approaching Peder and Elsa. "I owe you my life, sir."

"Nonsense, man," Peder said, shaking his head. "I did what any man would have done for you, yet ignored my duty to my ship. I take no pride in what was done." He squared his shoulders and stared into the mate's eyes. "We will not speak of it again. Tell the men. Not one word, ever again."

Riley nodded once, understanding, as Peder walked off. Elsa had kept after Riley until he had told her all of it, leaving no detail to the imagination. Her heart pounded in fear for her husband, for Riley, for how close they had both come to following Edmundo's path into the deep.

"I told you, missus, and now I will keep my promise to the Cap'n," Riley said solemnly. "Do not ever tell 'im I told you about it. But to my mind, it is good for a wife to know of what stock her man is made. Our cap'n is a fine man."

"I know, Riley. Do not worry. Your secret is safe with me."

She looked after Peder, watching as he sighed heavily and looked out to sea. He would wrestle with his decision for years to come. But not one of his men would ever speak of it again.

thirty-four

*T*ora and Trent were invited to a harvest dance, but few involved had ever handled seed or rake, she mused. Not that she had either. She simply saw the irony of it all. It was like having a ship christening with no ship. Despite its ironic nature, and true to form for the Saint Paul upper class, the ball was at the Gutzian mansion and being given by people of discriminating taste. She mourned the fact that it would be her last in Saint Paul, yet did everything she could to hide it from her escort.

Trent had agreed to her plan, an unpleasant surprise, and was allowing her to go west. Why had he not reacted as she had anticipated? Tora was sure that her threat of going would make him propose. Perhaps he was bluffing, playing his last card. Perhaps when she actually stepped onto the Northern Pacific tomorrow, he would bend his knee and ask her to be his wife. Yes, that was it, she decided. Surely he did not intend to let her go. He simply was curious to see if she herself was bluffing.

Well, I'll show him. I'll go all the way to Montana Territory if I have to, to earn his respect. She found herself alternately excited and horrified at the idea. Tora could see herself doing as she had said to Trent, performing as liaison for Storm Enterprises in setting up new ventures in new towns. Yet she also had been reading dime novels of late, and *Captives of the Wild Frontier,* gunfighters, Indians, and the United States Cavalry filled her head. Was she prepared to face the dangers ahead? Part of Tora wanted to toss her head at the challenge—of course she could handle it; the other part made her toss and turn at night in her sleep, or lack thereof.

"Why, good evening, Mr. Storm," said a coquettish blond as they passed.

"Good evening, Miss Grant," Trent said benignly.

It had not taken long for Tora to notice that her beau drew the eye of every available young woman in the Twin Cities and beyond, nor that all those women looked down their noses at her. They hated her. Hated her for what they could not have. Trent Storm. Yet if he did not propose, did Tora truly have him? It nagged at her soul. Was she doing the right thing in leaving?

She looked up into his eyes as he whisked her onto the dance floor. The small orchestra, a tight group elegantly dressed for the occasion, played a lovely, soothing waltz. He held her so confidently, looked at her so intently, that Tora was able to think of no one else. What was this within her? She wondered at the feeling that made her at once sick to her stomach and high as a kite at simply being on Trent's arm. It went beyond what she had once felt for Kristoffer. That was more like friendship. This was . . . She abruptly stepped away from him.

"What? What is it? You look pale, Tora."

"Forgive me, Trent," she said, as he led her off the dance floor. "I think I need to sit for a moment. Excuse me while I go find the ladies' sitting room."

"Certainly."

What was wrong with her? she wondered as she left him. Perhaps she needed to eat. Knocking briefly at what she knew was a ladies' lounge, Tora entered. Three young women looked up at her: Alicia Hall, Giselle Gutzian, and Audrey Campbell. *Oh dear.* She had stumbled into a private lounge, not the one most of the guests used. Alicia moved to block her view of the coffee table, but not before Tora saw a pile of white powder.

"Excuse me," she said hastily. "I was in search of the ladies' sitting room and the necessary."

"In there," Audrey said with a nod toward a door. Her eyes were hazy, as if she were sleepy.

Tora rushed past and closed the door. After pouring some water from a pitcher into the basin, she splashed her face, and felt a bit better. She stared at her features in the gilt-edged mirror, wondering what Trent saw in her. The girls outside were giggling, but Tora ignored them. She had to figure out what she was feeling. Was this love? She felt desperate to remain with Trent, but furious that he would let her go. It was more than what he could provide her, she decided with some surprise. It was the man himself. She was falling in love with Trent Storm!

Tora smiled and saw something in her eyes she had never seen before. Joy? Was this what she had been seeking all along? A knock startled her.

"Just a minute. I'll be out shortly." She opened her beaded purse and dabbed on some lip cream and powder. Then, taking a breath, she opened the door.

It was Alicia. Her eyes now held the same gauzy haze as Audrey's.

"It's all yours," Tora said, brushing past to make her way out.

"No, you don't," Alicia said with a giggle. "We want some answers."

Tora turned to face her. Alicia was about the same height. She felt the other young women come up behind her and felt trapped. "I beg your pardon?"

"Oh, relax, darling," Alicia cajoled. "Why don't you come on over here and share in the bounty first?" Her tone was light, inviting. Her words easy, if a bit slurred. Too much champagne? Tora wondered. She had been dying for a glass herself, but Trent was a teetotaler. Perhaps they had a bottle in here. No doubt the Gutzians had purchased only the finest from France.

Alicia led her by the elbow to the coffee table. Tora felt simultaneously suspicious and lured by the chance of sharing something with these women she wanted to befriend, not fight. She glanced at the white powder on the table, uneasy. "I really should get back to Trent."

"Trent!" Audrey cackled. "Why, the matter must be very serious if you are on a first-name basis with Mr. Storm."

"Of course it is," Alicia answered. "Our little Tora Anders has snagged the heart of dear Trent. You must tell us how you've done it, Tora. We are amazed at your ability."

Tora searched her face, but she seemed honestly interested.

"But first, to be a part of our circle, Tora, you need to partake." Alicia handed her a sterling silver tube as if she knew what to do with it. Seeing Tora's confusion, Alicia said generously, "Through the nose, darling. Take a big sniff of the laudanum up your nose. Inhale as deeply as you can. It will take care of your headache."

"I do not have a headache," Tora said. For the first time in her life, she felt as if she definitely did not have the upper hand. She looked around the room as if casting about for an anchor.

"Well, of course you don't, silly," Audrey said. "None of us had a headache either, and now we won't until morning! Think of it as a precautionary measure." She tilted her head down and giggled.

Audrey looked free, easy, happy. If all these fine, upstanding women of society were doing it—whatever *it* was—why shouldn't she? She had been trying to get in their good graces for months, and now they were welcoming her. She dipped her head and inhaled.

The powder burned as it entered her nostril, and she twitched her nose and shivered. That set the women to laughing hysterically. Within seconds, Tora felt lightheaded, free. She giggled along with them, and when Alicia gripped her arm, she did not pull away.

"Tell us," Alicia said conspiratorially. "Tell us the truth, Tora. How did you come to Minnesota? And how did you snag Trent Storm? We want to know it all, darling. Start at the beginning. I bet it's that adorable accent that got to him. Norwegian, isn't it? Why, you sound just like my own beloved."

A warning bell rang in Tora's head from a great distance. But feeling as she did, nothing could hurt her, she decided. Suddenly she felt she had it all—wealth, beauty, and apparently, by their reaction, wit. She was welcome! She was a part of them. And so, Tora began to tell them her story as if she were speaking with her sisters, trying hazily to stick to the story she had told Trent.

Alicia sighed and snuggled closer to her on the love seat as if they were dear friends. "But before that, darling. Before that horrible disaster on the sea. You're from Bergen, are you not? I believe you once knew my fiancé, Karl Martensen."

What is the harm? Tora asked herself, having a more difficult time focusing by the minute. She giggled. "Of course. He was in love with my sister," she said. She frowned as Alicia stood, her eyes narrowing. What had she said? Why was she so angry?

"Your sister . . ." she dimly heard Alicia repeating. "Well, isn't that interesting?"

And then Tora fell into a blessed, deep sleep.

Karl approached the group of men encircled by a ring of smoke from their Turkish Orientals, the cigarette of choice. In their offices most seemed to chew tobacco, but the women preferred them to smoke in their presence rather than spit. Karl refused either form of tobacco, as well as the glass of Monongahela whiskey that John shoved into his hand.

"No, thank you," he said, passing the glass to a waiter.

"Nonsense, man," John said, staying his hand with a laugh. "If you're to work with these men," he said, waving at the crowd of businessmen, "you drink with these men."

Karl said nothing, just held on to the glass. The men laughed uneasily and raised their glasses in silent cheers. After a moment, he was again forgotten.

"As I was saying, John, I thought it quite striking that Parker pulled out of the Sullivan warehouse deal so suddenly." The man's tone was full of innuendo. *He dares to say it because he has no direct business dealings with John,* Karl thought. The fellow was foolish to dare his future father-in-law. Sooner or later, every businessman in Saint Paul would deal with John J. Hall.

"Indeed," John said, full of bravado. "I always say that a man has to look after his assets close to home before he looks to foreign soil. The fortress walls, I call them."

Karl thought of the image, and his mind went back to a story his father had told him as a young child. He remembered little of the tale other than that it was of a Norwegian king who had conquered a city, and in retribution for the townspeople's resistance, ordered ten men killed and buried within the walls of his new fortress. Were Brad and Parker victims, laid to rest in John's fortress walls? Karl stepped back and watched Hall as he spoke, as if seeing him in a dream. *Who have I become?* he asked himself. Was he the knight for an evil king? Driven by money and the need to succeed, he had done John's bidding.

He caught himself shuddering as Trent Storm walked up and joined the group.

"You all right, man?" Trent asked in a low voice.

Karl nodded.

"Say, the lady I have been courting disappeared into Alicia's room. Have you seen your fiancée lately?"

"No," he said, choking on the word. *Tora and Alicia in the same room!* "I'll ask a maid," he said. Spotting Alicia's maidservant passing a tray of champagne, he waited until he could catch her eye. She hurried over. "Jonquil, would you check on Miss Hall and Miss—"

"Anders," Trent interrupted, assuming Karl did not know.

"Yes, Miss Anders. We have not seen the ladies in quite some time and wanted to make sure they were all right."

"Certainly, Mr. Martensen." She curtsied shallowly, then hurried off to follow his instructions.

Within minutes, Jonquil emerged from the lounge, and shortly thereafter, the women did too. Karl frowned as they made their way over. He did not like it. He did not like it at all. Alicia smiled, but it was all lip and no eye. Tora seemed tired, woozy, as if she had . . . Karl narrowed his gaze and looked at his fiancée. She evaded his glance, but he saw enough to know. Alicia had been into the laudanum again, and from the look of her, so had Tora.

"Headache, dear?" he asked under his breath.

"No." Alicia laughed, looking at him, challenging him. "I did earlier, but it's all gone now. Karl, darling, have you met Tora Anders? Your fellow Bergenser."

"Why, yes," he said without missing a beat. "We caught up at your sister's wedding." *Stick to the truth,* he coached himself.

"But, darling, she told me something quite amusing," Alicia said, her eyes catlike. For a moment, Karl could see a tail swishing beyond her. "Tora says you once loved her sister."

Karl laughed it off, hoping he sounded convincing. "Love! I know the entire Anders family but can only claim friendship with any of them. Why, Tora was just a girl when I left, hardly the young woman she is now. Perhaps she was remembering a girlish fantasy." Karl hated the defensiveness that crept into his voice. She was the one who should be questioned, not him.

Suddenly he felt as he had that day in John's office when Brad was fired. The shadows were deepening, threatening to swallow him. His job aside, what had he gotten into with Alicia? Was she the woman he wanted for a wife? The idea seemed ludicrous. Yet what was he to do now?

"I am simply curious, darling. Why was there no reunion between you two? I would think we would have dined with Trent and Tora by now, in that you two have so many things to talk about." Her tone was innocent. Her look was not. Alicia was onto something like a cat and would never let it go.

He would not be the mouse. Karl smiled apologetically at Trent. "Tora and I have a shared background, but we have little in common." He glanced at Tora, but she seemed confused. How much laudanum had Alicia given her?

Trent apparently shared his concern because he bent down and said a word in Tora's ear, to which she shook her head.

"Forgive me, sir," Karl said to Trent, "and my fiancée for her impolite manner this evening. Excuse us."

With that, he pulled Alicia to the doorway and down the hall to a private alcove.

"It is over," he said to her.

"What are you talking about?" Alicia asked, looking bewildered.

"We are wrong for each other, Alicia. It is over," he repeated, pacing before her.

"Yes, it is," her father said, striding through the deep shadows of the hallway. He exhaled, smoke dancing in the air about his face, which remained hidden in the relative darkness.

Alicia sputtered, indignant, but Karl could not keep his eyes off of John.

It had been a long time since Karl had feared anything.

But suddenly he was very afraid.

"I am hurt and discouraged that you were less than honest with me, Miss Anders," Trent said the next morning. "That was why you dropped the coffee that first day in my car, was it not? You recognized Karl Martensen. Why hide your association?"

"I thought it improper," she pleaded. "And then it was awkward. What were we to do? Please, Trent. I did not know you would take it this way."

Trent handed her bag to the porter and pressed a coin into his hand. "I want Miss Anders settled into your finest, cleanest stateroom," he directed.

"Yes, Mr. Storm." The man disappeared.

Trent turned back to Tora. "What was there between you two? Were you in love?"

Tora laughed. "No. He was in love with my sister."

"The one who died?"

She shook her head. How was she ever to get through the web she had woven? Trent was angry now. What would he do if he ever found out the truth? "Trent, I . . ." The train whistle blew, and she lost her courage. "There's something I need to say. Something I have not told you."

"Say it."

"You see, I uh . . . Well, I wanted to . . . Oh, never mind."

"Say it, Tora. Tell me now."

The train whistle blew. "Miss Anders?" the porter said from behind her. "May I show you—"

"In a minute!" she interrupted. Leaning out the doorway, she kissed Trent full on the mouth, in front of anyone who looked their way. But Tora saw only Trent. "Trent, whatever happens, remember this. I love you, Trent. I never knew it could be this way, and I never meant to hurt you."

His jaw was slack, and his eyes filled with pain. Did he know? Did he have an inkling of the secrets she held within? The train whistle blew again, and the engine began its slow churning. Trent walked beside her, holding her hand.

"I'll come to see you soon, Tora. We will talk more then."

"Until then, Trent."

"Until then, love," he said, so softly that she wondered later if he had ever really said it at all.

thirty-five

The *Sunrise* entered New York's busy harbor on a day in late November, barely making it before a northeaster ransacked the upper East Coast. It seemed to Elsa that the entire town had been waiting for their arrival, since as soon as Peder brought the *Sunrise* to dock, they were inundated by reporters.

"What on earth—" she began, emerging from their cabin with her valise. Peder was shouting and directing his men to hold the crowd back, and when she came out, the crowd went wild.

"Mrs. Ramstad! I wanted to talk to you about—"

"Mrs. Ramstad! Tell us about the Horn!"

"Mrs. Ramstad! We want to hear—"

Peder came striding back to her, his face a mixed mask of concern and delight. He handed her an edition of the *New York Times,* turned to a page that had her image, sketched as if she were looking heroically over a ship's bow like a figurehead. The headline read "Heroine of the Horn to Return Home."

"What on earth?" she repeated, dumbfounded. She looked back to the crowd, and even that glance set them all yelling again.

367

"You are a celebrity, it seems. The first woman to captain a ship around the Horn. News must've spread overland from San Francisco. Remember when Riley spoke with that reporter there at the dock? They have been waiting on you for weeks." Peder laughed as if enjoying an inside joke.

"It's not funny, Peder! What are we supposed to do about . . . Well, about *them?*" She waved at the reporters as if gesturing toward a pack of wolves.

"Think of it as making it past the Horn," he said, picking up her valise and taking her by the arm. "The only way through it is through it." And with that he led her toward the gangway. Sailors pulled the crowd apart like Moses parting the Red Sea. The high mood was contagious, and Elsa was soon laughing along with Peder. They hurried across the pier and through the shipping terminal, anxious to get to a carriage before the sailors could not hold the reporters back any longer

Peder looked over his shoulder. "Uh oh," he said, "we'd better move a bit faster." They hurried outside.

"Cabby!" Peder yelled, hailing a coach. But the driver went right on by, apparently otherwise employed.

"Cabby!" Peder urgently yelled again. The reporters were running now, determined to catch up with them. A grand state coach pulled up before them, handsomely painted a deep blue and pulled by a matched span of white horses. "Get in!" shouted an elegantly dressed man within, opening the small door for them to enter.

Elsa looked at Peder, who shrugged slightly and then followed her in, just as the reporters surrounded them and shouted more questions. The man tapped the roof with his cane, and they were off.

Elsa breathed a sigh of relief, still not quite able to believe that what had just happened was real.

"We owe you a debt, sir," Peder began.

"Nonsense," said the graying man with a wide, engaging smile. "Why, it was a coup! Allow me to introduce myself. Alexander Martin, editor in chief of the *New York Times.*"

Elsa laughed in surprise. "Out of the frying pan and into the fire, I'd say."

"Hardly, my dear. I intend to put you two up in the finest suite the Marquis Hotel has to offer. For a day, for a week."

"We only intend to—" Peder began.

"In exchange, all I ask is that you give me an exclusive for my paper."

"Perhaps, sir," Peder said firmly, taking charge again, "we wish to keep our stories to ourselves."

"Nonsense!" Martin said jovially. "Your wife's picture is on every paper across the country. She's the Heroine of the Horn! Isn't that a fine headline? Came up with it myself. Anyway, our readers are clamoring for her story. They want to hear what it was like to be there, to *be* her. Now be a good sport and let her tell me the details."

Peder shook his head, obviously as flabbergasted as she. "It is up to my wife. If she agrees, I will go along with it. If not, I will thank you to allow us to leave your presence without further ado."

Martin studied him silently for a moment. "Agreed." He turned back to her. "My dear?"

"But why . . . why on earth is my story so fascinating?"

"You beat the Horn! A woman! *And* lived to tell about it. Captained the *Sunrise* when your husband was incapacitated and the mate was in irons! Think of it, Mrs. Ramstad. You are beautiful," he said, turning to Peder. "If I may be as bold to say so, sir." Then back to Elsa, "And strong. You embody the American spirit. Our people want to hear more!"

"But I am Norwegian."

"You are an American now," he said. "You, my dear, *are* America."

Elsa shook her head and touched her brow. "It's all so much to take in . . ."

"There's more."

"Listen," Peder interrupted. "Perhaps this is not such a good idea."

"I've spoken with a dear friend, Fergus Long. I believe you know him?"

"Fergus! Of course!" Elsa relaxed a bit in the presence of someone with whom they shared a mutual friend. If Fergus liked him, Alexander Martin must be trustworthy, she thought.

"Fergus tells me that you are a talented artist and anticipate traveling with your husband on future ventures."

Elsa glanced at Peder. "It is my hope, if Peder agrees."

Peder scowled as if pushed into a corner. "This is a private issue."

"Of course, of course," Martin soothed. "I only wished to offer Mrs. Ramstad a unique opportunity."

"Which is?" Peder asked.

They all leaned as the coach turned a corner.

"I would like a firsthand account of her travels by your side, sir. With illustrations, of course."

Elsa laughed, incredulous. "You want me, *me,* to do that for the *Times?*"

"Yes, my dear. I think it is a delightful concept."

Elsa shook her head, unable to believe it. She looked at Peder, and he smiled at her.

"It sounds like something you would wish to do," he said quietly. "Are you sure, Elsa? This is it. Are you sure you do not want to stay at home in Camden-by-the-Sea? Is there nothing about that idea that is welcome?"

Elsa gripped his hands in hers and looked deeply into his eyes. "I want nothing more, Peder, than to travel with you. Past the Horn, wherever. I only want to be with you."

"Then it's settled!" Alexander Martin enthused. His expression was immediately cowed by Peder's warning look.

Peder turned to Elsa as she held her breath. His eyes softened. "I guess it is," he said quietly. He laughed. "I never knew the Heroine of the Horn would be sharing my cabin," he teased.

"Enough of that," Elsa warned. "So tell me, Mr. Martin. Tell me exactly what your expectations are."

A week later her unexpected interview with Alexander Martin was fading in memory, but the impact of their decision was not. Elsa left Peder in their bed and rambled about their Camden cottage in her nightdress. She eventually settled up in the turret, watching the starlight dance over the frigid Atlantic on a moonless night. She was unable to sleep, thinking about her next voyage with Peder. Where it would take them, what she would draw, how she might write a story for the American people that captured their imagination . . .

What if they could go home again? Perhaps in the spring Peder would consider a voyage to Norway. How grand it would be to see Mama again! And dear Carina. Elsa's thoughts went to Tora then back home to Papa. What would it be like to go to Bergen and not have him waiting there with open arms? How she yearned to speak with him, to tell him of her adventures and lessons of the last year! Despite his own desire to see her safely lodged at home, Elsa believed that Amund Anders would have grudgingly agreed that she could walk no other path than the one to which she had been led.

"It's right, Papa," she whispered, kneeling at the window, resting her elbows on the sill and her chin on her hands. Her hair was down about her shoulders, and she felt like a girl again. The cold air seeped around the windowpane, urging Elsa back to her warm bed, but for some reason, she felt hesitant to leave. The water was uncommonly quiet for a winter's night, and Elsa stared and stared at the deepest indigo of the night sky and the inky blackness of water beneath. It was to the water that she had been called. To her husband's side, wherever that might lead.

On the northern horizon, a green ray waved above the water. She thought she was seeing things for a moment, but then no, there was another. Elsa smiled, quick tears coming to her eyes. A fluorescent turquoise and brilliant blue alternated as within minutes the blanket of northern lights stretched toward her, as if calling her, talking to her. Elsa laughed through her tears, thinking of Our Rock and her family, of Kaatje and Karl. Most of all, she thought about her father.

"Hello, Papa," she whispered. She laughed silently and wiped aside her tears. "I have missed you."

Deep Harbor

Prologue

June 1886

Tora Anders strolled down the wooden sidewalk of Helena, Montana, with purpose. She walked everywhere with purpose these days, but today was special. Trent Storm was in town again. And he had invited her out for supper. She needed to get back to her fine Queen-Anne-style home—the pride of Helena—to bathe and change. Tonight would be different; she was sure of it. Tonight Trent would propose at last. Hadn't she waited four years for this day?

She nodded at two towering cowboys who nodded back appreciatively, touching fingertips to hat brims, and then at two women she had not yet met. Tora had been in Helena for only a little over a year. Having built her last roadhouses for Storm Enterprises in the vicinity, she decided it was time to make some semblance of a home for herself. And in the process, she hoped to entice Trent west by her blatant refusal to return east.

This hard, energetic place was rife with trouble as well as opportunity, and it fit Tora to a T. She loved the gently sloping mountains in the distance, the rolling hills that gave way to plains. Montana was Tora Anders territory if she had ever seen it. Surely Trent would eventually fall in love with it just as he had fallen in love with her once. In the distance she heard the train whistle and quickened her step. She doubted that Trent would come early. It was more likely that he would take care of some business and observe Helena's Storm Roadhouse—one of the finest restaurants Tora had set up for him—before coming to call.

There was little to fear from his examination. Tora had become a difficult, perfectionist of a boss. Frequently she made impromptu inspections of her facilities herself. If a table was not set with pristine linens or the utensils were not placed just so, she was known to take hold of the cloth and pull the whole table setting to the ground, often firing the manager on the spot. Consequently the roadhouses she had begun for Trent—sixteen over the last five years along the tracks of the Northern Pacific—had the best reputation of them all. She smiled and felt smug for a moment. With any luck at all, Trent had heard the critics' reports just as she had. At twenty-two years of age, Tora Anders was a force to contend with. And her fame as the "Storm Roadhouse Maven" was rivaling her sister Elsa Ramstad's fame as "The Heroine of the Horn."

She laughed under her breath, thinking of her father and what he would have thought had he read the American papers himself. Had he lived. *The old bird probably would have been scandalized,* she thought. *He never really did embrace what America was all about: freedom and opportunity.* Certainly his younger two daughters, Elsa and Tora, had not turned out as they had been raised to be. Carina, the eldest, was the only one to do as their parents had planned; only she had stayed at home in Bergen, Norway, married a Bergenser—Garth Ramstad—and raised children.

Tora frowned briefly as she thought of her own child, Jessie, then banished the idea from her mind. It had been a long time since she had allowed herself to think of the girl, and she quickly decided it would be a long time before she thought of her again. It was a tad more pleasant to think of her sister Elsa's son, Kristian, who had to be about two by now. Perhaps there was another one on the way. It was difficult to know, since she had not corresponded with Elsa for over four years and had only found out about her nephew by chance.

She turned off the sidewalk, on to an intricately laid brick pathway, and walked through an ornate iron gate in front of her home. Walking up the steps, she peeled off her white kid gloves and pulled at the wide ribbon that held her French straw hat to her head. It was warm for June, but the heat felt right somehow.

Her maidservant Sasha—one of three in the huge house—opened the door as if she had been waiting for her. This pleased Tora to no end. "Good afternoon, Sasha," she said primly, stepping through the massive doorway. Inside it was cool; the tall ceilings and thick mahogany paneling kept the place darker and thus cooler than out-of-doors. She handed Sasha her gloves and hat. "I trust you completed your task of oiling the staircase woodwork today?"

"Yes, Miss Anders," Sasha said with a deferential curtsey. She was short in stature, had drab brown hair, and spoke with a slight Russian accent. In a town full of Chinese and Irish, it had been difficult to find the right servants, Tora mused. But Sasha was one of the best. An excellent maid and none of Tora's gentlemen callers would look her way twice. *Perfect.*

"I did the paneling in the dining room as well," the maid added hastily as Tora immediately walked to the staircase and peered closely at the hand-carved balustrade, looking for traces of dust. But Sasha had done an impeccable job. All the way up the grand, sweeping staircase—which Tora hoped to descend soon in a fine French wedding gown—there was not one speck of dust to be found.

"Good," she muttered, heading at once to the dining room. Tora loved this room. After the heavy, dark paneling of the foyer and hallway, entering the dining room was like entering dawn. Everything was different. The panels were outlined in white-painted wood, their interiors covered in coordinating velvet which was padded from behind. Tora likened eating in the room to dining on a massive bed fit for a queen, and the guests she entertained around the enormous, ostentatious table often agreed.

Absentmindedly Tora walked around the perimeter of the room, thinking of the many admirers who had sat at the table, gazing at her longingly. In the West, women were scarce, and women of quality and wealth were treasured like gold from the mountains. Men came here to the Montana Territory to farm the rich soil, help lay the tracks, or mine the high hills in the distance. The capital bustled as each day people entered and exited for other parts of the state, leaving their money in the townspeople's hands as they did so. Yes, it was a fine place for a woman to make her way, and men far and wide admired her for her tenacity. Gentlemen came to call at all hours of the day, and her maidservants turned many away without an excuse.

Because Tora's heart belonged to one man: Trent Storm.

He was the man who had made her the woman she was today.

She was the woman who would make him a man of true power in the future.

And it would all begin tonight.

Trent Storm made his way through the throngs of people at the train station, not surprised that Tora was absent rather than there to greet him. It was not their pattern to have a cheerful reunion at the station. Instead, Tora would want him to come to her, in her corner so to speak, giving her the advantage. She would be dressed to the hilt and smelling of her intoxicating cologne—a mix of vanilla and flowers from the Orient— and smiling at him in a way that melted his heart. What he wouldn't give to see her in a plain dress like the simple farm women around him! He yearned for the chance to slip his hands into her hair and release the pins, setting free those thick, black waves to cascade down past her shoulders. They would frame her face and those incredible blue eyes, and it would take every bit of his control not to kiss her . . .

"Mr. Trent!" the porter said again, clearly irritated by now. "Your valise! You forgot this back there."

"Oh, thank you. I don't know where my mind is," he started lamely, fishing in his pocket for two bits for the man's trouble. Of course he knew exactly where his mind was. And it was time to clear it. He had spent four years waiting for Tora Anders to be honest with him, to reveal the reason she had made up the story of her family's death on the high Atlantic seas and the reason for her lies since then. Why hide a perfectly respectable past? His private detective had discovered that she had a mother and sister alive in Bergen, Norway, and a sister who was married to a prosperous sea captain named Ramstad. "The Heroine of the Horn" they called her. Trent often found himself spellbound by the stories she wrote for the *Times* and the exquisite drawings she included. Apparently Tora had come across with Elsa; however, curiously her name was not on the *Herald's* manifest. Was that the reason for her secrecy? he wondered for the thousandth time. Had she stowed away?

For a brief time she had been the housekeeper for a shipmate of Ramstad's, caring for his two sons. Then she had come to Minnesota and sought Trent's employ. Why the duplicity? The questions drove him nearly mad. And as attracted as he was to Tora on the outside, he was disappointed with how she had degenerated on the inside. What were once guts and gumption were now greed and gall, in his mind.

All in all, his relationship with Tora had soured. And it was time to end it. Tonight. Tonight he would expose the truth he had held within for four long years and demand an explanation. If she was honest, he might give her a chance. If she tried her old games with him, it was over. At forty-five, he was too old to live life in such a manner.

"Trent!" Karl Martensen called, trying to shout above the din of the crowd. "Trent Storm! Storm!" Trent did not pause, obviously deep in thought. Karl dipped and turned through the throngs, trying to hasten his steps across the platform to reach Trent. What was he doing here in the wilds of Montana? The answer came to Karl a moment later. Of course. The reputation of the roadhouse that Tora Anders had set up for Storm Enterprises last year was the talk of the line. In fact, it was rumored that all of the roadhouses she had built and run for Trent in the last four years were among the finest anywhere. Curiously, Tora had stopped here in Helena, electing to build a home and make some investments of her own. Trent had obviously rewarded her generously for work well done. Was there still something between the two of them?

Karl could not imagine letting one's heart wander so far as Tora Anders. Perhaps the affair had faded as so many others had for Tora. Trent was perhaps the conquest of the past. Now, with some gold in the bank, Karl was sure she had set her sights higher than even Trent Storm would ever reach. What would appease that girl? Nothing, he answered himself sourly.

"Trent! Trent Storm!"

At last the man turned, his eyes searching the crowd for the one who had called his name. His hair had gone more gray at the sides but was still full and wavy on top. He was a distinguished gentleman through and through, Karl thought, admiring the way Trent held himself and the cut of his clothes. Everything was just right on the man, except . . . except for the slight slump of his shoulders today. Was he aging? Weary from the trip? Karl doubted that. Trent owned one of the most extravagant of the Pullman railroad cars and traveled alone in it. It was as close to the lap of luxury through the Dakotas as one could find.

"Martensen!" Trent smiled sincerely and stretched out his hand as soon as he spotted Karl.

"Whew!" Karl said, shaking his hand heartily. "Is this town getting busy or what?"

"Statehood's on the wind," Trent said, looking around as if he himself had discovered the place. "It's a fine land with plenty of opportunity. Unfortunately we're not the only businessmen to have found her."

"Ah well, I think she's big enough for all of us. Especially since we're two of the first. The gold's pretty well tapped out, but there's more to this land's riches."

Trent smiled with him and then gestured toward a hired coach. "Need a ride? Where are you heading?"

"Oh, I'm to wait here for the next train from the Washington Territory. Bradford Bresley's due in on the four-forty."

"Bresley? Glad to know you're still doing business with the man."

"Exclusively. When John Hall and I parted ways, it was a natural thing to develop business with Brad."

"You are fortunate," Trent said. "I always wished there had been a man I could trust as friend as well as partner."

"The railroads are a tough place to find such an animal," Karl said with a laugh. "Say, are you in town for long? We should talk about a couple of things Brad and I have rolling."

"I'd be glad to. Staying at the Hotel Bravado for a couple of days, then it's back to Minnesota. Look me up there tomorrow."

"I will." Karl gestured as if he had just thought of something. "Oh, and are you going to see Tora Anders by chance?"

Trent nodded once, his face inscrutable.

"Give her my best, will you?"

Trent stared him in the eye for a moment, then nodded once again. "Tomorrow, Martensen. And bring Bresley along with you. Let's talk over dinner, shall we?"

"Sounds fine."

Karl watched as Trent tapped on the coach's roof, and the driver set off at once. Whatever business Trent had with Tora, it was apparently not of the heart. And as Brad would say, something was definitely rotten in Denmark.

Elsa laughed as Kristian bent down and buried his face in a jasmine bush full of white, fragrant blossoms, sniffing theatrically. "Look, Mama," he said. "I smell."

"Yes, you do," she said with a giggle. Elsa picked up his squirming body and buried her face in his neck for a kiss. "You smell just like the flowers!"

"Down, Mama! I want down!"

"Kristian, we must hurry. Can you find your papa? He's right up there, at the corner." She knelt and pointed, hoping to distract the toddler from the intoxicating Hawaiian flora and fauna. She had just extracted him from a fissure in a rock, trying to get at a gecko lizard, and now he was entranced by the flowers! It would be impossible to get him all the way through town without carrying him, kicking and screaming.

Elsa glanced up, looking for her husband, hoping he could help with Kristian. Peder was up ahead, gazing across the busy dirt road at the mercantile. Did he see someone he knew? As she watched, he took a step back, into the shadow of the porch above the sidewalk.

"Go, Kristian! I'll race you!" Elsa whispered. Kristian spotted Peder at last and took off in his direction. She smiled at his delighted giggle and followed along at a leisurely pace as her son raced toward her husband. Elsa winced as he squeezed between two natives and shoved aside a little girl in his efforts, then smiled again as he reached his father, embracing the tall man's leg. It was a glorious day to be in port at Honolulu, and she reveled in the chance to smell the fragrant flowers with her child and to gaze up at the towering green mountain at the point. Diamond Head, she thought it was called. A volcano, she had heard. What a wild, idyllic place!

Most of the people in town were Hawaiians and merchants, plus a few trailing whalers. The whalers spent half of their year in the vicinity, harpooning their kill and taking the cargo home to Japan, America, or even Russia. Soon the last of them would leave for distant shores, as the migrating whales had done months before. It would be nice to visit the place when it was as quiet as the natives usually enjoyed. Elsa grinned at the thought of a lazy day on the beach, combing the sand with Kristian for sand dollars and seashells and cuddling with her husband in a hammock for a nap beneath the palms.

Her smile faded as Peder grabbed up the child and looked for her anxiously. She reached him a moment later. "What? What is it?"

Peder took a step in front of her, as if posturing himself as protector, and nodded toward the mercantile. "There, just inside the window. Do you see that man?"

Elsa studied his profile, slightly obscured by the reflection of the glass. He was in uniform, a British uniform it appeared by the color and stripes. He stepped closer to the glass and bent to pick up a jar from the front window display. Elsa gasped. She edged closer to Peder, unable to believe her eyes.

Mason Dutton.

The pirate who had threatened her life and nearly burned the Ramstad's first ship to the water line.

A pirate, by anyone's account who had seen him that night.

"But," she mumbled softly, "he is in uniform!"

"Come. I'm getting you out of here." Peder took her arm firmly and led the way down the rough-hewn sidewalk toward the wharf.

Elsa hazarded one more glance over her shoulder toward the mercantile.

And Mason stared right back at her.

Kaatje blinked, her eyes stinging from the salty sweat of her brow, and eased her horse to a stop. With the back of her hand, she wiped her forehead and looked around for Christina and Jessie. They were near the house, making mud pies as they had been doing for over an hour. She smiled. *The industry of small children.* If only she could sell their wares for food! On the stone wall that bordered the well was pie after pie, testimony of the girls' busy morning.

All in all, life was good here in the Skagit Valley of the Washington Territory. The soil was more dense than North Dakota's and thus heavier to clear and plow but richer for growing. Here they didn't have the problem of drought that the dry-land farmers of the Dakotas battled; instead, they contended with rot. Still, it was easier to bring in a crop here, and Kaatje was glad for her move. In the four years since their arrival, she had managed—with the help of her dear Bergenser friends—to build some semblance of a home for her daughters in the one-room shanty and to bring in enough of a crop to sustain them through each year. With God's help, they would do it again in 1886.

If only it could be a bit easier, she thought to herself. Her neighbors had expanded their farms and their homes since arriving, whereas Kaatje found herself barely able to sustain what she and her friends had begun. She closed her eyes. *Forgive me, Lord. I am thankful for what we have been given. I'm just so tired. Ease my weariness.* Slowly, she unhooked the harness of the plow from her waist and chest and then released her horse. Her shoulders and back ached from the work, and she winced as the fabric of her dress moved over areas raw from the leather straps. She paused and gave in to her exhaustion for a moment, hand on neck, eyes closed, sweaty cheek to the slight breeze from the west.

"Mama! Mama!" yelled her girls in unison, glad Kaatje was taking a break for lunch. They hauled a tin bucket of water, and Nels, the draft horse, whinnied and took a step forward as if they brought refreshment for him instead.

"Poor horse," Kaatje soothed, stroking his giant sweaty neck. He was of good stock and had served them well here in the Skagit Valley. Certainly without Nels's help Kaatje would have accomplished little on this land.

When the girls reached her, Kaatje smiled broadly, invigorated simply by being near them as they chatted about business as if mud pies were a booming industry. "Give me a cup, child," she said to Jessie, who offered up a tin scooper. Kaatje drank deeply, scooped up another, and then nodded at Nels. "Give the rest to him, please. He must be very thirsty on such a day as this."

"Yes, Mama," Jessie said, happy to treat her big friend. Jessie had a natural way with animals. Some day, Jessie had announced the other evening, she wanted to be a shepherd like Jesus, caring for her sheep on the hills that surrounded the Skagit Valley. On the other hand, Kaatje's older child, Christina, seemed to fear the horse and preferred other chores which did not entail caring for Nels or their hog and sheep.

Kaatje walked to the shanty, eager to enter the shade and protection of their small home and rest a bit before returning to the field. She longed to sit in her rocker and close her eyes but instead opted to pull bread from the basket on the sideboard and direct Christina to get last night's leftover beef from the icebox in the cellar. As she placed forks and knives on the table with napkins and plates, the weariness overcame her. A blinding pain shot through her head, making her wince, and she stumbled toward her bed.

"Mama?" Jessie said, rushing over to her. "What is it? Are you ill?"

"No, child," Kaatje struggled to convince her. "Just very tired. Eat your lunch with Christina, and let your mother rest. I will be fine in a moment."

She awakened an hour later to both girls, settled by her bed, studying her intently.

"Mama! Are you all right?" Christina said, clearly frightened.

"Do you need Doc Warner?" Jessie asked, sounding like a small adult.

"No, children. I am fine." Pressing away the pain that racked her body from head to toe, Kaatje sat up. "I'm simply tired. It is not normal for women to do such work in the field."

"Because Papa is gone," Jessie said forlornly.

"If only he would come back!" Christina wished aloud.

"If he could find us," Jessie added.

If he's alive, Kaatje thought to herself. After hearing nothing for the last three years, she assumed the worst. Soon she would find the gumption to discover the truth. But not yet. Right now she still held the tiniest hope that Soren was alive. That he would return to them and make things right after all these years. That Kaatje would have the chance to rant and rave and let him know how difficult life had been without him and watch as he groveled for her forgiveness. That's all she wanted. A chance to let out all the fury that boiled beneath the surface. A moment of vindication. The day when all the things that were wrong in her life became right.

"All in God's time," she told her daughters. "Some day it will all be made right. In God's time." She closed her eyes, willing her body to rise. For her children, who gazed at her in such distress. For herself. The world would not beat Kaatje Janssen. She had too much to live for.

one

hen the knock at the door sounded twice, sure, quick, Tora's heart jumped. She swallowed and resettled herself in the chair, making sure the best side of her face was toward him and the flounce of her polonaise that fell to the floor was "just so." She could feel his presence before he came into view, and she wondered at this thing inside her heart, this thing that would not die, that stirred for him more than any other. What was it about Trent Storm?

He entered the room as if he owned it, looking elegant in new attire. He peeled off his gloves and coolly perused her. "Tora," he said with a nod and then a slight smile. There was something hopeful in his eyes, and Tora was glad for it.

"Trent!" she said as if surprised, as if she had forgotten he was coming, and went to him. He bent over her hand and kissed it, then held it in his warm, strong fingers as they stared at one another. Tora squirmed first. "It has been a while, Trent."

"Yes, well, things at home have kept me quite busy. It is a far piece to travel to Helena, mind you."

"Please sit down," she said with a grand gesture, hoping he would notice the neo-rococo furniture just in from France. He sat down without hesitation. "Yes, but we haven't seen each other for what? Five months?"

"Counting, darling?"

Tora frowned. His eyes were live with challenge, and the air was suddenly charged with energy. "No, not at all. I simply was commenting. I've certainly been busy enough with your new roadhouses not to have time to count the hours until we might meet again." She hoped the edge of sarcasm in her voice would deflate whatever dangerous balloon was rising between them.

"Quite. The facilities here are impressive. Not to mention this house." He glanced around. "Very nice. I trust you did this with only your own funds."

Tora scowled. This was not going at all as she had planned. "Of course, Trent," she said, hating the defensiveness in her tone. "I have built this home as some place to which I could always return. I had to borrow a certain sum from the bank, but they were happy to assist such a prominent—"

"A home to return to?" Trent interrupted, rising and walking to a window that stretched from the floor to the twelve-foot ceiling. He parted the velvet drapes and looked outside. "Hmm. A home. Something that reminds you of Bergen?"

Tora felt the blood drain from her face. "Bergen? Why it's been years since I've thought of Norway. No, I was thinking of some place—"

"Like Camden?"

"Camden-by-the-Sea?" she managed to ask without her voice rising an octave. Where was he going with this? "No, what I started to say was—"

"That you needed a home," he put in.

"Yes," she said, staring back into his eyes when he studied her.

"A sense of place."

"Yes, I suppose so."

"A sense of where you know who you are, and others do as well. That's the reason for this grand showcase of a home, correct? The three-story, overdone, showy Queen Anne of the Storm Roadhouse Maven?"

Tora rose, thoroughly alarmed now. "Trent, whatever is wrong with you? I had so hoped you would like it, so treasured the idea you might want—"

"What? To live here?" He shook his head once, decisively. "No, Tora. I do not even know who the Storm Roadhouse Maven is. You have not allowed it. How could I decide to marry you? To come and make a home with you? You have grown more distant in the time I've known you, wrapped up in your own vision of your future and a very tangled net of lies."

"Of . . . of lies?"

Trent pulled a yellowed paper from the inside pocket of his jacket and quietly unfolded it. "The Heroine of the Horn," he read aloud. He stared down at her. "Elsa Anders Ramstad. Your long-lost sister. Funny thing though. She apparently does not remember being lost. In fact, she seems to have a very solid idea of who she is and where she has come from."

"You . . . you spoke to her?"

He ignored her question. "You told me she was dead. Do you think that she claims the same of you?"

Tora sat down, hard. "Perhaps in some sense she does," she muttered, half to herself.

"That's the first honest thing I've heard from you in a long time."

Tora sighed and stared toward the window. She knew it was the end; this was the reason for Trent's growing distance all this time. He knew. He'd known for a long time. And her secrecy had driven him farther and farther away, even as she had sought to draw him closer. "How did you find out?"

"Some detective work. I so wanted you to confide in me, Tora."

He spoke as if he were talking about someone else, a distant relation. "Why didn't you tell me? Why the secrecy? Was I untrustworthy? What is so humiliating in your past that you could not simply tell the truth? Not enough drama for you? Tora Anders," he said with a shake of his head, "you could have been a star on the stage."

She could feel his stare but could not find it within herself to meet his gaze. "Tell you? You were my employer! You demanded no relationship outside of work. It was easier, cleaner if I came to you as an orphan. And as to Camden, and the baby, I couldn't tell you all of that. Trent Storm would never have hired an unwed mother."

When he did not respond, Tora quickly looked at him. He hadn't known! He hadn't known all of it! Looking suddenly ten years older, Trent sat down hard on the loveseat. Tora rose and went to him, kneeling at his feet and resting her face on his thigh. Tears came unbidden. "Trent, I did it to survive. If you had known I was less than the wholesome woman you hired to work in your facilities, would you have ever employed me, much less courted me? I had to do it! I wanted to do something important with my life. To do this," she said, waving about her. "And soon I was doing it as much for you as I was for me."

"At the expense of a child," he said numbly. "Where, Tora? Where did you leave your child?"

"In a good home," she said simply.

"Look at me," he said sharply, raising her chin forcefully. "The child lives?"

"I hope so," she whispered. For the first time in years, Tora felt a sense of relief in sharing the burden of her secret with another.

"You feel sorrow over your decision?" His eyes never wavered.

"Occasionally. But not for some time. There's so much more to my life now—"

Trent laughed a mirthless laugh and rose, as if brushing her off. "You are as heartless and empty as I feared. God wants a different woman for me, Tora. A woman with heart and passion. Not perfect.

I am far from a sinless man myself. But I fancy that I live up to my mistakes and face them. I expect nothing else from you."

So that was what this was all about? Some overblown sense of judgment? Why, he didn't know her! He didn't know what she had gone through to get to this station. If he didn't want her, fine; there were plenty of others who would step into line when they found out Tora Anders was available to court.

"You are dead to me, Tora Anders," Trent said simply, walking to the door as if both feet were laden with lead. "You are fired and no longer associated with Storm Enterprises."

Tora's mouth dropped, and her heart thudded dully. "I—I—"

"You are on your own," he said, walking to the doorway. He turned back once. "I sincerely hope, Tora, that one day you will find your way home."

And with that he was gone.

Dear Friends:

Thanks for reading *The Captain's Bride*. It has been my biggest project to date—delving into the historical realm of storytelling takes a whole new part of my brain! And telling all those characters' stories at once turned out to be somewhat of a puzzle. Hopefully, my readers and editors helped me get them all straight.

I know, I know. It was mean of me to leave you with so many questions. But fortunately, books two and three in the Northern Lights series are available now, ready for your reading pleasure! So ask for *Deep Harbor* (Book 2) and *Midnight Sun* (Book 3) if you care to find out what's going on with the Bergensers.

As I followed their stories, it became apparent to me that sin not only affects the sinner but the innocents around them as well. It's like a pebble dropped into the water; the concentric circles just keep getting bigger and bigger. I was led to explore that further in *Deep Harbor* and even more in *Midnight Sun*. See what you think! Tora Anders just might get her due. What will that mean for her? Will she discover the Deepest Harbor of all? I was eager to complete my story and find out myself.

At the time I wrote this novel, my first child was only two and a half years old. Now my second baby, Emma, is two and a half. How time flies. Between them and my husband and an editorial job that I'm finally saying goodbye to, it's been hard to write any faster than I do. But life is good and rich and so sweet. God has blessed me indeed, and I'm so pleased to be a part of the Bride of Christ. I hope each and every one of you can rest in that knowledge as well: You are treasured. You are prized. You are special. And the greatest Bridegroom of all longs to stand beside you. What joy!

Every blessing,

Lisa Tawn Bergren

Check out Lisa's Web site:
www.LisaTawnBergren.com
Or write to her:
c/o WaterBrook Press
2375 Telstar Drive, Suite 160
Colorado Springs, CO 80920

Printed in the United States
by Baker & Taylor Publisher Services